Praise for
TRIPLE CROSS

"A smart, prescient thriller that makes one wonder why the bottom really dropped out of the stock market. The story snaps and twists like a cracking whip, you can't help but root for Mickey Hennessy and his kids, and I defy you to guess the ending. Mark T. Sullivan has written a super-charged bestseller and surefire motion picture!"

—Robert Crais, *New York Times*
bestselling author of *The First Rule*

"Crisply written, breathlessly paced, suspenseful...an almost-addictive page-turner."   —*Booklist*

"Sullivan delivers a slam-banger. The novel cries out to be a movie. In today's economy, many a reader might root for the bad guys against the greedy hostages."

—*Cleveland Plain Dealer*

"Crack *Triple Cross* and get ready to drop off a cornice and schuss the mountain at heart-stopping speed. A real thriller with strong characters, fast pacing, and suspense enough for the most demanding reader. Don't miss this one!"   —Douglas Preston, *New York Times*
bestselling author of *Impact*

"Everything a first-rate thriller should be—fast-paced, compelling, and brilliantly realized. If you haven't read

Sullivan before, you're in for a rare treat —*Triple Cross* is not only HIS best, it is one of THE best."

—Tess Gerritsen, *New York Times*
bestselling author of *Ice Cold*

"If you're watching your real-life stocks tank because of the real-life greed of some investment bankers and mortgage brokers, you might take a malicious pleasure in sitting down with *Triple Cross* for the fictional payback."

—*St. Louis Post-Dispatch*

"*Triple Cross* crackles with tension and imagination from the first page. A riveting, heart-stopping adventure. You're there, amidst the action, feeling, hearing, even smelling the tension. Well done." —Steve Berry, *New York Times*
bestselling author of *The Paris Vendetta*

"A scathing indictment of corrupt politicians and unscrupulous Wall Street kings." —*Bozeman Daily Chronicle*

"A page-turner of the first order, a tale that will get the blood pumping and keep it that way." —Bookreporter.com

"The [story] could have been pulled straight from today's headlines about corporate greed and financial market manipulation." —*Helena Independent Record*

"Tense, compelling, and thought-provoking with razor-sharp detail and taut writing." —*Billings Gazette*

TRIPLE CROSS

MARK T. SULLIVAN

St. Martin's Paperbacks

This is a work of fiction. All of the characters, organizations, and events portrayed in this novel are either products of the author's imagination or are used fictitiously.

TRIPLE CROSS

Copyright © 2009 by Mark T. Sullivan.
Excerpt from *Brotherhood of Thieves* copyright © 2010 by Mark T. Sullivan.

For information address St. Martin's Press, 175 Fifth Avenue, New York, NY 10010.

Library of Congress Catalog Card Number: 2008035867

ISBN: 978-0-312-53415-8

Printed in the United States of America

St. Martin's hardcover edition / April 2009
St. Martin's Paperbacks edition / November 2010

St. Martin's Paperbacks are published by St. Martin's Press, 175 Fifth Avenue, New York, NY 10010.

10   9   8   7   6   5   4   3   2   1

To my boys, the best a dad could have

ACKNOWLEDGMENTS

Triple Cross has had many friends, teachers, informants, and champions.

My brothers, independent investor Richard Vietze and James Sullivan of Lincoln Vale, helped me more fully understand the stock markets, their instruments, and their movement. Thank you, Jokers.

Russell Mann of Lincoln Vale graciously helped me "game" the financial strategies at play in the book. Without his aid, I never would have figured it out. Any mistakes of math, faults of logic, or descriptions of big-time market movements and their players are entirely my own.

A special thanks goes out to Jim "Spyder" Finnerty for graciously inviting me to ski inside TYC. It was a great deep-powder day and, ultimately, the inspiration for *Triple Cross*. The Jefferson Club, it must be said, bears no resemblance to TYC, nor do its members. All characterizations in the novel are entirely works of fiction.

My old and dear friend Tom Bowman, Pentagon Correspondent for National Public Radio, helped me game the political effects of the attack, and to understand the sentiment among soldiers returning from Iraq. Thanks, Tom. In addition to looking and speaking like a Kennedy, you are one smart guy.

At the same time, I'd like to acknowledge Columbia University Professor Joseph E. Stiglitz, author of *Globalization and Its Discontents,* and David C. Korten, author of *When Corporations Rule the World,* for shaping some of the themes at work in the novel. I am deeply indebted to the Southern Poverty Law Center for helping me to more fully grasp the anti-globalist movement. All depictions of Third Position adherents and their personal beliefs, however, are purely fiction.

I am thankful for the time and insight given to me by Roger Nisley, former head of the FBI's National Hostage Rescue Team and its Critical Incident Response Group. Ron Minard helped me understand the workings of military police and the Diplomatic Security Service. Thanks, Ron.

A Herculian dose of gratitude goes to my agent, David Hale Smith, who took a chance, and to my foreign agents, Linda Michaels and, subsequently, Danny Baror, for keeping me afloat and writing.

Thanks to fellow novelist and friend Gregg Hurwitz for being the first reader. I owe you, bud.

If they're lucky, writers get to work with one great editor in their careers. Keith Kahla at St. Martin's Press is my one great editor. He, too, took a chance, and coaxed and cajoled and prodded the final form of this novel out of me. Along the way he was smart, funny, invested, and discerning. Keith, I can't thank you enough.

I am also deeply grateful to Sally Richardson, publisher of St. Martin's, for having the guts to look beyond the numbers. And a deep bow goes to Andrea Diederich and all the wonderful people at Fischer-Verlage, my German publishers.

Friend and novelist Joe Finder never let me give up. Neither would my wife, Betsy. Your encouragement got me through some dark times. Bless you both.

There is inherent in the capitalist system a tendency toward self-destruction.

—*Joseph Schumpeter*

CHAPTER ONE

True winter hit around eleven a.m. that New Year's Eve. North winds slanted in, bearing temperatures in the low teens. Iron clouds followed, casting a pale and crystalline-gray glow across the west flank of the Jefferson Range in southwest Montana.

Three construction helicopters chugged east toward the remote mountains over a valley cut up into cattle ranches and spliced by a river that ribboned through it. As they closed on the foothills, hail and snow peppered the choppers. Visibility worsened. The pilot in the lead airship grew agitated.

"We're gonna hit big-time snow and crosswinds," he said into his microphone, glancing at the hard-looking man riding next to him, dressed head to toe in snow camouflage and wearing a climbing harness. "Sure we can't postpone, General?"

The general turned his head, revealing the rocky

face of a man in his early forties framed with shoulder-length brown hair. "We have a schedule," he replied icily. "It will not be compromised."

The pilot felt the general looking at him and glanced his way again. What he saw in the general's eyes rattled the pilot, made him feel like he was expendable.

"Get ready for one hell of a ride," the pilot said finally.

They gained elevation and entered the clouds. Visibility was less than two hundred feet. Crosswinds buffeted the chopper and it lurched sideways. The pilot fought for control as the helicopter bucked, shuddered, and jolted. Several of the fifteen other snow-camouflaged passengers in the bird's hold muttered and cursed.

"Gonna be worse at ten thousand feet," the pilot said, gritting his teeth. "I can't guarantee you'll get on the ground alive."

"Abort the first landing zone," the general said. "Use the secondary."

"It's a long hike," the pilot said.

"It is what it is," the general said.

The pilot got on his radio and called the orders to the other two helicopters. He turned south with the winds. The buffeting ebbed, but visibility remained pea soup. Twice the pilot got too low in the dense clouds and almost clipped the tops of lodgepole pines with his struts. Despite the icy air seeping in the doors of the helicopter, sweat kept beading on his forehead and dripping down his nose. The pilot had flown fifty missions in Iraq and had been twice engulfed in sandstorms in the air, but those experiences were nothing compared to the white-out conditions he was facing.

The general, however, seemed largely unmoved by their predicament. His expression was burned in place, an attitude of calculating, grim determination. He peered back into the chopper's hold. There was an acidic odor wafting from in there and he recognized it as the scent of soldiers contemplating their mortality. His attention swept over the men and women sitting on benches, strapped to the helicopter's inner hull. The majority of them wore one version or another of the general's facial expression—expectant and focused.

Three of them, however, looked out of place—more fearful, more tenuous than the rest of the crew. One man, two women. All of them sitting together, their eyes darting from one to the other. The general caught the eye of the woman closest to him. Early twenties. Cute rather than pretty, short and athletic, her sandy hair was roped up in dreadlocks and a hoop ring pierced her nose.

"Are you ready, Mouse?" the general asked.

Mouse gazed at the general as if he were some kind of prophet, saying, "It's time to make them pay for the hell they've inflicted on people."

Approval rumbled through the helicopter's belly. The pale blond man beside Mouse spoke with a thick French accent. "Time to light the fire under their fat asses."

"It is, Cristoph," the general agreed. "Rose? Are you not well?"

The miserable-looking brunette with the big nose sitting next to Cristoph said, "If this shaking keeps up, I'm going to puke all over myself. I'm not used to this kind of crap. I don't know if I can do the rappel into the second zone."

The general's features hardened. "You'll do it or I'll throw you out the door."

Rose moaned and hung her head between her knees. The general's attention moved deeper into the cavity of the helicopter to a massive black man with a basketball-like head sitting atop crossbar shoulders.

"Truth, get your troops ready," he said. "Landing zone two."

Truth wiped a boxing mitt of a hand across his muzzle. "Lighten loads?"

"We're already stripped to the essentials. We're just going to have to suck it up."

The pilot shouted, "Quarter mile, General!"

The general twisted back to look out the windshield. The snow was falling like hundreds of white whirlpools on the radically steep, shale-strewn hillside. The footing would be treacherous.

"Hundred and seventy-five yards and closing," the pilot said, watching the readout on his U.S.-military-spec GPS.

Truth and two men moved several large rubberized duffel bags toward the side door, which they slid open. Frigid air and swirling snow blasted the inner cabin and brought with them the piney smells of the forest.

"There's your cliff!" the pilot cried.

The general spotted a narrow balcony of rock jutting from the woods, off the side of a gorge two hundred feet deep. He pointed at gnarled old pines growing off the near side of the point.

"Come about and keep your nose on those trees," he

told the pilot. "If you're on your game, you won't shear the rear blades and kill us all."

The pilot squinted in fear and eased the stick forward. The chopper hovered forward over the stone balcony. Ever so slowly, trembling like a compass confused by magnets, the nose of the ship came around.

"Go!" the general roared.

A pair of climbing ropes were flung out the door. Truth lifted the rappelling rack attached to his chest harness, clipped it to the rope, and went out the open side door. He carried a heavy pack with several grenades strapped to the back. He slid from view. The others followed.

The general shouldered his pack last, put on goggles, and leaped out the door, sliding down the rope, swinging wildly in the wind. Truth held the rope at the bottom and helped the general off.

The general walked the razorback, holding his hands out from his sides like a tight-wire artist, then reached the main cliff and entered the woods on a game trail, moving toward voices ahead. Behind him, the rubber duffel bags were lowered successfully, the first helicopter lifted away, and a second chopper took its place, disgorging more troops and supplies.

The general slipped through the trees toward the bottom of the rockslide where his soldiers were gathering. He tugged at the brim of his white wool hat, transforming it into a hood with holes cut for eyes, nose, and mouth. He crept into the embrace of a snow-laden fir tree. In his camouflage, the general was for all intents invisible, listening, gauging the people he was leading, looking for any weakness.

In the clearing, a lanky man in his late twenties with dark features and a gold front tooth yanked off a glove and with his free hand tugged up the collar of his coat. "We're taking this to a whole other level now," he said in an Oklahoma twang. "This is goddamned throwing down the gauntlet. Declaration of fuckin' war."

Cristoph removed his round wire-rimmed glasses and wiped the snow off them. "The general is right, Dalton," he said. "We must act."

A tall, attractive Latina woman in her thirties put her pack down beside them, saying, "If not, the world will be doomed. Our children will be doomed."

"I've heard the speech, Emilia," Dalton said. "I'm here, aren't I?"

"Are you, Dalton?" asked a pit-bullish man with a glare like an axe falling and teardrop tattoos under both eyes. "'Cause if you aren't, you should get the fuck out before the shit hits the fan. Start hiking. Town's only, what, forty miles?"

"Cobb, there's a difference between stepping inside the nuthouse and thinking about it," Dalton shot back. "We'll see who keeps it together when it goes psycho."

"Yeah, we will," Cobb said, giving Dalton a snake's half-lidded expression.

"This is no time for measuring penises," Mouse said, her voice rippling with emotion. "We can't lose sight of what this is for." She raised her fist. "Remember Seattle! Change the world!"

"We change it now!" Cristoph cried and pumped his fist.

The general smiled.

Truth and the men from the third helicopter came into the clearing dragging the rubberized duffel bags behind them. They opened the bags and distributed black 9mm Sterling submachine guns and bandoliers of ammunition.

The general stepped into the clearing, took his gun, loaded it, and then said, "Okay. Let's go teach the world a thing or two about justice, Third-Position-style."

CHAPTER TWO

Nine miles north, it was snowing an inch an hour. Fresh powder lay on Hellroaring Peak and the ski trails of the Jefferson Club, a twelve-thousand-acre ultra-private resort for the super-rich and powerful, the only kind of people who could afford membership.

Initiation fees were six-point-five million and afforded the member a twenty-five-acre parcel on which to build one of the alpine castles that dotted the property. There was also unlimited use of the spectacular facilities: the lodge, the spas, the golf, the stables, the fishing ponds, the hunting grounds, and the exquisite cuisine.

But the skiing was really why they came. Four hundred and fifty inches of light powder fell on Hellroaring Peak every year. With fewer than eight hundred members and most of them living elsewhere much of the year, the snow inside the club was often deep and untracked for days.

At noon, Michael "Mickey" Hennessy swooped off the high-speed six-man chairlift atop Hellroaring Peak and ran his telemark skis straight into the newly fallen fluff, laughing when it burst around his boots and shins, light as goose feathers.

Tall, broad-shouldered, copper-haired, and in his mid-forties, Hennessy was an expert skier and he arced smoothly through the powder to the entrance of Fortune's Alley, a two-thousand-vertical-foot run that snaked down the flank of Hellroaring. Hennessy had loved to ski ever since he was a boy growing up in Vermont. Ordinarily, he would have headed into the trees to sample his favorite powder stashes. But he had important guests trailing him, so he sliced to a stop.

Up the hill toward the lift, a man and a boy snowboarded hesitantly in the powder. The boy lost his balance and fell. A woman on skis pulled up beside him and helped him up while the man skidded to a stop only to fall as well. Hennessy cursed silently. This could take all day and he had a dozen tasks to attend to more important than leading a tour. But orders were orders and at least it was snowing.

A voice buzzed over the radio strapped to the chest of his black parka, *"Boss, you reading me?"*

Hennessy reached up and tugged the microphone from its clip. "Loud and clear."

"Grant and his family just entered main gate. That's all of them."

"Roger that. I'll tell Mr. Burns as soon as I get off the hill."

Hennessy clipped the mike back above a nameplate

that identified him as the Jefferson Club's vice president of security and director of privacy and then scanned the woodline up and down the trail. It was old habit. Hennessy was a former agent with the U.S. Diplomatic Security Service and had served on the detail that guarded the U.S. Secretary of State for six years. He took his job at the Jefferson Club just as seriously. Members paid for the finest safety measures on earth, and it was Mickey Hennessy's job to oblige them.

Especially that day. With the arrival of Aaron Grant, the seven wealthiest people in the world were on club grounds, along with the chairman of the U.S. Senate Appropriations Committee and several former athletic greats and Hollywood celebrities. He had sweated the details of this weekend for months. Which was why Hennessy felt at cross-purposes as the snowboarders and the skier made their wobbly way toward him. On the one hand, he'd be better off finalizing the details of the evening's security team instead of leading a tour of the facilities. On the other, it wasn't every day you got to ski with Jack Doore, the richest man in the world, his wife, and his only son.

"God, we're spastics!" Jack Doore announced when he finally reached Hennessy's side, the big grin the only part of his face visible below the helmet and goggles. "I thought growing up surfing would have helped me."

"It should help tomorrow," Hennessy assured him. "There should be thirty inches up here. Maybe more."

"Thirty inches?" asked Stephanie Doore, the skier, as she skidded to a stop with her young son, Ian, in tow. "My God, what do you do if you fall?"

"Flail a lot," Hennessy said.

She laughed. So did her husband, who said, "That'll be me, Sir Flailalot."

Stephanie Doore chuckled. "Who does that make me?"

"Lady Flailalot," Jack Doore said.

Her son tugged on her sleeve. "Ian surfs, Mom," he said.

"Yes, you do, honey," Stephanie Doore said sympathetically.

Ian fell silent.

"I think he's getting hungry," his father announced.

"The main restaurant's closed for tonight's party, but the café is open," Hennessy said. "It's right off the base of the lift next to the chocolate room."

Ian perked up and said, "Mmmmm."

"That does sound decadent, doesn't it?" Stephanie Doore said.

"Only to the waistline," Hennessy said. "By the way, Mr. Grant and his family arrived a few minutes ago."

"Fashionably late, as usual," Jack Doore said. "Let's rip it up!"

To their delight and Hennessy's, the Doores stayed on their feet. They skied down Fortune's Alley, past the terrain park with its tabletop jumps, rails, and half-pipe to the base area in front of the lodge.

The Jefferson Club Lodge was the architectural crown jewel of the resort. Five stories high and constructed of granite, timber, and hand-sawn plank siding, the lodge had been designed to reflect an Adirondack great camp updated with a Japanese influence that was both beckoning and formidable. It featured two wings that ran out from a heated terrace below the ski lifts. Where the two wings met, a semicircular glass wall soared upward fronting the ballroom and, atop it, a grand atrium that was the building's centerpiece.

To the north there was a skating rink and to the south were the lodge's famous pools. The pools were carved to affect a trout stream with granite rock formations at each end that soared several stories high and were bored through with waterslides.

After stowing their skis and snowboards with a valet, Hennessy led the Doores toward the heated terrace, taking the opportunity to explain the other benefits of membership, including the snowmobile trails, the cross-country ski facilities, the eighteen-hole Jack Nicklaus–designed golf course, the hunting grounds, the fishing ponds, and the stables. Then there was the legendary lodge with its fine Italian cuisine, the spa, tennis courts, saloons, the trading floor, the media center, and the grand ballroom available for special functions like tonight's ball.

After he finished, Stephanie Doore asked, "How much is membership?"

Hennessy explained the package, finishing with, "Of course, full membership with one of the more spectacular home sites triggers a surcharge of five million."

"So if we want a primo lot, we pay eleven-point-five million?" Jack Doore said. "That's not bad."

"No annual fee?" Stephanie Doore asked.

"If you come in at the premium level, you pay nothing more. Ever."

Stephanie Doore still seemed unconvinced. "How many homes do we need, Jack? Wouldn't an associate membership do? You can stay here as an associate, right?"

"You can," Hennessy allowed. "A suite will always be available to you, as will the rights to use suites at other Jefferson Club facilities worldwide, including the yacht in Crete, the castle near Royal Troon in Scotland, and, when it is finished, the Celadon resort on the south coast of Thailand. Associate membership, however, comes with yearly dues of fifty thousand dollars."

"Ian's hungry, Mom," Ian said.

Hennessy pointed across the terrace at the bowed glass room. "Café's right there."

Jack Doore hesitated. "You said the trading floor has real-time execution?"

Hennessy nodded. "I can take you there while your wife orders."

Doore nodded to his wife. "A chili bowl."

"You're on vacation, Jack," she chided. "Can't you think of something more extravagant?"

"No," Doore said. "I like good chili." He looked at Hennessy. "It is good, right?"

"Excellent, sir."

"Make sure they put cheese on mine."

Hennessy led Jack Doore through a door off the terrace into a warm room where they shed their helmets, hats, goggles, parkas, and boots, which a valet took. In return, the valet handed them each a pair of reverse sheepskin booties.

"I like these," Jack Doore said, examining them.

"Everyone does," Hennessy said, studying the man again.

Doore was roughly his age, but he had the looks and build of a surfer in his late twenties, including lank blond hair that was always falling in his eyes. It was hard to believe that someone who looked so boyish could be so brilliant. He had revolutionized the world in a matter of a few years with his YES! operating system. YES! flawlessly linked almost every machine to computers. The lodge was YES!-controlled. So was the club's security system. Virtually everything these days was YES!-controlled, and Doore had the $80 billion to prove it.

For a moment, Hennessy felt a pang of jealousy and anxiety. Despite his government pension and the investments he'd made over the years, his portfolio wasn't where it should have been. Thinking about it always made him upset.

That fact haunted him as he led the way into the grand atrium where the nonglass walls were hand-troweled and painted to look like distressed saddle leather. Antique Navajo rugs covered the rough-sawn fir flooring. Original Rod Zullo sculptures, Russell Chatham paintings, and other works by modern western masters adorned the tables and walls. The room smelled of pine from the blaze roaring in a stacked-stone fireplace that soared five stories up the center of the room. Water seeped from the rocks.

"Someone had a great eye for detail building this place," Doore commented as they headed for the staircase at the rear of the atrium.

"Mrs. Burns oversaw most of the construction and decorating," Hennessy said. "She'll be happy to hear you like it."

"I'll tell her at the party tonight," Doore promised.

"Hennessy! Come here! Now!"

Hennessy turned at the high-pitched voice, finding a Chinese man in his fifties, wearing black slacks, turtleneck, and tinted glasses, standing imperiously near the bar.

Hennessy stiffened and reddened. "Excuse me a minute, won't you? I've been working on some special security issues for Mr. Hoc Pan."

Jack Doore looked over at the man. "Chin Hoc Pan? Is he a member?"

"Two years," Hennessy replied with a hint of exasperation. "I'll be right back."

Hennessy went across the room to Chin Hoc Pan, bobbed his head, and stuck out his hand. The Chinese man looked at it distastefully and did not offer his as he announced, "My Gauguin remains unprotected."

Hennessy took a deep breath. "Mr. Hoc Pan, as I explained last night, raising the security on your villa will take time."

"You've had time," Hoc Pan said. "I pay much for membership. I expect action."

Hennessy took another deep breath. The Hong Kong real estate developer was currently the fourth-wealthiest man in the world. He was also one of the club's biggest pains in the ass. He was a bachelor and a germophobe and lived most of the time aboard a Boeing 747. Hoc Pan was also a passionate art collector and had recently purchased a painting by Paul Gauguin that had not been offered for sale in nearly seventy years. For some reason, Hoc Pan had decided to hang the painting in his house at the Jefferson Club and he'd expected Hennessy to drop everything and see to its well-being.

"Sir," Hennessy said firmly. "I assure you that our system is more than adequate to protect your Gauguin until the necessary consultants can be brought in."

"Not good," Hoc Pan barked. "Someone steals it, you got sixty million to cover?"

Hennessy reddened and countered, "If you wish, I can arrange to have it placed in the vault downstairs until—"

"How can I see Gauguin's genius locked in a vault?" the developer shot back. He made a spitting noise, then barked, "I call Foster. You give me Foster's number."

Gregg Foster was Mickey Hennessy's immediate boss, the director of security for all of HB1 Financial, the parent company to the Jefferson Club. For the last year, however, Foster had been in Thailand overseeing construction and security installation at the corporation's new Celadon resort. The last fourteen days he'd been trekking in Patagonia, unreachable.

"Mr. Foster's on vacation, sir," Hennessy said wearily. "As I told you last night, I haven't heard from him in two weeks and I don't expect to for at least another week."

"Burns, then," Hoc Pan insisted. "I speak to Horatio Burns!"

Hennessy took another breath and said, "I believe he's downstairs in the ballroom, sir. But it's off-limits until six by order of Mrs. Burns."

"No off-limits to me," Hoc Pan said, then made a cluck of disgust and marched off.

"He seems upset about security," Jack Doore said when Hennessy returned.

Hennessy had to control his anger. "He shouldn't be. And if you'll allow me a detour on the way to the trading room, I'll show you why."

CHAPTER THREE

On the second floor of the lodge, north hallway, Mickey Hennessy stopped at a fir door with a black bubble mounted above the jamb. He rang the bell. A matrix of blue light erupted from the bubble and scanned his face. The door slid into the wall.

He and Doore entered a cramped room dominated by monitors, three rows of them, six screens a row, arranged in a tiered console above keyboards manned by two Jefferson Club security officers in club uniform.

The screens showed real-time images of various parts of the resort: the covered entry driveway, the pools, the chairlifts, the skating rink, the hallways on every floor, the service entrances, the stables, and the gate at the club's main entrance.

"Inside the lodge and in each home, sensors monitor precious artworks, such as Mr. Hoc Pan's Gauguin," Hennessy explained. "If they're moved without warning, an alarm sounds in the security center and we respond. And as you can see, cameras watch most of the club's public areas, as well as the driveways and entries of every member's home. The cameras are linked to motion detectors that I admit are often triggered by the abundant wildlife on the grounds. Thank God the same isn't true of the fence."

Hennessy went on to describe the barrier that separated the Jefferson Club grounds from the wilderness. The fence was the first of its kind and boasted no barbed wire or posts or cement walls to mar the club's aesthetics. Instead, it was based on an optical sensor web that had cost a fortune to engineer and construct. The sensor web was ten feet high, two feet wide, and based on a YES!-controlled laser matrix that "read" any animal or large object passing through. More to the point, the fence was programmed to ignore horses and wild animals.

"But a human form?" Doore asked.

"Exactly," Hennessy said. "We've had only two breaches this year, both during hunting season back in November."

"Impressive," Doore said.

Hennessy looked at one of the guards staffing the system. "Activity?"

Krueger, the younger and more serious of the two, looked up from his keyboard. "Main gate was busy early. It's quiet now except for delivery vans leaving."

Lerner, a happy guy in his early thirties who had a picture of his two-year-old daughter taped to the console, turned in his chair and nodded. "With this snow, nothing's moving, boss. Not even the elk."

* * *

The Jefferson Club's trading room was in the south wing of the lodge on the first floor. Hennessy used his electronic master key to open matching cedar doors with a depiction of a bull elk fighting a grizzly bear carved in them.

The doors slid back, revealing a space pulsing with activity, much more crowded than Hennessy had anticipated for early afternoon on New Year's Eve. The twenty trading turrets were jammed. The place buzzed with members and guests muttering orders, trading information and gossip at the cappuccino bar at the far end of the room and the booze-and-shellfish bar at the near end. Almost everyone in the room looked frantic. Some appeared downright scared.

"What's going on?" Jack Doore demanded, looking suddenly nervous.

"Just the usual last-minute, last-of-the-year hedging, shorting the markets to offset any turbulence that might occur over the holiday," said a man waiting in line for the closest turret. He had a British accent and was sniffing a fresh Davidoff cigar. His hair was lacquered black in an expensive pompadour, his nails were manicured, and his skin appeared inordinately taut and scrubbed for a man in his mid-sixties, which led Hennessy to believe he had gone under the scalpel recently. His ski suit was one-piece and fit him as if he were the sixth-richest man in the world. Which he was.

"Sir Lawrence," Hennessy said. "How are you enjoying the club?"

"This room is certainly a positive," Sir Lawrence said crisply, not even glancing at Hennessy.

Hennessy swallowed it and said, "Jack Doore, this is Sir Lawrence Treadwell."

Sir Lawrence gaped and then stuck out his hand vigorously. "Brilliant to meet you, Doore. I'm sorry I didn't recognize you in your, uh, jibber togs."

"No worries, and excellent to meet you too," Jack Doore said as he shook Sir Lawrence's hand. "You're in oil, aren't you?"

"At GlobalCon we work with all facets of the business," Treadwell said. "You thinking of joining the club, Jack?"

"Seems like a cool place for my son. And I hear the pow-pow gets pretty deep."

"Pow-pow?" Sir Lawrence said, confused.

"Powder snow," Hennessy said.

"Ah, yes," Sir Lawrence said, irritated. "A bit out of my league. I can barely stand on the damn things. Say, Jack, might we talk business at some point?"

Doore looked uncomfortable. "I promised my wife I was on vacation."

"Won't take more than ten minutes," Sir Lawrence insisted.

Doore shrugged at last. "Ten minutes. But I have to place an order first."

"Brilliant!" Sir Lawrence said.

Hennessy stood there a moment, doing his best to ignore the fact that the British tycoon had never once looked his way. Then again, Sir Lawrence knew who

Hennessy was in the greater Jefferson Club scheme of things: a minion with a small bank account. That thought flustered Hennessy and he wondered what sort of end-of-year moves his financial advisor was making to his portfolio.

"The system will execute immediately?" Doore asked Hennessy.

Hennessy nodded and said, "The phones are dedicated, secure hard lines direct to all the major exchanges worldwide. The quotes are all level three. The servers are MegaDatas running YES! Six satellites connect us online. Mr. Burns wanted members to have the full power of the Web available, no matter what the situation. So in a long answer, yes. They will execute immediately."

"Impressive," Jack Doore said, nodding. "Extremely impressive."

Doore excused himself and went to one of the turrets. Sir Lawrence simply walked after him, never acknowledging Hennessy. Rather than get annoyed, the club's security director backed up against the wall between the doors and a bank of tall plants that separated the trading area from the lounge, trying to be as inconspicuous as possible. It was another old habit. Blending in and watchfulness were part of his job.

He'd been there almost ten minutes, growing increasingly concerned about the wild pace of the trading, when he heard a man with a thick German accent say, "I just got off the phone with Zurich. There are more shorts on the markets than anyone expected, much beyond the normal hedging for this time of year."

"How many players?" another voice replied, this one American and hoarser.

"No one knows," the German said. "But there are suspicions that Treadwell is among them."

Hennessy glanced sideways through the plant branches, seeing the broken forms of the two men sitting in club chairs and drinking from espresso cups. Even though they had their backs to him, he recognized them immediately.

The taller and older of the two was Albert Crockett, the infamous corporate raider and fifth-wealthiest man in the world. Crockett was in his seventies, a stoop-shouldered man with thin gray hair, a strained face, and a mortician's aura. The other man was the seventh-richest man on earth: Friedrich Klinefelter, the chairman of Mobius Hedge Funds LLC, the most profitable in the world the past three years running. Klinefelter was in his late fifties and boasted hawkish, aristocratic features amplified by his silver hair, which was slicked back against his scalp like a Ralph Lauren model. He wore casual clothes, wool pants and a sweater, but his posture was stiff, and he had a habit of darting his eyes.

"You're sure about Sir Lawrence?" Crockett asked.

"These are the rumors," Klinefelter replied. "But there is such large volume others have to be involved. They know something, I think."

"They know nothing," the takeover artist growled. "They're insane. The markets are strong. The U.S. economy's on a tear. This thing's not going south anytime soon."

"What about Burns?" Klinefelter insisted. "He's gone

to cash like Ross Perot did before Black Monday in '87."

"So he told Lou Dobbs and everyone's taking shots at him for it," Crockett said dismissively. "The *Journal*'s story was scathing . . . There's Treadwell now. Who's that he's with? Is that Doore?"

Hennessy startled and looked across the room to find Sir Lawrence and Jack Doore already returning. His mind whirled. *Horatio's gone to cash and Sir Lawrence and a bunch of others are shorting the market.* He had learned many things working at the Jefferson Club the past four years, but one seemed paramount at the moment: When financial markets implode, the amateur investor gets killed and the smart investor makes a fortune. He wanted to talk to his financial advisor. Now.

But then Jack Doore and Sir Lawrence paused in front of him and shook hands.

"I'll get back to you," Doore said.

"Don't wait long," Treadwell said. "This really could do well."

"I won't," Doore said before turning to Hennessy. "Chili and cheese?"

Hennessy bobbed his head. "Of course. Absolutely."

They left the trading room and walked the long hallway toward the grand atrium. Hennessy said, "What do you think of the economy, sir?"

Doore raised an eyebrow. "You're the second man in ten minutes to ask me that."

"I'm sorry. It's just that I heard many people were shorting the markets."

Doore shrugged. "I don't know what to tell you other

than I don't see anything but good fortune for YES! in the foreseeable future."

"Sir Lawrence is shorting the market," Hennessy said.

"Is he?"

"Just what I heard."

"I was buying up YES! stock because I think it's undervalued," Doore said. "But what do I know? Sir Lawrence is one of the shrewdest investors in the world and I'm a creative guy."

Hennessy chewed it over as they passed through the atrium again and entered a hallway on the far side. *But what if Sir Lawrence and Horatio are right? What if the markets are going south?* He took a hard left and led the way into the café, which was decorated with the remains of a soda fountain from Cheyenne, Wyoming, circa 1939.

They found Doore's family sitting at a table by the window looking up at the ski mountain. Without her helmet and goggles, Stephanie Doore was a willowy blonde in her late thirties, with a pleasant smile and gracious manners. Ian looked about eight years old and was slightly barrel-chested with short-cropped blond hair. He was happily wolfing ice cream, and it was hard to detect that he was mildly autistic at all.

Jack Doore took a seat beside his wife and was about to say something when he glanced out the window and his head snapped back in shock.

Hennessy looked out toward the ski slope and felt his stomach lock tight. Three snowboarders had entered the terrain park at warp speed. All three appeared to be carrying automatic weapons.

CHAPTER FOUR

Across the country in midtown Manhattan, FBI special agent and financial crime specialist Cheyenne O'Neil sat in her gray cubicle on the twenty-sixth floor of 26 Federal Plaza, staring at a churning sea of stock quotes, bids, offers, and trade confirmations on the large computer screen scrolling in front of her. Beside them in split screen were copies of various corporate documents. She'd been studying the numbers and legal mumbo jumbo for so long the letters and numerals had begun to swim.

Cheyenne sat back in her chair, took off her glasses, and rubbed at her eyes. She glanced at the television bolted into the ceiling above the intersection of four cubicles. It was tuned to the Bloomberg report and muted. With two hours of trading left in the year, the Dow Jones Industrial Average was up 87 points and stood at 16,180.

The NASDAQ Index and the Standard & Poor's 500 had posted similarly impressive gains.

Cheyenne didn't need to switch on the sound to know what the financial pundits were saying. She could see from their joyous-ape expressions that they were hooting on as they had been for months about the strength of the charging bull market and the vibrancy and resilience of the U.S. economy, not to mention the resurgent dollar.

Her fingers massaged her lower back as she announced, "I know it's there, but I just don't see it."

FBI Agent John Ikeda, a wiry Japanese-American man in his thirties and Cheyenne's partner of three years, pushed back from his desk and rolled into the doorway of the cubicle across from hers.

"It'll pop at you eventually," he said. "That's the thing about money, it leaves lots of fingerprints if you know what you're looking for."

"I don't know exactly what I'm looking for," she replied.

"Anomalies," Ikeda said. "With that kind of dough, the big boys are very careful. You're not going to find glaring incidents, just repeated patterns that are out of sync with the rest of their trading."

"You make it sound like chasing ghosts," she said.

"*You are chasing ghosts,*" snapped the short, fit, balding man in the gray suit and suspenders who'd walked up behind them.

Cheyenne stiffened, then pivoted in her chair to find Special Agent in Charge Pete Laughlin looming over her.

"It's there, Cap," she said. "I can feel it."

"Six months and nothing," Laughlin said.

"It takes time to expose fraud on a massive scale," Cheyenne retorted.

"Time you don't have, O'Neil," Laughlin said sternly. "Wednesday, I want you back on the Twindle case and your obsession back-burnered. Start the new year right."

"Cap . . . ," she protested.

"That's an order, O'Neil," Laughlin said and made to turn away.

Cheyenne jumped to her feet. "What if I can make something happen?"

Laughlin stopped and eyed her. "Like what?"

"I don't know," she fretted. "A significant break in the case?"

Laughlin laughed caustically. "Over the holiday?"

"Sure," she said, stiffening her lip. "Why not? All it'll cost you is a plane ticket."

Suspicious, he asked, "Where?"

"Montana," she replied. "Crockett and Klinefelter are both staying at a ski resort out there. The Jefferson Club. Klinefelter's leaving the country on Tuesday. Who knows when I'll get a chance to talk to them both together again?"

Laughlin made a dismissive flip of his hand. "And ask them what? You've got nothing. So you get nothing. No plane ticket."

"Cap, c'mon," she pleaded.

He walked away, saying, "End of discussion. Wednesday, you're on Twindle."

Cheyenne gritted her teeth, twisted her hands into

fists, and was about to go after her boss when Ikeda grabbed her by the wrist, shook his head, and muttered, "Not a good idea to piss him off. He'll have you on shit that'll make Twindle seem like Ivan Boesky land. Go take a breather. Better yet, take off. It's New Year's Eve, for God's sake."

She shook her head furiously. "They're going to get away with it."

"Take a breather," Ikeda said in a firmer tone.

Cheyenne sighed, knowing he was right. It was no use getting on Laughlin's bad side any more than she already was. She felt suddenly exhausted. She walked off through the cubicles and down the hall to the women's room, where she went to the sink and splashed water on her face.

She patted her face dry with a paper towel, appraising herself in the mirror. *Though dateless and alone on New Year's Eve, Cheyenne O'Neil remains a confident, well-educated, tough babe. Thirty-one, but doesn't look a day over twenty-nine. Summa cum laude, Syracuse University. Northwestern MBA. Third in her class at the FBI Academy. Superbly fit even though she hasn't yet worked out today. Stunning green eyes. Luxuriant auburn hair. Creamy skin except for the zit developing at the hairline. Wicked sense of humor. Insanely dedicated to the job. Insanely fixated on this case.*

Asking herself if she might be obsessive-compulsive, she returned to her desk and sat down. For a moment she considered quitting for the day. Then that voice in her head shouted that her instincts were right. Somewhere in that mountain of financial transactions, there was evidence of racketeering between two of the wealthiest men on earth: Albert Crockett, the corporate raider, and Friedrich Klinefelter, the manager of Mobius LLC.

Prompted by evidence sent to the FBI anonymously back in May, Cheyenne had come to suspect that Crockett and Klinefelter were acting in grand collusion and in gross violation of U.S. securities and racketeering laws. She believed Crockett would target a company for takeover, then slip word to Klinefelter in Zurich, who would buy up shares of the target company through his various hedge funds. In each case, Klinefelter would take care not to buy enough shares with any particular fund to trigger a 13D filing report with the SEC, which is required of any individual or company acquiring more than five percent of any U.S. public corporation's stock.

When Klinefelter's various funds were positioned with an aggregate of twelve percent of the target company's outstanding stock, Crockett would start buying aggressively through his various holding companies. He would disclose his position to the SEC once his position in the target company exceeded five percent, and then he would continue buying up to fifteen or twenty percent. At that point, he would send an irate letter to the target company's board of directors, accusing them of mismanagement and demanding that the corporation be sold off for its assets or that Crockett be given a seat on the board so he could begin the process of firing the executives and replacing them with his own people.

If anything, Cheyenne had decided, Albert Crockett was a shrewd judge of undervalued companies and the market knew it. Once word of his hostile takeover bid had spread, the stock of the target company would almost inevitably soar. Friedrich Klinefelter's private-equity funds would see significant gains. Cheyenne also believed Crockett had major money invested with Mobius, which meant any gain in the funds profited him too. And Klinefelter's twelve percent ownership would be there to back Crockett should his hostile takeover be challenged.

It was business by siege and incredibly profitable. It was also insider trading, collusion, and racketeering way beyond one investor scratching another's back.

The problem was, Cheyenne could not establish the backroom deal part of the scenario. She'd never talked to Klinefelter, who was one of the most secretive men in the world. And the one time she'd managed to question Crockett, he'd been accompanied by a cadre of attorneys sporting dated documents showing his independent analysis in support of the investments. Klinefelter's interest was nothing more than good business.

"Smart men think alike," Crockett had told her dismissively.

And that's where it had stood for the past three months. Stalemate. Then Ikeda recommended she try to investigate possible meetings or phone calls between the two men. But the assistant U.S. attorney working with her on the case had been unable to convince a judge to subpoena phone records and access to their computers. Cheyenne had been furious. *If you're suspected of terrorism, you have no rights,* she thought. *If you're suspected of being a thief, as long as you're loaded, you're still protected.*

Those gripes aside, she knew she had to find a better way to deal with the sea of stock transactions that pitched before her. There were hundreds of thousands of shares involved, all bought through various trading houses and off the Web. Billions of dollars being bet in ways that made it difficult to figure out just what the wager was.

It's a big poker game to them, she thought bitterly. *They don't care who they hurt. He who's got the most chips wins.*

Cheyenne sat there, chewing on that and scrolling down through the documents, seeing data on Crockett's takeover of Harrison Timber, an Oregon lumber company.

Then she thought, *There's lots of ways to win at poker.* That idea grew in her, transformed and seized her. She slammed shut her laptop and stuffed it in her briefcase. She grabbed her coat and struggled to put it on.

Ikeda noticed her. "Where are you going?"

"The airport," she said.

Ikeda stood, alarmed. "Bad idea."

"No, good idea," she said.

"What do you think you could possibly do out there?"

"I can play a game of bluff poker," she said, heading toward the elevators.

CHAPTER FIVE

As he stood in the Jefferson Club Lodge's café, staring up into the terrain park beside Fortune's Alley ski run, Hennessy's face turned pale. The first snowboarder wore a white anorak and launched off the tabletop with his pursuers, one wearing green and the other yellow, in hot pursuit. Fifteen feet in the air, the chasers raised their guns and opened up. Even at one hundred yards, Hennessy could see flashes of orange in the snowy air as the paintballs splattered off the white anorak of the quarry.

The first snowboarder managed to land clean. He carved away into the half-pipe and ripped up the far wall. The boarders behind him were not as smooth and had to crank their edges to make the turn. It gave the leader the chance he needed.

He soared off the lip, flipped, spiraled, and landed back in the half-pipe, heading right at his pursuers, blasting them with paintballs that hit them in their goggles. One of them sprawled. The other skidded and tried to return fire.

But their opponent was already swooping away, heading toward the base area. He leaped onto a rail and grinded it neatly, hands raised overhead in victory.

"That dude can ride!" Jack Doore said. "They all can ride!"

"Yeah, they can," Hennessy said, his face sour. "But the same three clowns crashed a snowmobile yesterday. I have to put a stop to this before they hurt someone."

Hennessy barged out the doors onto the heated terrace in only his red Jefferson Club fleece pullover and sheepskin slippers. He put his hand up to shield his eyes from the driving snow and headed up the stairs toward the ski lift, trying to intercept them before they got on.

The three snowboarders zoomed into the base area. Their anoraks were splattered with orange paint. They were laughing like idiots. The big one fell on his back, he was laughing so hard. The others followed suit, ignoring the looks they were getting from the members getting into the lift line.

Hennessy walked up, his hands on his hips, grimacing as the snow bit his face, ears, and hands. "Remove your helmets so I can see you and you can see me," he said, fighting to control his anger.

The snowboarder wearing the green anorak said, "Busted again, kid."

"Completely," the big one in white said, raising his goggles to reveal a freckle-faced boy of fourteen beneath a mop of red unruly hair. He looked at Hennessy with a *What did I do?* expression.

The snowboarder in green raised his goggles, revealing darker hair, blue eyes, and a knowing smirk. He was also fourteen, thinner and stricken with acne. The smallest snowboarder, the one wearing the yellow anorak, took her helmet off completely. She was fourteen too, sturdily built, with dirty blond hair that fell about her shoulders from beneath a brown wool cap pulled down level with the brows of her soft hazel eyes.

"I told them it was a bad idea," she said sullenly in a Boston accent.

"And yet you went along?"

"They forced me."

"It was her idea," the freckle-faced one said. He also had a Boston accent.

Hennessy grimaced and said to the girl, "I thought you said it was a bad idea."

"It was *my* bad idea," she retorted. "Inventing a sport is usually a bad idea. Look at Jake Burton. No one wanted to let him in at first."

"Snowboard paintballing, pretty cool, huh?" the bigger boy said.

"Bet no one's done that at the Jeff Club before," the one in green said.

"No, I expect not," Hennessy snapped.

"Don't be so wound up, old one," the girl said, unbuckling her binding.

"Yeah, Dad," said the one in white. "You know this stuff comes off in the wash."

Hennessy shook his head. "Gimme the guns, go to the locker rooms, take your clothes off, and do the laundry. You're going home first thing in the morning and you're not putting painted clothes in your suitcases. Your grandma would have a cow."

The three were Hennessy's only children, triplets, and entering the rebellious stage of their adolescence. Connor, the one in green, the thinner one with the acne, Hennessy's youngest son by five minutes and the most wanting-to-please of the three, handed over the paint gun silently. Bridger, his oldest, the one in white, the bull in the china shop, always acting in the moment, grumbled, "Grandma's used to it. *She* takes us to tournaments."

"I'm sure she does, but guilt will get you nowhere," Hennessy said.

Bridger slapped the gun in his father's gloved hand. Hennessy's daughter, Hailey, gave him a look of disgust and tossed hers to him, saying, "Take the guns, but let us keep riding. C'mon, Dad, it's dumping! The afternoon's gonna be great."

"Pity you'll miss it. I want you packed and presentable for the party. No rapster hats. No butts hanging out of your pants."

"I'm not going," Bridger said. "It's for rich kids."

"And for tonight, deprived children such as yourself. We're all attending the party. Understood? And you'll wear the clothes your mother packed."

Bridger yanked on his helmet and got his board. "Understood, Sergeant Hennessy."

"Sergeant Hennessy. That has a nice ring to it."

"When can we have the paintballers back?" Connor asked.

"Before you leave for the airport. Locked in their cases."

Bridger scowled and stomped away through the snow past the lift, heading toward the doors at the far end of the lodge. Connor followed, board flung across his shoulder. Hailey brought up the rear, her nose in the air.

Hennessy watched them for a moment, wondering why he seemed to know them less than ever, then started to shiver. He hustled back toward the door to the café. He'd made it no more than ten feet across the heated terrace when he heard a woman's familiar voice call after him.

"Hennessy!" she cried. "Mickey!"

Hennessy stopped with a baleful glance at the doorway and the warmth inside, then turned to meet a woman rushing toward him across the terrace. She wore a form-fitting one-piece white ski suit with a fur fringe around the hood. Her goggles were mirrored and she dragged a girl younger than Ian Doore behind her on a blue plastic sled. The girl wore a snowsuit that matched her own.

"Ms. Wise," Hennessy said, shifting the paintball guns to one freezing hand.

"I have to be at the jetport by noon tomorrow and I want to avoid the paparazzi. I don't want any pictures of Andriana. Is that clear?" she asked.

"As clear as it was yesterday," Hennessy replied.

"Then why were they at the gates, trying to get pictures of us as we arrived?"

"Maybe because you're one of the most famous actresses in the world?" Hennessy said, immediately regretting it.

Cheryl Wise leaned closer to Hennessy. "The most famous. Don't you forget it!"

"No, ma'am."

"Mommy!" the little girl on the sled whined.

The actress ignored her daughter. "If you can't assure me she'll get on the jet without having a camera shoved in her face, maybe I better talk directly to Mr. Burns. In fact, I want to talk to Horatio Burns right now!"

Hennessy was acutely aware of the icicles now building on his mustache.

"You and everyone else, Ms. Wise," he said wearily. "You and everyone else."

CHAPTER SIX

The Hennessy triplets trudged through the falling snow past the outdoor pools and waterslides, heading toward the locker room at the far end of the south wing of the lodge.

When they went by the snowmobile garage, Connor said, "Kinda sucks we only got to use them just that once."

"How was I supposed to know snowmobiles don't do jumps like that?" Bridger shot back.

"I dunno," Hailey said. "Your brain, maybe?"

"I landed it," Bridger said.

"On a rock," Connor said.

Near the kitchen, the smells of garlic and onions filled the air. An older man with a pale white beard and weathered, olive-tone skin, dressed in a snorkel-style winter coat, white pants, and rubber boots, trudged out the door carrying a bucket in his gloved hand.

Bridger got excited. "You going to feed them, Chef Giulio?" he asked.

The old cook pondered the teenagers' attire. "What you do? Paint yourself?"

"Sorta," Connor admitted.

"No good paint yourself," Chef Giulio said firmly.

Giulio Cernitori, commander of the Jefferson Club's renowned kitchen, was an outstanding if temperamental cook who had trained in the great restaurants of Milan, Como, and Tuscany. After a moment's stern pout, he grinned at Hailey and her brothers. "You want see me feed them one more?"

The triplets looked at each other. Connor said, "You heard what Dad said."

Bridger shrugged. "You never get to see this back home. Right, Hailey?"

His sister nodded. "Not exactly feedin' pigeons in Copley Square."

Chef Giulio climbed the bank, following a well-worn path in the snow.

"Dad's gonna flip," Connor said to his brother and sister.

"You're such a wiener sometimes," Bridger replied, starting after the cook toward the tree line. Hailey threw her board in a drift and followed.

Connor hesitated, then dropped his board next to his sister's and brought up the rear. In minutes they were in the trees. The snowfall was lighter here. In places the pine-needled forest floor still showed and threw forth a dank tangy odor. They came to a clearing and the teenagers stopped. Chef Giulio kept going, shaking the bucket of scraps.

A magpie called and darted off a tree branch, coasting in a lazy circle above the cook. Two ravens flushed from their roosts and then settled around the old Italian man, strutting on the freshly fallen snow, their jet-feathered heads cocked as he reached into the bucket, took out a fistful of scraps, and tossed them on the ground. The magpie landed. The ravens pecked at the magpie's long black tail, driving the competitor off the meal before wolfing down meat scraps.

Chef Giulio reached into the bucket again and threw more scraps. Soon the air around him was filled with raucous birds. He laughed and held up a strip of meat. One raven winged toward the meat, its beak open, searching. Chef Giulio almost let the bird take the scrap, but then he lowered it while reaching up with his other arm cocked just so. The raven hesitated, then landed on his left forearm. The cook broke into a beaming smile and fed the meat to the raven before shaking it from its perch.

The raven soared, prize clasped firmly in its beak, trying to outrun two magpies chasing him, croaking their pursuit. Chef Giulio threw the rest of the bucket scraps on the snow. "Is a good one, no?" he said, smiling.

"Best yet!" Hailey said, clapping. She'd seen the cook feed the birds five times since she'd been at the Jefferson Club and still could not get over it.

"Definitely the best," Bridger said.

"Good. Good," Chef Giulio said, patting him on the shoulder and then heading down the hill. "Now I go find Mr. Burns and talk about the menu." He stopped at the entrance to the kitchen. "You come back summertime?"

Hailey shrugged. "If my mom and dad are still talking."

Connor got annoyed. "We're coming back."

"Good," Chef Giulio said. "I teach you to cook, especially you boys. That way you eat well even when no woman wants you."

He laughed going through the door. The triplets heard a clatter of pans and were blasted with savory garlic and onion smells that left them wanting to follow the cook.

"Let's go," Connor said first, trudging away. "We gotta get packed."

"I wish we could stay here longer," Bridger said, following.

Hailey said, "Our flight leaves Bozeman at nine a.m. and there's nothing gonna stop that no matter how much we wish it. School starts Wednesday, and Mom'll be back from her honeymoon with Ted."

"Aww, kid," Bridger said. "You're killing me."

"Just giving you the facts," Hailey said.

"I'm just saying I wouldn't mind some catastrophe hitting," Bridger said. "Like an avalanche or something that would trap us up here."

"Keep dreaming, cartoon idiot," Connor said. "Keep dreaming."

CHAPTER SEVEN

After lunch, Mickey Hennessy left the Doores, who'd decided to catch the last runs of the afternoon, and headed downstairs to the grand ballroom, which had been off-limits the past twenty-four hours as Horatio and Isabel Burns, the founders of the Jefferson Club, decorated for the New Year's Ball.

He checked with the sentries he'd posted at the door and was pleased to hear that they'd turned away Chin Hoc Pan and Cheryl Wise when they tried to see Horatio Burns.

Hennessy entered and came up sharply, amazed at the transformation from just this morning. Thousands of crystal icicles now hung from the ceiling. Leafless poplar trees wrapped in silver pinpoint lights ringed the room. It struck him as a scene right out of Narnia and the Ice Queen's palace.

The rest of the ballroom, however, was a chaotic

maelstrom of final preparations. Men lugged pieces of staging in the back door. The band hauled instruments and the components of a sound system. The banquet crew set tables with the finest crystal and silverware. The florists had just delivered the elegant centerpieces, dominated by silver leaves and ruby roses.

In the middle of it all, Hennessy found Chef Giulio arguing with Horatio Burns.

"Whatchew mean, you no like my sauce?" Chef Giulio demanded.

"Too much garlic," Burns replied. "I don't want my guests having to brush their teeth after the first course. End of issue."

Burns wore ironed Wrangler boot-cut jeans, a starched chambray shirt, and black hand-tooled boots and matching belt with a silver buckle. Even in his late fifties, Burns was a formidable man, six foot five, lean, athletic, ruggedly handsome with pewter-gray hair and jade eyes that were constantly appraising the value of any object in front of him, which in this case was the club's cook.

Hennessy figured Chef Giulio would cave. Most people feared Burns as much as they respected him. How couldn't they? Burns's story was the stuff of wild legends.

Horatio Burns's father died working an oil rig in Gillette, Wyoming, when his wife was pregnant. She died in childbirth, leaving Horatio a newborn orphan. Horatio was smart, obstinate, and scrappy as a child. He bounced from orphanage to foster home to foster home before finally running away for good at seventeen to follow his dead dad's dream of wildcatting natural gas wells in the Powder River country of Wyoming and Montana.

He hit gas on his first try and made his first million by the time he was nineteen when he broadened his scope, using his profits to buy up old mineral rights and claims, mostly phosphorus and bauxite, which he mined. He sold his first company, Burns Minerals, when he was twenty-four for $257 million.

From there Burns branched out into global real estate development, and then transportation and food. He had a brain that never stopped plotting, the physical constitution to outwork his opponents, and a hyper-charismatic personality. Indeed, many an opponent had fallen under Burns's spell and paid for it. Those who crossed him soon learned that the tycoon was, above all, a competitor. He hated to lose at anything.

Hennessy's boss had climbed the seven tallest peaks in the world, including Everest twice, solo-circumnavigated the globe in a sailboat of his own design, and made a sizable fortune recovering gold from Spanish shipwrecks he discovered off Majorca while scuba diving. He also had a temper. An explosive one. And, according to the most recent Forbes ranking, he was currently worth somewhere in the neighborhood of $64 billion.

Chef Giulio seemed unimpressed. He flipped his hand at the tycoon. "I talk to your wife. She know foods better than you."

"Do it, Giulio, and you're fired," Burns growled.

The chef spun on his heels and walked away, saying over his shoulder, "You can't. You already fire me Christmas Eve."

"Then why the hell are you here?" Burns roared.

"Your wife, she hire me back Christmas morning."

Many in the room heard the last part of the argument, and several broke out laughing. Burns sputtered in indignation, then smiled sheepishly. The cell phone on his hip rang; he ripped it off his belt.

"Horatio," he snapped, then listened several moments before asking, "Yeah, Bill. What's the NASDAQ Spyder trading at?"

He listened again, his attention casting radarlike around the ballroom, finding Hennessy and locking on. He crooked a finger at the security director. Hennessy strode up as his boss said, "Okay, if you think you can lay it off, place another hundred million on puts on NASDAQ Spyders at the money, January expiration. Same with the DOW and the AMEX. We're looking for a fix of fifteen to eighteen percent. Use Isabel's LLC account this time."

"Good to see you, Horatio," Hennessy said when he'd hung up.

Burns checked his watch. "Are all the guests on the property?"

"The Grants were the last to arrive. They came through the main gate about an hour and a half ago. They're staying in the hillside cabin next to the Doores."

"How many on staff tonight?"

Hennessy knew that question would be asked. Burns liked to know what he was spending down to the nickel.

Hennessy told him there were fifteen men working security, three on the hill grooming the slopes, twelve on kitchen staff, twelve waiting tables and busing, and a skeleton crew of four manning the lodge.

"You're coordinating with the various bodyguards?" Burns asked.

"Only Mr. Crockett brought his," Hennessy said. "The rest probably heard about our security system and thought, why bother?"

"Of course," Burns said, the barest smile on his lips. "Best money can buy." The smile vaporized back into the poker face. "You're keeping up with Foster's duties?"

With his immediate boss on vacation trekking in Patagonia, Hennessy was overseeing HB1 Financial security worldwide.

"It's been pretty quiet, except in Hong Kong," Hennessy replied. "Some glass windows at the office were broken during the New Year's celebration."

Burns nodded absently and started to turn, already on to the next item on his list.

Hennessy cleared his throat. "Can I ask you something, Horatio?"

The multibillionaire got that confused look about him again, as if his planning for the next moment had been exploded. "What can I do for you?"

"Were you serious, I mean what you told Lou Dobbs about going to cash?"

Burns studied Hennessy a moment, then replied, "Cashed out three weeks ago, Mickey. I'll figure out what to do once I see some logic to the market."

"Would you recommend I do the same?" Hennessy

asked. "With my retirement portfolio, I mean. And the kids' college funds? If the markets tanked, I wouldn't be able to pay for their schooling."

Burns's posture shifted as if he wanted to leave. "I don't ordinarily give investment advice to employees, Mickey. But actions speak louder than words. You know where I stand on the issue."

"I heard talk in the trading room. There's an inordinate number of shorts on for this time of year. I was wondering, in your opinion, should I short it too?"

Burns studied him again, his hand traveling to his lips, before he shook his head vigorously. "That's a dangerous play, Mickey. Shorting a market is for someone who has a lot of balls and can take the risk. I'm sorry. That just isn't you."

Hennessy felt offended that his boss didn't think he had the stomach for that kind of risk, but before he could say anything, a woman's voice shattered the hubbub in the ballroom: "Ho-ra-tio!"

Burns's wife, Isabel, a stunning Italian woman in her late thirties, rushed across the floor in her latest daytime couture from Milan. "Giulio's right! The garlic is perfecto in the pesto for the crab cakes. Even my mother would say so, God rest her soul."

She raised herself on her toes and kissed her husband on the cheek.

"Isabel, your mother burned off her taste buds with cayenne by the time she was thirty," Burns replied. "Giulio will reduce the garlic or the sauce is off the menu!"

His wife's fists clenched. "Don't you have enough to

do without adding Giulio's job? Why don't you go jump off the mountain and parachute down or something?"

Burns cocked his head toward the windows. "Kinda snowing and windy out, in case you hadn't noticed, my sweet."

"Then go in your padded room and bang your head against the walls, because you are driving everyone here crazy. Especially me."

The squabbles between the Burnses were legendary and ordinarily very entertaining, but Hennessy took his leave and hurried from the ballroom.

Hennessy retrieved the paintball guns from the concierge and took the elevator to the fourth floor, north wing. In moments he was inside his office. He laid the paintball guns on the desk, and with a look out the window at the guests skating on the ice rink, he plopped in his chair and sighed.

His attention flickered to the photo of him graduating from the academy. Beside it was a framed letter of commendation, citing Hennessy for bravery and being wounded in the line of duty while protecting the Secretary of State. Hennessy shook his head, having for what seemed the millionth time an internal argument over whether he should throw both the picture and the letter of citation out. They had saved him, it was true, but more often than not he felt trapped by them. Then again, they'd gotten him this job and he'd healed here, hadn't he?

But what about the future? Where am I going to end up? He made good money working for HB1 Financial.

But even if he saved twenty percent a year, he wasn't going to retire secure. He'd lost too much in the divorce and its aftermath. He flashed on an image of himself cooking Dinty Moore beef stew over a hot plate in a single-room-occupancy hotel while Horatio Burns's reply echoed in his head: *Shorting a market is for someone who has a lot of balls. That just isn't you.*

Hennessy looked at the clock: one-thirty p.m., three-thirty on the East Coast. The markets closed in half an hour. He snatched up the phone and dialed the number of his financial advisor. The answer was immediate.

"Mickey, what the fuck?"

"Hey, Jerry," Hennessy said, smiling.

"Market's bulling out the year," Jerry said. *"You're making money."*

"Good," Hennessy said. "How much?"

There was a pause. Hennessy heard computer keys clacking, then Jerry said, *"You're up eleven percent on the year."*

"That's good," Hennessy allowed. "But I want you to sell it all. And go to cash and use it to buy puts on the NASDAQ Spyders, the DOW, and the AMEX, on the money, January expiration. Fifteen to eighteen percent fix."

There was dead silence on the other end of the line. Then Jerry groaned and said, *"Mickey, have you picked up again?"*

"No!" Hennessy said, feeling hot under the collar. "I heard some serious players out here saying the markets could tank and there are all sorts of shorts on them."

Another dead silence. *"What serious players?"*

Hennessy knew he shouldn't say, but blurted, "Sir Lawrence Treadwell, for one."

"Sir Lawrence fuckin' Treadwell told you he was shorting the markets by buying puts on the Spyders at the money with a fifteen to eighteen percent fix?"

"Not exactly, but yes. And so are many others. I heard Friedrich Klinefelter say there were huge short positions appearing."

"Mickey, the market's a bull with testicles like A-bombs. If you short at the money and the bull's boner continues to rise, you could be ruined in a matter of hours. Everything you and I have built for your retirement and the kids' education. Not to mention you· nest egg for that cabin you want down on the Big Hole."

"I know, Jer, but maybe I should listen to some of the greatest investors in the world, have some balls, and take a risk." He paused. "In fact, I'm ordering you to do it."

"Your money, Mick," Jerry groaned. *"But I'm telling you this isn't easy to do. It's New Year's Eve. Market closes in twenty-five minutes."*

"But not impossible?"

"No."

"Do it and call me back to confirm."

"Mickey—"

"Do it, Jerry." Hennessy slammed down the phone, feeling giddy with the excitement of the unknown. Just the way he used to feel before being deployed on a big security detail—on the edge, flirting with danger and chance.

Then he broke into a cold, paralyzing sweat.

"Have some balls," he said, jumping to his feet, grabbing up the paintball guns, and heading into the hallway before he could change his mind. "Have some balls."

He walked the hallways, checking the cameras and the doors, heading in a haphazard pattern toward his small apartment on the fifth floor of the south wing. Twenty minutes later and ten feet from his apartment door, his cell phone rang.

"What the fuck?" Jerry said. *"It's done. You went to cash for $533,680 and change and I used it to buy puts on the money, NASDAQ, DOW, and AMEX Spyders. Sixteen percent fix. January expiration. There were three minutes of trading left after your orders were executed and in that one hundred and eighty seconds, every single index rose. Happy New Year's, fuckhead, you just lost yourself twenty-three grand."*

Jerry hung up.

Hennessy's gut churned. His head pounded. He threw his hand out against the door, feeling dizzy and the urge to go have a drink.

Oh, my God, he thought. *What have I done?*

Like a zombie, Hennessy passed his electronic master key over the reader. The door clicked. He pushed it open.

Beyond the kitchen, he saw his son Bridger sprawled on the living room floor, eating pretzels and watching the Boston College football game. Connor snoozed on the couch. Both boys were still in their long underwear. Their snowboard parkas and pants were hung on the backs of chairs in the kitchen and dripping diluted yellow paint on the floor. Hailey appeared in the kitchen in her robe, her hair up in a towel.

She looked around, saw the mess, saw her father, and said, "Uh-oh."

"What the Christ is your problem?" Hennessy roared.

"Not my bad, Dad!" Hailey said, holding her hands up.

Connor's head shot up from the couch. "Shit."

Bridger scrambled for his clothes. "We didn't think you'd be back so soon."

"Look at this place!" Hennessy yelled. "Didn't I tell you to go to the laundry?"

"I did," Hailey said.

"We took the initiative of doing it in the bathtub," Connor said.

"Maybe we shouldn't have," Bridger said.

"Gee, do you think?" Hailey shot back.

Hennessy fumed, "Get this place cleaned now!"

He slammed down everything in his pockets on a small table by the door—wallet, cell phone, master key—and then, paintball guns in hand, stormed down the hall into his bedroom and slammed shut the door.

"You'd think we lit the place on fire," Bridger said. He had a roll of paper towels and was on his knees wiping up the kitchen floor.

Connor stuffed clothes haphazardly into two open duffels. "Yeah, the old one's really on the ragged edge. I guess being security for this party's a big deal."

"So maybe we better not tell him we don't want to go," Bridger said.

"Yeah," Hailey said. "That would be a major ballistic mistake."

CHAPTER EIGHT

All through the afternoon and into early evening, the storm intensified in power and scope. The gale winds gusted and turned the snowflakes to needles that slashed at the lenses of the night-vision goggles the general and his men wore as they fought through thigh-deep drifts high on Jefferson Peak behind the club. The loose snowpack sloughed and slid around them as they made their way north. At their passing, the snow made soft groaning noises as if in misery.

"This thing could slide, General," Truth barked into his headset.

The general was ahead of Truth, sideslabbing across the head of a ravine. Below and to his east two miles, the lights of the lodge glowed through the storm.

"Then we move harder," the general ordered. "Quarter mile now. Double-time."

Several voices grumbled as the pace quickened to

that of a hunting pack that scents its quarry just ahead. Cobb led, breaking trail at a relentless pace through thickets of fir trees that grabbed at their packs and slings. They passed through a glen of towering ponderosa pines, which gave way finally to a steep, open sage slope that faced southwest across the valley toward the ski slopes on Hellroaring Peak. On that mountain's lower flank, the headlights of a snow-grooming machine bobbed and cut the storm.

Truth and the general crept forward together, peering through their night-vision goggles, making every movement minute. The general made to take another step when Truth stopped him.

"Three feet in front of my chest," he muttered.

The general stepped up beside Truth and squinted. In his night-vision goggles the pride of the Jefferson Club's security system was revealed as scores of undulating violet laser beams twisting and spiraling in a space two feet wide and ten feet high.

"Like snakes in a pit," Truth said admiringly.

"Spread out according to plan," the general called through his headset to his soldiers. "Two-point-two seconds. Any one of you misses, they'll have the dogs on us."

The Dirty Shame Saloon, off the mezzanine south wing of the Jefferson Club Lodge, featured real leather saddles as barstools and a kitschy cowboy motif. Bridger and Connor Hennessy slouched through the swinging doors, their hands buried in the pockets of their cargo pants, which hung across their mid-butts, revealing boxer shorts. They glared uncertainly out from under their Red Sox caps at the children and grandchildren of the super-elite who were wolfing gourmet pizzas, guzzling sodas, and gunning down life-sized three-dimensional bad guys on high-def video games. Hailey stood beside her brothers, wearing jeans and an orange long-sleeve T-shirt that said BOARD LIKE A GIRL. On her head, she wore the brown wool skullcap that covered her eyebrows.

"Thought I told you not to wear that," her father said. Hennessy had taken a shower, a nap, and put on a tuxedo. He'd also decided to give his money back to Jerry first thing Wednesday morning, the twenty-six-thousand-dollar loss a lesson learned.

"Will you get off my case, Dad?" Hailey muttered back.

"I'm not on your case."

"Ever since we got here, you've been telling me how to act and what to do."

"C'mon, Hailey," he protested. "It's just that you're pretty and with that hat you look like . . ." He didn't know what to say.

"Snoop Dog's biatch?" Connor said.

Hailey punched him in the arm. "Jerkewitz."

"Stop it, all of you!" their father hissed.

"What'd I do?" Bridger asked.

"I expect perfect behavior from you," Hennessy retorted. "Now go in and have a good time. Many of the games inside have never been played before tonight."

"No way," said Bridger, looking into the saloon with renewed interest.

"Way," Hennessy said. "And pull up your goddamned pants. One of you farts, you'll knock someone over."

Hailey looked disgusted.

Connor started cackling. "Okay, so maybe we'll stay awhile."

Hennessy nodded. "I'll swing back in an hour. And I'm on my cell."

Bridger tugged his pants a begrudging two inches higher. "Upstairs is off-limits?"

"Completely."

"We need money?" Hailey asked.

"All paid for. Have a good time."

Hennessy watched until they'd each snagged a slice of pizza and found a free game to play, and then he left, heading back into the grand atrium, empty now save a maintenance man vacuuming.

As Hennessy climbed the stairs toward the ballroom, he spoke into the mike on his lapel. "Central, how we doing?"

"Looks like the rich folk be having a shindig," a voice replied in his earbud.

Hennessy smiled, but replied, "Let's cool the sarcasm on radio, Krueger."

"Roger that, boss. Sorry."

Ahead, through the open doors, the ballroom came into view. In the corner, a string quartet played a Bach sonata against the happy roar of a prosperous crowd. The men looked at ease in their tuxedos. Some clutched highball glasses, others unlit Havanas and wine goblets. Their wives were dressed to kill in original evening gowns from Tom Ford, Carmen Marc Valvo, Stella

McCartney, and a dozen other top designers. They wore ballroom slippers from Linda Pritcher, Jimmy Choo, and Manolo Blahnik. Their jewels were equally spectacular. Waiters moved among them, offering mouthwatering canapés, puffs, and other delicacies from Chef Giulio's kitchen.

Some hundred and eighty people had RSVP'd. At first sweeping glance, it seemed to Hennessy that there were probably another twenty to twenty-five guests yet to arrive. Isabel Burns had left strict instructions that she be notified when everyone was inside the lodge so Chef Giulio could time dinner.

Hennessy spoke with the armed security guard at the door, then eased his way over to check the terrace doors. Locked. He made his way along the row of floor-to-ceiling windows, pausing now and then, his attention casting over the crowd.

As he slid toward the bar, he heard a drawling, baritone voice boom over the din, "President can do what he likes, call for all the programs he likes. He's got the bully pulpit. But, gentlemen, when it comes to the country's power of the purse strings, I hold 'em. And let me say what a humbling honor it is for this poor, grateful son of Alabama."

Hennessy spotted the source of the voice: a walrus of a man with biscuit-colored hair and pastry folds of skin that sloughed about his eyes and drooped in curtains under his chin, hiding the collar of his tuxedo shirt and most of his bow tie. He was in his early sixties, holding the lapel of his tux where it strained at his prodigious belly, and grinning at the men waiting with him in line for the bar. Albert Crockett, Friedrich Klinefelter, and Chin Hoc Pan all looked as happy as wet terriers.

Hennessy understood. Senator Worth Stonington had made him feel the same way the day before. The chairman of the U.S. Senate Appropriations Committee had almost immediately crowded his personal space, throwing an arm around Hennessy and calling him "son." He'd also smelled of whiskey and breath mints and struck Hennessy as one of the most self-satisfied men he'd ever met.

But that wasn't surprising: Stonington did indeed hold the purse strings of the U.S. Senate, and was thereby the most heavily lobbied politician on Capitol Hill. A graduate of the Crimson Tide and Duke Law School, the senator had a reputation of being as brilliant and ruthless as he was corpulent, a consummate political player who always somehow managed to portray himself as a champion of the common man, the son of a simple cooper who'd made good.

The senator from Alabama turned to the bartender and said, "Two fingers of Maker's Mark, neat, my good man. He glanced at his companions, then added, "Make it four of 'em and sides of branch water."

"Will our own springwater do, Senator?" the bartender asked.

"Oh, hell, yes," Stonington said, breaking into a wet, throaty laugh. "Who drinks the goddamned water anyway?"

Albert Crockett held his hands together in a way that reminded Hennessy of a cemetery director greeting the bereaved. "Not I, Senator," he said. "Not I."

That's when Hennessy spotted Crockett's personal bodyguard standing off the tycoon's left shoulder. Alex Patton, a brawny African-American, nodded his way. Hennessy nodded back. Patton had worked in the Secret Service for twenty years. He was old school and good and Hennessy had liked him right away even if his boss looked like he wanted to sell you a hole in the ground.

The young, tough-looking blond woman standing next to Patton was another story. Helen Johnson was a sergeant with the U.S. Capitol Police, and in charge of protecting Senator Stonington. She'd made no bones about the fact that she would not yield to Hennessy or his men in case of a threat. In fact, she'd acted as if everyone on the property would be better served by having her take charge of security. The hard glance she shot him told Hennessy she still thought so.

"Senator, if you don't mind, I'd prefer something besides whiskey," Friedrich Klinefelter said. "One of the fine Italian reds reputedly stocked for the evening."

"I prefer wine as well," Chin Hoc Pan said.

Senator Stonington scowled. "Now, ya know, ya'll insult a man down in Alabama when you won't drink fine bourbon when he offers it to you."

Chin Hoc Pan looked unperturbed. "I rarely drink liquor, Senator."

Klinefelter smiled weakly. "I'm a wine lover as well."

A sheen of sweat appeared on the senator's upper lip, which curled with mirth. He took one of the shots of bourbon off the bar top, sipped it, swallowed, then licked the booze and sweat off his upper lip with a neat little flick of his tongue before saying, "Seems like I remember you're bidding on rebuilding our embassy in Beijing, Mr. Pan."

Silence held several moments before Klinefelter broke and said, "Bourbon sounds good, Senator." He took his glass, sipped it, and quivered lightly.

"Kinda lights ya up inside, don't it?" Stonington said as he handed a glass to Crockett. "Trick is never to drink too much. Kick ya worse than a mule. Right, Mr. Pan?"

Chin Hoc Pan nodded unhappily. He accepted the proffered shot glass, examined the rim for cleanliness, and then poured a brief stream of the caramel liquid into his mouth, careful not to let the vessel touch his lips. He shuddered. His eyelashes closed.

"How's that?" Stonington asked.

"Like the kick of the mule, Senator," Chin Hoc Pan said.

Mickey Hennessy took a deep, calming breath, willing himself not to study the bottles behind the bar, and moved on.

He snagged a crab cake in pesto sauce from the plate of a passing waitress and popped it in his mouth. He thought the taste incredible, and then spotted Isabel Burns, breathtaking in a Versace original black evening gown and diamond necklace and earrings insured for eleven million dollars. Hennessy always got an inventory of the jewels Isabel would be carrying with her at the club. He walked up to her as she finished speaking with one of the waitresses.

"Anything I can help you with?" he asked.

"Everything seems covered, thank you, Mickey,"

she replied, her attention moving past him, examining the crowd. "The celebration is well received?"

"Everyone seems to be enjoying themselves. And I've heard several comments that the food's fantastic."

Isabel smiled appreciatively. "Of course it is. The best money can buy."

The wife of the third-wealthiest man in the world was born in Palermo, the awkward, bookish daughter of a judge who prosecuted the Mafia. As legend had it, the summer of her seventeenth year she grew into her beauty. At twenty-three, while studying law in Rome, she entered a Miss Italy contest on a lark and was soon named the country's entrant to the Miss Universe Pageant.

Horatio Burns had been in the audience when Isabel stepped out during the swimsuit phase of the competition. He was about to turn forty, and when he saw her he fell head over heels in love. He tracked her down after she finished second, showered her with clothes and jewels, and married her a year later. They had rarely been apart since.

Burns once told Hennessy that Isabel was his soul mate, the only one who'd ever been able to keep up with him, physically and intellectually, his closest confidante and advisor. From his own experience, Hennessy knew that Isabel Burns could be the nicest person in the world. But you did not cross her. She had the king's ear and knew it.

So Hennessy noticed when her practiced genial expression suddenly hardened, as if she'd spotted someone in the crowd she really didn't want to see. He turned to find Sir Lawrence and Lady Alicia Treadwell coming toward them. A slender British blonde of indeterminate age and extensive cosmetic surgery, Alicia Treadwell wore a green silk gown that shimmered as she walked and highlighted the emerald accessories on her fingers, wrist, neck, and ears.

"Isabel," Alicia Treadwell gushed, grabbing her hands and blowing Euro-kisses past her cheeks. "What a marvelous, marvelous soiree."

When Alicia Treadwell released Isabel, her husband stepped in her place. Sir Lawrence caught Isabel beneath both forearms and blew kisses at her as well, saying as he withdrew, "We're so glad we accepted your kind invitation. The heath is much too dreary this time of year and somehow Bora Bora feels obscene."

The brief contact with Sir Lawrence did not put Isabel Burns at ease. Indeed, the embrace seemed to rattle her. Hennessy swore her hands trembled and she had to quickly reach out with the other to stop it, bowing her head away from the oil tycoon, while saying, "Thank you, Larry. I had much help. Horatio inspected every detail."

Alicia Treadwell tittered as if she couldn't believe it. "Horatio has time for party favors? I'd think he'd leave that to the professionals."

"In case you do not notice, he can be the controlling bastard," Isabel said, getting hold of herself and projecting her beauty pageant smile.

"Where is your alpha male?"

"Upstairs, I think. Seeing that the children are entertained."

"A party for the children, what a magnificent idea," Sir Lawrence commented.

"Brilliant!" Alicia Treadwell said. "Isabel, this party is a smashing—"

The lights flickered and then died into blackness.

CHAPTER NINE

"Now!" the general barked into his headset.

Inches from the optical barrier fence, the long line of snow-camouflaged men and women erupted from their crouches and hurled themselves forward into a roll that threw them far down the steep sage-covered slope. They landed on their packs, boots and arms splayed wide in self-arrest.

Far below them, the lights came back on in the Jefferson Club Lodge. Through binoculars, the general watched the guard shack out front for sign of alarm. He could make out someone exiting the shack, but there were no sirens and certainly no indication of gathering forces.

"Okay," the general said after several minutes' observation. "We're clean."

"Game's on," Truth said. *"Total silence until we hear from Radio."*

The armed troops split up wordlessly.

* * *

Inside the ballroom, the lights came on low and gathered power. Many in the crowd began to chuckle with relief and look all around as if seeing the decorations anew.

Isabel Burns said, "Thank God for generators. The storm must be very bad."

The security director was already moving away from her, speaking into his lapel mike, "This is Hennessy, what the hell was that?"

Krueger's voice came back over the earpiece, *"Something big must have blown on the line between here and Bozeman. We've already called Northwest Energy."*

"Generators?" he asked, leaving the ballroom for the short hallway before the stairs up to the atrium.

"Everything rebooted pretty as you please."

"I'm coming up anyway," he said. "Everyone in here?"

"The Grants pulled in just before it went dark. They were the last."

Hennessy entered the grand atrium in time to find Horatio Burns coming down the hall from the direction of the Dirty Shame Saloon. He didn't look happy.

"What the hell was that?" Burns asked. "I thought we upgraded the line last year."

"They're only as good as the power lines they're tied into."

"How long was security down?" his boss demanded.

"Two-point-two seconds."

"My wife?"

"Chatting up the Treadwells."

He studied Hennessy a moment, then clapped him

on the shoulder before saying, "Yes, well, then. Duty calls." He strode off toward the ballroom whistling.

Outside in the storm, huddled in an aspen grove by the side of Fortune's Alley ski run, the general, Truth, and Cobb waited as the snowcat turned and headed back their way. They stayed well hidden until the snow-grooming machine was almost upon them. Cobb coiled himself and sprang as it passed. He got alongside the snowcat and leaped up over its spinning treads onto the fender. The thud of his landing caused the operator to slow and then to stop. The operator opened the machine's door. In a vicious series of motions, Cobb grabbed the man by the chin and the base of the neck and broke his spine before he could even scream.

Mickey Hennessy entered the security control room. Krueger and Lerner were typing on their computer keyboards, going through a series of checks.

"Update?"

"Northwest Energy says a transformer blew on the Norris Road," Lerner said.

Hennessy caught motion on one of the surveillance screens. The snowcat drove by the base chairlifts toward the storage barn. He watched the machine a moment, then looked at the clock. It was ten-thirty. "Fred must have set the record for grooming."

Krueger shrugged. "On a powder day folks don't want too much groomed."

Hennessy relaxed. It made sense. "Okay, I'm out of here."

"Someone's bringing us food, right?" Lerner asked.

"I'll make sure of it," Hennessy promised, and shut the door behind him.

Four miles away, inside the arched stone and steel gatehouse to the Jefferson Club, Al Curtis and Pete Tompkins, the guards on duty, two regular Montana guys with wives and kids and mortgages, were drinking whiskey from their coffee cups, watching a comedy on the DVD player, and laughing their asses off.

The snowcat's headlights appeared up the hill from the gate, herky-jerky in the storm and coming down the slope toward the gatehouse very fast.

Curtis frowned. "What the hell's got Fred down here?"

"Probably heard there was free booze," Tompkins said, slurping from his cup.

Curtis got up from his seat. "He's going like a bat out of hell."

Indeed, the snowcat was now roaring at them. They could hear the growling of the diesel engines over the blare of the television. The snowcat's front blades were raised. The headlights were flaring like the eyes of some monster gone amok.

Tompkins jumped to his feet. "Idiot's gonna crash."

Curtis grabbed his coat and followed Tompkins. The snowcat downshifted and flung sideways into a power slide toward the gate.

"He's gonna hit!" Curtis yelled, moving backward fast.

The machine skidded, rocked to rest, and cut to idle not two feet from the steel bars of the gate, headlights on high, blinding the security guards like deer.

Hearing the doors to the snowcat open, Tompkins called out in a scolding tone, "Fred, you been huffing the chronic or something?"

A silenced round from Cobb's pistol caught Tompkins between the eyes. He fell backward. Curtis saw his partner die and tried to run while fumbling for his pistol. Cobb's gun thumped again, catching the guard behind the ear, dumping him in the snow.

Down in the Dirty Shame Saloon, Hennessy stood behind his children watching Harry Armstrong, the famous magician, performing close-up magic tricks. Armstrong was dressed in black leather and chains and making objects disappear and then appear inside empty soda bottles.

This time Ian Doore had given Armstrong his Hot Wheels fire truck. When the truck disappeared from the magician's hands, the boy began to fidget anxiously. When the toy reappeared inside an empty bottle of root beer, he turned, agitated, and twitched, looking for his mother.

"I don't want my truck in there," Ian said in a tremulous voice. "I want my truck."

Hennessy felt a tug on his heart. Poor kid. He looked at his sons, upset too. So was Hailey, who stared at the ground.

"Wait, wait," the magician said, calming the boy. He showed him his truck was now gone from the bottle. And then he plucked the toy from Ian's pants pocket.

Everyone gasped, then clapped, even Bridger, the natural cynic.

"He's good," Bridger said. "Not Mindfreak good. But real good."

Ian ran to his mother. Stephanie Doore wore a conservative black evening dress, with Tahitian pearls at her neck and earlobes. Ian went into her arms and hugged her tight, his right hand finding her left ear and stroking it.

"It's okay," she said. "It's just magic. Mommy's got to go upstairs now."

Ian's teal-blue eyes watered. He shook his head. "You stay."

Hailey walked over and said, "Would you like to sit with me and watch the show? My name's Hailey." She reached out her hand.

Hennessy said to Stephanie Doore, "My daughter. An accomplished babysitter."

"Okay, Ian?" Stephanie Doore said. "You'll stay with Hailey?"

Hailey smiled and nodded. Ian hesitated, then nodded grudgingly.

Hennessy glanced up at the clock. It was almost eleven. "We've got to go eat with the muckety-mucks. I'll be back for Happy New Year's."

When Hennessy and Stephanie Doore reentered the ballroom, they spotted Horatio Burns talking with her husband and his business partner, Aaron Grant. To Hennessy's amusement, he noticed that Doore was wearing sneakers with his tuxedo. Grant, a bearded bruin of a man wearing thick-lensed glasses, was more conventionally attired. This was not surprising given that Aaron

Grant was the business brains behind YES! while Doore was the visionary. Grant had a plate of hors d'oeuvres in one hand and was munching greedily as they walked up.

"Slow down there, cowboy, you've still got five courses to go," said Grant's wife, Margaret, a stout Korean-American woman, patting her husband's girth.

Grant shrugged, swallowed, and stabbed one of the pesto crab cakes from his plate. "Maggie, you've got to try one of these, the sauce is incredible."

Margaret Grant sighed, then opened her mouth, accepting the morsel. She broke into a moan of pleasure. "That is good. Just the right amount of garlic."

Horatio Burns grimaced before he turned again to Doore. "So you're not concerned about the economy, Jack?"

Doore shrugged. "It's not where my attention is. I think YES! will continue to do well because we focus on innovation, not worrying about the price of our stock."

"You won't last long at number one with that kind of attitude," Burns warned. "The markets can be brutal."

"We pay attention to our stockholders," Aaron Grant assured him. "And no one I've heard is griping lately."

Burns still seem dissatisfied. "What about Congress and the election?"

Doore smiled serenely. "Political tides ebb and flow, left and right, Horatio, but I'm not positioned along those spectrums. Like most Americans, I'll vote for the best person for the job. The collective consciousness always rules. I can live with that."

Grant nodded. "Jack and I believe the world is on

the verge of the greatest creative period in the history of man. Politics can't get in the way."

Burns's disapproval deepened. But then he caught sight of Hennessy and said, "Reasonable men can agree to disagree. If you'll excuse me?"

He came around to Hennessy, saying, "Walk with me." When they were out of earshot, Burns said, "I've been meaning to tell you to relax. I know how hard you've been working and you deserve a break when Foster gets back from South America."

Hennessy nodded. It had been almost a year since his last vacation. "I could use it and early January is slow."

They arrived at the kitchen door, where they were greeted with the aroma of the appetizer coming out of the ovens. *Sfinciuni di Montana,* a Sicilian-style pizza stuffed with a conza of minced elk and antelope, dry white wine, and ricotta and fontina cheeses.

"Smells incredible," Hennessy said as a waiter passed with the first serving.

"It does, doesn't it?" Burns replied. Then he said, "Go on and have yourself a drink, Mickey. Enjoy the festivities. See if there's a rich widow in the room to woo."

Hennessy's affable manner hardened. "I don't drink, Horatio."

Burns looked mortified. "My God, I'm such an asshole at times. I'm sorry, Mickey. I completely forgot. It's a testimony to your sobriety that I forgot."

"No problem," Hennessy said. "I'll look for a teetotaling rich widow."

Burns chuckled, made a gun with his fingers, and

pointed it at Hennessy. "There you go. Cheryl Wise is divorced at the moment, I believe."

"Oscar-winning actresses are kinda out of my league."

"Don't know until you try," Burns said. "And the more times you try, the more times you win. Take a risk, make the big play. That's always been my motto, Mickey. If you're going to shoot, shoot for the moon. Why not? Someone's gotta win. Someone's gotta be number one. And no one ever remembers the guy who comes in second or third."

"Right," Hennessy said. He'd heard the speech before.

Burns pushed through the kitchen doors, calling, "Isabel! Are you in here?"

Hennessy ate dinner with several honchos in the global security business and their wives. He made small talk with them as he ate his way through bison tenderloins served rare with a Chianti sauce and ruffed grouse in rosemary and thyme. He kept up the pretense that he was not upset all the way through dessert: six different kinds of cannolis Chef Giulio had crafted himself.

But after coffee was served, waiters coursed through the crowd, pouring Aristona and Collard champagnes into crystal flutes. Hennessy waved his waiter off, unable not to think about the fact that Burns had told him to have a drink. *What's with that?*

Burns had known from the beginning that he was a recovering alcoholic and prescription drug addict. When Hennessy interviewed with Burns and Gregg Foster for his job, a discussion of his addictions had dominated the conversation.

Does anyone remember anything about me? Hennessy asked himself, feeling suddenly bitter. *Am I that invisible in this world?*

He looked around. Nearly everyone was sipping the rare champagne and smacking their lips against the sweet, cold, biting satisfaction of it. Suddenly Hennessy swore he could taste it, champagne, and his tongue arched at the anticipation of more. An alarm went off in his head.

Feeling morose in crowded places with lots of people drinking was one of his triggers. It always had been, from his first drink in high school and on to the end. He folded his hands and looked down at the dregs in his coffee cup, feeling pursued by beasts he thought he'd long ago locked up for good, but now baying at him to take the merest sip of the champagne, just to taste it for real.

It was like his friends in recovery always said: Even for people with twenty years' sobriety, the desire to get wasted can hit at any moment. Hennessy had the five-year anniversary of his last drink and his last pill coming up in March. *I won't screw that up.*

He excused himself from the table. He had to take a walk, talk to his Higher Power and get his head on straight.

From a knoll four hundred yards above the Jefferson Club Lodge, the general crouched with his men, huddled against fir trees, watching the entrance through binoculars and the driving snow.

The general turned to look at one of his troops. "Radio. You're up."

Radio stood without hesitation, left his pack, and began wading downhill through the snow, unzipping his parka as he went. A hundred yards from where the lodge lights reached, he took off the parka, pants, and heavy boots. He wore a tuxedo underneath.

As Mickey Hennessy made his way toward the staircase to the grand atrium, Horatio Burns jumped up on the band stage. The tycoon flashed a grin and cleared his throat, looking about at the audience like the master deal-maker and marketer that he was.

"I trust you've all enjoyed the dinner," Burns said, waving toward the kitchen door where Chef Giulio stood in the doorway lit by a spotlight. "It was courtesy of Chef Giulio Cernitori, master of our kitchen here at the Jefferson Club."

The ballroom erupted into applause. Hennessy stopped at the ballroom door. Several people had risen to their feet and were cheering, *"Bravisimo!"* The cook grinned and clasped his hands overhead in victory. He brought out his staff for a bow.

When the hullabaloo died down, Burns said, "For the gratification of those of you who are already members of the Jefferson Club, Giulio has told my wife, Isabel, that he has agreed to stay with us for another three years."

"For a better salary and many trips home to Como paid for!" Chef Giulio shouted.

Laughter broke in a wave across the room. Burns chuckled. "For a much better salary and many trips home to Como paid for." He paused a beat, then said, "We have a lot of fun here at the Jefferson Club. I think the members present would agree."

Light applause rippled through the crowd.

"The Jefferson Club is a retreat from a busy world," Burns went on. "A place for the accomplished to come and relax in luxury, yet rugged enough to challenge the most hard-core skier and alpinist."

Burns was delivering his standard sales pitch for the Jefferson Club, so Hennessy felt no compunction about heading toward the staircase up to the grand atrium. The elevator opened and one of the waitresses pushed a dessert cart out and he had to stand aside before climbing to the atrium and crossing to the cloakroom in the lobby, where he retrieved his parka and boots. He went out the door and climbed down the massive stone steps beneath the timber canopy that covered the Jefferson Club's main entry. The driving snow billowed in beneath the roof, swirled, and stung his eyes.

A man in his late thirties, handsome, came in out of the storm from the direction of the stables smoking a cigarette. Snow clung to the sandy hair that hung in his eyes. Snow caked the shoulders of his tuxedo too. He wove a little on his feet when he saw Hennessy, then kept walking, raising the cigarette and saying drunkenly in an Aussie accent, "Shitty habit. Froze my ass off for a bloody cancer stick and a piss."

Hennessy hadn't recognized him at first, then thought he did. Marc Singer, an Australian clothes manufacturer. "Mr. Singer, you can smoke on the terrace. It's heated."

"Will do next time, mate," he said and went inside.

Hennessy watched the door close behind Singer, thinking there was something odd about the man's actions. Was it the way he held himself? Were his mannerisms exaggerated? *He's shit-faced, what do you want?* Hennessy thought at last.

He put up his hood and walked by the security shack. Peters, a beefy young guard that he'd recently hired, stepped from the shack and said, "Tough night for a walk, boss."

"Just needed some air," Hennessy replied. "I'll be back in time to ring in the New Year with my kids."

"They're going home tomorrow?"

"Yup."

"Seem like good kids."

"Yeah, they are," he said and walked out to face the full brunt of the storm.

CHAPTER TEN

As Radio passed the woman manning the lodge's reception desk, he held up the wet pack of cigarettes and in that Aussie accent delivered the same line about it being a bad habit and that he had to quit. He went straight to the atrium staircase, climbed it quickly for a man supposed to be hammered, and reached the second-floor landing. He entered the north hallway, where he began to stagger happily toward the door to the security control room. He did not look at the camera bubble when he banged on the door with his fist.

"Hey, Tina, dear," he yelled. "Open up. Forgot my bloody key."

He kept banging. "C'mon, Tina, I'm sorry what I said about us not belonging here. C'mon! We'll join, okay? We'll join. Whatever, love."

"Sir?" a voice called from back down the hall.

Radio glanced left. A waiter wheeled a room service cart toward him.

"That's not—" the waiter began.

The security center door opened. Krueger leaned out. "Sir, you're in—"

Radio raised two arms in a V position, one toward the guard, one toward the waiter. From under his cuffs, on spring-loaded slides, silenced .25-caliber pistols jumped into his hands. He pulled the triggers simultaneously, hitting the guard and the waiter in the face. The waiter rocked backward and landed with a thud on the carpet.

Radio caught Krueger as he fell, then used his corpse to batter open the door. Then he heaved the body at Lerner, who was rising from his chair. The live guard crashed back onto the console, pinned by his dead partner's weight. Lerner had one terrifying moment before Radio's third shot hit him on the bridge of his nose.

The bodies fell in a heap on the floor. Radio retreated into the hallway, grabbed the dead waiter by the scruff of his white coat, and dragged him into the security center. He got the door closed, put on latex gloves, and stacked the bodies in the corner. Finished, he studied the screen that showed the hallway outside the security center, saw it was still empty, and then went out and got the food off the cart. It was going to be a long night.

He shut the door again and bolted the lock. He dropped into Lerner's chair and slipped on his headset. He typed on the keyboards and accessed programs that allowed him to add a new frequency to the Jefferson Club's mobile communications system.

Finished, he said, "Three minutes to midnight. Main gate?"

Cobb's voice instantly crackled over his headset, *"Set. Snowcat in place."*

"East flank?"

"Affirmative."

"West?"

"Affirmative."

"North."

"Ready."

"General, this is Radio."

"Go, Radio."

"We control the perimeter. Attack at will."

In the Dirty Shame Saloon, Harry Armstrong, the Las Vegas magician, yelled, "Two minutes to midnight, boys and girls!"

The children blew noisemakers and sprang confetti-filled poppers. Bridger exploded one under Connor's chin, causing a shout of outrage followed by a chase over couches until Connor got his revenge with a confetti popper to his brother's neck.

"You two! Stop horsing around!" Armstrong yelled.

Bridger rubbed the base of his neck and frowned. "He talking to us, kid?"

"No," Hailey deadpanned. "That's not why everyone's looking at you."

"Where's Dad?" Bridger said, ignoring the looks. "He said he'd be here."

"He's got a minute and a half," Connor said. "He could still make it."

"Unlikely," Hailey said, hardening. "Old habits are hard to break."

Out in the snowstorm, the gale subsided to intermittent gusts. Hailey's father felt each snowflake as a stinging reminder to walk the line and stay sober. He did so by avoiding the negative and seeking the positive, a way of thinking and believing that had helped him greatly in the aftermath of his addictions.

As he walked, head down into the wind, he made a list of everything he was thankful for, especially his children and the time they'd spent together the past two weeks. Then, after some inner struggle, he made his only plea for the new year: that he find a woman and be spared further loneliness. It had been five years since the divorce, and the two relationships he'd attempted had been . . . *What time is it?*

He yanked back the sleeve of his parka, seeing it was nearly midnight. Hennessy spun around. He'd walked nearly three hundred yards from the lodge. He started to run, thinking, *I'm gonna miss it. I'm going to break a promise to them. On their last night!*

In the club's security center, Radio's focus leaped from security screen to security screen, catching fleeting evidence of the army closing around the lodge: the security guard Peters shot in his shack; another guard garroted on patrol; armed, white-camouflaged men racing at the lodge from three different directions.

Radio typed a code that unlocked the lodge's exterior doors, then called into his microphone, "Clear for entry. Take them down fast."

The crowd in the ballroom, still sweaty from dancing, was on its feet, clapping and shouting in unison with the bandleader, "Five! Four! Three! Two!—"

Machine guns opened up from four different directions, pounding the ballroom ceiling tiles and shattering the chandeliers and crystal icicles. Glass shards fell like tiny daggers on the panicked revelers. People started diving for cover as masked men in white stormed into the room, screaming at them to get down. Several partygoers, including Aaron Grant and his wife, Margaret, tried to run for the exits, only to find them blocked.

Albert Crockett's wife, Lydia, took off toward the terrace doors. Alex Patton, her husband's bodyguard, came up with a Glock to cover her and shot two of the attackers before he was cut down in a hail of machine gun fire. Two of the camouflaged men grabbed a hysterical Lydia Crockett and threw her down next to her dead bodyguard. Jack Doore was booted in the stomach and driven to the floor. Stephanie fell beside him, struck with the butt of a gun.

"Down!" the biggest of the attackers roared. "Hands behind your back. No cell phones! No PDAs!"

Everyone was on the floor now. Many were whimpering and crying.

One of the masked attackers jumped on the band stage. He strode to the middle of the stage in a military swagger. He wore a wireless headset with a microphone somehow linked to the ballroom's speakers.

In a voice that sounded electrically altered, he growled, "My name is General Anarchy of the Third Position Army, and all of you corporate, capitalist swine are prisoners of war!"

CHAPTER ELEVEN

From two hundred yards away, Hennessy heard the shooting inside the lodge like a distant chorus of hammers striking wood.

"Shit!" he screamed, going for his pistol. *The kids!* He sprinted pell-mell at the lodge. He got the pistol free. He heard the shooting stop. He triggered the mike on his tuxedo collar. "Central, this is Hennessy! What the hell's going on in there?"

Radio's voice came back. *"Chief, where are you?"*

"Running toward the main entrance, what am I getting into?" He kept sprinting, closing the ground. There was no reply. "Central?"

Seventy-five yards from the guard shack at the end of the lodge driveway, Hennessy slowed when he spotted two men wearing Jefferson Club Security parkas and caps running out the lodge's main entrance. He breathed with relief. He had backup.

Then he saw the automatic weapons they held low at their sides. Jefferson Club security did not issue automatic weapons. He dodged for the embankment that fell away off the south side of the access road, trying to get his pistol up. They sprayed fire after him. A bullet caught him through the triceps of his right arm. The shock of it spun Hennessy around and hurled him backward off the embankment. He fell, bounced, twisted, and back-somersaulted before bouncing again, rolling and crashing into a sopping-wet thicket of cedars that grew at the bottom of the embankment.

Lying there, the wind knocked from him, swallowed by the cedar limbs, Hennessy miraculously still held his gun. He heard voices coming toward him on the road atop the embankment.

"I hit him good," one said. "He won't go far."

"If he's still moving he'll be leaving blood and footprints," the other said. "Let's get on him. The order was to neutralize."

Through the snowy cedar branches, Hennessy saw flashlight beams playing atop the embankment. He forced himself to try to squirm away without making noise. He managed to put fifteen feet between himself and the open slope before getting up. The snow hung heavy on the tree limbs and when he took a step downhill, it set off an avalanche that slid off an entire tree in a wet rustle and *plop!* He peered back, seeing one of the guards step into a clear shooting lane, silhouetted against the driveway lights.

Hennessy raised his pistol left-handed. He steadied, let the tritium sights align on the chest of one of the attackers, and shot. At the report, the man jerked and fell. His partner jumped forward, blazing rounds down on the thicket. Bullets snapped tree limbs around Hennessy. One whined by his ear.

Hennessy spun and barreled downhill, legs plowing through the snow, his left forearm busting branches, doing everything he could to put distance between himself and his pursuer. The snow was deep in the woods and deeper in the meadow when he broke from the tree line. He ignored how wet and cold his legs were all the way to his crotch. He had to keep moving. He skirted the edge of the clearing, heading east toward the main gate, some five miles distant. He felt light-headed and then dizzy as the adrenaline that had saved his life now trickled his system toward shock. He fought it, forcing himself to take stock of his situation. He had eight rounds left in his Beretta and a second clip of twelve in his pocket. He was wounded. How bad, he didn't know. He needed to know.

He stopped on the far side of the clearing, got his coat off, and felt the blood that drenched his entire right side. He found the wound. The meat of his triceps. He got his belt off and around his upper arm below the shoulder. He grabbed the strap end and hauled on it, cutting off the circulation to the arm.

He got the parka back on, with only his left arm through the sleeve, and somehow got the coat zipped back up around him, thinking, *The kids are back there!* But he had no chance trying to rescue them, wounded like this, a single pistol against machine guns. He had to get out, get help. Or should he loop to the south, well away from the lodge to one of the members' houses? His master key would open most of the places. He would use the phone. Call for backup.

No! He'd left the club's master key in the apartment.

Cell phone! In the madness of it all, he'd forgotten it was even in his tuxedo pants pocket. He stuck his gun in his parka pocket, fished the cell phone from his pants, dialed 911, and said a prayer. It hissed, then engaged and rang.

"Jefferson County Sheriff's . . . nature . . . emergency?"

The connection was crackly. He yelled, "This is Michael Hennessy at the Jefferson Club. There's been an attack. Men with automatic weapons. I've shot one of them and—"

Nine-millimeter cartridges exploded to his left, intense brilliant flashes in the falling snow followed by cracking as slugs struck the trees around him.

Hennessy lunged away, dropping the phone and groping for his pistol. He got it, spun, shot twice in the direction of the muzzle flashes, and then took off again. Machine gun fire followed, raking the snow and vegetation around him.

He ran zigzag in a crouch, deeper into the trees, grateful that the snow was shallower there. He ran until he thought his lungs would burst, and then broke out into a second clearing, dizzy again and knowing that he could not keep up the pace. With the loss of blood, he'd be caught eventually, certainly before he reached the gate.

Hennessy looked around, seeing only shadows in the clearing, before concentrating on an island of white poplar trees thirty yards away. The plan came to him in an instant.

He took off along the edge of the timber again, passed by the grove of poplars, and then button-hooked back and stood just inside the tiny island of woods.

Standing there, he remembered to open the tourniquet for a minute, all the while peering across the forty yards of meadow to where he figured the man tracking him would come. He'd no sooner cinched the belt again when it happened.

In his snow camouflage, the Third Position soldier was all but invisible in the storm. But then Hennessy caught a faint green light issuing from beneath the man's hood. Night-vision goggles.

Hennessy eased into a shooting crouch, raising his Beretta, finding the pale red glow of its tritium sight and moving it toward the green, glowing goggles. He squeezed as the two colors lined up. The Beretta bucked. He lost sight of the green glow and reacted by diving on his belly. The machine gun opened up, raking the trees above him. Hennessy emptied his gun at the muzzle flashes.

The machine gun fell silent. He heard his enemy's death groan.

Gasping, Hennessy got to his feet, stumbled forward, and found the man dead on his side. He took his night-vision goggles and strapped them on. Immediately the landscape turned otherworldly and green.

Hennessy gave himself no time for emotion. He was in pure survival mode now. He took the Third Position soldier's machine gun and spare banana clips. He was less than two miles from the gate, but then realized they had to be controlling it. He'd go around and start walking toward the highway, flag down the first car he saw.

Go! he goaded himself. *Get help for the kids!* With that singular, overwhelming thought driving him, Hennessy began to run again.

Inside the Dirty Shame Saloon, the magician lay face down on the wood floor, hands behind his back. A hooded man in white camouflage cinched plastic zip restraints around his wrists. The children were all lying face down too, some crying, all of them petrified. The Hennessy triplets lay next to each other, hardly daring to raise their heads as hooded men walked among them, putting plastic restraints on all the adults. Ian Doore lay beside Hailey, holding on to his head and moaning.

Mouse walked into the room and said from behind her hood, "Do what we say and no one will get hurt."

But the younger kids and Ian kept sobbing. Hailey felt on the verge of crying too, though she refused to show it. Suddenly, Ian Doore pulled away from Hailey and got to his feet. His fingers were pinched together as he went for the door.

"Hey, little boy!" Mouse called after him. "Stop. Lie back down!"

But Ian Doore kept walking. Mouse went up and grabbed the boy roughly by the arm. He started twisting and whining. She shook him. His teal eyes turned wall-eyed with terror and he slapped at her.

Mouse reached back with her machine gun as if to

batter him with the butt. Hailey jumped up. "Don't!
He's autistic or something! He doesn't understand!"

Mouse glared at her, then at two of her comrades.
"Put them both in restraints. If he whines, gag him. If
she stands up again, shoot her."

Two men wrestled Ian Doore to the ground and hog-
tied him. He started screeching and whining. They put
duct tape over his mouth. Another two soldiers threw
Hailey down, cuffed her, and cinched her ankles. They
smelled horrible. When they left, she couldn't help whimpering to her brothers. "Why are they doing this?"

"I don't know," Bridger whispered back. "Just keep
your head down."

"Don't challenge them, Hailey," Connor said.

Hailey's lower lip quivered in fear and in anger.
"Where's Dad?"

"I don't know," Connor said, tears welling in his eyes
and his throat feeling like a tennis ball had been rammed
down it. "There was a lot of shooting earlier. I don't
know."

Downstairs in the ballroom, Third Position soldiers
threw the band members off the stage and onto the floor
while others worked to place the entire crowd in restraints.

"If you try to escape you will be shot," General Anarchy said in that strange electronically altered voice.
"If you try to use a cell phone or a BlackBerry, you will
be shot. If you have any communication device, put it
on the floor in front of you. When you have been placed

in restraints you may get up from the floor and take your seat."

On the floor close to the kitchen, Horatio Burns bled from a gash to his forehead. He looked around wildly, spotting Alicia Treadwell several yards away hunkered down with Sir Lawrence by her side.

"Alicia?" he called in a frantic whisper. "Have you seen Isabel?"

"I thought she was with you," Alicia said.

On the opposite side of the room, Stephanie Doore grimaced as Third Position soldiers cinched plastic cords over her wrists. She looked at her husband wretchedly.

"What about Ian?" she whispered.

Jack Doore twisted over and tried to get to his feet. Truth put his boot on Doore's back and grumbled from behind his hood, "Try again and I'll kill you gladly, Mr. Doore."

Doore gritted his teeth. "My son. He's got emotional problems. He's—"

Truth threw his gloved hand across Doore's mouth, then duct-taped it shut before putting him into restraints behind his back. "Your son'll be fine," the soldier said, hauling Doore up and slamming him in a chair. "If you cooperate. Cell phone?"

Doore stared at the huge masked soldier sidelong, then looked over at his wife as she was lifted and placed in a chair. He nodded and looked down at his tuxedo jacket. Truth reached inside, threw the phone on the ground, and crushed it with his boot.

* * *

In Jeffersonville, at the Jefferson County Sheriff's Office, Gracie Lawlor, the dispatcher, swiveled in her seat to look at Sheriff Kevin Lacey, who'd just come in from patrol and was removing his jacket and hat. It was 12:32 a.m. mountain time. Deputy Mike Rowdy was with him.

"Anything?" Sheriff Lacey asked the dispatcher.

"Nothing you don't know about," she said. "Oh, we got a crank call about fifteen minutes ago from someone claiming he was Mickey Hennessy up at the Jefferson Club. Said there'd been an attack up there. They lit off firecrackers and then hung up."

"You call the club to check?" Deputy Rowdy asked.

"Mike, I think I know a prank when I—" the dispatcher began, only to be cut off by the 911 line ringing again.

Gracie Lawlor punched a button and said, "Jefferson County Emergency."

A tense woman's voice came over the speaker, *"This is Sergeant Helen Johnson of the U.S. Capitol Police, assigned to protect Senator Worth Stonington. I'm at the Jefferson Club. We've been attacked. They're dressed in white camouflage and carrying Sterling submachine guns. There are at least thirty of them. Maybe forty. I'm in the first-floor women's room off the—"*

Banging and voices shouting cut her off. The line went dead.

Sheriff Lacey started running toward the door, shouting, "Call the goddamned state police in Helena and the FBI hotline in Salt Lake City. Rowdy, get the shotguns. Happy New Year son-of-a-bitch!"

* * *

Inside the lodge's cold storage unit off the kitchen, Isabel Burns heard the thudding shots through the walls. She clutched her cell phone like a weapon. Chef Giulio held a meat cleaver. Patron and cook were crouched and shivering behind boxes of whole filets of beef and Copper River salmon steaks.

"Call the 911," Chef Giulio said.

"I'll call someone better," Isabel replied, punching speed dial. "Tammy Walters."

"Who's that one?"

"My publicist. She'll get us real help quicker than any local 911 call."

In Manhattan's Tribeca neighborhood, it was 2:39 a.m. EST, and Tammy Walters, a buxom blonde in her mid-thirties, heard her phone ring as she came out of the restaurant Nobu. She was slightly blotto at the time and almost didn't answer.

But when she saw the caller was her biggest client, she hit SEND, as Jim Erickson, a young, handsome, single on-air reporter for MSNBC, and Tom Bowman, who held a similar position at CNN, stood aside for her to climb in the taxi. Both men were drunker than she was and chortling at some idiocy overheard earlier in the evening.

"Tammy?" Isabel Burns cried. The connection was faint.

Tammy Walters slid across the seat. "Isabel, is that you? How's the A-list of the A-list party going?"

"Tammy, they're shooting! Killing people! We've been attacked by a bunch of crazy men in white clothes

*with machine guns. I'm with Giulio. We're hiding in
the kitchen! They've got Horatio!"*

Tammy sobered instantly. "What?"

*"Tell someone what's happening to us, Tammy!
There are dozens of them . . ."*

Tammy heard shouting and then Isabel screaming
before the line went dead.

"Isabel? Isabel!" The publicist turned to her friends,
shocked to her core. She told them about the phone call,
then said, "It's a Forbes Who's Who out there tonight.
Jack Doore and Aaron Grant from YES! Albert Crockett.
Horatio Burns. Senator Stonington, the appropriations
chairman. And Cheryl Wise! She's there with her daughter. They're all hostages!"

Jim Erickson bolted forward in his seat, barking at
the cabdriver, "Rockefeller Center, NBC studios."

"CNN first," Tom Bowman said. "It's on the way."

"My God," Tammy said, clasping her hands together
as the taxi driver floored the gas, heading uptown. "This
could be the biggest story ever."

CHAPTER TWELVE

Two Third Position Army soldiers dragged U.S. Capitol Police Sergeant Helen Johnson by her hair into the ballroom.

"She got a call out," one said. "Local sheriff."

The kitchen doors boomed open. Two Third Position soldiers brought in Chef Giulio and Isabel Burns at gunpoint.

"This one got a call out too," one said. "Someone in New York. The old coot tried to stick a meat cleaver in me."

"Should have split your head open like cheese," Chef Giulio said.

Onstage, General Anarchy pointed at the Capitol Police officer and said, "She used a cell phone. Kill her."

Her captor drew a pistol, put it to Helen Johnson's head without hesitation, and fired. She jerked and fell to the floor. Screams of horror filled the ballroom.

Horatio Burns struggled to his feet and shouted, "This is barbaric. Stop!"

A Third Position soldier grabbed Burns and threw him back in his chair.

"Tell us what you want!" Aaron Grant's wife, Margaret, shouted.

General Anarchy said, "We want justice." He shifted his attention to Isabel Burns. "Now, Mrs. Burns, are you ready to face punishment so your fellow prisoners can learn the lesson of trying to contact the outer world, truly, deeply, and madly?"

Horatio Burns shot to his feet again. "Please! No! We've learned! We've all learned. Have mercy, for God's sake!"

A Third Position soldier hit Burns with the butt of his gun, sprawling him back in his chair a second time.

"I don't believe in God, Mr. Burns," General Anarchy said before pausing. "But just to show you that even Anarchy has a heart, I'll grant that wish. Your wife lives." He paused. "But her chef dies."

The soldier guarding the cook shot Chef Giulio at point-blank range through the back of the head. Isabel Burns began to screech and squirm while two other soldiers threw her in a chair beside her husband. They taped her mouth as she sobbed and stared at the old cook's body.

"The following men step forward," General Anarchy ordered dispassionately. "Albert Crockett, Jack Doore, Aaron Grant, Friedrich Klinefelter. Chin Hoc Pan. Senator Worth Stonington. Sir Lawrence Treadwell and Horatio Burns."

Jack Doore stood first, glaring at General Anarchy in defiance. Aaron Grant stood next. Then Burns. One by one, the rest of the billionaires followed their lead. Soldiers went over to them, pulled black hoods over their heads, and led them roughly to the stage, where they threw them at the base.

"Where's Stonington?" General Anarchy demanded.

Third Position soldiers began to search for the politician. They found the respected gentleman from Alabama and his wife, Olivia, hiding under one of the tables. They hauled them out and to their feet. Sweat gushed off Senator Stonington's brow. He was making choking noises.

"Hood him," General Anarchy ordered. "Get him up here with the others."

"Please, no blindfold," the senator begged, backing up. "I'm claustrophobic. Won't be able to breathe. I . . . I . . . I get asthma."

General Anarchy's electronic laugh was acidic. "Honestly, we couldn't care less, you corrupt, gluttonous bastard of a whore."

It was almost one a.m. in Montana and still snowing hard when a Jefferson County Sheriff's Chevy Suburban patrol rig pulled up to the main gate of the Jefferson Club flashing its blue lights. Sheriff Kevin Lacey was driving and nervously stroking his silver goatee, pistol in his lap. Deputy Mike Rowdy held a shotgun and had his head craned forward, inspecting the scene.

Deputy Rowdy noticed the snowcat. "What the hell's that doing here?"

The sheriff said, "I don't know. Where's the guards?"

"There's one," Deputy Rowdy said.

The Third Position soldier who called himself Dalton stepped out, dressed in Jefferson Club Security coat, hat, and pants. He came to the window, the hood on his parka up as the sheriff lowered his window.

"Evening, gentlemen," Dalton said agreeably. "Welcome to the snowy Jefferson Club. What can I do for you?"

Lacey said, "We got calls saying there was an attack up here."

"An attack?" Dalton replied, sounding confused. "What're you talking about?"

Deputy Rowdy leaned forward, disappointed. "There was no attack?"

Dalton laughed good-naturedly. "I suppose there's been a booze attack up at the big New Year's bash. That's about it."

The sheriff said, "Mickey Hennessy called. Said he'd killed a man."

"Gimme a break, what is this?" Dalton said, frowning. "I just spoke to the chief two minutes ago. He said the party's breaking up and he's heading home to sleep. And he sure didn't say anything about killing anyone."

Sheriff Lacey stuck his pistol out the window. "Step back. We also got a call from a U.S. Capitol Police officer. We heard shots."

Dalton threw up his hands and stepped back. "Hey. There's no need for guns. I don't know what you're talking about. You probably heard fireworks. They had a show."

"No one answers at the lodge," Deputy Rowdy said, climbing out the other door.

"Whole system went down when we lost electricity. We're on walkie-talkies."

"You got an answer for everything," Lacey said as he opened his door.

Dalton shrugged. "Look, I'm telling it like it is. You don't want to be going in there and waking up those kind of people to make yourself a fool over crank calls."

Lacey climbed out, saying, "I'd like to talk to Horatio Burns in person."

"I'll call him and tell him you're coming. But you'll have to walk to the lodge. That snowcat's dead. Be mid-morning before it's fixed and out of the way."

Rowdy came around the car hood, shotgun held loose. "What's wrong with it?"

Dalton picked his head up and tracked him, saying, "Engine trouble."

The deputy headed toward the guard shack. "My dad's a diesel mechanic. Why don't I take a look?"

"Probably not a good idea," Dalton called after him. "Folks in the shop are real particular about who works on the equipment."

The deputy did not break stride. "Humor me."

Dalton glanced at the sheriff, who stood behind the open door to his cruiser.

The corners of Dalton's mouth twitched before he said, "Knock yourself out."

The deputy stepped to the gatehouse and found Cobb

aiming a silenced pistol at him from six feet away. Cobb shot twice. Rowdy reeled and fell dead.

Sheriff Lacey ducked, swung his gun toward the gatehouse, and started shooting. Dalton dove to one side, bringing up his own pistol. His first round shattered the driver's-side window. The sheriff kept shooting, but leaped back in behind the wheel and rammed the patrol vehicle in reverse.

His windshield exploded into spiderwebs. He hammered the gas and ducked.

The Suburban fishtailed back from the gate, off the access road, and out onto the sagebrush flat below the club grounds. A shot blew out his left headlight. Another shattered the rear window. The truck slammed through the snow, across the flat, lurching, bouncing, and shaking the glass from the window frames.

Lacey picked up his head and looked over his shoulder. He plowed the Suburban back up onto the country road, shouting, "Son-of-a-bitch! Son-of-a-bitch!" He hit the road and kept the truck in reverse, the accelerator still mashed to the floor.

When he could no longer see the lights at the gate, the sheriff punched the brakes and threw the wheel around. He skidded through a one-eighty, rammed it in low gear, and took off toward Jeffersonville. Lacey grabbed his radio. "This is county four ten. Shots fired! Officer down! Shots fired and Rowdy's down at the gate to the Jefferson Club."

In the Suburban's single remaining headlight, a man lurched off the bank up ahead. He wore a Jefferson Club parka and carried a machine gun. The sheriff mashed the gas and drove straight at him. The man threw up his hand, blinded in the headlights' glare. He wove on his feet, staggered, dropped the gun, and then pitched forward on his face in the snow. Lacey slammed on the brakes and came to a stop a foot away.

The sheriff got out, chest heaving, pistol in hand, ready to blow the man's head off if he moved. He stalked up to him, then got the tip of his boot under the man's chest and kicked him over. It was Mickey Hennessy. His face was deathly gray. The sleeve of his coat was soaked with blood.

Hennessy's eyes fluttered open and focused in recognition.

"You gotta help me, Sheriff," he croaked. "My kids are in there."

The lights were dimmed in the Dirty Shame Saloon.

"Get some sleep," Mouse said.

"I want my mommy!" a girl's weepy voice called across the room from the Hennessy triplets and Ian Doore.

Other kids' voices took up that same tremulous complaint. Another called, "I need my favorite pillow to sleep."

"Shut up, you spoiled little brats!" Mouse roared. "Or your parents will die and you'll be left orphans. Do you have any concept of what that's like? Of how most children live in the world?"

Evidently they did, for the room fell into silence

marred only by the soft cries of young children and the sighs of older ones. Hailey lay next to Ian Doore, arms cinched up behind her back, feeling like a tremendous weight was pressing down on her body. Ian was looking into her eyes and making soft whining sounds behind his tape.

"It's okay," she whispered. "Just stay calm, Ian. Breathe through your nose."

Connor whispered over her shoulder, "Dad's out there somewhere, right?"

"He wasn't here to wish us a Happy New Year's," she whispered back.

"Do you think he's . . ." Bridger began. He couldn't finish.

Connor hissed, "Dad's out there and alive. He's too good not to be."

Mouse stepped up and put the barrel of her gun against Connor's head. "One more word out of you and I'll find your parents and kill them. Is that what you want?"

"No," Bridger said. "He'll be fine. We'll all be fine."

Mouse looked at them all as if in understanding, before pulling the gun muzzle away from Connor's head. "No more warnings. One more word and your father dies."

Downstairs in the ballroom, General Anarchy stood in a military at-ease position on the band stage. "If you must use the toilet, tell the guards. If you need water, tell the guards. If you move without a guard, you will die."

With that, he marched offstage, giving barely a glance to the corpses of Chef Giulio and Sergeant Helen Johnson as they were slid out the door into the snow.

Truth followed General Anarchy through the crowd toward the exit to the hallway. Many of the hostages were laying themselves down on the floor or were pitched over on the tables.

He passed Stephanie Doore. She said, "Please, my son. He has special needs."

General Anarchy gave her a cold appraisal. "We all do, Mrs. Doore."

He went out the door of the ballroom and up the stairs to the grand atrium, deaf to her further entreaties. Out of sight, he ripped off the white wool hood. His hair was matted with sweat. His eyes ran bloodshot as he watched Truth remove his hood and scratch at his shaved scalp.

"I'll take five hours' rest now," General Anarchy said. "You, too. We're going to have a busy day."

"I'll check sentries, then catch a few hours," the big black soldier promised.

Both their earpieces crackled with Radio's voice: *"General, we've had an incident at the main gate. Cobb had to kill a sheriff's deputy. The sheriff escaped."*

Truth stepped back as if expecting an eruption of rage, but General Anarchy merely rubbed at his temples before saying into the mike, "In a way, that only helps in the long run. Tell Cobb if he sees more law enforcement, he's to retreat with the snowcat to the top of the knoll and notify me. Do not shoot unless fired upon."

"Roger that," Radio said.

They entered the atrium. General Anarchy gave his surroundings scant attention, as if he'd seen it all before, saying, "This is good. By this afternoon, we'll have everyone in the game."

CHAPTER THIRTEEN

CNN and MSNBC interrupted regular broadcasting at 3:15 a.m. EST with first word of the attack on the Jefferson Club. Due to the large number of deep-pocket political donors inside the club, the President of the United States was awoken at Camp David at four.

The President decided normal protocol did not apply and immediately ordered in the FBI's Critical Incident Response Group, or CIRG. Developed in the wake of the standoffs at Waco and Ruby Ridge, CIRG was designed to help the FBI better manage crises such as large hostage situations and complex terror investigations.

An advance CIRG team lifted off in a government jet from Virginia two hours after the President's order. The ten-man team landed at Gallatin Field near Bozeman at nine-fifteen mountain time, a half hour before a Northwest Airlines jet from Minneapolis touched down. Snow had fallen all night in the mountains, but on the valley floor sun shone through breaks in the clouds and glistened off the tarmac.

FBI Special Agent Cheyenne O'Neil spotted the CIRG team unloading equipment into rental trucks while her plane taxied to the gate. She'd heard about the hostage situation from news reports in the Minneapolis airports and knew her plan to try an ambush interview on Friedrich Klinefelter and Albert Crockett was dashed. But she was here and thought she might be of help.

So even before the jet came to a full stop, Cheyenne stood and pulled down her carry-on. The airline attendant closest to her shouted. "Ma'am, sit down!"

Cheyenne walked toward her, badge up. "FBI. I'm supposed to be with those men with the trucks. I need to be off this plane first."

Many of her fellow passengers stared and chattered after her when she went and stood at the exit door, waiting impatiently for it to open. When it did, she held up her ID to the National Transportation Safety Administration officer who met the jet, then pointed at the locked door to the staircase outside the jetway.

"I need to talk to those FBI agents," she said.

He called his supervisor, who approved it. Cheyenne stepped out into cold dry air that took her breath away, so clean after Manhattan. She shivered going down the stairs, then hustled toward the jet and the trucks, trying desperately not to fall on the slick spots of black ice. She came around the nose of the jet and saw the men were almost finished loading their gear.

A tall African-American in his early forties, well over six feet tall, built like a track star, with a shaved head and smooth good looks, spotted her. He wore a leather bomber jacket with a sheep's-fleece collar and wraparound sunglasses. He came at her with gloved hands up. "You can't be in—"

"FBI," she said, holding up her badge. "Agent Cheyenne O'Neil. I wanted to see if I could be of help. Who's the special agent in charge?"

"I am," he said skeptically, then stuck out his hand to shake hers. "SAC Willis Kane with CIRG. Who exactly sent you here, Agent O'Neil?"

Cheyenne frowned. "Well, no one, exactly. I was coming here to interview two of the hostages inside the Jefferson Club on a case I've been working out of Manhattan Financial Crimes. Friedrich Klinefelter and Albert Crockett."

Willis Kane cocked his head. "You think they're connected?"

"No," she said. "At least I can't say that for sure. But I figure with the kind of wealth that's in that club, there's got to be a financial angle to this. Probably the motive. I'd like to help."

Kane shook his head. "We have our own people coming from DC and twenty agents from Salt Lake City. If I were you, I'd just head back to New York. If they need your special help, they'll call."

"Sir, with all due respect," Cheyenne replied, "I'm here. I'm a good agent. There must be something I can do to be of help."

The hostage rescue leader studied her a long moment,

then nodded. "Okay, Agent O'Neil, go to the Bozeman hospital and find Mickey Hennessy, the Jefferson Club's security director. He was shot in the takeover and stitched up last night. He should be coming around. Interview him. Find out everything you can about the buildings, the security system, and the likely location of the hostages."

"Straightaway, sir," she said. "Thank you, SAC."

She started to leave. Kane said, "Agent O'Neil, you'll need my phone number to make your report before you fly back to Manhattan."

"Oh," she said, reddening and taking the card he proffered. "Of course."

By ten a.m. that New Year's Day, the blizzard had slowed to snow showers. Thirty inches of powder blanketed the flanks of Hellroaring Peak, which remained shrouded in clouds that cast a flat light through the windows of the grand ballroom at the Jefferson Club Lodge.

Inside, hostages sat groggily in their banquet chairs, or gnawed at the baskets of stale bread the Third Position soldiers had thrown on the tables, or drank from the pitchers of water they'd brought in after dawn.

Stephanie Doore looked at her husband in his black hood sprawled against the base of the stage with the other seven men and choked back sobs. "What are we going to do?" she whispered to Aaron Grant's wife, Margaret, who was staring into her lap.

Margaret's makeup was smeared with tears. "I'm praying," she said simply.

"I haven't been away from Ian like this his whole life," Stephanie said.

"My girls are downstairs too, Stephanie," Margaret said, fighting for control. "My husband's right there beside yours."

She'd no sooner uttered those words than children's voices shattered the fearful malaise. Mouse came into the ballroom, hooded, and leading the kids. There was a rush of joy as they ran to find their parents and grandparents, hearing their shouts and going to them, hugging and crying.

Ian Doore, still in wrist restraints and the duct tape across his mouth, but freed of his ankle cords, jumped into his mother's lap. She nuzzled and kissed her son, tears streaming down her cheeks. "Oh, Ian," she whispered. "Thank God."

At the rear of the room, Bridger and Connor helped Hailey up onto a chair so she could help them look for their father. A Third Position soldier had cut her ankle restraints shortly before leading them upstairs.

After several long frantic moments, Bridger said, "He's not here."

"He's got to be," Hailey said, regretting every bad thought she'd had about him.

"He isn't," Bridger insisted. "I can't help thinking—"

"He's not," Connor said emphatically. "How do we know they just haven't taken him prisoner and put him somewhere else?"

Before either of Connor's siblings could answer, Truth, General Anarchy, and Cristoph, who carried a laptop computer, entered the ballroom, hooded. The Hennessys looked right through the holes in General Anarchy's hood and into his eyes, seeing charcoal irises boring back at them, sizing the teenagers up like some predator considering a kill.

But the triplets refused to avert their attention, trying not to show any outward sign of insecurity or intimidation. It was something their father had taught them: "If you act afraid, you are afraid and you have become prey, something a predator will pick up on. It's true in the wilderness. It's true in a city. Fifty percent of staying safe in your life is projecting an attitude of confidence, an absolute, zero, lack of fear. No matter what the situation."

All three Hennessy children remembered their father's teaching in that moment, but when General Anarchy had passed, they felt weakened.

"That dude's crazy evil, kid," Bridger whispered.

"Like Tony in *Scarface*," Connor agreed.

General Anarchy marched up onstage, tugging on his headset. In that buzzing, electric voice, he said, "I trust you all slept well?"

Grumbling built among the hostages. Henry Mendoza, the famous retired bicycle champion, stood and shouted, "What do you want from us?"

General Anarchy held his glove to his brow, peering back to identify the man. "From you, Mr. Mendoza, I want nothing but your silence." He gestured at the blindfolded men seated on the floor below him. "From these men, I want everything."

The Third Position Army leader motioned to Truth, who stood before the blindfolded hostages. "Restraints and blindfolds off," Anarchy said, then walked over to Cristoph, who had put his laptop on a waiter's table and was typing intently.

General Anarchy leaned over to speak with him. "Ready?"

"For what you need this moment, General, yes," Cristoph responded. "But I am slow getting the Web site live. It takes longer to load than I expected."

"First things first," General Anarchy said, then turned to find Truth and three of his men removing the hoods and cutting the restraints of the eight men on the floor at the base of the stage. As the hoods came off, each of the men squinted at the light. They groaned when their wrists were released from behind their backs.

Senator Worth Stonington snuffled and hacked, sweat pouring from his brow and dripping off his waddles. "I need somethin' to eat," he said, gasping. "I got a sugar condition. Look at me here: I'm tremblin'." He raised a quivering hand. "Ask my wife, Olivia. Sugar condition."

Olivia Stonington shouted, "It's true."

General Anarchy did not react at first. Then Jack Doore called out, "Geneva protocol, General. You have to feed and water prisoners."

General Anarchy marched up to Doore. "You have a lot to say, Mr. Doore."

"Generally," Doore said, gazing evenly at him. "And whenever I can."

General Anarchy made a flicking motion toward one soldier. "Bread and water."

Several of his men brought bottles of water from the kitchen and more baskets of bread left over from the New Year's bash. The men all guzzled the water first, except for the senator, who chomped down on one roll and fed another in after it before quenching his thirst, belching and saying, "Not enough sugar. There must be a slice of pie around here. Good piece of pie, I'd be fine."

General Anarchy reached back with his boot, as if he meant to kick the distinguished senator from Alabama, then thought better of it and said, "Find him pie."

As Horatio Burns ate his bread, Bridger saw him making soothing expressions toward his wife, who sat twenty feet from him, unsuccessfully fighting back tears.

"We gotta find Dad," Connor said.

"You honestly think they've got him hidden somewhere?" Hailey asked.

"Or he's hiding somewhere, yeah, I do," Connor said. "That soldier downstairs said she'd kill dad if we weren't quiet. She knew we were his kids."

"How we gonna find him then?" Bridger said. "I counted twenty-five machine guns between us and the door. Who knows how many are outside?"

Before Connor could reply, General Anarchy turned and paraded in front of the eight hostages sitting against the stage. "I want you men to know that there is a way for your loved ones to leave here unharmed."

"Ransom?" Albert Crockett demanded immediately.

"If you wish to call it that, Mr. Crockett, though we think of it as a donation to our cause," General Anarchy replied archly. "Here are our demands: Each of you will go to that computer and transfer one hundred million dollars of your personal fortune into ten numbered bank accounts. Ten million in each."

"Cannot be done," said Chin Hoc Pan.

"Impossible," added Friedrich Klinefelter. "It is the holiday."

"Not impossible, Mr. Klinefelter," General Anarchy said. "Only difficult. And not even so difficult for men of your staggering wealth."

Aaron Grant leaned forward. His shirt was pulled up out of his pants. His face was welted with the seams from the hood. "And if we refuse your demands? What then?"

Third Position soldiers all around the room began grabbing people from their seats and dragging them forward. Olivia Stonington was brought up. Aaron Grant's eleven-year-old daughter Katherine was dragged from her seat. Her sister, Sophie, started to sob. Albert Crockett's wife, Lydia, and Alicia Treadwell were taken. Isabel Burns and Ruth Klinefelter, too.

Stephanie Doore began to shriek when Truth wrenched Ian from her arms and marched him by the nape of his neck toward his father. He threw the boy on his knees.

General Anarchy stood in front of Jack Doore. "Your business partner poses an interesting question, Mr. Doore."

Truth cocked the pistol and pressed it to the back of the boy's head.

"One hundred million dollars in return for your son's life," General Anarchy said. "Less than a single percentage point of your net worth. What do you say, Mr. Doore? Deal or no deal?"

CHAPTER FOURTEEN

When FBI Agent Cheyenne O'Neil was granted access to the intensive care unit at the Bozeman hospital, she found Mickey Hennessy sitting nearly upright in bed, surrounded by a web of IV lines, electrical wires, and beeping monitors. Bandages swathed his upper right arm. His eyes were closed, his skin looked sallow, and his cheeks were quivering.

The nurse on duty had told her that Hennessy was very lucky to be alive. The bullet passed completely through the triceps, nicking the brachial artery, but causing little damage other than loss of blood and the contusions surrounding the wound track. Three inches to the left and the bullet would have taken out both lungs.

"Who are you?" asked a gruff voice. Cheyenne glanced to her right to find Jefferson County Sheriff Kevin Lacey sitting in a chair against the wall.

Cheyenne identified herself, then said, "I'm here to interview him."

"Not before I do," the sheriff said. "I lost a kid—only twenty-three—up there last night. I almost died getting out of there. I got dibs on answers."

"Don't know any," Hennessy slurred. He lifted his head, seemed to think better of it, and laid it back down. "They were just there."

Hennessy's face twisted in pain and he tried to lift his head again. "My kids were inside. Hailey, Connor, and Bridger." He teared up. "What's happened to them?"

Cheyenne went to his bedside and put her hand on his forearm. "There's no news, Mr. Hennessy. Can you tell us what happened? In as much detail as you can."

"I said I got first—" Lacey began.

But Cheyenne cut the sheriff off. "I'm here working with the hostage rescue unit. I know you have concerns for your dead, but I'm trying to help save the living."

Sheriff Lacey's jaw stiffened, and then he nodded.

There was a knock at the door. Hennessy's nurse, a battleship named Edna, interrupted to take his vitals. "BP's getting better," she announced, as she stripped the blood pressure cuff off his arm. "You took four pints, you know, even with the tourniquet. Wound looks good. You need something for the pain?"

Hennessy shook his head. "Nothing narcotic."

"You shouldn't try to be a hero," Edna insisted.

"Nothing narcotic," Hennessy said again.

Cheyenne was impressed. You had to be damn tough to turn down painkillers after being shot. She pulled a chair up next to Hennessy's bed, made sure he had a glass of ice chips within easy reach, and patted his forearm again before settling down, opening a notebook, and saying, "Tell us what happened from your perspective."

Cheyenne spent the next hour listening closely, prodding him for more details when necessary. All the while Edna the nurse bustled in and out, making sure his vital signs were stable and Cheyenne wasn't pushing Hennessy too hard. When he'd finished describing how he'd clawed his way to the club's entry road after killing the attacker with the night goggles and submachine gun, she asked, "How many are in there?"

Hennessy shook his head. "I don't know. I saw only the two who shot at me."

Sheriff Lacey said, "I heard Sergeant Johnson of the U.S. Capitol Police say there were at least thirty, maybe forty, and they were all carrying machine guns. Cable news is saying that Isabel Burns managed to get a call out. She said there were dozens of armed men in there."

Cheyenne asked Hennessy about the security system. "Impressive," she said when he finished his description.

"Not impressive enough," Hennessy replied. "They got around it. Someone inside had to be helping, someone who knew the system enough to know there was a two-point-two-second gap between the loss of power and the takeover of the generators."

"And who would that be?"

Hennessy grumbled in exasperation. "Probably anybody who took the time to look at the generator specs. They're posted in the generator room in the basement."

"On public display?"

He nodded. "I think it's by law."

"So it could have been anyone," the sheriff said. "Employee or guest."

"You background-check your employees?" Cheyenne asked.

"Agent O'Neil, I worked Diplomatic Security in Beirut, Syria, Colombia, Iraq, Kuwait, and a dozen other hot zones," he said. "What do you think?"

"I think you checked," she said, smiling. "Nothing out of the ordinary before the attack? No one snooping around? No one acting strangely? New employees?"

"We have a very stable crew," Hennessy said. "You can say a lot of things about the club, but people are paid well. And no one was acting strangely, at least no one who stands out. Then again, half the people at the New Year's Eve party were invited guests, not members of the club, so I wouldn't know if they were acting strangely."

Cheyenne thought about that. "Are there maps of the club available online?"

"Inside the club's computer system. I can access it."

"Any way to shut that fence down from the outside?"

Hennessy thought about that, then replied, "I think so. I've got the codes."

Cheyenne said, "You didn't use the codes last night, did you?"

Hennessy startled, then gave her closer appraisal. "You think I was part of this?"

She shrugged. "Gotta ask."

"The answer is no," he said, his face screwing up in anger. "Why would I ever do something to harm my own children?"

"I don't pretend to understand people's motives," she said.

"Well, I do," he shot back.

The tension was cut by a snuffling and chomping noise. Cheyenne glanced in the direction of the noise to find Sheriff Lacey with his head back against the wall, eyes shut, snoring deeply.

She looked back to Hennessy, then got up from her seat beside his bed.

"I think I'll leave now so you both can rest," she said, putting away the notebook. "I hope you feel better, Mr. Hennessy. I'll pray your kids will be returned to you safely. I know the experts are doing everything they can."

"Where are you going?" Hennessy demanded.

"Wherever Critical Incident Response is set up. I have to file my report."

Hennessy kicked the blankets off his legs. "I'm going with you. They'll need me. I know every inch of that place."

"You're not going anywhere," said Edna, who was coming in the door. "Doctor says you're here until at least this evening. Tomorrow, more likely."

Cheyenne said, "I can call you with updates if you like."

"I don't like," Hennessy said, glaring at the nurse. "I'm fully transfused and sewn up. My blood pressure's within normal range. Take the IVs out and give me any meds I need for infection. My kids are up there and I'm going to help get them out."

Inside the Jefferson Club's ballroom, shocked silence reigned as Jack Doore watched his son whine at him from behind the duct tape, oblivious to Truth's pistol an inch off the back of his head.

Bridger Hennessy felt sick to his stomach. All along he'd been telling himself that this was just like a good video game, scary, but ultimately harmless. But now the consequences of it all threatened to crush him.

His sister whispered, "They won't kill him, will they?"

Bridger did the only thing he could think of: He took Hailey in his arms as Stephanie Doore screamed, "For God's sake, Jack! Say yes! What do we care about a hundred million? It's Ian!"

Doore seemed to shake free of some awful trance and then looked to General Anarchy. "Deal."

Bridger felt like he could breath again. Hailey shuddered, then lifted her head off his chest. Truth made a show of flipping the safety on the pistol, withdrawing the gun, and sliding it into a holster. He reached under the boy's armpits and carried him wriggling to his mother. Doore went to the computer and said, "I'll need a phone."

Cristoph handed him a headset and said, "Give me the number."

As Doore put on the headset, General Anarchy said, "We will be listening. Make sure this is a simple transaction, Mr. Doore. No talk of where you are, why you are being held, nothing. Do you understand? Break the rules and we will execute your son."

Doore blanched and nodded. He gave Cristoph a number in Raleigh, North Carolina, where YES! was headquartered. The banker had heard about the attack and asked if this was ransom. Doore glanced at General Anarchy and told him it was more of a business transaction, then provided the banker with the necessary codes and passwords. It only took ten minutes for a hundred million dollars to vanish from Doore's accounts into the financial ether. Soldiers led Doore away while Cristoph typed on the keyboard. He called to General Anarchy, "Transfers complete and moving."

"Smartly done, Mr. Doore," General Anarchy said. "Glad you came to your senses. Who's next? Mr. Burns?"

Horatio Burns got to his feet seething with resentment. "You cold bastard. I guarantee you won't get away with this."

General Anarchy chuckled. "In case you hadn't noticed, we are getting away with it. And for calling me 'cold' your wife's life will cost you two hundred million."

A Third Position soldier grabbed Isabel by her hair and yanked her to her feet.

"Pay them!" she screamed. "Pay them, Horatio! He tears the scalp out!"

Burns blanched and held up his hands in surrender. "I'll do it. Let her be. Please."

General Anarchy said, "Let her down."

Isabel dropped back into her seat, weeping, her face wrenched with pain. Her husband shakily gave Cristoph the phone number of his bank in Ireland, reached the duty officer there, gave passwords and codes and account verification numbers, received voice recognition, and authorized the transfer of two hundred million into ten separate accounts, twenty million in each.

One by one, Friedrich Klinefelter, Albert Crockett, Sir Lawrence Treadwell, and Aaron Grant accessed their accounts and transferred one hundred million each to the Third Position Army's accounts. When Grant was finished, General Anarchy turned his attention to the bitter-lipped man who sat beside Senator Stonington, dipping the napkin from the bread basket in a glass of water and scrubbing at his hands.

"Mr. Hoc Pan?" General Anarchy asked. "Your turn."

The Hong Kong multibillionaire did not stop his scrubbing when he spat back, "You have no leverage on me. I have no wife, no family, and I am Buddhist, already at peace with my death. Shoot me if you will, but I not give you one penny."

Truth put his pistol to Hoc Pan's head. A distinct click echoed through the silent ballroom as the pistol's hammer cocked. The fourth-wealthiest man in the world hesitated, and then started scrubbing his hands again.

"Wait, Truth," General Anarchy said casually. "I believe there may be a more creative way to get him to comply." He called across the ballroom, "Bring it in."

Two of the Third Position soldiers closest to the Hennessys exited the ballroom and swiftly returned, carrying a large rectangular object wrapped in a yellow blanket.

They stopped in front of Chin Hoc Pan and turned the object upright. General Anarchy stepped forward to remove the blanket, revealing an oil painting of rich brown tones, soft whites, vivid reds, and a palette of blues. It depicted a cocoa-skinned girl in her early teens with long jet-black hair and an orchid behind her ear. She stood three-quarters turned away from the painter, naked from the waist up, the swell of her left breast just showing, a colorful sarong cast loosely about her hips. Her left hand rested against the trunk of a coconut tree. An orchid jungle framed her right side. She gazed across a white sand beach to a turquoise sea.

When he saw his beloved Gauguin, Hoc Pan's skin turned waxy.

"Looking Out to Sea for Her Lover," General Anarchy announced. "A masterpiece. You can feel the emotion in her, can't you? It's like you've stumbled out of the island jungle onto this nubile girl, caught in the trance of her first primitive longings."

Hoc Pan's lips parted. He looked mesmerized. General Anarchy tugged a knife from his utility belt. He held the blade at the nape of the painted girl's neck.

The Chinese tycoon snapped back to reality with indignant rage. "You would not dare! The painting is without price!"

"Tonight this painting has a price that will not be negotiated," General Anarchy retorted. "It will cost you the same penalty as Mr. Burns: two hundred million."

Hoc Pan stewed on it, his lip twisting like a worm after a drenching rain.

General Anarchy pressed the knife tip beneath the painted girl's chin. "I think I'll start by severing her head, and shoving it down your throat."

The Hong Kong billionaire's mouth hung open several beats, before arching and then spitting out, "Two hundred million."

Fifteen minutes later the transfers were complete.

"We paid you the money, now let us go," Margaret Grant yelled.

General Anarchy said, "You will be released when it is time. Besides, there's someone who has not yet paid his financial penalty: Senator Stonington?"

The chairman of the U.S. Senate Appropriations Committee had been dozing and startled awake at Margaret Grant's shouting. He sat up now, rubbing his rheumy eyes and twisting his head up at General Anarchy for several beats before getting his meaning.

The senator from Alabama rolled his great head side to side, and then drawled, "I'm a poor public servant. I don't have any hundred million to give you, and that's a fact. Hell, you'd be more likely to get duck soup from an armadillo than cash from me."

General Anarchy laughed. "Duck soup from an armadillo. That's a good one. And no, Senator, you don't have a hundred million. But let's face it, you're more corporate whore than public servant and you always have been, whether your party has been in power or not. And you do have a secret bank account, number A514CH221BZ, in the Hauptman Bank in Basel. What is the most current balance, Cristoph?"

Cristoph glanced at his computer screen. "Twenty-seven million euros, General."

Muffled surprise coursed through the crowd of hostages. Bridger was impressed. That was a lot of money no matter who you were.

"Twenty-seven million euros," General Anarchy was saying. "I want all of it."

Senator Stonington made a gurgling noise. Then he choked, hacked, and turned so red-faced it looked as if he were having a heart attack. But then the politician rolled over onto his left butt cheek, grunting with anger, and pushed himself up to his feet in a squat. He split the seat of his tuxedo pants and let loose a thunderous wet fart. People sniggered all over the room. Bridger rolled up his lip.

But instead of chagrin, Senator Stonington adopted a knowing, practiced pose, the one he'd used on thousands of campaign stops and in the well of the U.S. Senate: a relaxed posture, right leg back, head cocked just so, a knowing, easy smile. His right hand held his suspenders. His left hand was slightly raised, palm out. He looked about the ballroom, regarding his fellow hostages as he might a grand jury poised to indict.

"My friends, I may be a fat old boar of a man, and at times a little windy, but my reputation is impeccable," he said. "I have no such secret bank account. Anyone says otherwise is a damned bald-faced liar. No better'n a wolf or a skunk or a rabid possum."

"Rabid possum," General Anarchy said. "Pity. Tell me, Senator. Do you like olives in your martinis?"

"Olives?" Senator Stonington snorted, confused. "I don't drink martinis."

"How about Olivia's brains splattered all over the floor in front of you?"

With that, Truth wrenched the senator's wife to her

feet and dragged a squealing Olivia Stonington by the nape of her neck, pistol muzzle against her temple. He brought her in front of her husband. Her eyes were bugging from her head and running tears. Snot bubbled at her nose.

"Worth?" Olivia Stonington choked out.

The senator wouldn't look her way. "I don't know what account you're talking about. Nor does my wife."

Olivia Stonington went rigid, and then berserk. She flailed and lashed out at her husband with her evening shoes, her kicks just missing as Truth held her back.

"You fat cracker son-of-a-bitch," she shrieked. "You'd let me die? After everything I did for you! Coaching you every part of the goddamned way!"

She looked out into the faces in the ballroom and shouted, "It's true."

Her husband turned apoplectic, sputtering, "Olivia!"

She ignored him as she spilled the rest of it. "He has an account at that bank in Basel. We both put money in it. Twenty-seven million euros sounds right."

"This will mean my office!" Stonington roared. "My chairmanship!"

"Screw your chairmanship and screw you," his wife shot back. "I see what you're made of now, Worth, and I don't care anymore."

The senator kept digging at the collar of his soaked undershirt, looking at his wife as if she were some demon of betrayal he never knew existed. Then he dropped his hand and gathered it into a fist. He glared at her, then started past her, just out of range. When he passed, he spit at her feet.

"Disloyal, low-life, trailer-trash bitch, I shoulda left you in Tuscaloosa," he grunted.

CHAPTER FIFTEEN

At four p.m. that New Year's Day, Cheyenne O'Neil drove her rented sedan down a lonely stretch of Montana highway west-southwest of Bozeman, beyond the Ruby Range toward Idaho. Mile after mile of stubble wheat fields bordered the road. A pale winter light fed the landscape. In the distance, clouds tore themselves free of the Jefferson Range and raced across the horizon on high-altitude winds.

Sitting beside her, Mickey Hennessy was feeling unhinged by the fire in his arm, by the talk radio station out of Butte that was rehashing the events at the Jefferson Club, and by the blizzard of thoughts blowing through his brain. *What'll I say to Patricia if something bad happens to the kids? Permanently happens? To any of them?*

He felt gut-shot at the idea and then refused to consider it any longer. He snapped off the radio. His children were tough and smart. They'd survive. He knew he should try to contact Patricia. But he balked at trying to track down his ex-wife on her honeymoon until he knew more.

"This your first time in Montana, Agent O'Neil?" Hennessy asked.

"Yes," she said, gazing all about. "It's beautiful. Reminds me of home."

"Where's that?"

"Gunnison, Colorado, originally," she replied. "My parents have a horse ranch there, but I live and work in Manhattan now."

He frowned. "I thought CIRG was based out of Quantico."

"It is," she said, then explained how she'd come to be in Montana as they skirted Jeffersonville and took the turn onto Montana Highway 151, fifteen miles from the club.

"How did you figure on getting inside?" he asked after she'd finished, and thinking that she was something of a loose cannon to jump a plane for Montana without a concrete plan in place.

"I figured the badge would get me in," she said defensively. "What do you know about them, Crockett and Klinefelter?"

He shrugged. "Crockett's creepy. Klinefelter's Teutonic. Crockett's been a member four years. Comes for a week or two around Christmas and then again in March. Klinefelter was with the contingent invited as part of the membership drive. Doore, Grant, and Sir Lawrence too."

The road started to climb and twist into a pine and

spruce forest laden with new snow. Cheyenne had to focus through several hairpin turns and it was several moments before she asked, "Nothing odd about any of those people before the attack?"

Hennessy's wound flared and for a beat he thought about the vial of painkillers the doctors in Bozeman had pressed upon him as he left the hospital. He willed himself not to reach for them, however, as he considered her question. He was about to say no, but then told her about Klinefelter's concern about the number of shorts on the market.

"There's always a lot of shorts at the end of the year," Cheyenne said.

"To offset any catastrophe over the holiday," he agreed. "But Klinefelter said the shorts were much heavier than normal. Much heavier. He thought Sir Lawrence was—"

Yellow lights flashed ahead on the highway. A Northwest Energy truck was parked off the shoulder. A cherry picker blocked the road. Two men atop the picker's basket were struggling to move a blocky piece of equipment onto a utility pole at the height of the wires.

"Pull over," Hennessy said.

"What?"

"Pull over," he repeated. "I think this is how they got inside the club."

She came to a stop ten yards from the cherry picker. Hennessy was out the door before Cheyenne rammed the transmission in park and hurried out after him. One of the Montana Power workers watching the installation saw them. His face clouded.

"Hey, you don't want to be here while they're rigging," he yelled. "Get back."

Cheyenne trotted in front of Hennessy with her badge displayed. "FBI," she said. "Special Agent O'Neil. What happened?"

"Someone blew it up," the worker said. "Looks radio-controlled. Probably C-4."

"How do you know that?" Cheyenne demanded incredulously.

The line worker's face darkened. "I worked ordnance first Gulf War. Recon sapper. C'mere. I'll show you."

He led them around the utility van away from the cherry picker. He stopped ten feet down the bank, pointing in the snow at a jagged, charred hunk of metal. "That's not how transformers look when they blow on their own. Most times, transformers heat up, melt, then catch fire. A few will explode out with a bunch a sparks, but most of the thing remains in one distorted piece. This son-of-a-gun was blown to smithereens. There was pieces way the hell down the road when we got here. And I found this."

He dug in his pocket and came up with a scorched electrical component.

"What is it?" Hennessy asked.

"Part of a remote triggering system. One of ours. U.S. ordnance."

O'Neil and Hennessy reached Wolverine Creek and the Jefferson Club access road. The way wound up tight to the creek under dense pines over a saddle and down onto a broad sagebrush flat that stretched more than a mile to the main gate, a huge stone arch patterned after the northern entrance to Yellowstone National Park.

A third of the way across the flat, Montana State Police troopers had erected barriers across the road. Four cruisers idled behind it. To the north of the barricade, parked in a turnaround where trash and recyclables were taken from the club, Hennessy made out four motor homes parked among five satellite television trucks.

"Spokane, Salt Lake, Billings, Bozeman, and Missoula," Hennessy said, reading the signage on the trucks. "Whoever's in charge is facing a real shitstorm."

"Willis Kane's the SAC," she said, as one of the state troopers came to the window. "Seems like he can handle it."

"Willis Kane," Hennessy repeated slowly. "Great."

"You know him?" she said.

Hennessy flashed on an image of himself throwing down the Secretary of State before he was shot. He said, "One of life's bitter ironies I'd rather not talk about."

Cheyenne rolled down her window, showed her ID, and told the trooper she was bringing Hennessy to talk with the CIRG team. The trooper waved her through. Ahead, parked in an area bulldozed free of snow, Hennessy could see dozens of law enforcement cars and trucks, including FBI and Montana State Police SWAT vans. Eight large outfitter's tents were set up near the vehicles. Smoke belched from the flues of woodstoves and propane healers sticking out the tops of the tents.

Sitting off by itself, facing the gate, was a customized armored truck about thirty feet long with four slide-out panels fully extended along the sides and a large satellite dish and antennas crowding the roof.

"That got here fast," she said. "They must have brought it up from Salt Lake."

"What is it?" Hennessy asked.

"Mobile command center," she said, pulling over and parking next to a Butte sheriff's cruiser. "Homeland Security built them after 9/11 for situations like this one."

She climbed out into deep snow. "Goddamn it, I need my boots."

Hennessy climbed out, feeling woozy. She must have noticed his imbalance because she rushed around the nose of her vehicle and caught him beneath the armpits. He was six inches taller than she was and outweighed her by at least fifty pounds, but she kept him upright.

"So help me, Mr. Hennessy," she said, "if you collapse on me here after defying the hospital's orders—"

"Just a little light-headed, that's all. And call me Mickey."

"Mickey," she repeated. "Cheyenne. Okay, let's pay SAC Kane a visit. Sounds like he'll be overjoyed to see us both."

They made it to the door of the command center and found it guarded by an FBI agent from Spokane, Washington. Cheyenne showed her ID and he let them in.

The doors whooshed back and they climbed a narrow staircase into a large work space. The first half of the space was set up like a conference room, with table and chairs, a whiteboard on the right wall, a fifty-inch flat television screen attached to the left. Beyond the conference room, there was a galley and computer workstations, four on each wall. Above each hung a smaller flat-screen display. The rear of the command center was a floor-to-ceiling wall of electronic communications equipment and screens.

Special Agent in Charge Willis Kane stood at attention in front of a camera mounted on that rear wall. A short, intense bald agent that Cheyenne recognized from the airport stood beside Kane. So did a stocky man in black SWAT fatigues. To her surprise, the creviced face of FBI Director Tim Griffith filled the screen next to the camera.

"Figure out what we're dealing with before you make any move," the FBI director was saying.

Cheyenne stopped Hennessy from moving forward. They stood and watched from the conference area.

"Yes, sir," Kane said. "But I've taken the precaution of ordering Rapid Deployment Logistics to provide support for my team and for both Hostage Rescue Teams en route."

"Why two?" Griffith asked.

The stocky man in the SWAT fatigues stood up straighter and said, "Sir, based on the number of armed men believed to be inside, I thought it prudent to bring in two teams. They'll come in staggered. One this evening. One sometime tomorrow afternoon."

The FBI director nodded. *"And they're still not talking?"*

The short bald agent at Kane's right shook his head. "I have people calling all the inside numbers, but no one has picked up yet."

"Stay on it," the director said. "The President is very

concerned about this. You'll have whatever you need to get those people out of there unharmed. In the meantime, I want updates every four hours. Understood?"

"Yes, sir," Kane said.

The screen went dead. Kirk Seitz, the short bald agent and the FBI's top negotiator, said, "You think we're settling in here long-term?"

Kane shrugged. "Gotta be prepared for it."

He looked past Seitz to a gaunt, darkly featured man sitting at the closest workstation. "Anything, Pritoni?" he asked.

Agent Pritoni lowered his headphones around his neck. "Every once in a while I'm picking up a transmission. Bring this here. Guard that. Nothing to hang your hat on."

"They know we're listening?"

"Could be disinformation," Pritoni allowed.

"How about the frequency they're running?"

"Common U.S. military, but pretty random," Pritoni said. "Lot of units use it. And none in particular."

"Keep listening," Kane said. "We'll see about getting you some unidirectionals, give you better ears."

Gordon Phelps, the agent in the SWAT clothes and the team's hostage rescue leader, nodded. "I can have my men take them in with them. I'm sending in two recon teams, one to the north, and one to the south of the club grounds." He pointed at the computer screen to the left of Pritoni's. It displayed Google Earth's rendition of the club's terrain. The hostage rescue leader tapped on the screen. "They'll go in here and here."

Kane bent down to get a closer look. Hennessy started

walking toward the incident commander. Cheyenne startled and hurried after him.

"When do you want your men in position, mid-April?" Hennessy asked.

Irritated, Kane twisted from the computer screen, saw the Jefferson Club's security director, and stiffened. "Hello, Mickey."

"Willis," Hennessy said.

"You're supposed to be in a hospital."

"They let me out."

Kane glanced behind Hennessy and spotted Cheyenne. "I told you to report by phone and go home, O'Neil. This is no place for number crunchers or wounded civilians. Did you bring him up here?"

Cheyenne started to sputter a response, but Hennessy cut her off, saying, "If you send your teams in from those entry points, they'll end up with an obstructed view of not much. It's all blown-down trees on both routes. In deep snow like this, a femur buster."

Phelps studied Hennessy with distaste. "Who are you?"

"The director of security at the club," Hennessy said, moving to the computer screen and pointing to two slopes that ran in toward the wilderness.

"These knobs will let your men watch Wolverine Creek to the headwaters on Hellroaring," he said. "They can hike from right here and not trigger the fence."

"Fence?" Kane asked.

"Optical sensor fence," Hennessy replied. "You've got to figure they're monitoring it. I can plot the fence on your maps. Maybe even disable it."

"Can't be difficult," Phelps said. "They seemed to have foiled it with ease."

"They figured out the flaw," Hennessy agreed.

Kane shrugged and said, "Whatever. I can't be running a hospital ward. Give us the plotting of the fence, then you and Agent O'Neil leave. Why don't you go somewhere warm and recover? Recovery. That's how it's done."

Hennessy glared at Kane. "I know what recovery is, Willis, and I'm not going anywhere. I'm going to help you. They blew a transformer down the highway with radio-controlled explosives. A U.S. military bomb. Our system was down less than two-point-two seconds. They entered in that gap."

"Two-point-two seconds is a fuckup in my book," Kane said.

"Lot of things in that book of yours," Hennessy said. "Always have been."

"And don't you forget it," Kane shot back. "So sit with Agent Phelps and help him plot the fence line. Agent O'Neil, I want a written report of your discussion with Mr. Hennessy, then take him back to Bozeman where a doctor can watch him. And then you will get yourself on a plane and go back to New York."

"I told you I'm not going anywhere," Hennessy said.

"You want me to place you under arrest, Mickey?" Kane said evenly.

"Connor, Bridger, and Hailey are inside, Willis. They're hostages."

In the heat of the moment, the meaning did not sink in at first. Then it did.

"The triplets?" Kane said hollowly.

Hennessy nodded. "I can help, Willis."

The CIRG leader kneaded his temples. He craned his head around and held his breath for several beats. Then he seemed to come to some kind of a decision and pointed harshly at Hennessy. "First time you question my authority, Mickey, I call an ambulance and have you hauled out of here in restraints."

CHAPTER SIXTEEN

Twenty minutes later, Hennessy hit ENTER on one of the keyboards inside the FBI command center and groaned, "They've blocked all access to the club's computers. I can't get in. Even through the Web site."

Willis Kane stood behind him. He growled, "Which means?"

"I can't disarm the fence," Hennessy said. "They've put a firewall around it."

"We'll get people working on breaking it back at Quantico," Kane said. "In the meantime, plot the barrier on Google Earth."

Kirk Seitz, the hostage negotiator, threw down his headset at an adjacent workstation. "They've shut down the phone system completely," he said. "I keep getting a recorded message saying the numbers are no longer in service."

Cheyenne O'Neil sat at the terminal on the other side

of Seitz, where she was supposed to be writing up her notes from her interview with Hennessy. Instead, she was looking at an avalanche-warning site. Kane demanded, "What are you doing?"

"Checking the likelihood of avalanche," she said. "I figure your men climbing up there would want to know the danger is off the charts."

Phelps, the hostage rescue leader, blinked, then snapped up his radio and called the warning to his men.

"Finish your report," Kane ordered before turning his attention to Hennessy. "Is there any other way to beat the fence besides blowing up a transformer? Short-circuit it?"

"It doesn't work that way," Hennessy said. "There are twelve laser emitters per station, one hundred and twelve random receivers, all turning off and on according to a mathematical algorithm that I frankly don't understand. Except for a two-second gap between main power and backup, it's the most foolproof system I've ever seen."

"Any way to shut down the generators?" Phelps asked.

"You need a key to the switch box in the lodge basement. When the generators go down, the battery banks take over for thirty-six hours. Or they run out of fuel to run the generators, but that's not going to happen for a week. The tanks are huge up there."

"Who did the engineering?" Phelps asked.

"White Hawk Security out of Reston, Virginia."

"If anyone knows how to break the system, they will," Phelps said.

Kane nodded, then looked around the command center, seeing all of his agents already working on one of his orders. He turned to Cheyenne. "Can you find White Hawk?"

"Straightaway, SAC," Cheyenne said, happy to be given orders.

"I can call White Hawk for you," Hennessy offered.

"I'd rather have Agent O'Neil do that, because I imagine you now have a legitimate beef with their work," Kane said.

That was not true. He'd worked for White Hawk before jumping ship for the Jefferson Club. But Hennessy got the subtext: He wasn't FBI. He wasn't anybody. He gave Cheyenne the company's tech support number, and said he was going to go outside to get some air.

He struggled to his feet, waited for the black dots to disappear in front of his eyes, managed the stairs, and stepped outside into the cold, blowing snow. He pulled up the hood of the jacket and walked through knee-deep snow away from the encampment toward a man building a bonfire in the fading light, sensing the vastness of the landscape around him as acutely as his own emptiness. Connor, Bridger, and Hailey were inside. He'd never felt so helpless. His mind drifted again to the painkillers in his pocket. He almost reached for them, but willed his hands to stop. He wasn't going there, not now. Dreamland would only yield nightmares.

Sheriff Kevin Lacey was feeding the fire. As Hennessy closed the distance, his attention drifted across the seven hundred yards to the Jefferson Club's main gate and the snowcat. He looked at the barren knoll beyond the gate and the cliff behind the knoll, fifty feet high. The snowy trees on top seemed to form the upper wall of a battlement.

Desperately trying to stay on an even keel, Hennessy greeted Lacey and thanked him for helping save his life. Lacey nodded, but sounded bitter.

"I lost Rowdy right there against that gate last night," he said, throwing logs in the fire. "I should have some say on what happens here. But don't work that way. State police's got no use for me. FBI, same thing. I thought having a bonfire would give me some say in what's happening here. Those hostages come out of there, they're going to need a fire to keep warm."

"You going to keep it burning until they come out?"

"Every last one of them," Sheriff Lacey promised.

Hennessy liked Lacey. "Need some help?"

Lacey looked at him, then nodded. "Appreciate the offer, but sit yourself on that log and get yourself warm. My brother's bringing up a load of cordwood and I gotta make sure he doesn't get stuck."

The sheriff trudged off toward the road. Hennessy squatted down, picked up a chunk of log, and threw it in the fire. The flames danced, swirled, and sent sparks into the gloaming light. Hennessy felt the fire's wavering heat against his face and the ache of wanting to hold his children far more acutely than his throbbing wound.

"Mickey?" Cheyenne called.

He glanced over his shoulder to find she'd changed, put on pac boots, wool pants, and an insulated anorak and wool cap. "Kane sent me to be your nurse."

"Lucky you," Hennessy said and threw another chunk of wood on the fire.

She walked to him. "I talked to the support tech on duty at White Hawk. She's trying to track down the guys who designed the fence."

"Faber and Japrudi." Hennessy nodded absently. "Smart, smart guys."

She got a log and sat on it beside him quietly for several minutes before asking, "What's with you and Kane?"

Hennessy glanced at Cheyenne. With her face lit by firelight it was the first time he'd really noticed that she was beautiful. She gazed at him expectantly. He felt exposed despite the fact that only four people in the world knew the truth.

But for reasons Hennessy could not quite explain and never would be able to explain, coming under Cheyenne's sympathetic gaze he felt compelled to come clean and tell a fifth person. There in the cold air by the fire, in the waning light of New Year's Day, he laid out the threads of the story.

Kane and Hennessy had known each other since their days as Marine Corps military police. They'd trained and served two tours of duty together in Rwanda and Colombia, where they worked with U.S. Embassy personnel and members of the Diplomatic Security Service. When their second tour was up, Kane joined the FBI. Hennessy chose Diplomatic Security. While Kane worked through his first years at the Bureau as a junior agent, Hennessy was training full-time as a counterterrorist.

He worked U.S. Embassy security details in political hot spots around the world: Somalia, Colombia, Kuwait, Syria, and Pakistan. He met Patricia in Boston while on leave from Beirut. They fell in love, were married, and had the triplets after resorting to artificial insemination. Patricia came to hate living in politically unstable places. When the kids were approaching school age, she told Hennessy she couldn't take it anymore. She was moving back to Boston, where the triplets would have a more normal childhood.

Hennessy agreed, but then applied for and won a post on the security detail that covered the Secretary of State. The move brought him stateside and Patricia and the children moved down to the Washington, D.C., area.

In the meantime, Kane qualified for the FBI's Hostage Rescue Team, headquartered in Quantico, Virginia, not far from the Hennessys' home in Alexandria. Kane came to the house all the time. He wrestled with the boys, flirted with Hailey, and played poker with Hennessy every other Saturday night.

Then Hennessy compressed a couple of vertebrae in training. It left him in nagging pain. The doctors recommended surgery, but he knew he'd be off the detail if he followed through with their recommendation. So he opted for a steroid injection and OxyContin. The treatment helped. But in six months, he was abusing the pain medication and augmenting it with liquor. In a year, he felt like he couldn't live without either.

"Those days were the depths of my denial," he said, speaking to the bonfire more than to Cheyenne. "I was convinced I could pull it all off: hard charger by day, drinker and prescription doper by night. Then my moods started swinging."

He got angry with Patricia. Their fights turned nasty. Hennessy responded by drinking and drugging more.

"That's where I was five years ago," he told Cheyenne. "Then the Secretary of State announces that she's going to give a speech at the University of Hawaii regarding North Korea during a meeting of the Pacific Rim nations."

Almost immediately the CIA and the NSA began to pick up chatter about an attack on the Secretary of State. The Secretary was apprised of the threat, but decided to go forward with the speech anyway. The President ordered the FBI's National Hostage Rescue Team to Hawaii to back up the Diplomatic Security Service.

"Kane and I worked the same detail," Hennessy recalled. "It was like old times."

The first two days of the meeting passed uneventfully. The Secretary of State attended all her panels and gave her speech on the second evening. It was controversial, a resounding condemnation of North Korea's totalitarian regime, signaling a shift to an even more hawkish position regarding the communist state.

"We put Madame Secretary in her suite for the night around midnight," Hennessy recalled. "I came off duty more wrung out than I've been in my entire life. I mean, for three solid days we'd been treating everyone as a threat. It wears you down. So I went to the bar to blow off steam and stayed until closing even though I was due back on duty for the wrap-up luncheon at the Sheraton Honolulu."

When he got to his hotel room, it was three a.m. Hennessy took a pain pill and passed out. When he awoke twenty minutes before his shift, he had the shakes and the sweats and did the only thing he could think to do: He made coffee in his room, put two vodkas in it from the minibar, and threw in two OxyContins as chasers.

Kane was part of a sniper team set up on rooftops around the Sheraton when Hennessy walked to the Secretary of State's vehicle. After getting the all-clear from Kane, Hennessy opened her door. Honolulu police were keeping back the crowd.

"I was waffled and that's why I didn't see him right away," Hennessy said. "Craig Brooks, this fringe character with a history of mental illness, is standing at the barricade. When we're ten feet away, Brooks brings up a camera with his left hand. I see it, but miss the gun in his right hand until it's swinging at the Secretary of State. I manage to knock her down just as the shooting starts. I get hit once in the back of my Kevlar vest and then take one in the thigh. Everything goes to shit. I'm down, covering the Secretary with my body. Guys on my team try to get Brooks, but he's out in the crowd shooting. He wounds four people before Kane kills him from the roof.

"When I wake up in the hospital, I have plates and screws in my femur and people are calling me a hero," Hennessy said.

Cheyenne cocked her head. "I remember this. You were that guy."

"I was that fraud," he said. "The day after I woke up, Willis and Patricia come in my hospital room. She tells me she's through with me and wants a divorce. The way Willis is looking at me, I can tell we're no longer friends or comrades."

The doctors had told Patricia that Hennessy was legally drunk and on opiates at the time of the shooting. She showed the results to Kane, who felt compelled to tell Hennessy's boss, who in turn felt compelled to inform the Secretary of State.

Due to the politics of the situation, and the positive publicity the Diplomatic Security Service had received due to his "heroic and selfless" act, Kane had been empowered to make his old friend an offer he could not refuse: In return for not being exposed as a drunk and an addict and a tarnish on the DSS's reputation, Hennessy would instead receive several letters of commendation and be known as a hero the rest of his life. He would also announce his retirement from DSS effective immediately.

"When Kane left my hospital room, I had nothing left," Hennessy said softly. "No family. No job. A disgrace to my wife, my closest friend, and the people I'd worked for. It was the bottom for me. I haven't had a drink or dropped a pill since. I went into rehab and have worked at sobriety ever since. It's been hard, real hard, but I've done it. Nearly five years sober and I fully intend to stay that way, which is why I'd appreciate it, Nurse O'Neil, if you'd keep an eye on these little babies for me."

He dug in his pocket, came out with the prescription

pain medication, and handed it to her. "I'll only ask for one if I can't stand it. Okay?"

"Okay," Cheyenne said, looking unsure as to why he'd told her his deepest, darkest secret. But then she asked, "How'd you get to be working here?"

Hennessy shrugged. "Because of the commendations, when I'd healed up and felt ready, I went looking for work and was hired by White Hawk. I'd been there about six months when Horatio Burns hired the firm to design and install the security system at the club. I was asked to oversee the project. I fell in love with Montana and when Gregg Foster offered me this job I jumped at it. But now look at where it's got me. My kids are in the hands of madmen."

Hailey Hennessy was only vaguely aware of the light changing outside the Jefferson Club Lodge as clouds that had gripped the mountains blew out while Senator Stonington completed the transfer of his money to the Third Position accounts.

For the last few minutes she'd been watching Stephanie Doore as she rocked Ian in her arms and thinking of her own mother. *Does she know?* Hailey felt guilty. She'd been sullen and resentful during the wedding the weekend before she and her brothers came west. Ted, her mom's new husband, was okay, but she'd felt like she was being discarded at some level. Now all Hailey wanted to do was hug her mother, just hold her and smell her and know everything would be okay.

"I'm so hungry I could eat a magpie," Bridger whispered.

Appalled, Hailey muttered, "They're like vultures."

"I'm so hungry I could eat a magpie," Bridger repeated.

"Forget your stomach for once," Connor shot back. "Where's Dad?"

One of the waitresses was sitting in a chair next to Hailey. She turned to look at them. "Are you Mickey Hennessy's kids?"

Bridger nodded. "Do you know where he is?"

She shook her head. "I saw him leaving the ballroom shortly before the attack."

"Going where?" Hailey demanded.

"I don't know," she said. "Up the stairs, toward the atrium. But I haven't seen any of the security guards since the attack."

"So he's in the lodge somewhere," Connor said. "They're holding him prisoner."

"Or he's hiding somewhere, wounded, needing us," Hailey said.

"I don't know," the waitress said soberly. "There was lots of shooting."

"So you're saying he could be dead?" Bridger asked, a tremor in his voice.

"Don't say that," Connor said, elbowing his brother. "Don't ever say that."

Before the waitress could add anything, on the opposite side of the room Cristoph looked up at General Anarchy and nodded. *"C'est fait,"* he said.

General Anarchy left the computer and bowed before Senator Stonington. He grinned and said, "You've helped so much, I can't bear to let you go, Senator."

"What?" Stonington sputtered.

As if on cue, several Third Position soldiers rushed toward the eight men sprawled at the base of the stage. "You said you'd let us go," Horatio Burns cried in rage.

"I never said I'd let *you* go, Mr. Burns," General Anarchy replied evenly. "I said I'd let your relatives go. You'll face justice before you leave this courtroom."

A soldier grabbed the founder of the Jefferson Club and threw Burns roughly on his stomach. They bound his wrists, and then hooded him again. Others were following suit with Friedrich Klinefelter, Jack Doore, Senator Stonington, Aaron Grant, Chin Hoc Pan, Albert Crockett, and Sir Lawrence Treadwell.

Shouts erupted among the other hostages. "You said you'd release us! Let us go!"

General Anarchy looked about as they shouted, then nodded. "The rest of you are free to leave. You will be released from your restraints and then you can walk to the front gates. There are FBI agents waiting. You will not be harmed."

Gasps and cries of relief went up across the room. But Stephanie Doore stood up and shouted, "I'm staying with my husband!"

"So am I!" Margaret Grant said, rising beside her.

Isabel Burns looked like she didn't know what to do, then jumped to her feet. "And I am too!"

Alicia Treadwell rose more reluctantly than Albert Crockett's wife, Lydia, did. Friedrich Klinefelter's wife, Ruth, made it to her feet last, but no less resolved. Olivia Stonington remained in her seat.

All around Hailey and her brothers, Third Position

soldiers were cutting the plastic restraints off the hostages. Other soldiers were already moving into the anteroom off the ballroom to guard the staircases and elevators. People were buzzing with some relief now. The first were heading toward the anteroom under the watchful eye of other attackers, moving a little too fast in their ballroom shoes, desperate and determined to be free of the terrible place where they'd been held sixteen hours.

General Anarchy said to the wives of the remaining hostages, "Embrace the fact that we do not hold you culpable in your husbands' crimes and leave. Now."

"What does that mean?" Margaret Grant cried. "Crimes?"

"Margie!" Aaron Grant yelled from under his hood. "Go! Take the girls and go!"

"Take Ian, Stephanie," Jack Doore shouted. "Get him out."

"Isabel, save yourself," Horatio Burns ordered. "If you love me, you will."

Albert Crockett said, "Lydia, please. It's for the best."

Reluctantly, one by one, the wives turned from their husbands and found their children and grandchildren and joined the throng pushing and jostling toward the exits. Stephanie Doore was last. Tears streamed down her face as she led Ian toward the staircases. As a Third Position soldier cut her restraints, Hailey kept looking over at her, then fell in with her brothers moving with the crowd.

"What about Dad?" Connor asked. "We've got to find him."

"We've got no idea where he is," Bridger said. "He might be—"

"Needing us," Connor insisted, fighting back tears.

Hailey felt a ball of emotion burrowing in her throat. She'd given her father a hard time the past two weeks and felt awful about it. *Where is he? We can't just leave without knowing what's happened to him.* And then it occurred to her what they had to do.

"We gotta get away and find him," Hailey said as they squeezed through into the anteroom. The place was packed with people shoving toward the staircases.

"There are Third Position soldiers everywhere," Bridger said, nodding toward the troops at the foot of the staircase and others on the landing above.

Hailey looked ahead and saw that on the right-hand wall of the anteroom, catty-corner and behind the right staircase, the janitor's closet was open.

"In there," she said and pushed along the edge of the crowd behind a soldier and ducked inside. None of the escaping hostages paid the slightest attention. Nor did the soldiers standing on the landing watching the exodus. Her brothers came in behind her. The closet was cramped and there was barely room for them. Hailey took in the space and its contents at a glance: a sink, buckets, mops, brooms, vacuum cleaners, and shelves packed with cleaning supplies.

"What good does this do us?" Bridger demanded. "We can't get out of here. Those soldiers will find us eventually. Let's go."

"We need a diversion," Connor said.

"I guess," Bridger said with little conviction.

Hailey sniffed, catching a chemical odor. She looked up and spotted a small can of paint thinner on one of the shelves. She gazed around, spotted cleaning rags, and said, "This will do it, I think."

She grabbed the rags and threw a handful of them in the sink. She doused them with the paint thinner, then stood back, saying, "I think it will spontaneously combust if we give it time."

Bridger grabbed a can of cleaning solvent and doused it on the rags, saying, "This should speed it up."

"We've got no time for that," Connor said, digging in his pocket and coming up with a lighter. A gold one set with jewels.

"Where'd you get that, klepto?" Bridger demanded.

"On the floor in the ballroom," Connor said. "I was gonna turn it in."

He lit the lighter and threw it at the rags. A minor mushroom cloud of toxic-smelling flame exploded upward. Hailey threw herself backward, but felt her eyebrows singe and smelled hair burning.

"Get out!" she screamed. "My hair's on fire!"

Connor yanked open the door. He jumped out with Hailey and Bridger moving behind, all of them coughing. Flames and smoke followed them. Fleeing hostages still packed the hallway and staircase. The fire alarms went off in whoops.

People started screaming, "Fire! Fire!"

The Hennessy triplets dodged into the crowd, yelling, "Fire! Fire!"

The Third Position soldiers guarding the ballroom atrium staircases came pushing their way toward the fire. So did those up on the landing. Halfway up the staircase, Hailey and her brothers had to press against the wall and let a group of the attackers pass, praying they didn't see their burnt hair or smell their singed clothes. But General Anarchy's men went right on by and the triplets kept climbing. When they reached the atrium, it was unguarded and in pandemonium as club members and guests attacked the cloakrooms looking for coats and boots. Others weren't bothering. They ran out the front door in their formal attire.

"The apartment," Connor said, taking the staircase toward the upper hallways.

"Told you it'd work," Hailey cried, racing behind him, grinning wildly, and feeling more alive and more scared than she'd been in her entire life.

Upstairs in the security control room, Radio searched for the sensor that had triggered the fire alarm. He knew it was in the anteroom off the ballroom and he was trying to shut it down while watching the monitors that showed the last of the hostages rushing past the soldiers battling the blaze.

He never saw the screen behind him showing the Hennessy kids climbing the atrium staircase and disappearing into the passage to the fifth-floor south hallway.

Five miles away, in the glowing light of the bonfire, Cheyenne watched Hennessy's head droop at the thought of his children still trapped inside the lodge. She felt confused about him. He'd just admitted he'd been inebriated while serving on the security detail that guarded the Secretary of State. But he'd still saved the Secretary's life. He took a bullet for her. That counted for something in Cheyenne's mind. And she could feel how much he loved his kids and how much he was suffering.

"They're going to be all right," she soothed. "I'm sure of it."

A red pickup truck with a bed full of cut cordwood rode off the road embankment and inched its way through the sage and the snow toward the fire. Sheriff Lacey sat in the passenger seat beside a younger man, driving. They parked, threw the lift in gear, and as the bed dumped the wood, Cheyenne heard shouting.

"Mickey!"

It was Kane, with Phelps and his hostage rescuers following. They ran up, breathing hard. "I just got word from my men climbing the north ridge," Kane said. "There's at least two hundred people coming down the access road. They're free!"

CHAPTER SEVENTEEN

Inside the gatehouse, Cobb stripped off his Jefferson Club security attire, dressed again in his white Third Position Army camouflage, went out, climbed in the snowcat, and keyed the ignition. It coughed, strained, and then roared to life. Dalton climbed in beside him.

"Got the banner?" Cobb asked, spinning the machine around.

Dalton reached behind him and put his hands on the rolled banner. "Right here."

Cobb shifted gears. They rode uphill away from the club's gate, churning snow behind them. Dalton looked out the rear window with his binoculars.

"They see us moving," he said. "Bunch of them coming away from that fire."

"How about the TV crews?" Cobb asked.

"Can't see. Wait until we get to the top."

Cobb checked his watch. He spoke in his headset, "How long, Radio?"

"You should be seeing the first of them any minute now," Radio replied.

"We'll be out of daylight soon enough."

"The general says use the headlights."

A thousand yards behind them, Hennessy watched the snowcat climb the hill, feeling his heart pound at the thought that his kids would soon be in his arms.

Phelps said, "You want us ready to enter?"

Seeing the snowcat come to a broadside stop, Kane dropped his binoculars. "We need to debrief everyone who comes out first. Everyone talks to a law enforcement officer before they're released. No exceptions. Then we'll figure out a way to enter."

Sheriff Lacey said, "It's eighteen degrees and about to drop another ten. I can get school buses up here to haul those people somewhere warm. And build more fires."

"Thank you, Sheriff," Kane said. "That will be a big help."

The first hostages appeared on the knoll, running past the stopped snowcat, which had turned on its headlights. They shone on Cheryl Wise, the actress, who was in the lead, carrying her daughter. Behind them, a band of about fifty people appeared. Half wore no coats and were shivering violently. Women hobbled along in their gowns, their evening shoes lost somewhere in the snow behind them.

Kane and his men moved forward cautiously,

backed up by twenty-five Montana State Police troopers in SWAT gear. Cheyenne O'Neil trailed after them with Hennessy in tow. He cradled his arm, looking ahead anxiously, trying to spot his kids in the waning light.

The media camp had spotted Cheryl Wise through binoculars and gone wild. They'd been ordered to remain behind barricades, but several cameramen left the encampment and looped to the north and then toward the gate, parallel and behind Kane's men. A gaggle of soundmen and reporters followed, all desperate to get close enough for a clear shot of the exodus.

Three Montana State Police troopers peeled off to intercept them and finally succeeded in stopping the pack three hundred and fifty yards from the gate. The location offered them a dramatic wide-angle shot of the hostages escaping through the arched gate while the FBI and state police closed from the opposite direction. All of it against the backdrop of the stunning Jefferson Range at sunset.

Thousands of miles away, producers in Atlanta and New York saw the streaming footage. Within seconds of each other, CNN, MSNBC, and Fox News cut to it live, showing Cheryl Wise running through the arched gate. That set off an uproar among the reporters, who babbled into their lenses that it was somehow fitting that the great actress was leading the hostages to freedom. Millions of people all over the country tuned in. With every minute the Nielsen ratings climbed.

* * *

It was mass hysteria when hostages met rescuers less than one hundred yards from the cameras. People were suffering from frostbite, exposure, and hypothermia.

"Move toward the fires!" Kane shouted over a bull-horn. "You'll be taken somewhere warm just as soon as we can. Move toward the fires! We'll help you there."

Far behind them, with sirens and flashing lights, ambulances appeared, followed by fire trucks from Jefferson, Madison, and Gallatin Counties.

The FBI and troopers moved to help the weakest and the elderly. Soon the firefighters and emergency technicians joined them. People began to describe what had happened inside the club. Cheyenne was closest when Margaret Grant and her two daughters came through. From them she learned about General Anarchy and the Third Position Army, the billion-dollar ransom, and the eight men still being held hostage.

"What are they going to do with your husband and the others?" Cheyenne asked, hurrying them toward a pickup brought up to ferry people to the buses.

"I don't know," Margaret Grant said, fighting for control. "But you can tell they have an agenda. They kept talking about justice being served."

Hennessy, meanwhile, stood on the side of the road, watching the horde pass, calling out to the members he knew, and getting scowls in return. Up on the hill beyond the gate, the number of people coming had slowed. Most were out now and moving past him. *Where are they?* he kept asking himself every time a child or a teenager passed.

He spotted Isabel Burns coming toward him, her arms locked in Alicia Treadwell's. Both women were dressed in chinchilla coats. Both had been crying.

"Isabel! Isabel, it's Mickey Hennessy!" he cried.

She appeared in a daze, but spotted him and came toward him as if she were surprised to see him alive.

"Mickey," she said, bewildered. "Where were you? Where were your men?"

He gestured at his arm. "I believe my men were killed. I was shot outside and hunted, but managed to escape last night. Have you seen my kids?"

"I see them in the hallway before the fire broke out." She stopped. Her eyes hardened. "Horatio's still in there. Blindfolded, arms tied behind his back. I had a gun put to my head for making a cell phone call and my hair almost torn out. They killed Giulio. You're fired, Mickey. You're lucky I do not scratch your eyes out."

She stomped away. Hennessy had had so many shocks in the past twenty-four hours that he took this one in stride. He'd just lost his job and didn't care. Others would blame him. He didn't care. He watched the stragglers coming down the hill. Stephanie and Ian Doore were the last to pass through the gate.

When she passed, he asked, "Mrs. Doore, have you seen my children?"

Stephanie Doore shook her head and made to leave with her son, when Ian began to make a whining noise and gathered his hands into fists.

"Upstairs," he managed, his eyes sweeping the snow. "Hailey went upstairs."

"What stairs?" his mother asked, kneeling next to her son. "Where?"

"Upstairs," Ian said and then began to tremble from the cold.

"I've got to get him warm," Stephanie Doore said. "I hope you find them."

Hennessy watched her walk away, hearing that word *upstairs* ring in his head. He felt a rushing in his ears and then everything started to spin.

"Mickey?" Cheyenne called. She'd come back to help the last people toward the fires. "Where are your kids?"

He collapsed on one knee. She ran to him. He was panting and staring wildly at the ground. "They didn't come out," he managed. "They're still in there."

No," she said. "The hostages I've spoken with said they let everyone go except for eight men. They must have gotten past you. They're probably by the fires."

"No," he said hoarsely. "I looked at everyone who came past me. Jack Doore's son just told me they went upstairs, meaning in the lodge. They're not out. I thought they were coming out. I thought this was over."

Cheyenne put her arm under his good shoulder and tried to get him to his feet. Shouts rose from the news cameramen to their right. "Up on the hill! Up on the hill!"

Up on the knoll beyond the gate, the snowcat's headlights shone on high beam, illuminating a banner strung up between the machine and a large pine tree.

The banner read: WWW.THIRDPOSITIONJUSTICE.NET.

"Mickey," Cheyenne said. "Something tells me this isn't over by a long shot."

* * *

On the fourth floor of the Jefferson Club Lodge, Bridger, Connor, and Hailey had figured out that their father had not returned to his apartment after the attack. His bed was still made. Their paintball guns were under it. Their luggage was still in disarray, though their snowboard clothes had dried. And the phone lines were all dead.

"Dad left his master key," Hailey said, picking up the electronic card from the kitchen table. "This could help."

"Definitely," Connor said. "Good find."

Bridger was at the living room window, looking out. It was dark. He saw nothing but the eerie blue glow of the heated pool throwing steam into the frigid air. It had been nearly half an hour since he'd seen anyone pass. The other hostages were long gone.

"Maybe we should surrender and get them to let us go too," Bridger said.

"What about Dad?" Hailey demanded. "You said he's still here."

"He's not here," Bridger shot back.

Connor shook his head violently. "Far as I'm concerned he's here until I prove to myself he's not."

"How are we gonna find him? Look in every room?" Bridger snapped.

Hailey held up the master key. "Why not?"

"They've got guns," Bridger said.

"We've got guns too," Connor said, then went back into his father's room and into the closet. The .22-caliber bolt-action rifle with the iron peep sight was propped in the corner behind the dress shirts. They'd used it several times during their stay with their father, going to the

rifle range and learning how to use it safely. He unlocked
the trigger guard with a key his father kept in his bed-
stand. He grabbed the paintball guns on the way out.

"Okay," he told Bridger and Hailey when he returned.
"Here's our arsenal."

"You call a .22 and three paintball guns an arsenal?" Bridger asked.

"Paintballs move at three hundred and fifty feet per
second. You hit someone where the skin's exposed, it'll
hurt. You hit them in the temple, it'll knock them out."

"It'll make them crazy!" Bridger shot back. "They
have machine guns, or haven't you noticed? We can't
fight them with paintballs."

Connor started loading the clip from the .22, saying,
"This may not be a big gun, but you heard what Dad
said: A .22 will kill you just the same."

"You planning on killing someone, Connor?" Hailey asked, increasingly scared.

Connor stared back at Hailey, finding a source of
strength he didn't know he had, before replying, "Only
if it'll save you, Bridge, Dad, or myself."

Inside the Jefferson Club Lodge ballroom, most of the
Third Position soldiers had long removed their hoods
and stripped down to T-shirts. The band's instruments
were tossed in a corner. The banquet chairs and tables
had been removed from the ballroom floor and stacked
along the wall and down the hallway toward the lobby
and atrium.

Circular saws whined and cut. Hammers fell. Drills
spun. Dead center of the empty stage a team of six men

built a large rectangular frame from two-by-fours found in the club's maintenance shop along with the necessary tools.

Directly behind the carpenters, a team hoisted the last of eight maroon curtains stripped from lodge rooms and fixed it with wood screws to the log posts that framed the windows. When they were finished, the curtains covered the windows floor to ceiling and twenty feet to either side of the stage.

Other men carried in trestle tables from the lodge library and placed them facing the stage twenty feet back and ten feet apart. They slammed down brass and green glass banker's lamps on them and then piles of books.

Behind the tables, scaffolding found in the basement had been erected to support a square platform with enough room for two Third Position soldiers—Mouse and Emilia. They were rigging two small digital video cameras to tripods and cables that dropped off the platform into a matrix of wires jutting off the back of desktop computers taken from the club's administrative offices.

Sitting before the screens, wearing her headset and microphone, Rose smoked a cigarette, her eyes flickering from monitor to monitor.

General Anarchy came up behind her with Truth trailing. "Will you be ready?"

"Yes," Rose said. "Question is, can they build the set fast enough?"

"They've done it twice before," he replied. "And please smoke outside."

She raised an eyebrow, took a deep drag, and then

stubbed it out and blew the smoke out the corner of her mouth away from General Anarchy.

"I consider you the weakest link, Rose," he said. "I hope you prove me wrong."

Rose glared back at him. "I grew up on a kibbutz and could handle a gun when I was six, General. I was lined up for execution in a Palestinian attack and I didn't blink. I consider myself the strongest person here despite getting airsick."

"You'll have your chance to prove it," he said and then spun on his heels.

"Asshole," Rose muttered.

General Anarchy heard it, but ignored it. Instead, he went to Cristoph, who sat at another table working on a desktop and a laptop at the same time. Cristoph heard him coming. "Everything's loaded on the servers, General. Servers are glitch-free. Satellite feed is strong. Bandwidth is huge. It'll handle anything we throw at it."

"Firewalls?"

"Best a billion can buy," Cristoph said. "Unattackable. It is as you described it: the Jefferson Club is a digital fortress."

General Anarchy smiled. He clapped Cristoph on the shoulder. "Well done," he said. "Take the site live at six-thirty."

CHAPTER EIGHTEEN

At six-twenty-eight p.m., a fleet of nine school buses arrived on the sage flat outside the Jefferson Club's gate to transport the freed hostages to the Jeffersonville armory. A new contingent of agents from the Salt Lake office went with them as part of a team with Montana State Police troopers and Justice agents who would interview the released hostages and collate the intelligence.

Inside the mobile command center, Willis Kane stood behind Kirk Seitz as the hostage negotiator kept typing www.thirdpositionjustice.net, hitting ENTER, and receiving a page that featured a painting of a forearm and hand wielding a hammer striking an anvil on top of the words, *"Pardon the wait. We're still under construction."*

Seitz threw up his hands. "Why tell us to look at a Web site if it's not up?"

"Keep trying," Kane said, then turned to his other men. "Anything?"

Agent Pritoni tugged down his headset. "They're moving stuff around in there: scaffolding, lumber, tools. I think something big's gonna happen at seven."

"Big what? Why seven?" Kane said.

"Can't figure it out. But there's a definite deadline."

"And therefore a plan," Phelps said. "No doubt a ruthless one: The witnesses all said they shot the chef and the Capitol Police officer in cold blood."

Cheyenne, who was standing back toward the galley, said, "SAC, that billion dollars was transferred somewhere. My partner and I can track it. It's what we do."

Kane thought for a moment, and then nodded. "Get on it."

Mickey Hennessy, who was sitting at the conference table looking pale and sick, said, "What about my kids? They're still in there, Willis."

Before Kane could reply, Seitz said, "Web site's loading, SAC."

Kane held up his hand in understanding toward Hennessy, and then turned to the screen. All around the CIRG command center, the agents operating the computers called up www.thirdpositionjustice.net.

Hennessy watched, feeling cold, then hot. He wanted desperately to sleep, but he pinched his bad arm to stay awake, seeing the Third Position Justice homepage open with a flash sequence featuring footage of the 1999 riots in Seattle during the first meeting of the World Trade Organization.

Thousands of protesters filled the streets, chanting

slogans against the WTO. They held banners that read DON'T HOMOGENIZE ME! and DOWN WITH CORPORATE TYRANNY! Another read GOVERNMENT SELLOUT! CORPORATE RULE!

Over these images a tenor's voice intoned, "The right and the left have failed us. Each end of the political spectrum has become corroded, corrupt, and beholden. Moderate citizens feel disgusted with their leaders and helpless to help themselves. As this disgust grows into rancor, people with widely different political backgrounds and philosophies are finding that their new worldviews overlap.

"We are opposed to communism, with its stultifying effect on thought, liberty, and ambition. But we are equally distrustful of global capitalism, with its tendency to concentrate wealth among a super-elite and to make people, cultures, and economies more and more alike, turning our planet into a polluted, bland, and materialistic McWorld where the dollar is all and freedom is bought and sold.

"We mistrust our politicians for their cozy relationships with global corporate powers. We value a pristine environment, a land unsullied by petroleum-based corporate agriculture and runaway urbanization. We fight for diversity—the future of our species and that of all creatures on earth. We fight for mankind's very survival.

"This is the age of new politics. This is the age of the Third Position, neither left nor right, allied against the capitalist system as it is currently practiced, completely pro-earth, revolting against global corporations, eager to forge a new society."

The images on the screen crash-cut to news footage of chaos as protesters in Seattle battled police in riot gear. The fights turned bloody. Tear gas filled the air. Guns went off. Protesters stampeded. Police beat them with batons.

The voice-over went on, "We soldiers of the Third Position are neither conservative nor liberal, just free men and free women fighting for liberty from forces that have chained the individual and made him a slave, forces that have gagged the artist and throttled her creativity, forces that have hamstrung the dissenter and dipped every man, woman, and child in corporate sponsorship, all of it rubber-stamped by a government gone prostitute."

Over images of politicians led away in handcuffs, the voice said, "Witness citizens fleeing the polls in droves. Hear the pervading cynicism of an electorate that believes that the government is no longer by the people and for the people, but by the corporation and for the corporation.

"As a result, greed has laid our common ethics to waste. The justice system is incompetent to turn the tide. If you have enough money these days, you can turn jail time into celebrity and use it to boost your portfolio upon your release."

Against a picture of a lobbyist smoking a cigar, the voice continued, "These days corporations have lobbyists with bulging checkbooks writing their own laws in the back halls of Congress, letting the shills of the left and the right make it all look legal, proper, and fit to read about in *The New York Times*. The buck doesn't stop here. It never stops moving. It's government by pass the buck, not principle, and we are sick of it."

Over images of fat American-looking children pigging out on hamburgers and fries, emaciated slum kids playing barefoot in the shadow of billboards advertising Nike, and vast oil slicks with birds and animals flapping in spilled petroleum, the narrator said, "Corporate influence has not just corrupted America. It has set its sights on corrupting every other nation on earth. The average citizen in the world is not long from a time when the principles of all nations will become subservient to the culture and law of whatever transnational company pays enough."

The screen jumped one last time to show a wilderness setting at sunrise. People wearing backpacks and carrying weapons walked away from the camera into the woods.

"But take heart, citizens," the voice went on. "Resistance grows. New alliances are forming between those who have thought of themselves as right-wingers, conservatives, and patriots, and those who have thought of themselves as left-wingers, progressives, and war protesters. Whatever their old politics, they see the evil that globalization and corporate domination have wrought on every facet of our society. The Third Position's goal is freedom from corporate tyranny, a cleansing of political corruption and the triumph of earth's needs over the tycoons' pockets. We hope you join us and help forge a new, third way to a better world."

The screen jumped to a plain white background and

an Internet link underlying the words, *Click to enter the Court of Public Opinion.*

Kane said, "They've shown their stripes. Anti-globalists. I thought we'd seen the last violence from that quarter. We need our best anti-globalists looking at this site ASAP and I want a direct line to an analyst in their office starting yesterday. We need immediate access to their database. Get Scotland Yard and Inter-pol looking too."

"For what?" Phelps asked.

"Anyone in the worldwide anti-global movement who's capable of orchestrating this," Kane said. "Some-one with extensive military training and a lot of money."

The room began to bustle as agents jumped to carry out Kane's orders.

Cheyenne pulled out her cell phone, meaning to call her partner's home number in New York, when Hen-nessy said, "Click that link," to the agent manning the computer closest to him. The agent moved his cursor to the Court of Public Opinion link and clicked on it. An MPEG movie downloaded and started to play. A white-hooded head appeared on the screen wearing dark sun-glasses and a headset and mike.

"My name is General Anarchy of the Third Position Army," he said in that electronically altered voice.

"Willis!" Hennessy yelled. "Anarchy. He's on!"

Everyone crowded in behind the screen, watching the hooded figure say, "In the name of Earth, Sky, Water, and Forest, and for the oppressed, the poisoned, and the dead, the following men have been indicted for crimes against humanity and the planet:

"U.S. Senator Worth Stonington, chairman of the U.S. Senate Appropriations Committee; Sir Lawrence Treadwell, chairman of GlobalCon; Albert Crockett, chairman of Crockett LLC; Friedrich Klinefelter, founder of Mobius Hedge Funds LLC; Chin Hoc Pan of Pan-Horizon Group; Horatio Burns, chairman of HB1 Financial; and Jack Doore and Aaron Grant of YES! Corporation.

"The trial of Senator Worth Stonington will commence at seven p.m. mountain time, nine p.m. eastern, live on this site," General Anarchy went on. Then he cocked his head as if in reappraisal before saying, "A warning to the police sworn to protect the corporate kings: Each and every soldier in here is ready to die for this cause and the remaining hostages are booby-trapped. Any rescue attempt will mean their death and yours."

General Anarchy's tone of voice changed, returning to a softer delivery. "Seven p.m. mountain, nine p.m. eastern, six on the left coast. The first trial in the Court of Public Opinion. You won't want to miss it. This is gonna be bigger than *Lost*."

The MPEG movie ended.

"*Lost*?" Kane said.

"Television show," Seitz said. "My kids watch it all the time. Big hit."

"Looks like Anarchy is anticipating a big audience," Hennessy said.

Kane digested this, then barked at Pritoni, "Get me Computer Investigations at Quantico. I want to know who's behind this Web site, who built it, who hosts it. Now!"

* * *

Inside her father's apartment, Hailey Hennessy listened as Connor said, "We need to take turns at sentry. Dad said you stay secure by first securing the area around you."

"Whatever," Bridger said with a dismissive flip of his hand. "I'm gonna watch TV, see what they're reporting."

"Are you whacked?" Hailey demanded. "Someone'll hear."

"Chill," Bridger said. "I'll use the headphones."

Connor moved the kitchen table until it faced the apartment's front door. He put a chair behind it, got pillows from the room where they'd been sleeping, and stacked them on the table. He put the .22 rifle on the pillow, muzzle facing the door, then sat down.

"What are you—" Hailey began.

A door slammed loudly somewhere in the hall outside the apartment. Then she heard voices coming closer. She felt panic drip into her bloodstream and she backed up toward the hallway to the bedrooms. There was a pause, followed by someone twisting the door to the apartment. Click-click, rumble, rattle, and again.

She glanced to her right, seeing Connor shaking as he got down behind the .22, pressed the stock into his shoulder, and aimed at the door. He flipped off the safety.

Five stories below, six television sets rested on tables in the atrium. It was six forty-five p.m. and General Anarchy and Truth were watching the coverage of the hostage release on the various cable newscasts. The footage proved quite dramatic, especially with the unforeseen bonus of having one of the world's most recognizable actresses first out through the gate. When the www .THIRDPOSITIONJUSTICE.NET banner went up, the snowcat's headlamps lit it perfectly. They showed the banner on every newscast. Some featured clips from the homepage.

"You couldn't ask for better than that," Truth said.

General Anarchy smiled in agreement. "A producer's dream."

MSNBC broadcast General Anarchy's MPEG message describing the hostages as capitalist criminals and announcing the trial of Senator Stonington. Fox News was reporting that two of the FBI's elite hostage rescue units were on the scene.

"But they're not coming in anytime soon," Truth said.

General Anarchy bobbed his head in agreement, gesturing at the televisions. "We're not the biggest story in the world yet. But give it a few hours. Noon tomorrow, our message will dominate the airwaves and the fiberoptic networks."

Cobb and Dalton trudged in, yanking off gloves, hoods, and camouflage coats.

"General," Cobb said, nodding. "Irving and Fork took our place on the knoll."

Dalton yawned. "I gotta sleep."

"You earned it," General Anarchy replied, then

handed them each an electronic passkey. "That'll get you into most rooms in the lodge. Find one, report your room number to Radio, and be back on duty at six a.m."

Dalton took his key and set off toward the lower hallway. Cobb shoved his in his pocket. "I'm okay, yet," he said, scratching at a day's growth of beard. "I only need a couple hours and I'm good to go."

"General?" Truth said. "You need to look at this."

General Anarchy looked back to the television sets. A bundled-up female reporter from the Butte station was doing a live stand-up outside the gates of the Jefferson Club.

"We are being told that of the two hundred thirty-two people said to be inside the Jefferson Club at the time of the attack, all but *sixteen* have been freed," the reporter said. "This is different from what we were telling you a half hour ago when we believed that all but *nineteen* were unaccounted for, including the eight men believed held hostage and several guards and club workers. But now we are getting word that fourteen-year-old triplets Connor, Bridger, and Hailey Hennessy, children of the Jefferson Club's security director, Michael Hennessy, remain missing and are presumed still inside the club's grounds."

Staring at the television screen, General Anarchy's carefully controlled facial expression twisted into a mask of rage. Without turning around, he roared, "Find them! Everyone was supposed to be out of here! No witnesses other than our cameras!"

Mouse appeared. "General? Truth? You're late for makeup."

General Anarchy's attention flashed in a rage to the clock: 6:47 p.m. He barked at Cobb, "Find them, Cobb! Find those goddamned kids and get them out of here!"

CHAPTER NINETEEN

The door to the apartment stopped shaking. Connor heard footsteps fading away toward the atrium staircase. He flipped the .22's safety on. He stood up sweating and so wobbly he had to use the tabletop for support.

He felt Hailey staring at him like she didn't know him. "Were you really gonna shoot whoever came through that door?"

Connor thought about it. "I wanted the option."

"Why?"

"They kill people. Why not us?"

"You're out of it, kid," Hailey said. She grabbed a banana from the counter and went into the living room.

Connor followed, feeling like he was a stranger not only to his sister, but to himself.

Bridger sat on the floor, oblivious to all that had happened. He'd plugged a pair of earphones into the television jack, turned the television on, and was channel-surfing. He stopped. His head shot forward, and he yelled, "It's on! We're on!"

Hailey slapped him on the shoulder and Bridger cringed. "What?"

Hailey yanked off the earphones. "Shut up!" she hissed. "There was someone checking at the door a minute ago."

"Really?" Bridger whispered, brows knitting.

"Yeah," Connor murmured, seeing over and over again the sight of the .22 aimed at the door in his mind.

"Check it out, though," Bridger said, lowering his voice and gesturing at the television. "It's the club's gate. There's like a bazillion people out there."

Connor turned numbly, then startled at the images of police barriers and lights and freed hostages in blankets heading toward the bus.

"What're they saying?" Connor asked.

"Did they mention Dad?" Hailey demanded.

Bridger grimaced. "Just that we were his kids and that we're still in here."

The three huddled together, pulling the headphones apart so they could all hear the newscaster talk about Senator Stonington's upcoming trial to be webcast on www.thirdpositionjustice.net at seven p.m. mountain, nine eastern.

Bridger looked at his watch. "That's like five minutes," he said.

Connor was already on his feet. He went to the cabinet under the television where his father kept the keyboard. He gave the keyboard a command. The television screen jumped not to Yahoo.com as it ordinarily did

when the service activated, but went directly to the Third
Position Web site, which launched into the flash movie
of the Seattle anti-globalism riots. The voice began,
"The right and the left have failed us. Each end of the
political spectrum has become corroded, corrupt, and
beholden . . ."

In the FBI's command center, Mickey Hennessy dozed
on one of the chairs in the conference area. Willis Kane
had offered him a cot in one of the tents outside, but he
had refused. Cheyenne put a blanket over him before
finding a phone and calling her partner at home in New
York.

"How'd you get in the middle of the reincarnation of
the Unabomber?" Ikeda asked by way of greeting.

"More like the Freemen," Cheyenne said, then went
on to describe the ransom transfers the eight remaining
hostages made. "They want us to track the money."

"Clear it with the boss and I'm on it in the morning," he promised. "Of course, he's gonna love the fact
you went to Montana without his okay."

"John, I told them we were the best. I need you to act
like it and get on it. Now."

Ikeda's voice hardened. "We'd need to work through
Treasury, through SWIFT in Belgium, and the banks or
firms that held the cash. They aren't open. It's a holiday.
If the transfers were wired, the reports won't file until
tomorrow morning anyway."

"The President is monitoring the situation, John," she
replied. "I've already got the number of the duty officer

at Treasury. And we've got the Strategic Information and Ops Center behind us."

"Okay, okay," Ikeda sighed. *"I'm on it. I'll start domestic and Hong Kong."*

"I'll call Treasury and see if they went SWIFT."

As she hung up, Cheyenne could hear protests from her partner's family, but felt no remorse. She believed bringing General Anarchy and the Third Position Army to justice would rely on the money. Whatever this trial was supposed to achieve, it was the transfer of the billion dollars and where the money landed that would haunt them.

She dialed the number Kane had given her and got the Treasury duty officer, who promised she'd have SWIFT numbers as soon as he was able to track them. Based in Brussels, SWIFT was a central clearinghouse for wire transfers and payments all over the world. If the Third Position had moved the billion dollars overseas, she'd be able to use the codes to follow. Ikeda was checking a similar clearinghouse in Hong Kong.

Suddenly every computer screen inside the command center showed the Web page with the hyperlink *Click here to enter the Court of Public Opinion.* But when the link was clicked, it did not jump to the MPEG video of General Anarchy announcing the trials of the hostages. Instead, it loaded a Web page done up to look like an old scroll that displayed a menu with two hyperlinks: *Hear the Charges! See the Evidence!* and *The Third Position v. U.S. Senator Worth Stonington.*

When the latter link was clicked, the screen showed

an animated movie stage, curtains closed, footlights on, with the shadows of people moving in the foreground.

"Hurry in," a woman's voice chided. "The trial's about to begin. Find your seats. The Court of Public Opinion wants your voice and vote. Take your seat, if you want the trial to begin on time. Take your seat."

The silhouetted figures sat. The curtains parted to reveal an elevated view of a courtroom of sorts with a raised judge's bench set on top of a stage. Beside the judge's bench, Senator Stonington slumped in a large leather chair, hooded, his wrists and ankles lashed to the stout wooden arms.

The senator was still in his tuxedo, though the bow tie and cummerbund were missing. His pleated shirt hung open and tugged out of his waistband. Stonington rolled his head with each breath and made weak apnea noises through his nose.

Inside the darkened ballroom, off the courtroom set, General Anarchy marched toward Cristoph at his computers. "How many hits?" he asked in a whisper.

Cristoph turned in triumph, hands raised overhead and his glasses slipping down his nose. "Two million and rising, General," he gloated. "We have the audience."

"The servers?"

"Not even a hiccup."

"Excellent. Now we'll make sure everyone else regrets not tuning in."

General Anarchy passed Rose sitting at her jury-rigged control booth.

"Ten seconds," she said.

*   *   *

The Hennessy triplets were watching the webcast on their television set, listening through the earphones. Senator Stonington started to choke and hack. He cleared his throat and spit.

"Uhhhh," Bridger groaned.

"I don't think he knows where he is," Connor said.

"You're a master of the obvious," Bridger said.

"Screw you."

The camera pulled back. Six hooded figures in white camouflage sat in the jury box. The cameras drew back more to reveal book-strewn tables for the prosecution and defense. The prosecutor stood with his back to the camera. He had a blond ponytail and was dressed in white tuxedo tails and gloves. The defender wore a black dress. A black lace shawl wrapped her shoulders and tangled in her long jet-black hair.

A small woman appeared from behind the jury box and stood next to Senator Stonington. Her hair was dyed red and slicked back against her scalp. Her face was painted like a mime's. She wore a waiter's white jacket and black pants and struck the hardwood floor three times with the butt end of a staff she carried.

She cried, "*The People of Earth versus U.S. Senator Worth Stonington.* All rise. The honorable Judge New Truth presiding."

A huge man in a black robe climbed up on the bench. The left side of his head was painted black. The right side was white. His left hand was white. His right was black. His eyebrows were bushy. His cheeks were ponderous and droopy as a Shar-Pei's.

Judge Truth picked up a mallet and pounded it on

the bench. "The Third Position Court of Public Opinion is called to order. Remove his hood, Bailiff Mouse."

Mouse went behind Senator Stonington and stripped off the hood. The gentleman from Alabama blinked, then squinted. His eyes refocused, and then he gaped at the bizarre scene around him.

Judge Truth said, "Mr. Prosecutor?"

Inside the FBI command center, the agents startled at the frontal image of the prosecutor.

"What the hell is this?" Phelps, the hostage rescue leader, grumbled.

Cheyenne wondered the same thing. And so did Hennessy, who'd roused and now watched groggily. The prosecutor's face was Kabuki-white. His eyebrows had been wildly exaggerated and rendered to look like a Japanese anime character. His lips were red, elongated, and twisted upward in a weird, knowing grin.

Senator Stonington stirred in his chair. "Who're you s'posed to be, the Joker?" He laughed and shook his jowly head.

The prosecutor said, "General Anarchy for the prosecution."

In the CIRG command center, Seitz said, "That's the face of Anarchy?"

On screen, Stonington continued to chuckle. "Where's Batman? What is this?"

Judge Truth rapped on his gavel. "This is your trial, Senator."

The Appropriations Committee chairman wriggled himself upright and harrumphed. "Son, I was a trial lawyer twenty-two years. This is no trial and you sure as hell are no judge."

Truth ignored him and said, "Charges?"

General Anarchy picked up a sheet of paper and read from it. "The charges are willfully defrauding the people, engaging in racketeering, using his elected office to enrich himself, accepting bribes, selling his vote, failure to file statements with the Federal Election Commission. And twenty-two other counts of porking the government and whoring himself to corporate interests."

The senator struggled against his lashes, fury rising in his face. "What in the name of sweet Jesus is this? Under what goddamned statutes?"

General Anarchy walked toward the senator. "We are not beholden to statutes or precedent or protocol here, Senator. We'll show the evidence and let the people decide."

Senator Stonington got perplexed, and even more so when he saw General Anarchy gesturing at a digital camera mounted on a tripod off to one side of the courtroom. "We on television or something?" he asked, suspicious.

"The Internet," Judge Truth said. "A real-time webcast."

Stonington turned wary. "You mean anyone in the world can watch this?"

"More than two million at last count. And every one of them's a potential juror."

New Year's night, indeed any holiday evening, is a guaranteed news vacuum. The government's shut down.

People are recovering from parties. The President's away. And other than the weather and the latest savagery from the Middle East, news directors are left with a gaping void they have to fill.

CNN filled its void five minutes into the Worth Stonington trial by focusing exclusively on it, going so far as to rebroadcast the footage streaming on the Third Position Web site. Fox and MSNBC soon followed. Word of the trial began to spread in earnest. Links began going up to the Third Position's URL.

Nine minutes into the webcast, the ABC announcers at the Tostitos Fiesta Bowl mentioned the crisis, and cut away for a report on the trial at halftime. NBC and CBS broke into their coverage with two-minute reports as well.

As a result, thirteen minutes into the webcast, the audience watching Senator Worth Stonington's prosecution on their computers and televisions quadrapled. It was an instant media phenomenon.

Hearing Cristophe relay that news over his earbud, General Anarchy smiled. He cocked his mocking features at the Alabama Democrat and said, "Senator, I'm hearing that our audience has gone global and now numbers almost eight million."

"Eight million?" the senator said, bewildered.

General Anarchy went to the camera closest to the jury box and spoke to it. "For those of you just tuning in, welcome, and don't worry: You haven't missed much. We're just getting to the nitty-gritty of the dirty dish. Then you'll get to vote. You personally will have a say in deciding Senator Stonington's fate."

"I have committed no crimes!" Stonington shouted at every camera he could find in the glaring light. "This is a goddamned kangaroo court!"

Judge Truth whacked his gavel. "One more outburst, I'll have you gagged."

For the next ten minutes, using a variety of multimedia effects, General Anarchy laid out the evidence against the senator in broad-brush strokes, including the secret bank account in Basel, Switzerland, and the method that filled it with tens of millions of dollars.

"Did you preside over the drafting of Senate Bill 462, the transportation spending bill last year?" General Anarchy asked.

"Sure did," Senator Stonington allowed. "But what's that got to do with the price a shrimp in Mobile?"

The prosecutor stormed across the room and stood in front of the legislator. "We're not after the price of shrimp," he said. "We're after the price of Allied Precision. An Alabama company, I'm told."

At the mention of the name, Stonington twisted against his bonds. "Allied Precision are mighty fine people. Great patriots."

"Great corruptors is more like it," Anarchy said, then went on to show how the senator used so-called "riders," hush-hush, last-minute attachments to the transportation bill, to get funding for Allied Precision projects. He laid out the evidence in a stylish multimedia show that featured video clips of Allied Precision's headquarters, the lavish homes and boats of its executives, the dubious projects that the riders paid for, and the coup de grâce: the documents surrounding the secret Swiss bank account.

When the camera cut back to Worthington strapped to the witness chair, the senator looked caged. He watched General Anarchy as if he wielded a whip.

"How much was in the account before we took it from you?" Anarchy asked. "How much were you willing to let your wife die for?"

The senator fidgeted in his seat, the fingers of his bound hands playing the instrument of his mind like a piano solo dwindling into a heartbreak ending. His chest heaved. He stared at his dancing fingers as if they were things apart from himself.

"Twenty-seven million euros," Stonington mumbled and then blubbered at the cameras, "I've shamed myself. I've shamed my office and drunk too damn much. I know it. I'm seeking the Lord's forgiveness. Jesus is the only one can forgive me now!"

General Anarchy stepped back, hand on his hip, then walked away from the witness, asking archly, "How many times have we heard that lately, fellow citizens? *I have shamed my office. Lord forgive me. Please, Jesus, forgive my wicked ways.*"

He stopped in front of the jury and snarled, "Let's keep God out of it, shall we? Let's focus on the moola. Twenty-seven million euros taken from the people to pad the senator's wallet. And more than six hundred million dollars for Allied Precision's pork projects."

The camera angle shifted to show the courtroom from above. General Anarchy pivoted to face the judge. "The Third Position rests."

Now Judge Truth filled the screen. He struck his

gavel and said, "Citizen's Defender Emilia, present your case."

The camera switched to the woman in the black dress, gloves, and shawl. She rose from her chair and lifted her head to reveal dark sunglasses perched on a face painted the opposite of General Anarchy's: black with garish ruby lips that suggested sorrow.

"I would gladly, Your Honor," she said in a slight Hispanic accent. "But there is no defense for a man who enriches himself through public office, offers the government for sale, and raids the people's coffers."

She sat down. Worthington looked at her incredulously, then started to protest. But Truth struck his gavel and then shook it at the camera.

"All you jurors out there in Internet land go to www.thirdpositionjustice.net and vote. There's no fee for voting online, but you must do so during our fifteen-minute deliberation period. Senator Stonington, servant of the people or screwer of the people? Check the evidence on the site, then you tell us. We'll be awaiting your verdict in fifteen minutes, starting now."

In the background, the senator was shouting, "That was no defense! This is America, I'm entitled to a defense!"

The screen cut to a Web page that said, *Court in recess until 10 p.m. eastern.* Below was a hyperlink that read, *Your Jury Vote Counts!*

The FBI agents all clicked it and saw their screens jump to a simple ballot that read, *U.S. Senator Worth Stonington. How say you? Guilty? Or Not Guilty?*

CHAPTER TWENTY

Hailey Hennessy watched Connor check *Guilty* and hit ENTER. She nodded. He was guilty. The screen jumped to a clip of Porky Pig, laughing and saying, "The, the, the, that's all, folks!" before turning to a Third Position presentation on the general corruption of the U.S. Congress.

She yawned, but watched until it ended with a plea for citizens to join the Third Position movement and to register online at the Web site. Connor instead typed on the keyboard and returned to the Web page that said *Enter the Court of Public Opinion*. He clicked it. The screen flickered to the courtroom, empty now except for Senator Stonington in the witness stand, his forehead resting in his hands.

The jurors filed back in. Judge Truth climbed up on the bench. General Anarchy and Citizen's Defender Emilia appeared at their tables. Bailiff Mouse shouted,

"The Third Position Court of Public Opinion is again in session!"

Judge Truth rapped his gavel. "Thank you, Bailiff Mouse. Mr. Foreman, has the Court of Public Opinion reached a verdict?"

The hooded and camouflaged figure closest to Senator Stonington rose and extended a piece of paper to the bailiff, saying, "It has, Your Honor. We and the eight and a half million other independent jury members who voted online in the last fifteen minutes at www.thirdpositionjustice.net find the defendant, U.S. Senator Worth Stonington, Democrat of Alabama, guilty."

Truth smashed his gavel, then intoned, "So be it."

"This is a mockery!" Senator Stonington shouted.

"Yes, it is," General Anarchy shouted back at him. "A mockery of justice for a man who made a mockery of his public office."

Judge Truth said, "Senator Worth Stonington, you are hereby sentenced to public humiliation and prison."

On the television screen, General Anarchy's face appeared in close-up. He said, "Stick around for Senator Stonington's punishment. But first, a word from our sponsor."

His image vanished, replaced by more anti-globalist propaganda, this time arrayed against the forces of corporate agriculture and its pernicious effect on the environment.

Connor shifted and sat up. "Did you know any of this stuff?"

"Nah," Bridger said. "Makes me not feel like eating a cheeseburger, though."

"Think it's for real?" Hailey asked, feeling confused. "That we're all controlled by corporations and people like Senator Stonington and Mr. Burns?"

"Yeah," Bridger said.

Connor reacted angrily. "Dad always says our country's about freedom."

"Dad doesn't know everything," Bridger said.

"He used to guard the Secretary of State," Hailey said.

"So?"

"So he'd know if we were controlled, don't you think?" Connor said.

Before Bridger could reply, the screen jumped to a snowy setting outdoors at night. Snow and stone and log pillars were visible.

"That's outside the front door to the lodge," Hailey said.

On-screen, the camera swung around to show the massive carved front double door of the Jefferson Club's main lodge and the six hooded jurors marching out with Senator Stonington between them, pleading for his dignity.

"You can't do this," the legislator choked. "It's not right."

The Hennessy kids immediately broke into gales of laughter.

The FBI command center erupted in gasps and laughter until Willis Kane growled, "It's not funny. He's still a U.S. senator. He deserves our respect."

The senator had been stripped of his clothes down to his boxer shorts, T-shirt, shoes, and socks. He wore a plastic pig's nose and ears. A sign was pinned to his T-shirt:

PIGGY AT THE PUBLIC TROUGH: GUILTY AS CHARGED!

Mickey Hennessy shook his head and bit his inner lip, wanting to chortle, but remembering the men who'd shot him and Chef Giulio and the others in cold blood.

General Anarchy appeared on the steps behind Stonington. "Senator, do you understand the terms of your punishment?"

Wild-eyed, Stonington nodded as if he didn't want to understand, but did.

"Let justice be done, then," Judge Truth cried. "Let him be made a mockery. Drive his fat ass to the gate!"

The senator looked around for a car to take him. But there were only two snowmobiles and two hooded Third Position Soldiers driving them. They revved their motors. Worthington shivered, but looked at them in resignation.

Then the jurors came up with slender wooden dowels about eighteen inches long. Bailiff Mouse had one too and she lashed Senator Stonington across the butt cheeks.

"You're not riding, you corrupt son-of-a-bitch!" she screeched. "You're gonna run all the way to that gate like your poor wife did leaving you."

The senator squealed in pain and stumbled out from under the entry canopy while the jurors took turns swatting at his bouncing backside, all of it lit by the headlights of the snowmobiles. A cameraman followed jerkily behind the senator, who bawled, "I have a heart condition. I can't run five miles. I can't!"

Anarchy's face suddenly dominated the screens inside the FBI command center. He leered and said, "If you enjoyed tonight's episode, please join us at seven-thirty a.m. mountain time tomorrow for the second trial. You won't want to miss it. I guarantee it's absolutely scandalous stuff!"

The screen returned to Stonington bawling, gasping, and waddling down the road.

Willis Kane said, "Get another ambulance up here. I think he's gonna need it."

General Anarchy climbed the stone steps to the lodge's front doors. Truth trailed him, pulling off his fake eyebrows.

"Few ad libs here and there, but not bad for a live broadcast," Truth said.

"We'll know soon enough," General Anarchy said, pulling open the doors. He walked through the lobby, clapping men on the back and shaking hands with others, handing out a "job well done" where it was warranted.

By the time they reached the lodge ballroom, the lights around the mock courtroom were off. General Anarchy went straight to Cristoph, who was on his feet doing a little dance step. "I just hacked into the Nielsen's," Cristoph said, shaking both fists over his head. "It climbed all night. Twenty-two million share!"

"We've got ourselves a real audience now for tomorrow's early matinee," General Anarchy said, pleased. "Keep a close eye on the firewall. They may try to cut off our webcast."

"Let them try," Cristoph boasted. "This system's like a bomb shelter."

General Anarchy went to Rose, who was leaning back in her chair, dragging on a Marlboro, satisfaction plastered across her face.

"Live broadcast, and I slayed 'em," she said in her gravelly voice. "That's why cable ran with it, General. They could see the dramatic eye at work in the shots."

"They could," General Anarchy agreed. "I apologize for my earlier comments."

Rose said, "I was so angry at you I put it into my work and it worked."

"Funny how that happens," General Anarchy said. "Get some food and sleep."

"Who's going on trial in the morning, General?"

"That's the mystery, isn't it?"

Lying in the family room of his father's apartment, Connor was still laughing at the image of Senator Stonington when something dawned on him. He jumped up, grabbed his father's binoculars from the bookcase, and yanked open the sliding glass door that led to the balcony. He stepped out into fourteen inches of snow and used the binoculars to peer through the trees and then he started laughing softly again. The senator was running the two-hour mile in the snowmobile headlights.

He handed the glasses to Hailey, who said, "That's awful. He'll never make it."

As if he'd heard Hailey, Stonington slipped and sprawled on the snowy driveway. The jurors kicked at him, but he didn't move. Finally, they lifted the senator onto one snowmobile, which took off. The second followed.

Bridger said, "They sure want him to make it to the gate."

"So everyone will see him," Hailey said.

Connor went back inside the apartment, teeth chattering.

Hailey and Bridger followed. Bridger said, "When are we looking for Dad?"

"Like an hour?" Connor said. "I figure we want most of them sleeping."

"I guess," Hailey said anxiously. "Where should we start?"

"Right here," said a man's deep growling voice from beyond the front door. *"I've got you, you little fucks, gone home to papa's place."*

The kids heard an electronic clank and saw the door handle begin to twist. Connor dove behind the .22 still lying on the table. He rammed his shoulder to the butt and peered through the iron peep sight. Bridger panicked, grabbed his paintball gun and retreated into the hallway to the bedrooms. Hailey panicked, grabbed her paintball gun, and retreated toward the living room, flipping off the lights.

The door swung open. For a moment, Connor had Cobb square in his sights about twenty-five feet away, silhouetted in the doorway. He wasn't wearing his hood.

"Come out, come out, wherever you are," Cobb called. He couldn't see Connor yet, crouched behind the kitchen table, looking over his sights, shaking.

Cobb came down the short entryway to the kitchen. He had his headset hanging down around his neck. His free hand groped the wall. Connor thumbed the rifle's safety off. Cobb heard it just as his fingers found the light switch. He flipped the switch even as he was throwing himself to the side and onto the floor.

Connor was blinded for a second. When he could see, Cobb was already on his feet, machine gun shouldered. Connor pointed his rifle at Cobb's balls.

"Put the gun down or I'll blow your head off, little man," Cobb said, slowing.

"You put your gun down or I'll shoot your dick off," Connor said in a quavering voice. He felt sweat gush on his forehead.

Cobb noticed. "You always sweat before you try to kill a man," he said. "Even if it's only a split-second decision. Life or death, you always sweat. Ready to try to kill me?"

"Where's my dad? His name's Hennessy. Mickey Hennessy."

"Haven't seen him," Cobb said, easing forward and swinging the muzzle of his machine gun toward Connor. "This here's full auto. I touch this trigger, it'll turn your head into such mush your mommy will wish you'd been decapitated."

Tremors seized Connor. He could no longer see his own sights, just the black hole of the muzzle. He tried to pull the trigger.

Cobb was quicker. He flicked his hand under the barrel of the .22 and pushed it aside. The rifle went off, a sharp clap in the confined space. The bullet shattered the oven door. Cobb ripped the gun from Connor's hands. "That's better," he said softly.

There was such unexpected reasonableness in his tone, such deep assurance in his eyes that for a moment Connor relaxed, thinking that Cobb would just let them go.

Cobb set the .22 on the kitchen counter, then turned back to Connor, smiling. "You honestly think you try to kill a man and he ain't gonna teach you a lesson?"

Before Connor could even think to reply, Cobb kicked him in the stomach with his steel-toed boot. The fourteen-year-old bucked up, choking at the incomprehensible pain and the speed with which all the air had left him. He could feel his spine from the inside before he crashed to the floor, gasping and moaning.

Cobb kicked Connor again, this time high in the left butt cheek, hitting some kind of nerve back there. The boy twisted in agony and one hand sought his hip.

"You try to kill a man, he definitely teaches you a lesson," Cobb growled. He touched the muzzle of his gun against Connor's temple. "Ever been shot, boy?"

Connor struggled for air and whimpered with fear.

"First thing happens," Cobb said, "right after you take the hit, it's like it didn't happen, you got so much adrenaline pumping. Then your blood pressure drops as you start to bleed out. Makes you feel like you're going down the drain. You ask yourself if you're going to die. That what you're asking yourself right now, boy? Am I gonna die?"

"Hey, shit-for-brains!" Bridger called from the hall-way.

Cobb twisted around. Bridger was less than ten feet from him, aiming down the barrel of his paintball gun.

CHAPTER TWENTY-ONE

Doing everything in his power to both stay awake and ignore the god-awful throbbing in his upper arm, Mickey Hennessy trudged through the snow and the icy air after Cheyenne O'Neil, both of them following Willis Kane and his men toward Sheriff Lacey's bonfire out on the sage flats before the Jefferson Club's main gate.

Up on the hill beyond the gate, the headlights of the snowcat were dying. But Hennessy could already see the crisscrossing headlights of the snowmobiles cresting the knoll. The snowmobiles stopped next to the snowcat in front of the Third Position's Web site banner. Senator Stonington climbed off, shaking with cold.

One of the snowmobilers seemed to talk to him. Stonington nodded, and then started down the hill, adjusting the pig snout on his nose. The senator's feet went out from under him almost immediately. He slammed onto his side and began to tumble and roll down the icy hill. He came to rest right under the arch of the gate and lay unmoving.

"Get up there and get him!" Kane shouted at his men.

Two pairs of hostage rescuers ran the ditches on opposite sides of the road, staying to the shadows. Hennessy lost them, and then picked them up again when they reached the walls of the lit gatehouse. One hostage rescuer from each side darted into the archway and grabbed Stonington. They got him in the firefighter's carry and dragged him away from the gatehouse lights while their partners covered the retreat.

They reached Kane. He threw two wool blankets and a space blanket around the senator, whose eyelids and hair were glazed white. Stonington was frostbit on the cheeks and chest. His jaw shook like a rattle.

"Where's the press?" Stonington said, looking over his shoulder into the darkness.

"An ambulance is coming, Senator," Kane said. "I'm the FBI agent in charge. When you're better I'd like to ask you some questions."

Stonington said shakily, "Where's the press. The—the cameras?"

"Senator?" Cheyenne said, stepping in front of Stonington. "Let me take those things off you." She reached for the pig nose.

The senator twisted violently from her and shouted, "No! I can't take them off until I show myself to the cameras. If you don't let me, I'm a dead man. They have snipers waiting to blow my head off if I try to leave before speaking to the media."

Hennessy felt chills on his neck as if someone were

aiming at him. The feeling climbed into his head, making him dizzy and ready to pass out. But he kept his feet and managed to walk behind Kane and his men as they helped the senator toward the barrier the state police had erected to keep back the cameramen and reporters. As they approached, the klieg lights came on, blazing beacons against the bitter Montana night.

"Senator Stonington! Senator Stonington!" a reporter cried. Then the whole pack of them began to bray and honk. *"Are you guilty? Eight-point-five million say you are. Will you resign your office? Senator Stonington! Senator Stonington!"*

They trained their cameras on him and fed the monster story its first sacrifice, beaming the images of the chairman of the U.S. Senate Appropriations Committee wrapped in blankets with piggy nose and ears. He stopped before them and shrugged off his blankets, revealing the sign hanging around his neck.

"Quiet!" the senator called out. "It's important y'all hear what I got to say."

He seemed to summon his last strength and recited, "I, Senator Worth Stonington of the great state of Alabama, am guilty of piggery at the public trough and do hereby resign my office in disgrace. Throw me in a sty. Feed me slops. It's what I deserve."

With that, he raised his chin, pivoted, and walked back toward Kane and his men, tearing the pig nose off his face and throwing it in the snow. The reporters' voices swelled like a tsunami after him: *"Senator Stonington! Senator Stonington!"*

Ten feet from the FBI agents, Stonington halted, appearing suddenly bewildered. He gasped, hunched up, and then listed to port like a ship taking on water. Then he changed tack and his weight surged starboard, throwing his body into irons for a split second before capsizing into the snow, keel up and unconscious before tens of millions of viewers watching the scene live worldwide.

Bridger took another step from the hallway to his father's bedroom, seeing over the sights that Cobb's initial concern had lapsed into amusement. Bridger felt an overwhelming urge to cry and run, but didn't, even when the Third Position soldier started to swing his machine gun toward him, saying, "Who you gonna hurt with that, *shit-for-brains*?"

Bridger mashed the trigger, aiming for Cobb's eyes.

Twenty feet away, crouched in the shadows of the living room, Hailey acted more out of instinct to protect her brothers than anything else. She yanked the trigger of her gun on burst mode, aiming for Cobb's temple at the same time Bridger shot.

Their guns made chug-popping sounds. Paintballs exploded against Cobb's eyes and in his ear, painting him a fluorescent green.

"Ahh!" Cobb yelled, dropping his own gun, staggering, and digging at his eyes.

He crashed against the kitchen counter and for a moment looked like he'd go down. Then he came up, left eye open, looking wildly for his weapon, which had clattered across the room into the entry hall. Cobb spotted it and made to go for it.

Connor's left foot lashed out, striking the Third

Position soldier across the shin. Cobb let loose a shout of blind rage and began to flail. He ran into the refrigerator, held to it long enough to regain his balance, before heaving himself again toward the front hallway and his gun.

Two feet from it, Cobb grinned maniacally, only to spot Bridger, who had circled him in the initial fray and was now standing between the Third Position soldier and the front door to the apartment. Bridger was aiming at him from less than five feet away.

"Step back, sit on the ground," Bridger ordered. "Hands up on your head."

The Third Position soldier hesitated before breaking into another grin. "Go ahead. I've taken worse and lived."

Bridger did not feel any urge to run or back down. He got angry, very angry, and opened up at point-blank range, hitting Cobb perfectly on the point of his nose and in his open laughing mouth with six direct shots. Blood spewed from Cobb's nose. He reached for it as he staggered backward into the kitchen, choking and spewing the paint. Bridger felt insane with anger and followed him, shooting the Third Position soldier in the Adam's apple.

Hailey had moved in to cover Connor, who still lay on the kitchen floor. As Cobb reeled backward toward her, she aimed for the base of his head where it met his neck. She squeezed her finger, sending a burst that exploded exactly where she wanted.

Cobb shuddered and then lurched sideways, still gagging on the paint. He smashed off the table, his hand groping the air for any purchase.

Bridger and Hailey kept firing. Cobb slipped off his

feet. The side of his head struck the edge of kitchen counter with a dull crack. He crumpled on the floor, knocked cold, blood and fluorescent green paint pooling on the tile beside him.

Five miles away, a Jefferson County ambulance backed up through the barricades. Two emergency medical technicians brought out a gurney, only to realize it wasn't big enough. They threw it aside and six hostage rescuers and the EMTs struggled to get the senator inside on the floor of the ambulance.

"O'Neil," Kane said. "Follow the senator to the hospital."

Cheyenne took a deep breath, wanting to protest, to stay and continue to work the money trail, but then replied, "Straightaway, SAC. I'll report when I know something."

The EMTs started packing Stonington in blankets and getting an IV in his arm. Kane's men jumped out and slammed the door.

Cheyenne looked at Hennessy, feeling oddly sad. "I gotta go."

"'Course you do," Hennessy said. "Thanks for everything."

"Take care of yourself."

"You too, Cheyenne."

"You could use some sleep."

"I could use my kids in my arms."

"You'll get that," she said, then thumped her chest above her heart. "I feel it here. Oh, your medicine." She pulled the vial out.

Hennessy blinked, then rubbed his arm. "A half a dose. You keep the rest."

She frowned. "What if I don't come back?"

"I don't know," he said.

The ambulance's engine fired up. Cheyenne hesitated, wanting to hug him, but instead putting her hand on his arm. "Take care of yourself, Mickey," she said.

He smiled at her as if seeing her anew. "You too, Cheyenne."

She wanted to linger, but then turned and started to run for her rental car. She got behind the ambulance as it pulled away. She drove right past Hennessy, who was watching her with a dazed expression. She wanted to stop again, to make sure he'd be all right, but forced herself to wave and go by.

Cheyenne felt like she had lived five lifetimes in the nearly twenty-four hours since leaving her apartment in Manhattan. It made her punchy. She yawned, then shook her head and opened the window a crack, letting in just enough cold air to keep her awake.

They pulled out onto the access road and were soon doing sixty-five through the dense forest, their headlights turning the snow-covered road into a white glare lipsticked with the flashing of the ambulance's red lights. She kept her eyes focused square on the rear doors of the ambulance, but her thoughts were not of the senator, but of Hennessy.

He obviously had suffered hard times and made serious errors of judgment, but he was essentially a good man. She could feel it about him, the way he talked about the importance of his sobriety, in the raw way he pined for his sons and daughter, in the way he handled Willis Kane. It was also there in the fact that Hennessy was still on his feet. Since they'd left the hospital in Bozeman he'd slept barely an hour. As far as she was concerned, Hennessy was an absolute machine and a good, good man.

Inside the FBI command center, Hennessy watched from the conference area while Willis Kane stood at attention in front of the camera on the rear wall, watching the telegenic face of Edward Jackson, President of the United States, on the computer screen beside it. They'd been patched through to the White House situation room within five minutes of Senator Stonington's heart attack and the CIRG leader had been on the hot seat ever since.

"Is this how they're going to treat all of the hostages?" President Jackson demanded. He was a craggy-looking man, in a white dress shirt under a blue sweater. "Expose them, humiliate them?"

"We can only hope, Mr. President," Kane said.

"What are they after?"

"Money, certainly," Kane replied. "A billion dollars."

"Then why stay and put on these trials?"

Hennessy knew he should stay out of the conversation, but he blurted from the conference area, "They're trying to sell their politics, Mr. President."

On the computer screen, President Jackson's eyebrow arched. "Who said that?"

Kane grimaced and looked over his shoulder. "Michael Hennessy, Mr. President. The security director at the Jefferson Club. His kids are the ones still inside."

"I want to hear what he has to say."

The CIRG leader reluctantly stood aside while Hennessy walked up and took his place, feeling oddly calm. "Mr. President, the whole thing looks like a marketing campaign to me. Look at their Web site. Listen to what they're saying. I think they're trying to turn people to their anti-globalist position using these trials to show the world the corruption in the system."

It irritated the President, but he nodded. "I think you're right, Mr. Hennessy. I think we need to be putting out a message portraying them as the killers they really are. Put Kane back on."

"Thank you, Mr. President," Hennessy said, then stepped away, feeling flushed and dizzy after talking with the most powerful man on earth.

"Mr. President?" Kane said, moving back before the camera.

"How close are you to launching a rescue attempt?"

Kane's features hardened. "With all due respect, sir. I don't know where the hostages are being held. Anarchy has warned us that they are all booby-trapped. I'd hate to go in there, get into a firefight with forty or fifty men, and lose the rest of the hostages because we acted too fast. And I haven't been able to debrief Senator Stonington. The doctors say he's unconscious, and will be through the night. I've got men on rotation at his bedside, waiting for him to revive."

President Jackson sat back in his chair. "What do you recommend?"

"Let us get up to fully manned and review all our options and the intel that's still coming in from the freed hostages," Kane said.

The President said nothing for several moments, then pushed his jaw forward. "Okay, Agent Kane. We'll do it your way overnight. But in the meantime, prepare for a rescue attempt. I want a plan for a counterassault on my desk in the morning before this second trial."

"Yes, Mr. President," Kane said, and the screens went black.

Kane turned to Phelps. "You heard the man. I want scenarios in place and ready to ship to the White House by five a.m."

"First team's here and settling in," the hostage rescue leader replied. "We'll work in shifts. But I gotta tell you, Deployment Logistics has got to be on it. We're going to need a lot of equipment here to do this right."

"Such as?" Kane asked.

"Snowmobiles, skis," Phelps said. "Helicopter, maybe. Definitely our own snow camouflage."

"You give me a tight plan, I'll get what you need," the CIRG commander promised.

Kirk Seitz, the negotiator, rubbed his bald head, before screwing up his face and saying, "We can't just focus on a counterassault, SAC. We need to draw them out, get inside their heads before we think about a battle, find out what they want."

"In case you hadn't noticed, they're not talking to

us," Phelps retorted. "They're talking at us. And I already know what I need to know about them—they're killers, kidnappers, and terrorists. And they want money and attention."

"We'll pursue both courses as they are offered to us," Kane said, ending the discussion. "Kirk, get in touch with Strategic Information and OPS and start building a profile of these guys."

Seitz bristled, but nodded and went to a computer station next to Pritoni. Phelps put on his coat and plunged out into the night. Kane crossed over to Hennessy, who was sitting down at the conference table, staring at the pain pill Cheyenne had left him.

Kane noticed the pill. His cheeks went taut. "What's that?"

Hennessy looked up at his old friend. "It's a dose of Co-Tylenol Number Four they gave me at the hospital. O'Neil took the rest with her. You don't know how much I want to flush it down the toilet, but my arm feels like someone's drilled through it and something that should be attached isn't any longer. Like it's got a dream of its own. Or a nightmare." Hennessy's eyes had gone watery. "Do you understand, Willis?"

Kane stood frozen, unable to reply at first. Then he said softly, "I always remember bouncing Hailey on my knee, playing horsey with the boys, and when you tickled them, how each of them tried to laugh harder than the other."

Hennessy grinned. A tear slipped down his cheek. "You should see them now. They're people with wills and their own ideas and yet they're half-brained. The whole judgment thing goes right by them. Especially the boys, who are big enough to do damage. Hailey's smarter than her brothers. She'll instigate them into something, then stand aside cynically observing. And then suddenly she's the voice of reason."

He shook his head. "I felt like I made a real connection with the boys this trip. But Hailey . . . I never felt like I closed the gap with her and . . ." He looked at the pill. "I feel so fucking helpless knowing she's still in there. I'm one step from tracking down O'Neil, finding my drugs, and buying a bottle."

Kane put a hand on Hennessy's shoulder. "Go to sleep, Mick. You're more good to your daughter and sons rested and sober than exhausted and smashed. Use one of the bunks in the tents next door. And take the pill so you can sleep."

Hennessy nodded. He got his jacket and went out into the pitch-dark night. No stars shone. The cold came after his exposed head and he hustled toward the closest outfitter's tent. A woodstove burned inside, and it was almost as warm as the command center. A gas lantern sent a soft glow that revealed ten sets of bunks, most of them already filled. He spotted an available lower bunk with a heavy sleeping bag. He wriggled himself into it and after a moment's hesitation gulped down the pain pill.

The man in the bunk overhead snored, choked, and then rolled over, shaking the bunk. Hennessy stared into the darkness, seeing fleeting images of the triplets as toddlers running around in their diapers, as happy and rough-and-tumble as three puppies. Then the three on snowboards yesterday, shooting each other with paintballs, lying in the snow, laughing so hard they could barely speak.

Hennessy closed his eyes and began to pray. *Bless them and keep them safe, Lord. Let them come out that gate and let me hold them again. Please, I don't think I can bear this new life you've given me without them. Give me the strength to get through this. Give me hope.*

He imagined himself holding his children, his arms wrapped tightly around their necks, and pulling them to him. He felt a warm, sure, familiar feeling start to crawl up his spine, the first hints of it at the back of his skull. The painkiller was kicking in. He closed his eyes and felt the sweet embrace of an old lover.

Then, for no particular reason, he remembered how Cheyenne had thumped her fist against her chest, telling him that in her heart she felt the kids would be all right. She was a little quirky, a lot brash, intensely smart, and she had a lot of style and guts. Beautiful too, he thought, then put those thoughts away. *I'm sixteen years older than her. That's a generation. I could be her father.*

But he kept that image of Cheyenne thumping her chest alive in his mind's eye. It comforted him as he plunged into narcotic sleep.

CHAPTER TWENTY-TWO

"Kid, he's moving," Bridger cried softly. "Tape them good."

Cobb's wrists were already bound together and his arms strapped to his chest with duct tape. Connor was wrapping the Third Position soldier's ankles. He was gritting his teeth and still hunched over. His stomach was killing him.

Hailey sat on the kitchen chair, watching her brothers, trembling. It was as if she'd gone through a door in a wall she didn't even know was there, and everything was slow motion and thoughtless on the other side. Either you did it or you died. Her mouth hung open at the metallic taste on her tongue, and she kept blinking, thinking they all might have died.

Cobb rolled his head. Most of his face and the left side of his skull were encased in a drying mask of fluorescent green paint. He muttered something unintelligible. He made chopping noises, opening and shutting his mouth. Then he started to spit out paint. He whispered hoarsely, "Water."

Bridger looked at Connor, who said, "No."

"We've got to," Hailey said, going to the sink, still feeling outside herself, watching the water fill a glass, something familiar that helped steady her.

Hailey knelt beside Cobb and held the glass of water to his lips. She dribbled the water on them. Cobb opened his mouth to it and drank until he coughed and sputtered. When Hailey tried to withdraw, Cobb whispered, "More."

Hailey leaned back over him. Inside the paint smear that masked his upper head, Cobb's eyelids strained, then tore open slits in the drying paint. His eyes rolled around, blinking, trying to get a clear vision. They found Hailey.

Cobb's shoulders jerked at the duct tape that wrapped his arms. His thighs strained at the tape that bound his ankles. He heaved himself at Hailey, trying to head-butt her. She rolled backward just in time. Cobb went berserk, squirming, wrenching himself side to side, finding his voice, straining against every word, "You little fucks, I'll eat your brains! It'll make the shit I pulled in Kosovo look tame!"

"Shut him up!" Hailey said.

"How?" Bridger said.

"Tape him!"

Cobb arched his head toward the apartment's front door. "Hey!" he shouted. "Hey, I'm fucking in here!"

Bridger tore six inches of duct tape and moved gingerly toward Cobb, who saw the reluctance in the boy's eyes. "Let her do it," Cobb said, jutting his chin toward Hailey, glaring with this insane look. "C'mon, little girl, I'll bite your fingers off and eat 'em. Then I'll bite your little tits off too."

Connor's face twisted with rage and he said, "Don't talk to my sister like that, asshole." Then he kicked Cobb as hard as he could in the stomach. Cobb doubled up, gasping for air. Connor put his shoe on the Third Position soldier's head and pinned him to the ground. Bridger slammed the strip across Cobb's mouth. And then another. And then a third before Connor removed his foot. Cobb sucked in wind through his nose, glaring at them, making furious whinnying noises.

He looked around and then mule-kicked a cabinet. The first blow cracked it. The second blew the door completely in and Cobb's bare feet punched into the cleaning supplies, sending them crashing around him. This time Connor kicked him in the head and knocked Cobb out again. He leaned back to kick a third time, when Hailey stopped him. "Don't," she said. "Take him back into Dad's room. It's the farthest from the hall."

They dragged the Third Position soldier by his feet out of the kitchen and into the hallway. He came to and started fighting again. But they managed to keep their grip. By the time they got him to the bedroom, they were soaked with sweat. They dropped him by the bed and Cobb went wild, thumping his heels on the floor.

"He's gonna kick until someone hears him," Connor said.

"So make it so he can't kick," Bridger said. He

started pulling the mattress off his father's queen-sized bed.

Hailey figured out what he was up to and helped. They put the mattress on top of Cobb and sat on his lump. Cobb finally quieted.

"We could pile the dressers on top of him," Connor said.

"That'll help," Bridger agreed. "But I was thinking we get the razor blades from Dad's utility knife and tape them inward between the toes of his feet so if he tries to kick again he cuts himself, like way badly. He won't do that too many times, now, will he?"

Hailey gave her sibling a look of repulsion. "You're disturbed, Bridge."

"What?" Bridger said.

"She's right," Connor said, grinning. "Disturbed but brilliant."

"Oh," Bridger said, smiling.

"I didn't say brilliant," Hailey said.

But she and Connor continued to sit on Cobb while waiting for Bridger to retrieve the utility knife and the box of replacement blades from the hall closet.

"I don't know about this," Hailey said. "It's like Abu Ghraib or something."

Connor looked at her blankly. "It just makes it so he doesn't want to move."

Hailey still didn't like it, but she helped when Bridger returned and they all shifted the mattress so Cobb's toes were sticking out. Connor and Hailey sat directly above the Third Position soldier's shins, pinning his heels to the floor.

Bridger ripped strips of duct tape and fitted them between Cobb's toes. Then he lowered a utility blade, cutting edge facing inward between the middle toes of each foot, and taped them in place. He positioned the last two blades on Cobb's heels and taped them in place too. When he was done, they lifted the mattress so they could see Cobb's head and shoulders.

"You got razor blades on your feet," Bridger told him. "You kick, you get cut."

Cobb's eyes flared in rage again and he began to growl at them, but he didn't kick. They dropped the mattress, and then moved the box spring on top of it. They piled their father's oak dresser and two end tables on the box spring.

Hailey said, "We gotta get out of here. Someone sent that lunatic after us."

"Where do you suggest we go?" Bridger demanded.

"Dad's office," Connor said. "He could be there."

"What if they're using the security cameras? They'll see us."

"Only between here and the utility staircase," Connor said. "No cameras in there, Dad said. Remember? We get to the utility staircase, we can move."

"What if there's someone watching the utility staircase?"

Connor went over and picked up the semiautomatic pistol they'd taken from Cobb's holster. He tossed it to Bridger, then picked up Cobb's machine gun. "We'll cross that bridge when we come to it."

Hailey felt instantly overwhelmed. "Now you're both acting disturbed."

Connor's face went stony. "I'm sorry, sis, but I'm not letting anybody kick me like that again. Ever."

Three floors below Mickey Hennessy's apartment, Radio's head bobbed with fatigue, and then drooped and rested on his chest. He'd been up close to thirty hours and couldn't keep his eyes open any longer.

Had he been watching the screen showing the fifth-floor south hallway, he would have seen Bridger Hennessy in his snowboarding pants, boots, and jacket exit his father's apartment, look both ways, and then run toward the east hallway carrying the pistol in one hand and his paintball gun in his other. Connor moved painfully after him similarly dressed, holding Cobb's machine gun. Hailey brought up the rear, the .22 held reluctantly in her hands.

The three sprinted around the corner and appeared on the security system's east hallway monitor. Bridger yanked open a gray steel door with an exit sign posted overhead. He waited while his brother and sister dashed inside, then slipped in after them and closed the door.

Connor and Hailey leaned over the railing on the cement landing, their backs to the laundry and trash chutes, listening. No noise. Bridger started to ease down the staircase. His skateboard shoes made squeaking noises on the metal risers.

"Take off your shoes," Hailey hissed. "Tie them together around your neck."

"Who made you queen?" Bridger said, his face rocky.

"You got a better way to stay quiet?"

Connor set his guns down and kicked off his sneakers. Bridger's nose curled. His brother's sneakers stank. Really stank. He stopped breathing through his nose, tied his own shoes together by their laces, and strung them around his neck. Connor did the same, and soon they had crept down the stairs to the fourth-floor landing without incident. Bridger opened the door to the hallway an inch, peering both ways before pulling the door open. It made a terrible creaking and scared the triplets into a blind sprint up the north hallway. They were thirty feet past the elevators, approaching the north hallway, when they heard a *ding!*

The elevator!

Bridger looked around in a panic and spotted a cow-hair divan set diagonally in the hallway corner before a coffee table. Hearing the elevator door start to open, he dove over the top of the couch, landing in the deep triangular space behind it. Connor landed on top of him, pinning Bridger's arm and smashing the cocking lever of Cobb's pistol into his brother's cheek. Hailey landed on top of Connor. Bridger saw stars and could feel blood trickling from his wound.

But he didn't dare move or cry out. Looking out through the gap between the sofa bottom and the carpet, he had a fleeting glimpse of a Third Position soldier exiting the elevator without his hood. He had short blond hair, round wire glasses, and a bony face.

Cristoph looked up and down the hallway. Then he adjusted his glasses and started walking toward them. Bridger felt sure that he was going to discover them. And then more soldiers would come and they'd all die. Badly.

Cristoph rounded the corner and was past them several feet before he stopped. Bridger heard him sniff and say, "Uhh!" as if he'd caught wind of something foul.

Connor's sneakers! Bridger thought.

He felt one of his siblings shift on top of him, grinding the pistol hammer deeper into his cheek. Then he heard the Third Position soldier say, *"Quelque chose est mort"* and continue walking.

Hailey peeked her head up and saw Cristoph enter a suite at the far end of the hall, toward the atrium staircase.

"He's gone," she whispered.

"Then get off me!" Bridger sputtered. "My face is speared!"

Hailey and Connor rolled back over the couch. When Bridger got up, blood dripped from a nasty square gouge on his right cheek, already turning black and blue.

"Oooh, that's gotta hurt," Hailey said.

"I'm bleeding," Bridger said. "They're going to find us."

Connor said, "It's not gushing or nothing, kid, just oozing, like hamburger."

Hailey dug in her pocket and came up with the lens cloth for her snowboarding goggles. She pressed it against her brother's cheek.

"I think you'll live," she said.

Bridger scowled at her. He hated it when Hailey acted superior. He replaced her fingers with the back of his right hand and then hurried after Connor. When they reached their father's office, Hailey set the .22 down, fished in her pocket, came up with the electronic master key, and used it. They entered and shut the door. Ambient light shone in the window from the skating rink spotlights three stories below. Connor slumped onto the couch, moaning softly, while Bridger let out a huge sigh and said, "Your feet stink."

"What?" Connor said.

"He smelled your toe punk," Bridger insisted.

Hailey laughed softly as she searched her father's desk drawers. She came up with a box of Band-Aids. With Connor's help she had soon fashioned a reasonable bandage over Bridger's wound.

"I got dibs on the couch," Connor said. "My stomach's killing me."

He took his father's cardigan sweater off the rack, kicked off his boots, and threw the cushions on the floor. He lay down on the couch and arranged the sweater for a pillow. He rubbed at his stomach.

"You okay?" Hailey asked.

"Fine," Connor replied, then smiled. "I just think about that guy with the razors between his toes and I feel better."

Bridger grinned and then winced. "One of my best ideas yet."

Bridger lay down on the cushions, his snowboarding coat over his shoulders, and suddenly felt exhausted. He closed his eyes and, despite the pain in his cheek, drifted slowly toward unconsciousness.

Hailey remained at the desk, looking at a framed photograph of her father, herself, and her brothers on a hike in the mountains the summer before. She picked up the photograph and studied the faces, especially hers and her dad's. He was behind the triplets, his arms wrapped around Connor and Bridger with their arms around her shoulders. Her head was tilted to the ground and she had this sad, brooding expression.

But her father beamed into the camera, looking like the happiest guy on the planet. Seeing that, right then, after all that had happened in the past day, something gave way in Hailey and she honestly felt how much her father loved her, loved all of them. She'd known, of course. But it didn't feel like this. And loving him hadn't ever felt like this before. She suddenly wanted to know her father, to understand him, to be his friend. She felt a raw, hollow ache in her chest that she believed could only be stopped by her dad holding her.

She set the picture down and jiggled the mouse. The computer screen lit up, casting Hailey's face in a pale blue glow.

"What are you doing?" Connor whispered from the couch.

"Sending Dad an e-mail," she whispered back.

"That's the dumbest thing I've ever heard," Bridger said from the floor. "If he's caught or wounded, do you honestly think he'll be checking his e-mail?"

Hailey ignored him. She accessed her e-mail box, hit COMPOSE, and wrote,

Dad? Where are you? We've been looking everywhere for you. Please don't be dead. We are hiding in your office. One of them found us in your apartment. He kicked Connor in the stomach and the head. Bridger and I shot him with our paintball

guns and knocked him out. He's tied up in your
bedroom with razor blades between his toes
(Bridger's idea, not mine). Please find us. Or leave
us a message anyway.   *Hailey*

She typed in her father's e-mail address and sent the
message. She yawned, then she went to the heating register and turned it up to seventy-five degrees. She shut
the shades, climbed into the reclining chair, and lay back
with her snowboard coat over her. Hailey wondered
where her mother was, whether she'd heard of the attack,
her honeymoon wrecked. She'd be falling apart. Hailey
was sure of that. That's what her mom did whenever she
or her brothers got hurt playing sports. Fell apart. But
now, instead of making her feel claustrophobic, Hailey
saw her mother in a different light. She was a little goofy
at times. A little too serious at times. A dictator about
homework.

"I wish we were home listening to Mom nag us,"
Connor said in the darkness.

"I was thinking the same thing, kid," Bridger murmured. "The same exact thing."

Hailey smiled and drifted into sleep.

CHAPTER TWENTY-THREE

At five that morning, General Anarchy descended a staircase into the basement of the Jefferson Club Lodge. He found himself below the ballroom and the grand atrium in a massive storage area filled with summer furniture and pallets of canned goods, cleaning supplies, and toiletries for the guests. On the far left wall, a door led to the boiler rooms, the backup generators, and the laundry below the north wing. On the right side of the storage room there were nine doors, all of them to storage bays. A Third Position soldier guarded the room. He had bright orange hair and a baby's face.

"General," he said in a soft Southern drawl.

"How are they, Carpenter?"

"Sleeping last time I checked," Carpenter said.

"Their televisions worked last night?" he asked.

The soldier nodded. "Every single one of them saw the show."

General Anarchy focused on the sixth door.

"Wake up Sir Lawrence," he ordered. "Feed him, let him use the head, then put him in the courtroom."

An hour and a half later, Mickey Hennessy jerked awake in his bunk in the outfitter's tent. He was coated in sweat and gasping, panicked by a nightmare in which he'd seen General Anarchy chasing Hailey down a long white hallway. He could still see the weird, mocking Kabuki grin painted on the terrorist leader's face.

Doughnuts had been set on the table. He ate two greedily, sucking them down with coffee. Then he grabbed his jacket and slipped out of the tent, finding the air before dawn hovering near zero. It gnawed at his face, turning it beet red before he reached the mobile command center.

He entered, finding Willis Kane where he'd left him—at the conference table. Phelps and Seitz were with him, along with a half dozen other hard-looking men in SWAT gear. They were all looking at the flat-screen monitor that displayed the Google Earth view of the Jefferson Club grounds.

"So we'll come in from four directions with air cover from a National Guard helicopter," Phelps was saying, gesturing to four spots on the screen highlighted with pushpin icons. "Only question I have is how long it will take us to get in position once the order is given."

"I like it," Kane said. He spotted Hennessy. "What do you think, Mickey?"

Hennessy smiled, but then shook his head. "Your other three points of attack make sense if we can beat the fence. But if you enter from the northwest, off the flank of Mount Jefferson, you'll find yourself on the nose. It's a virtual cliff. You'll have to rappel."

Phelps looked at him sourly. "I know. That's why they won't expect it."

"They catch you on the fence coming in, they'll mow you down on the cliffs."

"Not if we're getting cover fire from the helicopter," Kane said, annoyed. "I've requested a Blackhawk with fifty-caliber machine guns."

"They'll know you're coming," Hennessy said. "We put in radar this past summer for the heliskiing operation that was supposed to launch in February."

The front door to the command center whooshed open, letting loose a flood of cold air into the close quarters while Hennessy said, "Other than that it could work." He gazed at Kane. "My kids?"

"Nothing new," Kane said softly.

Cheyenne walked in and slid a CD-ROM disk across the table at the Critical Incident commander. "SAC, I thought we might be able to use this. A three-dimensional map of the lodge."

Hennessy knew there was one, but he couldn't believe she had it.

"Where'd you get that?" he demanded.

Cheyenne smiled. "On my way up here I met Sheriff Lacey and we woke up the court clerk in Jeffersonville, who took us to city hall to get the designs that accompanied the building permit. I found this instead."

"Nicely done, O'Neil," Kane said, taking the CD-

ROM and handing it to Phelps. Then he frowned. "Thought I asked you to stick with the senator."

"He's sedated," she answered quickly. "And the Bozeman resident agent is with him. He said he'd call when the senator regained consciousness. I'll get back on the money angle now."

Before Kane could reply, she slipped out of the conference area and grabbed an open computer workstation.

Kane's cell phone rang. As he answered it, he gestured at the disk in Phelps's hands. "Mickey, guide him through every conceivable way to enter or exit that building."

Hennessy nodded. "Anything I can do, Willis. Anything."

He and Phelps moved to a station near Cheyenne, who was busily scanning her computer screen. They slid the CD-ROM into a bay and after several moments' grinding, a computer-generated model of the lodge exterior appeared. They were looking at the atrium and ballroom from the perspective of the Hellroaring chairlift.

Hennessy moved the cursor to the right wing of the lodge. He clicked on the wall revealing all five floors and the basement in cut-away. He slid the cursor past the kitchen.

"Let's look at the wine cellar first," he said to the hostage rescue commander.

Before Hennessy could navigate to the wine cellar on the map, Kane snapped shut his cell phone and called out, "That was Computer Investigations at Quantico.

They say the Third Position site's registered to a Gil Tran Tepp, renter of a PO box in Kuala Lumpur. Malaysian authorities are trying to track him. The site itself seems to be hosted by servers inside the Jefferson Club. They brought the files in with them."

Pritoni tugged down his earphones. "Can the servers be shut down?"

"Not from outside," Hennessy responded. "They're protected by specially designed firewalls. The software guys told us they were impenetrable."

"Well, their method of wire transfers weren't," Cheyenne crowed, tapping the screen. "My partner's managed to track some of the money to accounts in Macau, Isle of Man, Isle of Wight, Liechtenstein, and Dublin, all well-known tax havens."

"Who owns the accounts?" Kane demanded as he and Hennessy crowded in behind her to look at her screen.

"They're registered to dummy corporations," she said. "But don't worry, Ikeda's an expert at untangling them."

Hennessy and Phelps moved back to the station showing the three-dimensional map of the lodge. Hennessy forced himself to think like a burglar and began to show Phelps the few ways a counterassault team might enter the lodge. Above them, televisions mounted to the ceiling above the computers blared with coverage of the siege on the Jefferson Club, the trial of Senator Worthington, and speculation about what hostage would next head to the Third Position's Court of Public Opinion.

Wooden staging had gone up overnight in the growing media encampment outside the gate. Despite the bitter cold, reporters preened before twice the number of cameras present the evening before, all of them swarming into the lingering news void early the day after a worldwide holiday.

Kane shook his head. "I don't get it. Why have a trial at seven-thirty mountain? I mean, what's the audience at seven-thirty in the morning on a workday? And back East it's nine-thirty. People have left for work. You'd figure they'd try to do it in prime time again, like they did last night."

Cheyenne had a scary thought. "The New York Stock Exchange opens at nine-thirty eastern. So does the NASDAQ."

Kane frowned. "You think they're tying this to the markets?"

"What better way to advance the anti-globalist cause than trying to influence the Dow Jones? You should call the director, let him know."

Kane shot back irritably, "No offense, Agent O'Neil, but who made you Maria Bartiromo? I'm going to have to have something a hell of a lot more concrete than a coincidence of timing before I go calling the director. What exactly do you think's going to happen?"

"I don't know exactly, SAC," she said, irked at his attitude. "But I can tell you that the markets aren't going to like one of their champions on trial in a kangaroo court. Uh-uh. No way."

Dawn broke. In the snowy fog that shrouded the Jefferson Club Lodge, the light was a dull pewter glow.

Connor heard a noise, opened his eyes, blinked at the light, and groaned at the pain in his gut. Bridger and Hailey were already up. They'd raised the blinds several inches. Bridger sat in his father's desk chair. Hailey sat on the little window seat behind him.

"Anything from Dad?" Connor asked Hailey.

"No," she said.

"There's a surprise," Connor said. "I'm hungry."

"Snacks in the fridge," Bridger said.

Connor got up and retrieved two packages of cheese snacks and a Sprite as Bridger worked his way through the Third Position Web site into the Court of Public Opinion's docket, finding a new hyperlink: *The Third Position v. Sir Lawrence Treadwell.*

Bridger clicked the hyperlink. The screen loaded the image of the courtroom and Sir Lawrence, hooded and tied to the witness chair in his disheveled tux. The bailiff in the mime suit stomped out from behind curtains to the right, carrying her staff. She struck the staff on the hardwood floor three times, then leaned back her head and shouted, *"The People of the Third Position versus Lawrence Treadwell, Chairman of GlobalCon.* Judge Truth presiding. All rise!"

The camera retreated to show the full cast of the trial: the six hooded jury members, General Anarchy on the right for the prosecution, and Citizen's Defender Emilia on the left. Judge Truth came in parading his harlequin self and rapped his gavel.

"Remove the hood," he ordered. "Let him face his accusers."

Mouse removed the blindfold. Sir Lawrence's hairdo

had cracked and hung in his face. He shook the hair away, blinked several times at the bright lights, and then gazed around him, taking stock of the situation, a man used to controlling crisis, defiant, ready to take all comers.

Judge Truth said, "General Anarchy, what are the charges?"

General Anarchy's Kabuki face filled the screen before intoning, "Mass murder, attempted genocide, and other acts of extinction."

Inside the FBI's command center, the agents went silent for a long moment as they digested the charges. Cheyenne was dumbfounded.

"Mass murder?" Willis Kane said silently.

"And genocide," Cheyenne said.

"And other acts of extinction," Hennessy said, his eyes glued to the screen.

On camera, Sir Lawrence appeared equally incredulous. He gaped at General Anarchy, then at Truth, thinking they were joking. Then he lost it.

"What the bloody hell?" he yelled, struggling against his restraints. "I've never murdered anyone and certainly have never participated in genocide! What in the Queen's name is an act of extinction? This is bollocks! Who the hell are you behind that ludicrous makeup? Why are you doing this? Wasn't the money enough?"

"Keep up the tantrums, Sir Lawrence," General Anarchy replied evenly. "As you know, we are webcasting this trial. Last night we had an audience and jury of millions. Now, I'm sure we don't have that many this morning, but certainly those with special interest are watching, probably your stockholders."

While Treadwell grappled with that idea, Cheyenne noticed the television above her computer screen. Out of habit, she stood and tuned it to the Bloomberg coverage. The Dow Jones Industrials had opened down eighteen points. GlobalCon was already off three dollars in heavy trading.

On the lower screen, Judge Truth whacked his gavel. He paused, then said, "General Anarchy?"

The prosecutor walked to the jury box, his gloved hands clasped behind his back.

"Ladies and gentlemen of the jury," he began. "On the charge of genocide, we the people of the Third Position will show beyond a shadow of doubt Mr. Treadwell's intimate involvement in the oil and gas business, his correspondingly utter disregard for the environment, and his personal contribution to the mushroom clouds of heavy-metal hydrocarbons that have been released into the atmosphere during the past twenty-five years. As a result, Sir Lawrence has become the sixth-richest man in the world, and earth as a sustainable ecosystem has been driven to the tipping point of catastrophe and the inevitable genocide of humanity by global warming."

Sir Lawrence had listened to all this slumped, looking out at General Anarchy and the jury from beneath hooded brows. He snorted. "Global warming? That's just some ridiculous theory by egghead liberals and that Nobel Prize sham Al Gore. No such thing. And attempted genocide? No court in the land would convict me."

General Anarchy looked at the oil tycoon, amused.

"That's because you've got the system rigged in your favor. You're wealthy enough, you can buy the best attorneys, hire the best PR strategists, and make the right discreet bribe. You'll have no such luxury here, Sir Lawrence."

He turned back to the jury. "The people will also provide evidence of Mr. Treadwell's willful acts of extinction and attempted extinction through his petroleum extraction, transportation, and refinery businesses."

"Name one," Sir Lawrence snarled.

General Anarchy arched an eyebrow toward the closest camera. "Arcane Bay, a remote little paradise in the Philippine archipelago facing the South China Sea."

CHAPTER TWENTY-FOUR

Inside his father's office, Bridger was transfixed by the scene unfolding on the computer screen. At the mention of Arcane Bay, the petrochemical billionaire looked like he'd just been kicked in the balls.

"Sir Lawrence sure knows where that place is," Bridger said.

"No doubt," Connor agreed.

General Anarchy was saying, "The Third Position will show that Sir Lawrence Treadwell not only caused the terrible events at Arcane Bay in September 2001, but then tried to cover them up. His actions resulted in the death of all marine life in the bay and the demise of thousands of birds, countless animals, and thirty-eight humans."

Sir Lawrence came out sputtering, "I had no bloody involvement in—"

Judge Truth hammered his gavel. "How do you plead?"

"Not guilty!" the tycoon thundered. "Not guilty to all of it!"

General Anarchy appeared in close-up. "Perhaps this will jog his memory."

The screen leaped to a shaky view of a tropical paradise blurred by clouds of black smoke. People were screaming. The video camera jerked through jungle toward a white sand beach. Near the high-tide line, the white sand was black and oily. The water itself was on fire. The flames curled like waves, all coming from an aging oil tanker called the *Niamey*. Then the camera came to bear on a long trembling shot down the beach where the screaming was coming from.

"Oh, my God," Bridger said.

"Jesus," Hailey said, while Connor looked away.

The beach downwind of the fiery slick was littered with the bodies of humans and animals in charred poses. People wandered in shock among the corpses, searching for loved ones, cloths over their mouths, squinting and holding their hands up against the heat of the flames, crying and coughing against the smoke. The screen froze on survivors whimpering with grief, some on their knees, others bent double, overcome.

It lingered there several seconds, then the coverage cut to Sir Lawrence in profile, his jaw locked, staring hatred at General Anarchy. "I've never seen that before."

"Quite possible," General Anarchy allowed. "It was supposed to have been destroyed as part of GlobalCon's settlement with the victims of Arcane Bay. But as you know, a billion dollars can work wonders to pry open the lid on even the darkest of secrets."

"I had nothing to do with that unfortunate accident."

General Anarchy's laugh was caustic. "Is that what you're calling it? That unfortunate accident? Thirty-eight people dead? An ecological gem destroyed?"

Sir Lawrence fought for composure. "It was a most unfortunate accident caused by the decisions of a low-level manager in one of my far-flung subsidiaries. I most certainly had no direct role in this matter."

General Anarchy shook his head in mock woe. "Really?" He walked over and picked up a document from the prosecution table. He held it up to the camera, saying, "I hold here a GlobalCon directive signed by Sir Lawrence. If you care to examine it closer, you'll find it on www.thirdpositionjustice.net.

"But the gist of the document reveals that our up-standing billionaire authorized a delay in overhauling all GlobalCon ships over twenty-five years old. The *Niamey* was twenty-nine when her rudder failed, she hit the reef, and broke up."

The screen cut to a close-up of Sir Lawrence, who glared through squinted eyelids, while General Anarchy introduced two other pieces of evidence. The first, a letter from Sir Lawrence, urged his attorneys to deal with Arcane Bay swiftly and quietly so as not to upset shareholders. The other, written by GlobalCon's own scientists, predicted it would be nearly a century before the visible effects of the spill and the fire were washed away by time and tide. The reef would never recover.

"Nor may the people of Arcane Bay," General Anarchy said.

Back in the command post center, Hennessy sat forward in his chair, glued to the drama unfolding on the screen. Sir Lawrence was visibly shaken up when the camera returned to him. "Where . . . ?"

"Like I said, a billion dollars sure speeds up the process of investigation," Anarchy said.

"SAC?" Cheyenne O'Neil called out. Hennessy took his eyes off the webcast to find her gesturing up at the Bloomberg report. "The Dow's off one hundred and sixty-six points, nearly a full percent of its value, since the trial began. The Standard & Poor's is almost down that much too. And the NASDAQ. I told you the markets wouldn't like this. You should recommend they suspend trading in all of the hostages' companies."

Kane's face screwed up in thought. Then he snatched up his satellite phone even as the computer screens jumped to a fuming Sir Lawrence.

"The survivors were cared for," Sir Lawrence cried. "We paid millions."

"You got away with murder because of 9/11," General Anarchy said.

"I don't know what you're talking about," Sir Lawrence grumbled.

"Don't you? The eyes of the world were completely on Manhattan and Washington in the weeks after the Trade Towers fell, not some tiny bay in a remote archipelago of the Philippines, and certainly not on your immoral deal."

"What was immoral?" Sir Lawrence demanded. "We negotiated. They agreed. End of story. It was business."

"It was dirty business!" General Anarchy shouted. "Six-point-seven million for the thirty-eight dead, their relatives, and the people who survived the fires? One hundred and forty-two people? One hundred and sixty-five grand apiece? For children with eighty percent of their bodies burned? For parents who watched their sons and daughters scorched to death in front of their eyes? For the orphans? The childless mothers?"

Sir Lawrence leaned forward and shouted, "Those people lived on less than a dollar a day before the accident. We paid them more than they'd ever dreamed of."

"You paid them a pittance, Sir Lawrence, and you went on with your life, eating crab cakes and garlic sauce."

Hennessy stared dumbly at the screen, then sat up straighter. "Crab cakes and garlic sauce were hors d'oeuvres at the New Year's party," he said. "How'd he know that? How could he possibly have known that?"

Cheyenne looked at him and shrugged. "Leftovers? Someone told him?"

"Or they found one of the menus," Hennessy said, seeing how it was possible, yet unable to shake the suspicion that someone inside had been feeding the Third Position information prior to the attack.

On the computer screens, General Anarchy strode before the bench.

"The Third Position rests, Your Honor."

Judge Truth rapped his gavel and said, "Citizen's Defender Emilia, your defense?"

She stood and said, "As far as I can see, there is no

defense, Judge. No logical reason for acting in such a thoroughly despicable manner, with such wanton disregard for life, wanting only to enrich himself further. The defense rests."

"This is preposterous!" Sir Lawrence sputtered. "You're fired!"

"You can't fire her," Judge Truth said. "She's court-appointed."

"This is insane!"

Judge Truth banged his gavel. "Enough!" he roared. The screen cut to his harlequin face in close-up. "Fifteen minutes, America. Is Sir Lawrence Treadwell victim of an unfortunate accident or an arrogant money-grubbing bastard who killed innocents while cutting costs? You tell us. Your vote matters to the Third Position. Polls are open now and for the next fifteen minutes!"

The courtroom scene disappeared from the screens inside the FBI command center, replaced by a Web page that said, *COURT IS IN RECESS UNTIL 10:30 EASTERN.* Below was the hyperlink that read, *Vote!*

While other members of the FBI team went to use the head or get coffee from the galley, Hennessy got up and paced nervously. "They're going to find him guilty."

"That video was enough to convince any jury," Cheyenne agreed. "How the hell did they get through the court seal?"

"Like the man said, with a billion dollars you can do just about anything."

Connor Hennessy clicked on the hyperlink that led to the jury ballot. Hailey read it over his shoulder.

Sir Lawrence Treadwell
Participant in Global Genocide:
[ ] Guilty [ ] Not guilty
Mass Murder and Acts of Extinction.
[ ] Guilty [ ] Not guilty
[ ] Victim of an Accident
[ ] Evil Money-Grubber

"Guilty evil money-grubber," Bridger said.

"On all counts?" Connor asked.

"No," Hailey said. "You can't convict him of genocide for global warming."

"Yeah, I guess not," Connor said, and then entered their judgment. "Everyone's responsible for that."

The screen jumped to a computer-generated reenactment of Treadwell's tanker exploding, the fire rising like a wave and crashing on the beach. At the end it said, *"Thanks! Your vote matters in the Court of Public Opinion!"*

Hailey looked at the clock on the wall. 8:17 a.m. Thirteen minutes until the verdict. Bridger walked out from behind the desk and picked up Cobb's machine gun. He put the stock to his shoulder and aimed down the optical sight at the window blinds.

"You got the safety on?" Hailey asked nervously.

"Think I'm a moron?" Bridger demanded.

"Sometimes," Connor said. "I gotta pee."

"Do you always announce your evacuations?" Hailey asked.

"I figured you'd miss me, Sis," Connor said, then went in the office's bathroom.

Before Hailey could answer, she heard something outside. She went to the window behind the desk and peered through the blinds. Several Third Position soldiers were walking away from a large black metal barrel in the middle of the ice rink.

"They put a barrel out there on the ice," she said.

Bridger ignored her. He was examining the machine gun, removing the clip and then reinserting it. "You know, I think I could shoot this thing."

"Don't even think about it," Hailey said. "You'd probably shoot us."

Connor came out of the bathroom and went to the refrigerator. All the Sprites were gone, leaving only diet Dr Pepper, one of his father's eccentric tastes. He grabbed it and the last of the peanut butter crackers.

He cracked the pop-top with a revolted expression. "I hate diet Dr Pepper," he said. "Especially with peanut butter crackers."

At that same time, their father was desperate for a diet Dr Pepper, but had to settle for a can of Pepsi he found in the command center's galley. He cracked the pop-top with his good hand, hearing Willis Kane still on the phone with Washington.

"Yes, sir, that's what she's saying," Kane said. "And the markets are sure backing her up." He listened, then nodded. "Yes, sir."

Hennessy walked past him into the command center. Cheyenne O'Neil was on her phone, taking notes on the computer. Hennessy felt useless and frustrated, unable to do a thing to find his children. *What were they thinking, running off like that? Why did they leave the main group?*

And then it hit him. He'd disappeared in the attack. *They're looking for me.* In the second it took for Kane and Cheyenne to hang up their respective phones, Hennessy felt desperate and proud and furious and more helpless than ever. He'd abandoned them to get help, while they'd refused to leave without him. Hennessy sat down at the conference table and put his head in his hands, barely aware of Kane moving to Cheyenne as she put her headset aside.

"The director agrees with you, O'Neil" Kane said. "He's calling the President to recommend suspension of trading in those stocks."

Hennessy raised his head. Cheyenne was beaming. "Yes, sir. That's good. And I've got more good news. My partner and I have been able to track the ownership of some of the companies that controlled the accounts the ransom money moved to. There's a common name on six of them: Gil Tepper, care of a PO box on the Isle of Wight."

"Okay?" Kane said, trying to place the significance.

Hennessy saw it. "Sounds a lot like the guy who registered the Web site."

"Gil Tran Tep," Cheyenne said, nodding at him. "I thought so too."

Kurt Seitz walked into the conference area. "Their site's going live again."

Indeed, every computer screen in the command center had jumped to a full frontal shot of Sir Lawrence Treadwell in the witness chair. His wrists were tied together in front of him. The multibillionaire sat up straight, trying to appear confident, but he was knitting his fingers together and worrying them, the movement his only fascination.

The camera retreated and showed the last of the hooded jury members returning to the box. General Anarchy and Citizen's Defender Emilia stood at their respective tables. Truth gaveled the court to order. "Do you have a verdict, Mr. Foreman?"

The hooded foreman rose. "We have, Your Honor."

"How say you?"

"By a vote of nine-point-five million to eight-point-two million, we the people of the Third Position find Sir Lawrence Treadwell not guilty of future genocide. Everyone who drives a car or burns fuel for heat is partially responsible for greenhouse gases and global warming."

On the witness stand, Sir Lawrence brightened and his head rose. "Good. See? People aren't stupid."

The jury foreman continued, "On the charges of mass murder and other acts of extinction for his role in Arcane Bay and its cover-up: By a vote of fourteen-point-eight million to three-point-five million, we the people of the Third Position find Sir Lawrence Treadwell guilty."

Inside the mock courtroom, Judge Truth looked to General Anarchy. "Penalty?"

"The Third Position believes special circumstances are warranted," General Anarchy replied coldly. "We seek death."

Sir Lawrence started to blink rapidly, then he

struggled against his bonds and his yelling bounced off the ceiling and floor of the ballroom. "Death! You can't do this! You'll never get away with this!"

Judge Truth rapped his gavel and spoke gravely. "Sir Lawrence Treadwell, Chairman of GlobalCon, a jury of eighteen-point-three million of your peers has found you guilty of mass murder and ecological atrocity. The Third Position sentence is death. You will be executed forthwith in an appropriate manner. May heaven have pity on you. I cannot."

The jury rose and filed toward Sir Lawrence. He squirmed in his chair, the fear and disbelief dancing across his face. He arched backward when they surrounded him.

"No!" he yelled. "No!"

The jury lifted his chair onto their shoulders, and then marched him past the jury box while he wrenched himself side to side.

"You can't execute me for crimes I didn't commit!" Sir Lawrence screamed. "They were policies! That's all. Good business practice! You can't kill a man for wanting to trim costs! For keeping shareholders happy! Help me! For God's sake, someone help!"

CHAPTER TWENTY-FIVE

Cheyenne O'Neil stood in the CIRG command center, feeling queasy as she watched Sir Lawrence Treadwell carried from the court, screaming for someone to come to his aid.

The screen cut to General Anarchy in close-up, speaking over the tycoon's fading cries. "The next trial begins at eleven a.m. mountain time, one p.m. eastern. You won't want to miss it. There'll be codefendants, and you won't believe what those bad boys of capitalism have been up to. But first, just punishment for Sir Lawrence Treadwell."

"They're not going to kill him, right?" Mickey Hennessy said beside her. "They're just trying to scare the shit out of him, right? Reduce him to a quivering mess. Send him before the cameras to plead guilty to his crimes."

"I don't know," Willis Kane said, arms crossed. "I don't like this."

"Neither does the Dow," Cheyenne said, pointing at the television screen above her. The Dow Jones had fallen three hundred and twenty-nine points. "It's lost almost two percent of its value since opening. Oh, there it is: They're freezing trade on GlobalCon, HB1 Financial, and YES!"

Before anyone could comment, the Web coverage cut to a jerky, handheld camera that caught Sir Lawrence being carried out the side door of the lodge. He was still struggling, pleading, "I'll pay anything. Anything. Don't do this. Please!"

The camera followed the procession from behind. Hennessy recognized their path.

"They're heading for the skating rink," he said. "Northwest side of the lodge. I can see it from my office."

Connor, Bridger, and Hailey realized what was happening as well. Hailey peered out from between the slats of the blinds behind the desk. Bridger and Connor looked out the window in front of it. The parade of jurors, with Sir Lawrence on their shoulders, marched toward the rink. General Anarchy, Truth, and Mouse followed. Citizen's Defender Emilia brought up the rear, black shawl over her head, like a widow behind a caisson.

They stepped onto the ice rink. The jurors' feet slowed to a shuffle. One cameraman moved parallel to the parade, his back bent over, holding his camera low to the ice. A second stood beyond the barrel.

"They really gonna kill him?" Connor wondered anxiously.

Hailey swallowed at the bitter taste in her throat, feeling rubbery in her joints. "They're not afraid to kill people."

"This is bad," Bridger said, not knowing what to do. "Real bad."

Outside, the procession had reached the barrel. Sir Lawrence began to shriek and buck against the chair when the jurors placed the chair on the ice. "No. I . . . I . . . No!"

The Third Position jurors cut the bonds that held the tycoon to his chair, then lifted him and, despite his wild thrashing, plunged him into the barrel. He sank to his sternum. Liquid splashed over the sides of the barrel and spilled on the ice.

The jurors stepped back to form a circle around Treadwell.

"What are they doing?" Connor asked, peering out the window.

His father was wondering the same thing inside FBI command center.

Even Sir Lawrence seemed baffled by what was going on, gaping dumbly at the liquid. Then his hands sought the barrel rim and he began to whimper at the members of the jury.

"You've made your bloody point," he managed. "I'm guilty. I'll give more money to the people of Arcane Bay. A billion. Two. Don't do this. Please don't do this."

General Anarchy came to the edge of the circle, followed by Judge Truth, who called out, "Sir Lawrence Treadwell, you have been found guilty and sentenced to death in an appropriate manner. So be it. Good people of the Third Position, see justice served."

The jury members all fished something from the pockets of their coats. Hennessy could not see what they'd retrieved at first.

But Sir Lawrence evidently could and he went stark-raving mad.

"No!" he screamed. "You can't! This is barbaric! Someone help! Stop them! Someone stop them!"

The screen jumped to a close-up shot of one of the jurors' gloved hands holding a match. Off-camera, Sir Lawrence screeched, "No! For the bloody love of . . . Help!"

"It's gas," Seitz gasped.

Standing at the windows in their father's office, the Hennessy triplets realized it too.

"Jesus!" Hailey said.

"We gotta do something," Bridger said.

"Yeah, we do," Connor said, grabbing the .22.

"What are you gonna do?" Hailey cried.

"Try to stop them."

"Yeah," Bridger said in a voice that sounded drugged. He took the machine gun and pushed up the window.

"No, don't do it," Hailey said, dancing on the edge of tears.

Connor took aim out the window saying, "We voted

him guilty, Hailey. We helped put him in the barrel and we're the only ones who can stop it. We have to."

Bridger nodded. "It's what Dad would do."

Inside the FBI command center, Hennessy's hand traveled to his mouth as the camera revealed gloved hands striking matches. A flat cracking noise like a whip sounded. The camera retreated, showing one of the jurors down on the ice howling in pain, clutching his leg even as the matches were thrown and hit the pool of gasoline around the barrel. Sir Lawrence tried to hurl himself free.

But it was too late. The gas ignited, swept across the ice, and a cold blue flame slithered up the side of the barrel. The flame vaulted the rim and contacted the gasoline. A fireball erupted.

Hennessy's jaw dropped open at the nightmare vision. "No!"

He'd seen films of the Buddhist monks who'd set themselves afire in Vietnam, but nothing as gruesome as Sir Lawrence arching backward as the fire settled into a pillar of flame ten feet high. His arms were raised. His mouth was open wide in a silent scream.

A machine gun opened fire from somewhere off-screen. The ice all around the burning man chipped and threw sprays of snow when bullets raked across it. The jury members began to run. So did the cameraman, who nevertheless captured the image of two jurors hit, buckling and sprawling on the ice.

There were shouts in the background and then the screen went black.

Bridger had Cobb's submachine gun braced against the windowsill, possessed by blind rage and wanting to shoot them all for what they'd done to Sir Lawrence. It was inhuman.

But he couldn't control the gun. The automatic's muzzle kept jumping and weaving. His bullets were hitting the trees on the other side of the rink, high above his intended targets. Beside him, Connor was aiming down the .22's iron sights. He touched the trigger. Ice exploded right behind General Anarchy's feet as the Third Position leader sprinted toward the trees beyond the ice rink.

Connor was running the .22's bolt when the machine gun's breech clanked open.

"I'm out," Bridger said. His face felt like it was burning as he stared out at Sir Lawrence's blackened corpse, arched backward out of the barrel in the dying flames.

"We're gonna die!" Hailey shouted hysterically.

"No, we're not," Connor said. He spun away from the window and started running toward the door.

Bridger tried to change the banana clip. Outside, General Anarchy yelled, "Fourth floor! Open window!"

Bridger whipped around and charged after his brother, still fumbling with the clip. Hailey had grabbed Cobb's pistol and was already ahead of her brother. The window and the blinds behind Bridger exploded. A hail of machine gun fire ripped the ceiling and the office walls, shattering the photo of them all hiking, their father's framed retirement commendation, and his diploma from the Diplomatic Security Service Academy.

General Anarchy's voice shouted into Radio's ear inside the security center on the second floor of the Jefferson Club Lodge, *"Radio, are you on them? Fourth floor."*

Radio was hammering the keyboard, calling up the cameras. Instantly he could see Hailey and the boys running down a hallway, then disappearing behind a steel door.

"They're in the utility stairwell, General," Radio barked into his headset and started typing again. "No cameras in there. You'll have to clear it top to bottom. Flush them out!"

"Flush them out and kill them," General Anarchy replied.

Hailey was dropping through the utility stairwell four steps at a time. Her brothers were right on her heels. When they reached the second-floor landing, Connor suddenly grabbed her by the hood of her sweatshirt and Hailey choked and spun around angrily. "What're you, trying to break my neck?"

Connor looked pale. "They'll be coming for us from below."

"Then we go up to the roof," Bridger said and made as if to start climbing.

Connor stopped him. "They'll trap us up there. No way are you jumping."

Bridger's hand went to his head. Then he looked over Hailey's shoulder and went around her. "We'll get to the basement," he said. He tapped on the large door to the laundry chute, which was on the outer wall beside the trash chute. "The door's locked down there with a dead bolt. Dad had to use a real key to get in there. They can't get in there without that key. At least not quick. We can get through the basement to the secret passage to the Burnses' house."

Connor looked at the chutes doubtfully. "That's gotta be a twenty-foot drop."

"But the laundry chute bends," Hailey said, seizing on the idea. "I saw it when we were down there yesterday washing our clothes. We'll land in one of those big hampers filled with silk sheets."

"What if the hamper's not there?" Connor asked.

"Broken leg's better than dying, kid," Bridger said. He took the machine gun and dropped it down the trash chute. He pulled open the doors to expose the laundry chute.

He grabbed Hailey and lifted her to the opening, feet first, while Connor threw the .22 into the trash tube. Hailey fit easily. She had a moment of panic, then forced herself to shove away from her brother without thinking.

Hailey plunged into darkness. It was everything she could do not to scream.

Kane was beside himself. "What the hell was going on there at the end? Replay it. Did anyone tape it?"

"They came under fire," Phelps, the hostage rescue leader, said.

"I'm not a dolt," Kane said. "Who? Why?"

"I've got it," Seitz, the negotiator, said. "I taped it all."

The computer screens inside the command center leaped to the image of the gloved hands striking the kitchen matches, then cut to the view of the jury members surrounding Sir Lawrence in the barrel of gasoline.

The first gunshot sounded like a flyswatter whacking a counter. A Third Position soldier dropped, holding his leg. Sir Lawrence arched inside the pillar of fire. The machine gun started up. The Third Position soldiers ran. Two jurors spun and dropped. The screen went black.

Phelps said, "The automatic sounds like a nine-millimeter, which is what the released hostages said the Third Position soldiers were carrying—Sterlings. Maybe they had a revolt in the ranks. Maybe it wasn't supposed to go down that way, killing him like that, and one of them had a conscience."

Hennessy was shocked to the core. "No," he said. "That first shot was a .22."

"So?" Kane said.

"I bought my kids a .22 for Christmas—so they could learn to shoot. It was in my closet with their paintball guns. Those were my kids shooting in there."

"How in the hell did they get a machine gun?" Kane shouted at Hennessy.

"How do I know?" Hennessy roared back. "You've got to go in there and help them. Now, Willis!"

Agent Pritoni tore off his headset and interrupted, "SAC, sniper team one saw the entire event from their position on the ridge. The kids opened fire from a fourth-floor north window. A machine gun and a .22. They saw the shooters: two boys. They hit three bad guys before the Third Position returned fire on the lodge."

"Were my kids hit?" Hennessy cried.

"They don't know," Pritoni replied. "But I'm hearing a lot of chatter. They're hunting them and they know who they are."

Hennessy pleaded, "Willis, they're hunting them."

Kane's satellite phone rang. He looked at the number, then bobbed his head to Hennessy. "I'll do my best." The CIRG commander walked away, saying, "Kane."

Hennessy was torn between wanting to trail Kane and wanting to listen to the radio chatter Agent Pritoni was monitoring. He chose the radio and listened to crackling descriptions of Third Position soldiers moving toward the utility staircase where they'd been seen last. When he realized where they were, his gut plummeted.

"They're trapped," he said. "There's no way out of there where they won't be seen."

Kane returned and said, "Second hostage team's in the air. We go in after dark."

"Dark?" Hennessy roared. "That's eight hours. Bridger, Connor, and Hailey could be dead by then. They could be dead right now!"

"Don't you think it's chewing me up inside?" Kane cried. "But I've got the AG, the FBI director, and the President looking over my shoulder and the last thing they said to me was to wait for the reinforcements. Go in after dark."

Hennessy jerked his left thumb at Phelps. "You've got some of the best hostage rescuers in the world here already. Get Montana State Police involved. The National Guard! Take a helicopter. Land it in there."

"And commit suicide?" Kane retorted. "My intel is

marginal and we're outnumbered. I'm sorry, Mick, but that's a recipe for getting my men, the hostages, and your kids slaughtered. I won't do it. And neither would you if you were me."

"It's Bridger and Connor in there, Willis. Hailey's in there. My little girl."

"It doesn't change the decision. It can't."

Hennessy felt ready to explode. He grabbed his parka and headed toward the door. "Then I'm going to have to go get them myself or die trying."

"Mickey!" Kane shouted. "Mickey!"

CHAPTER TWENTY-SIX

Hailey flew feet first out of the laundry chute and crash-landed in a pile of plush Turkish towels and silk sheets. Her feet caught and tangled, throwing her against the hamper's frame with a wallop. She lurched back, groaning. She doubled up, then realized her brothers were still coming. She rolled to her side just in time.

Connor plunged out of the chute in a spiral motion that heaved him sideways against the hamper frame. His head snapped left and smashed off his shoulder. He fell beside his sister, moaning.

"Out of the way," she managed to whisper.

Connor rolled over and Bridger shot out of the chute in a forward dive. He tucked his chin to his chest and rolled out of it flat in a thudding judo fall position. He seemed shaken for a second at the impact, then sat up, saying, "That wasn't so bad."

"Speak for yourself," Hailey choked. "I can't breathe."

"That sucked," Connor groaned. "My stomach and now my ribs."

The laundry was a windowless room lit with a single red bulb above the sink beyond the industrial washers. The metal staircase to their left led to a gray steel door locked with a dead bolt from the inside. Beyond lay the utility stairwell they'd just exited. To their right another set of stairs that led to a dead-bolted door to the loading docks.

Angry voices rumbled to them from beyond the stairwell door. Booted feet pummeled their way up the staircase. Bridger whispered, "We've got to get out of here. Someone will come looking quicker than we think."

"Let's just go out the loading dock and make a run for it," Connor whispered, getting to his knees.

"They're probably watching the lodge from all sides," Bridger retorted. "And we'd leave tracks in the snow. Burns's house is safer."

Hailey uncurled herself, and, rubbing her chest, she climbed out of the hamper and stood wobbly. "Think it'll work? The master key?"

Bridger moved toward the door beside the bottom of the staircase that led to the utility stairwell. "Fifty-fifty chance, right?"

Connor climbed out of the hamper, still woozy, saying, "Gotta be."

Bridger eased back the dead bolt on the door to the loading dock. He pushed it open and peeked outside into the icy air and weak sunlight. Seeing no one, he snuck out onto the loading dock and the dumpster below the trash chute. He pulled out the machine gun and .22, then glanced beyond the dumpster and froze. The bodies of the Capitol Police officer and Chef Giulio lay there, frozen. Beyond them were five other men, face down, all dressed in Jefferson Club security coats. Bridger's mouth chewed the air and he fought back tears while moving over to them. *Is that Dad?*

He felt outside himself and lost, but forced himself to push the biggest of them over. It was Lerner, the guard who worked the security control center. His eyes were open and frozen. There was a bullet hole between them.

Bridger doubled over, wanting to puke, but then staggered back toward the door to the laundry. He entered, feeling as if everything he'd known for certain before was now suspect, capable of transforming in a horrible instant.

He found his sister softly crying in the corner. "They're going to kill us," she was saying. "Why'd you have to shoot at them, Connor?"

Connor screwed up his jaw, tears coming to his eyes. "Because it's what Dad would have done."

"I think Dad's dead," Bridger said numbly.

Connor grabbed his brother by the collar. "Don't say that."

Bridger shook free and hissed, "They shot Chef Giulio and some lady. And a whole bunch of Dad's men. Their bodies are out there on the loading dock."

"Is Dad's?" Hailey cried, lurching to her side, trying to get up and feeling sick.

"No," Bridger admitted. "At least I didn't see him."

Connor took Cobb's pistol from Hailey and handed her the .22.

"Then he's alive," he said, "and he'd want us to try to get to the Burnses'. We can do this, we just go through the generator room to the storage area, the bakery, and then the wine cellar."

"What if it doesn't work?" Hailey asked, holding up the master key. "Dad said it works on every single lock in the lodge except one."

"And that's the vault," Bridger said.

"He never confirmed it."

"We've got to try, Hailey," Connor said. "It's our best option."

Hailey bit her lower lip, and then nodded and gripped the rifle tighter.

General Anarchy stormed up onto the second-floor landing in the stairwell. Truth and three Third Position soldiers were descending.

"Roof's clear, General," Truth said. "No tracks we could see, but it's blowing hard enough to drift snow pretty quick."

"You're saying they could have jumped?"

"Hell of a drop," Truth said. "I'll send a team to search the perimeter."

"Send teams to look in every goddamned room in this place."

"Every room," Truth promised.

General Anarchy pivoted to leave. But crossing the cement landing toward the descending flight of stairs, his attention swept the wall and caught a blip of red at the corner of the laundry chute. He saw it was a piece of torn fabric, shiny and thick enough to be used in a ski or snowboard jacket. He hesitated, then picked up the fabric bit and headed down the staircase, calling over his shoulder. "I'm going to check the basement."

"They couldn't have gotten in there—it's locked from the inside, General," Truth said. "Dead-bolted."

General Anarchy shrugged and said, "Call it a hunch, Truth."

"The next trial begins in less than an hour."

"More than enough time to eradicate the vermin."

The frigid north wind blasted Hennessy as he drove himself forward through the deep snow toward Sheriff Lacey's Suburban. He'd get a shotgun and fifty rounds, head south, and cross the fence in the thicker woods. If they were in control of the fence, they'd know he'd penetrated the grounds and would come for him. He welcomed it. He'd kill them all, find the kids, and take them home to their mother.

Patricia would know soon. And she would blame him. And she'd be right. In the moment of crisis, he hadn't tried to save his kids. He'd run away to save himself. Shot or not, he should have gone to get Hailey and the boys. He knew that's what his ex-wife would say. And she'd be right.

As he got closer to the sheriff's vehicle, he saw the media horde. He could make out reporters doing stand-ups in front of cameras. It dawned on him that maybe there was a better way to help his children.

"Mickey!" Cheyenne called after him.

He glanced over his shoulder to see her running from the command center, zipping her down coat and tugging on her wool cap. She caught up with him as he passed the barricade. Sheriff Lacey was snoozing in his truck with his shades on.

"Slow down, Mickey," she gasped. "Where are you going?"

Hennessy left the road, gesturing toward the stages and the lights. "I'm going to tell them that my fourteen-year-old kids have more balls than all the FBI agents gathered here combined."

She got around the front of him, putting her hands on his chest. "Maybe they do. But most of the time having a brain is better than having balls, Mickey. If you challenge Kane on this, if you challenge the Bureau on this, I guarantee you'll be kicked out. Then you'll be no help to your kids, who, by the way, I have good news about."

"What?"

"Pritoni said that according to the radio chatter they've disappeared," she replied. "Anarchy can't find them."

Hennessy surged with puzzled hope. *How did they get out of the stairwell?* But then he shook his head. "I've still got to do something."

Several minutes later, Hennessy entered the media encampment with Cheyenne by his side. They passed the Winnebagos and the campfires, and were instantly scrutinized as they worked their way toward the stages, where reporters were furiously chewing on the death of Sir Lawrence Treadwell and the heinous murder's effect on the markets, which dropped more than three percent of their value before rebounding nervously.

Hennessy jumped up on the stage with the most cameras in front of it and shouted, "My name is Michael Hennessy. I was director of security at the Jefferson Club. I was shot during the attack and escaped."

There was a moment's pause before the frenzy began. Every camera aimed at him, their klieg lights flaring in the winter morning light. Reporters started shouting questions at him about the attack and Sir Lawrence Treadwell's gruesome killing. He held up his good left hand.

"I'm here speaking to you as a father," he said after they quieted. "After what happened inside the grounds of the Jefferson Club this morning you may have heard some shooting and seen at least one Third Position soldier fall."

He paused to see the reporters pushing and straining to get their microphones and cameras closer, then said, "I believe the shooters were my children, two boys and a girl, triplets, fourteen years old. Their names are Bridger, Connor, and Hailey."

Cheyenne was standing behind the mob of reporters and cameramen jostling for position, and she heard and saw their reaction plainly. *Super-elite resort attacked by anti-global terrorists! Billionaires held hostage! Senator made mockery. Markets wobbling. The sixth-richest man in the world burned alive, and now three teenagers were inside the resort fighting back! It's the story of the millennium!*

Shouts went up: *"Where'd they get the guns? Are they inside? What do you think made them shoot?"*

"I don't know," Hennessy cried. "But please! My sons' and daughter's lives depend on you shutting up and listening to me!"

The unruly pack settled. He looked into as many camera lenses as he could, unable to say anything at first, feeling his face ripple from anger to confusion before settling on sincerity.

"General Anarchy and soldiers of the Third Position Army," he began. "I beg you to understand that young teenagers have underdeveloped brains—their frontal cortexes have not fully developed yet. The frontal cortex is where judgments are made. And, please, understand that . . ."

Hennessy faltered. Tears streamed down his cheeks. Many of the cameramen zoomed in on him as he choked out, "They're good kids. I love them. Please, if you find them, do not harm them. For the love of God, let them go. They're kids with their whole lives ahead of them. Show us that the Third Position is merciful. Show my children mercy."

As their father begged for their lives, the bruised and battered Hennessy triplets moved in a quiet shuffle from the laundry room past the lodge's heating plant and into the generator room, where two engines chugged and pistoned, feeding on natural gas, providing electricity to the lodge. The noise was almost deafening. The heat was like a sauna, the smell like stale fuel.

When they reached the east end of the generator room, Bridger saw that the door that led to the central storage area was ajar by a good two feet, propped open by a piece of lumber wedged under the handle.

Connor moved past him and hugged the inner wall, stopping at the doorjamb. He peeked his head around, taking in the storage room at a glance: It had almost the same footprint as the ballroom one floor above, but filled with the supplies and equipment necessary to run the lodge. The patio and pool furniture were stacked to the left of the door. Beyond them were pallets of restaurant supplies stacked six feet high. In the far northeast corner of the room, perhaps forty yards away, he could make out the pitch-darkness of the hallway that led to the bakery.

The basement was largely as he remembered it when they'd come down with their father the week earlier. Except for the piles of junk stacked in the center of the space: chunks of lumber, old mattresses, and cots; lodge uniforms, sheets, and towels; mountain bikes, baseball bats, and volleyball nets; and a thousand other things that had been thrown up in mounds between Connor and the Third Position soldier at the bottom of the stairs.

The soldier had his back to them and worked at a table, putting food and water on trays. Connor's attention swept to the line of doors on the opposite wall of the room.

He pulled back from the door and whispered to his siblings, "They emptied those little storage rooms on the other side and are using them as cells for the guys they're gonna put on trial. There's a guard about to feed them."

Hailey began to shake. "We're gonna get caught. They're gonna kill us."

Bridger hissed back at his sister, "No, they're not. We're going to get past him and out, do you understand?"

Hailey nodded, but there were tears in her eyes again.

"Do we try to save them?" Connor asked.

"Who?"

"Mr. Burns and them, who do you think?"

"No," Hailey said, panicked now. "You'll have to kill the guard. They'll hear the shots and come. If we get out, we'll tell somebody where they are."

The boys considered a moment, then nodded.

"We wait until the guard goes in one of the cells and then we run," Connor said.

"I'm right behind you," Bridger muttered, lifting the machine gun's barrel. He'd replaced the clip.

"Don't shoot," Hailey pleaded. "Whatever you do, don't shoot."

They heard a squeak as the guard rolled a service cart.

"Here we go," Connor whispered, seeing the guard open the third door.

Through the open door he could see Albert Crockett blindfolded and restrained on a bed. There was a television in the room with him. The guard went inside.

Connor ducked around the doorjamb and took off on tiptoe, his heart racing. He knew how life-and-death it all was, and was determined to live. But he was no more than ten feet into the room when he heard the musical rattle of lumber falling to the cement floor. The door to the generator room slammed shut with a resounding crash that cut off the pounding roar of the generators and left the storage room strangely quiet.

Connor skittered behind and partially beneath a chaise longue, panting. Bridger dove into the dark shadows beyond a pallet of soap boxes, while his sister jumped over him and sprawled behind a pallet stacked with soft-drink cans in twelve-pack boxes. Connor couldn't believe one of them had kicked out the brace. He bit his lips to keep from moaning.

The guard left Albert Crockett's cell, his head swiveling. He picked up his gun. But then the guard's head snapped right to look toward the stairs. He straightened.

Connor saw legs appear on the staircase and then General Anarchy descended into view. *He knows we're down here,* he thought, blood roaring through his temples. *He's hunting for us. The guard's gonna tell him about the door!*

"What's wrong, Carpenter?" General Anarchy asked.

The Third Position soldier relaxed and shook his head. "Door to the generator room slammed shut. I had it open to get some heat in here. Every time someone opens that door upstairs, it creates some kind of wind tunnel and slams the door. I thought I had it propped up, but guess not good enough."

"Have they eaten?" General Anarchy asked.

"Just started with Crockett," the guard replied.

Suddenly Albert Crockett shuffled into his cell doorway. His ankles were still tied, but the hood was gone and his hands were free. The corporate raider looked old, frail, and petrified, holding on to the doorjamb as if it were a mast in a hurricane sea.

"I'll give you another hundred million, Anarchy,"

Crockett said. "I'll give you five hundred million. Just let me go."

General Anarchy acted like he'd just been insulted. "I don't care about money, Mr. Crockett. It's not what drives me."

"Money drives everyone," Crockett shot back. "A billion."

General Anarchy took three quick strides to the tycoon and jammed his pistol's muzzle against Crockett's bony throat. "Money drives everyone except the man who lusts for power, Mr. Crockett. Power is my currency."

He drove Crockett back into his cell and pushed him sprawling on the bed. Crockett cowered and held his hands up, fearing he'd be struck. General Anarchy spun away and marched out, holstering the gun and barking at Carpenter, "Take him to the courtroom. Klinefelter too. We'll consider their crimes next."

Crockett started screaming behind him. "A billion five! A billion five!"

Then Klinefelter's deep muffled Germanic voice joined him from the cell next door. "A billion five! I'll match it in euros! A billion five!"

Chin Hoc Pan's call rang from behind the door to the fourth cell. "Billion five. I match it too. You let me go! Billion five dollars!"

Then Connor heard Jack Doore and Aaron Grant shouting that they would pay two billion. The teenager understood their terror. They must have seen Sir Lawrence's death on television and now feared their own.

General Anarchy ignored their pleas. "Where's Burns?" he asked Carpenter.

"Seventh door," Carpenter shouted over the billionaires' desperate pleas.

The general took a step, then seemed to think better of it. He stopped and bellowed at the hostages, "Silence, or you won't be fed or watered!"

The bids and cries died. General Anarchy nodded to himself with satisfaction, then asked Carpenter how to get to the laundry. The Third Position soldier pointed to the door twenty-five feet to Connor's right.

"You're clear on your assignment?" General Anarchy asked.

Carpenter answered firmly, "I'll do what has to be done, General."

General Anarchy nodded, heading toward the door to the generator room, drawing his pistol. He passed Hailey's hiding place behind pallets of Cokes, and then Bridger's behind a stack of soap boxes. Connor saw Anarchy coming right at him. Shaking madly, he got Cobb's pistol out in front of him.

The Third Position leader almost walked past Connor. But then he stopped, less than five feet away. Connor's heart battered his rib cage as he tried to aim at Anarchy's ankles.

CHAPTER TWENTY-SEVEN

"What are you doing for our husbands?" Lydia Crockett was demanding in a semi-hysterical pitch when Mickey Hennessy and Cheyenne O'Neil returned to the command center.

The takeover artist's wife was standing in the small conference room, dressed in warm winter clothes and looking like she hadn't slept an hour since her release the prior afternoon. Stephanie Doore was with her, looking in a similar state of duress. So was Margaret Grant. A brawny man in his late thirties with a blond mustache stood next to the wives, wearing a black Kevlar vest over a dull green fleece pullover.

They were all facing Willis Kane, who said, "Everything we can at the moment."

"Are you going to rescue them?" Stephanie Doore asked.

"I can't discuss that with you," Kane said.

"They burned Larry Treadwell!" Margaret Grant shouted, exploding into tears.

Kane looked stricken, and rubbed his hand across his shaved head. "I know. But they've said they've booby-trapped your husbands. If we go in prematurely—"

"Prematurely?" Lydia Crockett cried. "They're going to put my husband and those other men on trial and kill them one by one!"

"Mrs. Crockett," he said. "It takes time to get the necessary people on the ground. My advance team got here less than twenty-four hours ago."

The brawny man in the Kevlar vest said, "Agent Kane, I'm Harry Mann with Greenwater & Associates. Mrs. Crockett called me last night. I have twenty-five armed extraction specialists on the ground already as well as two of our helicopters. Shows what private sector security can do in a pinch."

"I don't care if you've got a hundred Arnold Schwarzeneggers out there," Kane growled, taking a step toward Mann. "You or your mercenaries go anywhere near the club grounds and I'll arrest you. Every one of you. Understand?"

Lydia Crockett squeezed her hands into fists. "We are not going to stand by and let our husbands die while you twiddle your thumbs, Agent Kane."

"And I'm not going to stand here and listen to threats, Mrs. Crockett," Kane replied coldly. "The warning stands. You interfere, you will go to jail. Now leave. I have to figure out how to save your husbands' lives."

The women and Mann stood there a second, their fury visible and palpable.

"We'll see what the press thinks," Stephanie Doore said, then turned on her heel and headed for the door, barely giving Hennessy a glance before plunging outside with the other women in tow.

Harry Mann picked up a parka off one of the chairs, then laid a business card on the table and said, "If you need me, I'm here."

"Comforting to know," Kane said, then turned his back on him, heading into the communications area of the command center.

The private security specialist appraised Hennessy and Cheyenne with a hard smirk, then left. Hennessy waited until the door to the center closed before following Kane. The CIRG commander was rubbing his eyes, looking beat. But he said, "I saw what you said out there, Mick. I appreciate you didn't try to force a confrontation. I've got all I can handle."

"Yeah, well, I was never one for pissing matches," Hennessy replied before looking to Pritoni. "Anything more about my kids?"

Pritoni tugged down his headset. "They're still looking for them."

"Have you told Patricia?" Kane asked. "She needs to know."

"I've left messages on her cell. I suppose I could leave her an e-mail too. Or maybe look up the name of the company that rented the sailboat to them. Is there a computer I can use?"

Agent Seitz gestured to his. Hennessy took the hostage negotiator's chair and called up Yahoo! He signed on to his mailbox and opened it. His heart skipped two beats.

"Hailey e-mailed me!" he shouted, clicking furiously on the link with the subject *Dad Where Are You?*

"When?" Kane said, coming in behind him.

"Last night, I think," he replied, waiting anxiously for the screen to pop up. And when it did, Hennessy devoured every word:

Dad? Where are you? We've been looking everywhere for you. Please don't be dead. We are hiding in your office. One of them found us in your apartment. He kicked Connor in the stomach and the head. Bridger and I shot him with our paintball guns and knocked him out. He's tied up in your bedroom with razor blades between his toes (Bridger's idea, not mine). Please find us. Or leave us a message anyway.   *Hailey*

"Jesus," Kane said, reading over Hennessy's shoulder. "Shot him with paintball guns and knocked him out?"

"Those kids got some serious balls," Phelps, the hostage rescue leader, said.

Hennessy reread the message. He felt a wave of gratitude splash over him. Some of what he'd tried to teach them had sunk in. They were trying to survive.

"Answer her," Cheyenne said.

Hennessy startled and typed:

Hailey, I am all right. I am in an FBI command center outside the club gate. I was shot the night of the attack, but managed to escape and bring help. Everyone here thinks you and your brothers are brave and you are and I'm proud of you for that. But, please, don't shoot at them anymore. Tell us where you are now. I'll wait by the computer. Write back. I love you all.

Dad

He hit SEND and saw the message blip into the ether, imagined it bouncing off the satellite and traveling like a beam inside the Jefferson Club Lodge. "Answer," he murmured to himself. "C'mon, now, Hailey. Answer."

"They used the computer in your office?" Kane asked.

"Must have," Hennessy said. He hesitated, asking himself how they got in. Then he answered himself out loud. "The master key. They've got it."

"Want to give us that in English?" Kane asked.

"I left my master key to the lodge in the apartment," Hennessy said. "They've got it. It opens every single electronically locked door in the lodge. Except one, anyway."

General Anarchy's white shoes and the bottom of the Third Position Army leader's tuxedo pants had not moved in ten seconds. Tears dripped down Connor's cheeks. Snot oozed from his nose as he tried to aim the pistol and not breathe. Then he heard a match strike and then cheek and lip popping sounds.

Connor craned his head around to look up through

the chaise longue's mesh. He could see General Anarchy's face blurred in profile lit by the match. He saw the stubby cigar's band: an ornate emblem in blue and gold. In the ember glow of the cigar he saw the Third Position leader in profile as he puffed. Connor thought General Anarchy's painted smile was right out of a horror movie. He closed his eyes and smelled the distinctive, acrid odor of Anarchy's cigar in his nose like the probing tentacles of some ruthless, predatory creature. He begged God to make the Third Position leader walk on.

General Anarchy took a step, the pistol held loosely in his right hand, puffing, billowing a cloud. He took several more steps and opened the door to the generator room. The pulsing engine roar returned and then died when the door shut behind him.

Connor's attention shot to the guard. He'd opened a cell near the stairs and gone inside. Connor scrambled out from under the chaise longues. His brother and sister were already dodging through the stacks of canned and dry goods toward the only other exit.

Connor reached the last open space they'd have to cross before the doorway. Bridger leaned out, then snapped his head back, panic in his eyes. They heard a key put in a lock and then a door swinging open on squeaky hinges. Bridger peeked again, just as Aaron Grant said, "That's all?"

As the guard went into Grant's cell, Bridger coiled and leaped out into the open, running across the floor. He disappeared into the dark hallway on the other side of the room. Hailey and Connor bolted after him. Connor saw the light shining from Grant's cell in his peripheral vision, before being swallowed by the shadows. Hailey slowed. He did too and padded carefully backward, gun raised, watching the light back in the basement, sure they'd be followed, until the passage doglegged left and the darkness became almost complete. All of them were breathing hard. Sweat beaded and rolled down Connor's face as he moved by Braille. It felt insanely long until they reached the staircase to the bakery, and he kept thinking he was going to hear a shout or a crash.

"Where's Hailey?" Bridger whispered. "We need the key."

"I'm getting it," she whispered frantically.

With a low buzz the door opened and the stairway flooded with soft red light. They went toward the light down a short hallway before stepping into the lodge bakery between two of the massive stainless-steel ovens. The smell inside was deliciously stale. Bridger spotted a tray of day-old oatmeal raisin cookies on the prep table. They all started grabbing the cookies and stuffing them into their mouths and into their pockets.

"Oh, these are good," Hailey whispered.

"The best," Connor said. "Just need milk."

Bridger wolfed another and grabbed two more. So did Hailey. Connor kept watching behind them as they passed through a stainless-steel swinging door into a hallway. This one had an arched tile ceiling. The walls were covered in cut limestone and the floor was terracotta bricks. It was like stepping into a cave tunnel. The air was chilly. The walls looked damp and shimmered in the pinpoint lights that lined the way to the lodge's vault and wine cellar. Connor turned off the light, plunging them back into blackness.

"Why'd you do that?" Bridger demanded.

"There's a camera over the vault, remember?" Connor replied, then felt his way down the left side of the hall to the wine cellar's massive oak door. Hailey fumbled a minute, but got it unlocked.

Bridger shut the door and flipped on the light, revealing a long sunken room with a high ceiling. The floors were limestone slabs quarried on the club grounds. The floor-to-ceiling ceramic bins on the walls overflowed with wine bottles. Aside from the oak table, chairs, sets of silver *tastevins*, and crystal glasses, the only decoration was a large framed original lithograph by Toulouse-Lautrec of a prancing court jester with the legs of a goat sticking out from beneath his regalia. The jester danced with two bottles of Bordeaux, drinking one. Red wine dribbled off his pointy beard and devilish smile.

Connor glanced out through the peephole in the wine cellar door, seeing the dim lines of the stainless steel bars that blocked entry to the vault and safe across the hallway. His brother and sister were already moving toward the lithograph. He followed, saying, "How come they haven't come for the stuff in the vault? There's got to be a lot of money and jewels in there."

"What do they want jewelry and stuff like that for?" Bridger said. "They've got a billion already. And jewelry can probably be traced."

"So can money," Hailey said.

"Right," Connor said.

"I don't know and I don't care," Bridger replied, rubbing his stomach. "Let's just find the lock and see if Dad's card works."

They reached the framed lithograph and started examining it. Bridger took hold of the edge of the frame and cautiously tugged. It didn't move an inch. Then he tried moving it upward. The frame didn't budge. It didn't move when he tried to move the lithograph laterally both left and right.

"I give up," Bridger said.

"Try twisting it," Hailey said.

Bridger sighed and tried to twist the frame to the left. No movement. But when he pressed hard on the lower left corner of the frame, the entire lithograph shifted by several degrees, revealing an electronic key slot.

He grinned, then looked at the card in Hailey's hand. "Okay, fifty-fifty."

"It's the vault the card doesn't open," Connor said. "Definitely the vault."

Hailey stuck the electronic key card in the lock.

At the opposite end of the lodge's basement, General Anarchy eased past the industrial-sized hamper set beneath the laundry chutes. He had the lights on and his eyes moved to the doors to the loading dock and the utility stairwell. Both were dead-bolted. He studied the hamper until he spotted a smear of blood on the frame. He touched it and found it just starting to gel.

"Conniving brats," he said, turning to the door that led outside. He stepped out onto the loading dock and shivered in the cold air long enough to inspect the snow in the parking lot and driveway. Not a track. But one of the corpses by the dumpster, one of the guards, was on his back, while the others were face down. He frowned, trying to figure out what that meant.

"General?" Radio called in his ear. *"We found Cobb. You won't believe what those kids did to him."*

"I'll be right up. Anything else?"

"A herd of elk passed through the fence, coming from the north, two miles from the gate."

Five minutes later, General Anarchy stood in the lodge's grand atrium with Truth. Cobb was still digging specks of paint from the corners of his eyes.

"Those little fucks are gonna die," Cobb said. "You mark my words, General."

"They sure handled you, Cobb," Truth said, amused.

Cobb stood up and snarled, "I won't be so kind-hearted again, Truth."

"Go to the basement and pick up their trail," Anarchy said. "I found blood in a hamper in the laundry down there and they didn't go out the loading dock door."

Truth nodded. "I had the perimeter walked fifteen minutes ago. They haven't left the lodge. They're still in here."

"Good," Cobb said, getting his combat knife from its sheath at his hips. He rubbed his thumb along the blade. "They wanted to play with guns and razors, they're gonna play with guns and razors."

CHAPTER TWENTY-EIGHT

Mickey Hennessy hit refresh on his e-mail box for the twentieth time since replying to Hailey's message. Nothing. His mind began to spin dark fantasies to explain why they hadn't written back. *Where are they? If the Third Position is manning the surveillance system, how did they manage to beat it?* He racked his brains trying to figure it out and nothing became clearer than the lack of change in his e-mail box: Empty.

"Which one?" Cheyenne said, setting a cup of coffee and a sandwich in front of him.

"Which one what?"

"You said your electronic master key opened every lock except one."

Bitterness spiced Hennessy's laugh. "The steel-bar door to the vault. Only Burns, Isabel, and I have that key." He dug in his pocket and came up with a key shaped like a stout sword with a pitted pattern on its blade. He laughed again. "Key to a fortune."

"Why's that seem funny to you and sad at the same time?"

His laugh was softer, shot through with loss.

"Because I wouldn't tell the kids which door the master key wouldn't open," he said. "They were pestering me about it all week, and I was good-naturedly ribbing them about the secret. You know, a game we were playing. They're good detectives. They narrowed it down to the vault and the entrance to the secret passage Burns built between his house and the wine cellar in the lodge basement. I was going to tell them it was the vault before I put them on the plane this morning."

"You'll get the chance to do it yourself."

"I hope so," he said and reached out to hit the RE-FRESH button on his browser. But his cell phone rang. He grabbed it and flipped it open.

A rough, anxious voice called to him over a staticky reception. *"Tell me they're going to be okay, Michael!"* said Patricia, his ex-wife, breaking into sobs. *"Tell me they're going to be okay!"* Patricia had always been prone to hysteria, but there was no exaggerating or undermining the anguish in her voice.

"They're gonna be okay," Hennessy soothed, feeling sick all over again. "They're tough kids. Where are you?"

It took several moments for Patricia to calm down enough to tell him she was in St. John, Virgin Islands. She and her new husband docked late last night. She went out early to get breakfast by herself. CNN was playing in the little restaurant by the marina. She'd seen him pleading for their children's lives.

"They burned that man to death," Patricia said hollowly. *"And then the kids started shooting. Why? Why would they do that? What would possess them?"*

"I don't know—outrage, maybe?" he said. "A desire to right some wrong."

"That's just the sort of nonsense I expected from you!" she shouted. *"They might be dead because of the nonsense you put in their heads!"*

"They might be alive because of what I've managed to teach them in the little time you let me be with them!" he shot back. "Hailey e-mailed me from my office last night. When the other hostages were released, they stayed behind looking for me. One of the Third Position soldiers found them in my apartment. He punched and kicked Connor and held a machine gun to his head. Bridger and Hailey shot him with their paintball guns, knocked him out, tied him up, and left him."

"They did?"

"They did, and they've managed to avoid capture while causing significant injury to the enemy," he said. "If you don't remember, in the military they call it *valor.*"

"I remember valor usually involves getting shot," Patricia retorted, her voice rising. *"Those maniacs are hunting them. It's all they're talking about on the news shows. Our children and the hostages. Whether they'll live or die."*

"Don't listen," Hennessy said.

"How can't I?" she shrieked back. *"It's everywhere!*

People are downloading the trial and the execution to their iPods and phones by the hundreds of thousands. They had one expert on just now who said that this might be the first global event to unfold primarily on the Internet. My babies are in the middle of it!"

Hennessy didn't know what to say.

"Ted and I are coming straight to Montana," Patricia said.

Hennessy sighed. "I wish you would, Patricia. I can't face this alone."

Inside the tunnel beyond the secret wine cellar door, the triplets crept toward Horatio Burns's house, feeling weak and jelly-kneed after the repeated surges of adrenaline that had doused them all in the last several hours. Part of Hailey wanted to rejoice. They'd gotten free of the lodge. But she kept looking back down the dimly lit, musty-smelling passage as it began to climb in elevation. *What if General Anarchy knows about the passage? He's known about everything else, hasn't he? Are we safe in here?*

"I think we're okay," Bridger said, as if reading her thoughts. "They'll look for tracks in the snow and find nothing. They'll think we're still in the lodge."

"Definitely," Connor said, smiling and yawning at the same time. Then he started shivering and grew morose. "We shot people. What if we've killed them?"

"What if we did?" Bridger asked coldly. "That guy in Dad's apartment would've kicked you to death for giggles. They burned Sir Lawrence alive. I feel good about shooting at them. I'll feel bad if I didn't kill them. I'll shoot again if I have the chance."

"No, you won't," Hailey said. "We're waiting this out until dark and then leaving. They won't know we're gone until we cross through the fence."

Ahead a heavy wooden door blocked the way. It had a small square window in it about head-high. Connor got to it first and looked through into a dimly lit office.

"It's clear," he said.

Hailey slid the master key in the lock. With a heavy click, the door swung open on its hinges several inches, revealing itself as a bookcase and the small square window as a two-way mirror. Connor pushed the door open slowly, with Bridger covering him with the machine gun.

They entered the room behind a massive desk that looked freshly rubbed with oil. The desktop was neatly cleared but for the desktop computer with a flat-screen display and a half-dozen pictures of Isabel Burns arranged around it.

The desk chair was distressed oxblood leather. So were the couches and chairs around the room. The shelves were filled with books and Western art. There was a gun case built into the far wall. Connor began shivering again. It was cold in the room. He went to the thermostat. *Fifty-two degrees?*

"Guy likes it freezing," Connor murmured, turning the heat up to seventy-two.

Bridger didn't respond. He was crouched at the outer door, listening. After several moments, he stood, raised the machine gun, and nodded to his sister. Hailey opened the door to the foyer to the mansion. The slate floor was laid out in a concentric mosaic pattern around a fountain drained of water. Overhead a crystal chandelier, dark.

Bridger bobbed his head out the door, then looked back. "No one's home."

He eased into the hall. Hailey followed, seeing a staircase built of wrought iron and split ponderosa logs on the other side of the fountain. Beyond that, she could make out a great room the size of a small house. There wasn't a light on that she could see in the entire place.

"No one's here," Bridger murmured to his siblings. Feeling confident now, he moved into the foyer, heading toward the great room.

"Where are you going?" Connor asked, hurrying after him, with Hailey behind.

"Kitchen," Bridger said. "There's gotta be a ton of food in there."

Hailey almost protested, but she was just as famished as her brothers. She hurried after them through the great room and past a dining table for twenty and a wet bar and into a kitchen fitted with an eight-burner stove in fire-engine-red enamel.

Bridger went straight to the matching fridge, saying, "I'm gonna chow." He yanked it open and his spirits sank.

"Whatsa matter?" Hailey asked.

"Nothing in here but like mustard and stuff," Bridger said.

Hailey got around the back of her brother and saw it was true: Besides the staple condiments, pickles, and jellies, the refrigerator was remarkably empty. A single half-drunk quart of orange juice. Not even an egg.

"Think they eat all their meals at the lodge?" Connor asked.

"Sure hope not," Bridger grunted, then he began opening doors and cabinets. They were filled with small appliances, dishes, glassware, and spices. But no food-stuffs.

While her brothers continued their search, Hailey set the .22 on the counter and wandered into the hallway off the kitchen, looking for another thermostat. She could almost see her breath, it was so cold. She flipped on the light in the hallway and saw a small alarm panel blinking red and flashing EXTERIOR ALARM ACTIVATED.

Next to the panel was the door to the pantry. She went inside and found it bulging with canned and dry goods. Delighted, Hailey grabbed four cans of chicken noodle soup, a box of dried spaghetti, a box of Tris-cuits, and a jar of Russian caviar. When she marched proudly into the kitchen with her loot, Bridger was still searching the cabinets.

"Pantry's in the hallway," she said, setting the booty on the countertop.

"Now we're talking," Connor said, tearing open the Triscuit box before frowning. "Caviar? That stuff's expensive."

"They got like twenty jars of it back there. They won't miss it."

Connor wrestled with the top to the caviar jar while Bridger set about heating the chicken noodle soup. Within minutes they were sitting at the kitchen counter devouring their feast. Bridger decided he liked caviar immediately. He went to the pantry and found his own jar. He scooped out a dollop and dropped it in his soup. And another.

Bridger grunted, looking delirious with the taste the caviar gave to his soup. He lifted the entire bowl and drank it.

"Slob," Hailey said.

Bridger put the bowl down with a satisfying belch. "Much better," he said. He grabbed a handful of crackers and poured more soup. He added caviar to it and began to slurp that down.

Hailey got up and headed back toward the great room.

"Where are you going?" Bridger called after her.

"Mr. Burns's office. I'm gonna see if Dad answered me."

"The next trial's starting in twelve minutes," Connor said.

"I know."

Hailey went to the desk and found the computer on with the screen dark. She turned it on. Connor drifted in with a dinner plate covered with crackers and a caviar jar.

"Don't be too freaked if he doesn't answer," Connor cautioned.

"Shut up," Hailey said. "He's gonna answer. You watch."

"I'll watch," he said, turning on the plasma TV in the corner. ESPN's roundup of the New Year's bowl games was playing.

Hailey watched the flat-screen monitor on the desk

glow blue and show a prompt that asked, *Are you sure you want to shut down?*

She hit CANCEL on the prompt and the screen jumped to a desktop format. She clicked on the YES! Internet browser. Soon she was at the prompt for her own e-mail account. She lowered her head, pleading with God to let her hear from her father, and then struck ENTER.

At virtually the same time, Connor changed channels to CNN and gasped.

Hailey saw her father's name on the queue of the incoming e-mail and leaped to her feet, hands raised high overhead, tears spilling from her eyes. "He's alive! He answered! Dad answered!"

Connor was pointing crazily at the television. "Dad's right there!"

Bridger ran in, crying, "Where?"

On the television screen, their father stood before a bank of microphones. Connor hugged Bridger. "I knew he was okay. I knew it!"

"They're kids with their whole lives ahead of them," their father was saying. "Show us that the Third Position is merciful. Show my children mercy."

Then the screen returned to a reporter with the front gate to the Jefferson Club visible in the distance behind her. "Hennessy has not seen or heard from his three children since the initial attack," she said. "But one thing is sure. They are being called heroes across the country for taking on the Third Position in the wake of Sir Lawrence Treadwell's brutal execution."

"Heroes?" Hailey said, bewildered and wiping her tears on her sleeve.

"Who cares?" Bridger said. "There's no reason for us to be here anymore. Dad's safe. We got to go out and run for it. It's only five miles."

Hailey sobered. "The exterior alarm to this house is enabled. It's in the hallway toward the pantry. If we go out any door we'll trigger it and they'll be on us. It's broad daylight. We'd never make it. If we're going to go, we go at dark."

Connor said, "Answer Dad. See what he thinks we should do."

General Anarchy paced in the ballroom, watching Cristoph loom over his computer. "What are the hits like?"

"Seven million unique visitors in the last two hours," Cristoph boasted. "All with cookies downloaded into their systems. We've struck a chord. They're ready for more."

"The servers?"

"Forty-eight percent capacity," Cristoph said, his attention drifting from General Anarchy to the Third Position soldiers leading Albert Crockett and Friedrich Klinefelter into the Court of Public Opinion. Both were hooded. The corporate raider walked stooped over. The hedge fund manager came behind him, his head swiveling at every noise. The guards lashed them in witness chairs in front of the bench, ten feet apart.

"Okay, people," Rose called out as General Anarchy moved toward the prosecution table inside the courtroom set. "We are live in six minutes!"

CHAPTER TWENTY-NINE

The hostage rescue leader snapped shut his satellite phone inside the FBI command center. "Team two will be on the ground in Bozeman in two and a half hours, SAC," Phelps said. "I've sent them the plan and the 3-D map of the place. Waiting for their comments. I'm requesting that Montana Air National Guard ferry them up here and give us backup."

Willis Kane glanced at the wall. It was 10:57 a.m. in Montana. He'd have the firepower and know-how he'd need in place by 3:00 p.m. at the latest. "Assume we are go at last light," he said. "Move your snipers in close without triggering the fence."

The FBI negotiator bristled. "You decide to attack without even letting me—"

Kane shut Seitz down. "If they'd start talking and stop killing people in cold blood, we would start talking, Kirk. If not, once team two arrives we're going in there. That came from the President himself. You don't like it, take it up with the man."

Seitz shook his head. "You attack, they'll all be dead," he said. "These guys are sociopaths. You won't save anyone."

Ten feet away, Mickey Hennessy said, "My kids are coming out of there alive."

Seitz looked at Hennessy, saw the emotion, and shrank. "I'm sorry, Mr. Hennessy. But when violent men isolate themselves, they tend to look at the world in a different light than you and me. They feel desperate and committed. And I want my opposition to the plan noted. I'm not taking the heat for it."

Hennessy's attention jumped to Kane and then to Phelps. "I have faith in these guys, Agent Seitz," he said. "I believe they'll save my children."

With that, Hennessy went into the galley, looking for coffee. But as he did, he worried about the things that could happen if the raid did go south. He imagined the Jefferson Club Lodge in flames or General Anarchy finding his kids. He wondered if he'd ever have the wherewithal to tell Patricia they were dead, if he'd ever be able to hear the words himself and actually understand them.

"Two minutes to the third trial and the market's getting jittery again," Cheyenne announced when he returned. She'd taken his seat at the computer and had just pulled up the Third Position homepage, again watching the protesters in Seattle in 1999. Hennessy looked from the Internet feed to the Bloomberg report, wondering how anti-globalism had gone from a street movement to a militant force capable of shaking world markets.

"Can I check my e-mail once more?" Hennessy asked.

Cheyenne bobbed her head and leaned aside so he could reach the keyboard. He hit REFRESH on the browser he had up and there it was.

"She answered," he shouted, arms thrown overhead, oblivious to the pain in his arm. "Hailey answered!"

Grinning, Cheyenne got up from the chair, letting him in. She watched over his shoulder while he accessed the message, scanning the words, then calling out, "They're in the Burnses' house. They used the tunnel!"

"What tunnel?" Kane asked, moving in behind him.

"There's a secret passage between the lodge and the Burnses' residence. I'm about the only person who knows about it other than Horatio and Isabel. I don't even think my boss knows. But I let it slip to the kids when I showed them the wine cellar."

Cheyenne was still reading the message. "We need the Burnses' alarm code. They want to turn it off so they can run."

"I don't know it," Hennessy said. "They were secretive about that kind of thing."

Kane looked at Cheyenne. "Find Isabel Burns. Get the number."

Hennessy typed his reply and hit ENTER.

In Burns's office, Hailey saw her father's answer and clapped her hands giddily. She and her brothers devoured the message, which concluded by asking if they had a working phone and with the news that their mother was worried sick.

"What else is new?" Connor asked, but felt his eyes were watering.

Bridger picked up the phone. "Dead," he said, dropping it in its cradle.

Connor studied how the phone line traveled with another attached to the computer down through a hole cut in the top of the desk. He ducked under the desk and tracked the lines to a round metal lid set in the floor. He pried up the lid and grinned.

"There's a VOIP line down here," he said, unplugging the telephone line from its socket and attaching it to the converter beside it.

"No way," Hailey said.

Their father had bought a voice-over Internet protocol line to be installed at their mother's house to save money on long-distance calls the year before. Using a VOIP line, a call travels through the Internet. They talked to their father on it all the time.

"Can't believe Mr. Burns cares about long-distance charges," Bridger said, going around the back of the computer and plugging the telephone's cable into the computer.

"Probably why he's so rich," Hailey said.

Connor got up, picked up the portable phone, punched TALK, and instantly heard the VOIP dial tone. "We're up!" he said, punching their father's number.

His siblings pressed in around him, hearing, *"Hennessy."*

"Dad!" they all cried, choked up again.

"Connor? Bridger! Hailey! I can't tell you how happy I am to hear your voices."

"Yours, too," Connor said, tears dripping down his cheeks.

"Yeah," Bridger choked. "What do you want us to do?"

"Have you found Mrs. Burns?" Hailey asked.

"Still trying to track her down. But I'm going to put you on the phone with Willis Kane, remember him? He's in charge and wants to talk to you."

Kane's gruff voice came. *"Who's on the line?"*

"We're all here, Mr. Kane," Connor said.

"You've all shown great courage and resourcefulness and loyalty to your father and I'm proud of you guys," Kane said. *"But right now I need your help."*

He started hitting them with questions: How many Third Position soldiers had they seen? That was hard to tell because they all wore hoods and makeup. Did they know where the hostages were being held? When they told him about the storage units below the ballroom, Kane's questions turned rapid-fire. How many guards were watching the hostages? What kind of weapons did they have? What hostage was where? How close were they to the generator room?

"We walked right through the generator room," Hailey replied.

Kane paused, then asked, *"Could you go back there and shut down the system?"*

All three of the teenagers looked sick. Then they heard their father arguing in the background, telling

Kane he wasn't going to let his kids take that kind of risk.

But Connor said, "If you think it's necessary, I'll go."

"What?" Bridger said. "No."

"We had the chance to rescue the hostages and we didn't," Connor said.

There was a collective silence that was finally broken by Kane. *"No. You do not move until we've got the code to the house alarm."*

"You just want us to stay here and wait?" Connor said, somewhat indignantly.

"You're going to be observers. Can you see the lodge from your position?"

Bridger went and peeked out one of the curtains. Through the trees, he could make out the loading dock door, the pool, and the access road. Kane told them to keep a watch. If they saw any movement, they were to report it immediately. Then he asked them what weapons they had.

Connor told him, then added, "And there's a whole bunch of hunting rifles and shotguns in Mr. Burns's gun case."

"Replace your .22 with a shotgun," Kane said. *"Semiautomatic if he's got it. I've got to go. We'll have you out of there and back with your dad in no time."*

Their father came back on the line. *"Do what Willis said. Limit your movement as much as possible and keep quiet!"*

"What do we do if they're going to kill someone else?" Bridger asked.

"You're going to stay put and be witnesses so we

can put these guys behind bars for life. Be aware. Of time. Of place, Of anything you see."

"We can't protect ourselves?" Connor said unhappily.

They heard the hesitation before he said, *"You're damn right you protect yourself. Look, the Third Position site just went live. The trial's starting."*

Hailey was already calling it up. "Dad," she said.

"Yes, noodle?"

"We were worried about you."

"I was too, Hailey."

"I love you."

Her father cleared his throat and said, *"I love you too, Hailey. I love all of you."*

"We love you too, Dad," Bridger said.

Connor started to cry again. "We thought you were dead."

"I know," Hennessy came back after a long pause. *"I thought I was too."*

But he's not! And we're not! Connor thought gleefully as Hailey got up from the desk chair, the back of her hands pressed against her lips. Bridger slid into the chair and clicked on the hyperlink to the Court of Public Opinion. The courtroom filled the screen.

Albert Crockett sat erect and blindfolded to the left of the bench, with Friedrich Klinefelter on the right toward the jury. The big-screen monitor sat dark on a stand at the base of the bench between them. Citizen's Defender Emilia was visible, standing in her mourning clothes. General Anarchy stood ramrod-straight across the aisle.

Bailiff Mouse entered behind Klinefelter. She struck

the floor three times with her staff, crying, *"The People of the Third Position versus Albert Maxwell Crockett and Friedrich Herman Klinefelter.* Judge New Truth presiding. All rise!"

Inside the mock courtroom, the harlequin justice climbed the bench, took his seat, and smashed his gavel before ordering the defendants' hoods and restraints removed.

Crockett raised his chin, blinking. The wrinkles around his eyes looked like fissures in parched sandy dirt. The remnants of his tuxedo were hopelessly wrinkled and dusty. His chin was stubbled, streaked with grime, and moved ever so slightly as he craned his head around, taking in the particulars of the court, a surreal expression spiraling through his face.

Klinefelter drew his head back into his shoulders like a turtle retreating. From this bunkered position he let his attention dance about, stopping on Citizen's Defender Emilia before taking in General Anarchy, the jury, and Judge Truth.

"I have done no crimes," the hedge fund manager declared. "None. Release us."

Crockett's daze evaporated. The corporate raider fixed his attention on the jury before finding the nearest camera and growling at it, "And neither have I. These men are barbarians. They burned a man alive! Don't believe anything they might say."

Judge Truth gaveled him into silence. "General Anarchy, what are the charges?"

Without a glance at the defendants, General Anarchy announced, "Vulturism, parasitism, racketeering, fraud, and murder. Lots of murder."

Klinefelter's head shot out from his shoulders. "I am innocent of these things!" he yelled at the hooded jury. "I killed no one. What is this vulturism? I make investments. No racketeering! No murder! I play the market. That is all."

"You are a parasite in the global intestine, Herr Klinefelter," General Anarchy said, moving from behind the prosecution table. He threw his left arm toward Crockett. "And your partner in crime is the king of vulture capital. Together you've plundered and laid waste to irreplaceable resources all over the world. You've taken the livelihoods and savings of tens of thousands. You've doomed children to poverty and ignorance. And you're both accessories before and after the fact in murder."

Judge Truth demanded, "How do you plead?"

"Not guilty!" Crockett cried. "I am not a vulture. I am not a murderer. I don't have one penny I have not earned fairly and legally! Not guilty, sir!"

"And I am no parasite!" Klinefelter roared. He was rocking back and forth against the restraints that still held his ankles to the chair. "Not guilty to all these charges!"

Judge Truth banged his gavel. "General Anarchy," he said. "Present your case."

Over the next thirty minutes, the Third Position leader again used a cutting-edge multimedia presentation that led the hooded jurors and the Internet audience through a story of high-stakes financial chicanery. He started with the tale of Harrison Timber.

Forty years before most people had heard of the concept of sustainability, Harrison Timber, a family-owned operation based in Friedleburg, Oregon, was practicing the art, selectively cutting trees as they matured, carefully planting new trees to replace them. A film of the Harrison lands revealed lush forested mountainsides. Anarchy said the Harrisons believed in managing their lands to produce lumber indefinitely and profitably. In that spirit the family decided to let their workers share in the company's good fortune, selling shares in a limited offering that was snapped up by Harrison employees and a select group of private investors. One of them was Albert Crockett.

Harrison Timber had been on Crockett's radar for years. The raider liked to analyze the underlying assets of companies and then figure out ways to get control of those assets at a discount and then sell them at a profit. In this case, Crockett wanted the timber. Within months of the offering, he bought out the shares of the other private investors and demanded a seat on Harrison's board. Once in a position of power, Crockett advocated that the company increase production to meet Asian demand.

Because of the advanced growing techniques Harrison used, the company actually could raise its yield and still keep the forest sustainable. The family reluctantly agreed to Crockett's demands. But to raise production, they had to borrow money to buy new equipment. In response to the sudden debt load, Crockett demanded more stock in the company be released on the market. He bought most of it.

"And then what do you think he did?" General Anarchy asked.

CHAPTER THIRTY

Inside the CIRG command center, Cheyenne O'Neil said, "I know what he did. He demanded more timber harvested and more stock sales until he controlled the company."

On screen, General Anarchy said as much, then activated a video that showed mountainous terrain stripped of trees, the soil chewed up by heavy machinery. Treetops and slash lay everywhere. Nothing had been burned, nothing had been cleaned, leaving a crisscrossing jungle of muddy debris.

"This is what Mr. Crockett did to Harrison Timber lands in three years," General Anarchy said in voice-over. "You see, before Mr. Crockett bought his first share of Harrison limited stock he had calculated the so-called 'breakup' value of the company. He knew that the timber on the privately owned land was worth roughly eight hundred million on the going market. He paid three hundred million for the company, giving him a profit of five hundred million."

The camera shifted to Crockett. "I know a bargain when I see one," he said, shrugging. "I had the vision and acted."

"Vision to pillage is more like it," General Anarchy snorted. "Vision to destroy a sustainable business for short-term greed. Vision to destroy a small town where the lumber mill has gone silent and the unemployment rate now tops thirty percent. Vision to rape the land and people and profit by it. The vision of a financial barbarian."

Crockett seemed to remember the cameras and turned to the closest. "I create efficiencies. That is life. Efficiencies. Nature grows more efficient every day, constantly adapting, one gene to the next, all in search of efficiency. I mimic nature. And if in that pursuit I am made wealthy, then nature, God, is rewarding me. Things happen for efficiency and I am an efficient man. But I am not a cold-blooded killer like these men."

"I know who he is, Albert," Friedrich Klinefelter suddenly announced. The camera shot to him. He was looking at General Anarchy. "I know who you are."

That seemed to throw the Third Position leader momentarily, then he looked menacing.

Watching the scene inside the FBI command center, Cheyenne's throat closed. "He's gonna kill Klinefelter. He's got to."

But General Anarchy composed himself and asked, "Who do you think I am?"

Klinefelter hardened and said, "Someone who

thinks he can turn the tide of history through violence. Like Robespierre or Hitler or Stalin or Mao—killing those who had the intelligence and the spine to challenge their authoritarian principles."

"I am none of those men, nor do I want to be," General Anarchy replied, his carriage visibly relaxing. "I am here only to show the truth, Herr Klinefelter. That's what anarchy does from an historical perspective. Anarchy uncovers buried truths. Anarchy cleans house of the corrupt order and the lies behind them."

"And replaces them with your lies?" Klinefelter said, nodding. "I think so."

"Is it a lie that you thrive on anarchy, Mr. Klinefelter? Volatility? Chaos?"

"I thrive in life as it strives for efficiency, to use Albert's term."

"One way to put it," General Anarchy replied. "Let's look at another."

The Third Position leader launched another multimedia attack, this one accusing the hedge fund manager of being a parasite that sucked the life out of sick, weak economies. The documentary-style presentation depicted Klinefelter acting in collusion with Crockett as they wagered on the price of the Haitian franc against the dollar.

It worked like this: At the same time Crockett was raping the Oregon forests to pad his pockets, he was busy buying a potash mine in Haiti and preparing to liquidate its assets. Crockett and Klinefelter knew that the mine pumped more than two hundred million dollars into the fragile Haitian economy and knew that the closure would be seen as a blow to the country's already dire financial straits. So they decided to sell short the Haitian franc three days before the announcement.

"What happened, Mr. Klinefelter?" General Anarchy said.

Cheyenne leaned forward in her seat. She knew about the Haitian mine, but nothing about a big currency wager.

The hedge fund manager seemed unable not to smile as he replied. "The Haitian franc devalued. We made some money."

"Some money?" General Anarchy cried. "You each pocketed one hundred and fifty million that you essentially stole from one of the most impoverished countries in the western hemisphere after shutting down a business that was profitable and vital to its economy. That's the evil of you guys: the way you murder countries and companies by gutting them and pecking at their bones as Mr. Crockett likes to do or gnawing at their guts, which is Herr Klinefelter's forte. It's the way you'll do anything to increase profits and shareholder value, but in so doing make life miserable for thousands."

Klinefelter was shaking his head vigorously. "If anything, we help these countries and the people who live in them. Exposing them to this kind of capitalism makes them understand what it takes to survive in the global economy."

"And I don't rape land," Crockett insisted. "I transform its economic potential."

General Anarchy's painted lips curled with disdain. "Then transform this: What did you do with the Haitian currency profits?"

The corporate raider's mouth puckered as if chewing something citrus and unripe. The hedge fund manager looked equally displeased, but answered, "We used it as collateral on an investment that could have made billions, but instead went sour. It happens. When you do as many deals as we do, it happens."

"You say that with such nonchalance, Herr Klinefelter," General Anarchy replied. "I learn new depths to your callousness and remove from the day-to-day life of the world's vast populace, sitting in your castle on the mountainside, far from the desperately poor who do your bidding even if they've never heard your trade orders."

The multimedia prosecution continued, revealing that Klinefelter and Crockett took their Haitian franc profits and added sixty million looted from the Harrison Timber pension fund and leveraged the bundle with junk bonds to buy TXC Corporation, a Brazilian-based multinational mining concern for two-point-two billion U.S. Six months later, the markets in several of TXC's mineral ore businesses collapsed. Bauxite prices plunged by half. So did the benchmarks for phosphorus and talc.

"Those junk bond payments must suddenly have looked enormous," General Anarchy remarked when the camera returned to him. "Mr. Crockett relied on his buzzard instincts and began to sell off TXC's unproductive assets and to exploit any that remained lucrative. Like the Fernandez gold mine."

Crockett stared as if his worst fears had been realized, while Klinefelter shifted hard in his seat.

Hennessy asked Cheyenne, "Do you know what he's talking about?"

She looked over at him in a slight daze. So much information had come at her so fast that she was having trouble processing it all. "I've never heard of it."

Inside Horatio Burns's office, Bridger Hennessy was still riveted on the drama playing out on the computer screen. But Connor walked away, saying, "This is boring."

"I don't know," Bridger said. "These guys look like they're getting ready to have their teeth pulled without Novocain."

Indeed, Crockett and Klinefelter seemed to revisit some private agony when Anarchy picked up a remote and aimed it at the television in the courtroom. The screen sprang alive, then filled the computer monitor in Burns's office, showing Fernandez, a shantytown near the gold mine deep in the rain forests of central Brazil. Over images of men wearing blue jumpsuits, hard hats, and headlamps entering a wire cage elevator and dropping into the earth, General Anarchy described how the Fernandez gold mine had been productive and profitable for the entire twenty years it had been in operation.

But as financial pressures mounted on TXC Corporation, Crockett and Klinefelter ordered the managers of the mine to boost production. They also authorized a shift in mining technique to allow cyanide leaching, a highly toxic method that allows gold to be extracted from rock faster than by more conventional methods.

Over images of graves in the jungle, General Anarchy went on to detail the deaths by cyanide of thirty people living near the Fernandez mine as the poison leached into the groundwater. Then he described how Crockett and Klinefelter began to ignore mine safety procedures in favor of cost-cutting measures.

The screen froze on a haunting black-and-white image of body bags being lifted from the mine elevator. The men carrying the bags were miners still in their hard hats and headlamps. Their faces were coated in grime and sweat, their eyes haunted and resentful.

"Consider this accident January twenty-fifth of last year," General Anarchy said as the camera returned to him in the courtroom. "A tunnel collapsed deep in the mine because Mr. Crockett had ordered a cut in shoring material. Fourteen men were missing. Klinefelter was in Zurich attending a ballet. Crockett was in Chicago, staying in a two-thousand-dollar-a-night suite at the Drake, preparing to take his wife out for an evening of fine dining."

The Third Position leader held a sheaf of papers in his hands and shook them at both men. "And what was your level of concern?" His gloved fingers nimbly plucked one piece of paper. "Here we are: a message from Herr Klinefelter's BlackBerry to Albert Crockett's, late that night. Quote: 'Albert, a rescue effort is futile and will only bring hysterical attention to the situation. TXC can ill afford the publicity of a rescue attempt. These men will not be found alive.'"

General Anarchy looked at the paper and sighed. "And so the decision was made not to try for a rescue.

The official line was that the collapse was too large. But the truth was different. Isn't that right?"

"No, it is not!" Crockett said.

Judge Truth pounded on his gavel, then shook it at Crockett. "You are one lying bastard. Tell the truth, sucker. For once in your life, tell the truth."

"I swear to God almighty!" Crockett said. "There was nothing we could do."

General Anarchy threw his arms up in the air. Behind him Citizen's Defender Emilia stood, her widow's veil hanging over her face, keeping it in shadow. She picked up a piece of paper from her desk.

"An e-mail from Crockett to Klinefelter dated the morning after the collapse," Citizen's Defender Emilia said in that Latina voice. "Subject: *Fiasco*. Quote: 'I agree, Friedrich. There is nothing good for you, me, TXC, or Mobius funds if we shut down the mine for a rescue attempt with little chance of success. Fernandez is TXC's best revenue producer right now. I advise we make sure the widows and orphans are compensated and get everybody else digging again.' Close quote."

Klinefelter squirmed against his lashes, saying, "Reaching them was an engineering impossibility given even the most up-to-date equipment. That was the official finding from LOPA, the Brazilian mine commission."

"We're not interested in the *official* finding," General Anarchy retorted. "We want the truth. Mr. Crockett? Is that the truth?"

"The report was stamped by the authorities," Klinefelter insisted.

"Mr. Crockett, was there one shred of doubt that those men were unreachable?"

"On my part? No," Crockett said.

"By anyone?"

"Not that I know of."

"How about Ricardo Luis Sarro, the first mining engineer to inspect the cave-in?"

"I don't know him."

"He used to work for TXC until shortly after the accident," General Anarchy said. "He told the Fernandez managers that the men could be reached in four days, five at the latest, by drilling at them diagonally from a shaft fourteen feet closer to the surface."

Crocket shifted in his chair. "News to me. I would have okayed that."

General Anarchy pinched at the bridge of his nose. "Mr. Crockett, you try my patience. We've seen mention of Mr. Sarro in several memorandums from you to the mine officials. Do you wish me to jar your memory with another dose of reality?"

Crockett looked trapped. "I don't know. We didn't . . . We didn't."

"We had no reason to believe those men survived," Klinefelter insisted.

"Oh, you had reason," General Anarchy said, shaking his head wearily. "But instead of acting out of humanity, you acted out of greed and put only a skeleton crew on the detail charged with finding the missing men. It took them thirteen days. They found three of the bodies crushed in the rubble. But the other nine men had lived for quite some time, praying for rescue. The last to die,

Himmy Lopez, left a note saying that one by one his comrades succumbed to the chill and starvation. The note was dated three days before his body was discovered. If they'd had the mine's best equipment and men, half the missing might have been saved. But Mr. Crockett and Herr Klinefelter left them to die and went right on grubbing for gold."

"That's a lie!" Crockett said, wriggling at his restraints. "These are the lies of men looking for money. Money's all they want. It's all anybody wants from us!"

"What about justice?" Judge Truth roared and hammered his gavel. "It's what the Third Position wants." He thrust the gavel at the camera. "It's what the world wants! Vote now! Decide their fates! You have fifteen minutes, starting now!"

The screen went blank.

CHAPTER THIRTY-ONE

Hailey suddenly felt groggy. She turned from the screen and said into the phone, "I'm tired, Dad. I'm going to lie down now."

"You're not going to vote?" he asked.

"No," she said.

"Me, neither," her father said. *"The boys?"*

She looked up to find her brothers walking away from her. Bridger shook his head and said, "I'm gonna get more caviar."

"I'm getting the shotgun," Connor said, stopping in front of the gun case.

Hailey yawned into the phone. "No one's voting. I'll keep the phone with me. Just yell. I'll wake up."

There was a moment's hesitation before she heard her father say, *"Okay, keep it right next to you."*

Hailey walked across the room to the sofa, wanting

to tell her father how much she wanted him to be there to tuck her in. But instead she said, "Dad, I'm sorry."

"For what?"

"Being such a bitch," she replied.

"You were never a bitch to me. Sweet dreams, noodle."

Hailey smiled and felt like everything was going to be okay now. At least for her family. She lay down with the phone in the crook of her arm. She fell asleep in an instant, unconsciousness rolling over her like a dark wind.

Connor, meanwhile, was examining the gun case doors. There didn't appear to be any lock or latch, and the glass was thick, probably almost an inch, much more heavy-duty than he expected. He put his hand on the frame and understood it was some kind of composite material stained to look like wood. It wasn't a gun case. It was more a vault.

So how does it work? he asked himself. *Electronic key?* But he saw no slot for it. He twisted the handles and pushed at them. Not a budge. He moved around books and the bric-a-brac on the shelves, hoping he might trigger something. Nothing. He ran his hand along the seam where the gun case met the bookcases to either side. Nothing.

Finally, he squatted and let his hands roam around the base of the gun cabinet and then along the beading on the shelf below the doors. On the shelf's left side, his fingers picked up the barest edge. An inch farther his finger found another.

With his thumb he felt around and then pressed. It barely gave. He heard a click. He looked up. The doors to the gun vault hung ajar.

Grinning and feeling very satisfied with himself, Connor grabbed a pump shotgun and a box of shells. He put the .22 in the shotgun's place and shut the doors. He carried the shotgun and the shells to the desk, and then tried to figure out the gun's action. It took him a minute to identify the safety and pump releases. He loaded the shotgun with five shells. One in the chamber. Four in the magazine.

He held the gun. It felt heavy and solid in his hand. The stock was inlaid with the carving of a bird-hunting scene. He wanted to show Hailey, went over to her, and almost woke her up. But she looked so peaceful, he just watched her a moment, feeling guilty for having gotten her into this predicament. It was his idea to go look for their father. If they'd just gone with the others they'd be safe now. All together.

Hailey moaned in her sleep and rolled over on her belly, the phone pinned beneath her. Connor turned from his sister, shouldered the shotgun, and swung it at an imaginary bird, oblivious to all danger.

Less than a quarter mile away inside the Jefferson Club's security center, Radio noticed a red code blinking at the bottom of every screen on the console. He frowned, not understanding what it meant. He clicked on the code and words played out on the screen: *Burns residence, library, gun cabinet. Intrusion. Silent alarm activated.*

He squinted at the message. He called up the six security cameras set around the perimeter of the Burnses' house. He used a joystick to maneuver the cameras, looking for tracks in the snow. Nothing. He checked the alarm system: Activated. Last known entrance or exit: 7:55 p.m., New Year's Eve.

And then, just as suddenly as it had started, the blinking red code disappeared.

Radio's jaw cocked to one side. Either it was a false alarm or someone had been hiding in the Burnses' house all along. But the intelligence was rock-solid. The general knew to a man the number of people inside the club and their whereabouts. Except for those three kids, given the head count as the hostages fled, there shouldn't be anyone else on the property. Except for those three goddamned kids.

Radio called into his mike, "Cobb. Give me your location."

Several beats passed. He was about to try again when Cobb's voice came crackling over the headset. *"I'm in the bakery. No sign of them."*

Radio said, "I had a silent alarm trigger in the Burnses' house on the hill above the lodge. The gun case. The exterior alarm system is activated and showing no entry. And no sign of tracks around the perimeter, at least from what I can see from the cameras."

Cobb replied irritably, *"Probably a goddamned false alarm. But I'll check it as soon as I've finished in the basement."*

"How much more down there?" Radio asked.

"Just the vault and the wine cellar."

Cheyenne O'Neil studied the jury ballot on the Third Position Web site and studied the charges against Albert Crockett and Friedrich Klinefelter: murder, conspiracy to commit murder, and being a vulture in the case of the takeover artist; and murder, conspiracy to commit murder, and being a parasite in the case of the hedge fund manager.

"You going to vote?" Cheyenne asked Mickey Hennessy, who sat next to her.

Hennessy set down his cell phone and shook his head. "I can't vote guilty because I fear the penalty. I can't vote not guilty because both of them are money-drunk ogres."

"Money-drunk ogres?"

"Better than cash-soused baboons."

Cheyenne chuckled. "Cash-soused baboons. I'll have to remember that."

"Please do," Hennessy said, then sobered.

Cheyenne caught his worry and said, "Kane says they'll be taken out first."

"That's good," Hennessy said, nodding and managing a smile.

Cheyenne glanced at the Bloomberg broadcast. The market had lost another hundred and sixteen points.

"Whew, it's getting clobbered," Cheyenne said.

"What is?" Hennessy asked, reaching for his cell phone, which was still connected by the VOIP line to the Burnses' library.

"The Dow," she said. "The markets. I've been talking about it all day. Haven't you been listening?"

Hennessy hesitated. And for the first time since hearing the gunfire that began the attack, Hennessy remembered he'd shorted the market. With the worry and anxiety over the kids, it had been shoved on the back, back burner. Now he looked up at the Bloomberg channel with confused interest.

"So if someone shorted the Dow, they'd have made lots of money, right?"

Cheyenne shrugged. "If the bet was big enough, I suppose a fortune. Why?"

Hennessy shrugged, unsure what he should say. Then he replied, "I heard several of the members say they were shorting the market as a hedge going into the new year. I guess they do it to protect themselves."

"Well, they certainly did themselves a favor on that," Cheyenne said. "The equities are getting hammered across the board. Having the shorts will save them."

Hennessy was asking himself whether he should call his broker when Agent Pritoni tore down his earphones. "The kids must have set off an alarm! The gun cabinet in the library at the Burnses' residence. They're not treating it as a fire. But someone's going to check sometime soon. Maybe very soon."

Hennessy snatched up his cell phone and yelled, "Kids! Pick up the phone!"

He waited expectantly, his attention leaping sharply to Kane.

The CIRG commander held up his hands and said, "I know. I know."

Hennessy felt ready to blow up. And then he realized he wasn't hearing anything on the phone at all. He fought the urge to puke. "Oh, my God," he said. "The line's dead."

"Call them back," Cheyenne said.

"You can't call in," Hennessy said. "Only out."

"They'll notice and call you," she said. "I'm sure of it."

Hennessy got up and began to pace. He opened his cell phone, inspected the number of bars it was receiving, and snapped it shut. Here he'd thought they were going to be okay. Guaranteed okay. *They are not okay.*

He heard Phelps say, "Team two's an hour out of Bozeman."

Then Kirk Seitz called out, "They're coming back with the verdict."

On the set of the Court of Public Opinion, hooded jury members filed into the box. Albert Crockett and Friedrich Klinefelter watched them, sweating, dry-lipped, their eyes flicking everywhere and nowhere, like men on the verge of a fit.

Bailiff Mouse called the court to order. Judge Truth reappeared. He slid into his chair, seized his gavel, and rapped it. "Mr. Foreman, do you have a verdict?"

The hooded foreman rose from his seat. "We do, Your Honor." He lifted a piece of paper and read from it. "Albert Crockett. On the charge of murder, we the people of the Third Position find by a vote of 6.2 million to 4.4 million: Not guilty."

The multibillionaire's head rose and he smiled and nodded to the hooded jury members and the cameras. "Yes," he said. "Excellent."

"Friedrich Klinefelter," the jury foreman continued. "On the charge of murder, by a vote of 5.1 million to 3.25 million: Not guilty."

The hedge fund mogul sighed and smiled, looked over at Crockett, beaming.

"Albert Crockett. On the charge of vulturism, by a vote of 8.01 million to 1.13 million, the Court of Public Opinion finds you: Guilty as charged."

Crockett glared at the foreman. "You think this is funny, don't you? Trying to humiliate a man? I won't be humiliated by you or anyone else. I am who I am."

"Friedrich Klinefelter," the foreman went on. "On the charge of being a parasite, by a vote of 9.23 million to 887,962: Guilty as charged."

The camera went close-up on Klinefelter. The Swiss magnate fumed at the verdict. His lips made slow snaky motions.

The foreman continued, "Albert Crockett and Friedrich Klinefelter, on the charge of acting as coconspirators to murder in the case of the Fernandez mine workers, by a vote of 5.75 million to 4.7 million: Guilty as charged."

"I am not guilty!" Klinefelter shouted. "It was an accident!"

"The LOPA report said we acted within reason," Crockett bellowed. "There was no conspiracy. I repeat. No conspiracy!"

Judge Truth banged his gavel. "Order! Order in the Court of Public Opinion!"

CHAPTER THIRTY-TWO

Bridger Hennessy returned to Horatio Burns's library bearing a plate piled high with crackers, mugs of soup, and two jars of caviar. He was sniffing the open jar. God, it was good. He'd never had anything that had tasted so good, so addictively good.

"New supplies," he said, walking by Hailey, who was still sleeping peacefully face down on the couch.

Connor looked up from the computer and said, "Verdict's in. Guilty."

"I missed it?" Bridger cried, hustling over to the desk.

Hailey let out a groan and sat up blearily. "Guilty?"

She was still holding the phone. She set it in her lap and yawned. Bridger handed her a mug of soup. She took it and the phone and followed him over to watch the chaos unfolding on the computer screen where Crockett and Klinefelter refused to stop shouting, "Not guilty! Not guilty!"

Bailiff Mouse waded in with a Taser gun and shocked Klinefelter in the knee. He rocked back and writhed in his chair. Crockett quieted and shrank.

"I will not tolerate any more outbursts," Judge Truth said. "General Anarchy, do the people have any recommendations regarding punishment?"

"The people do, Your Honor," General Anarchy replied. "We seek death by a method chosen to reflect the crime."

The cameras caught both Crockett and Klinefelter. The images played in split screen around the world. Their eyes had gone white and wide and their flesh was turning scarlet with fear. More Third Position soldiers appeared.

"You can't do this!" Klinefelter shouted. "You can't kill a man like this."

Crockett looked wildly at the cameras. "Help! Someone! Anyone! Help us!"

Hailey, Bridger, and Connor sat forward, their hands clasped in prayer poses. Inside they all felt that same helpless anger they'd suffered when they realized the Third Position meant to kill Sir Lawrence Treadwell.

"What do we do?" Bridger asked.

"Ask Dad," Connor said.

Hailey snatched up the phone. "Dad?" She listened and realized he wasn't there.

"It's dead," she said in a whine.

"Dial him again," Bridger said, snatching the phone from her and pounding in his father's cell number. To his relief, he heard it ring and gave his siblings the thumbs-up.

On the computer screen, Judge Truth stood behind the bench and thrust his gavel toward the defendants. "Albert Crockett and Friedrich Klinefelter, having been found guilty of vulturism, parasitism, and conspiracy to commit mass murder, the Third Position Court of Public Opinion sentences you to death by an appropriate method. May God have mercy on your souls."

The hooded jury members and their backups surrounded the two billionaires. They grabbed their chairs and despite their struggles hoisted them on their shoulders and marched from the courtroom.

Their father picked up. *"Hennessy."*

"Dad, what do we do?" Bridger said. "They're going to kill them."

"You do nothing!" his father shouted. *"The FBI picked up a radio transmission. You guys set off an alarm when you broke into the gun case. They're sending someone to investigate. You've got ten, fifteen minutes, maybe less. Clean everything. Put everything back the way it was, then get in the passage back to the lodge and wait. Don't hang up. Keep the line open. One of you watch. The others clean. Go. Keep me posted. Now!"*

"Okay," Bridger said, petrified all over again. He dropped the phone and gave his brother and sister their father's orders.

Hailey ran to the window and peered outside at the uncovered walkway to the house and the lodge beyond, seeing no one. The boys sprinted to the kitchen. Connor scooped up cracker boxes, mugs, and spoons. The sink was piled with pots, bowls, and plates. Bridger took them and shoved them in the refrigerator. By the time he finished, Connor had wiped down the counters.

Five minutes later, the door to the secret passage back to the lodge was open. Bridger raised the phone to his ear. "It's done. Connor wants to know if you want us to shut off the computer."

There was a long pause before he said, *"That will cut the line. Better idea: Shut off the monitor. We should still be able to talk. Get in the passage."*

"For how long?" Bridger said, not liking that idea.

Connor was watching the computer screen, which now showed an exterior shot in the snow under brilliant sunlight. Crockett sat in his chair, which had been set in the snow. Hooded jurors carried Klinefelter forward like some condemned Grand Poobah.

He grabbed the phone from Hailey and told his father, "Okay, we're going in."

Then he hit the phone's mute and kept watching the screen, where the cameras were focused tight on Klinefelter as the jurors set him down in a swirling, misty fog.

"What is going on?" Klinefelter asked anxiously. "What do you do back there?"

"We need to go," Hailey said.

Bridger felt like he could not budge. "We hear someone, we go in," he said, glued to the screen where the camera had pulled back to reveal jurors behind Klinefelter. They were working ropes through holes drilled in what looked like a length of lodgepole pine. They lashed the pole to the back braces of his chair.

The camera retreated to show Klinefelter sitting

right on the edge of the deep end of the Jefferson Club's outdoor pool. Steam rose and wafted in the winter light. The stout pine pole jutted out behind Klinefelter fifteen feet and rested over an oversized carpenter's horse. Four jury men took up positions on the far end of the lever. Several feet back, General Anarchy watched. So did Judge Truth, Citizen's Defender Emilia, and Bailiff Mouse.

"In the passage," Hailey insisted.

Bridger could not figure out what they were doing with that pole-and-seat thing.

"What is this?" Klinefelter cried, equally confused, on the computer screen, struggling to look over his shoulder. He fought against the lashes that held him to the chair. "What is this?"

General Anarchy stepped around beside Klinefelter, but kept looking back at the camera. "For the nonmedievalists among you, the predicament in which Mr. Klinefelter finds himself was once a form of punishment designed for wayward, immoderate women. It's called a ducking stool. We thought it appropriate to use the good old ducking stool with its rising and falling action as his appropriate means of punishment because this man has spent his life parasitically feeding on the up-tics and down-tics of the market."

"Nein!" Klinefelter screamed in terror. *"Mein got! Nein! Nein!"*

General Anarchy winked at the camera. "Oh, did I mention that Herr Klinefelter has a pathological dread of water due to the near-drowning he suffered as a child?"

"I don't want to watch this," Hailey said. "This is sick. Let's go."

Bridger held up his hand. "Just a sec."

Judge Truth held up his hand on the deck by the Jefferson Club's pool and intoned, "Brave jury of the Third Position. Carry out your duty."

Klinefelter went stark-raving mad, rocking and wriggling to be free, all the while screaming in German. The jurors threw their weight on the far end of the lever. The enterprise raised Klinefelter a solid foot off the cement coping. He dangled as they swung him out over the water. The chair twisted against the slack in the ropes.

"Nein!" Klinefelter sobbed at the water. *"Hilfe!"*

The sum of the jury let go of the lever. The Swiss magnate plunged into the water. The foam of the splash cleared around Klinefelter, showing him six inches below the surface, his head thrown back, his eyes silently screaming up at the air.

General Anarchy stood beside the pool, his back to the drowning man. He looked into the camera, and recited, " 'There stands, my friend, in yonder pool / An engine called the ducking-stool; / By legal power commanded down / The joy and terror of the town.' From the poem 'The Ducking Stool' by Benjamin West, 1780."

He wagged a finger at the camera. "You've got to love a method of punishment that spawns poetry. Let's see how Mr. Klinefelter's stock is doing!"

The jury men threw themselves on the lever. The

hedge fund tycoon rose from the pool, steaming in the winter air, sputtering and hacking, water drooling from his nose. His deflated gasps threw miserly clouds in the frigid air.

"Looks like he's only in a recession to me," General Anarchy said.

The jury let go of the lever a second time. In the foam that surrounded Klinefelter's reentrance, he whipped his head all around and made noises like a wounded horse.

At poolside, General Anarchy spoke to the camera again. "The ducking stool, pillories, the stocks, maybe even the whipping post. Everything's on the table at the beginning of any good revolution."

"You're savages!" Albert Crockett yelled from his position twenty yards back. "Savages! How could you even think to be a political movement?"

"We're not a movement," General Anarchy shot back. "We are a revolution. And every revolution requires a housecleaning."

Klinefelter's mad gyrations beneath the water had begun to slow.

"Check his ticker!" General Anarchy said, and then grinned at the camera. "I bet he's good for at least a couple more good dunks, don't you?"

The jury hoisted Klinefelter from the pool a second time. His head lolled to his left and then rocked backward as he heaved for breath. *"Nein,"* he gasped. *"Kein mehr.* No more." He coughed up water. "Pity."

Then the hedge fund mogul started taking in air asthmatically, snorting, straining, and gritting his teeth against some inner commerce. The veins on his neck popped against his skin and up the side of his face to the temples. He stayed that way for five seconds, muscles contracted and trembling, eyes bulging. Then he arched backward, his mouth open, his tongue lashing before he lost it all in a final convulsive crisis.

The last life within him drained. His corpse slumped forward against the ropes, dead and dripping above the pool.

Willis Kane hit the wall of the command center so hard Mickey Hennessy thought his hand would break. "Goddamn it!" Kane yelled. "Goddamn it!"

"Raid it now," Hennessy said, standing. "You know where the hostages are. Now."

Kane shook his head, looking whipped by circumstances beyond his control. "We can't save Crockett, if that's what you mean. And if we try before we're at full force we'll likely get the other hostages killed and lose a fair number of the men I've got here. My hands are tied, Mickey. And I'm the one who's going to have to live with it."

Hennessy wanted to fight him, but dropped it. The weight of responsibility on Kane's shoulders had to be enormous and he wasn't about to add to it. Instead he lifted his cell phone and said, "Are you in the tunnel?"

There was a long silence before Connor whispered, *"Right here, Dad."*

"Buttoned up tight?"

"Yup."

"Good," he said with relief. "Stay put and shut up."

Hennessy lowered the cell phone, seeing Cheyenne

staring up at the Bloomberg channel. He followed her attention, seeing that the Dow had dropped nearly seven hundred points and was trading at roughly four percent below its opener. The anchorman was reporting panic selling as investors around the world tried to limit their losses.

"I don't understand," Hennessy said. "They're powerful men, but powerful men die all the time. And you don't see the markets tank like this, do you?"

"This isn't about any one of them," Cheyenne replied, her arms crossed. "The Third Position's putting capitalism on trial here and capitalism's losing. I figure a lot of people around the world are thinking maybe the United States isn't such a safe haven for their money right about now. This keeps up, they'll stop trading."

"Who makes that call?"

"A computer," she said. "If the futures market goes 'limit down'—or loses a full five percent of its value—that market will shut down in an effort to stem more losses. The stock markets have 'circuit breakers' which trigger a different method of slowing down losses. Not surprisingly, gold's going through the roof."

"Limit down," Hennessy mumbled to himself.

"Frankly, Agent O'Neil, I don't give a damn about gold or the Dow," Kane growled. "What happened to those people who built the fence?"

Cheyenne reddened. "I'll call again."

"Has Isabel Burns gotten back to us with the code to the house?"

"No, sir, I left word with Mrs. Burns's secretary. She

said she did not know where Isabel was and she wasn't answering her cell phone."

"Call back. Keep trying. Phelps's second team is on the ground in Bozeman in fifteen minutes and I want a way in."

Hennessy said, "Let me call White Hawk. I can get through."

Kane hesitated. "Go ahead."

He sat down, picked up a phone, and dialed the number for White Hawk in Virginia. On the computer screen in front of him, Klinefelter's body hung in the steam, his face and hair beginning to ice up. Beyond him, the hooded jury carried Crockett up the knoll toward the woods above the kitchen. General Anarchy, Judge Truth, and the others followed at a solemn pace.

The scene cut to a handheld shot of the jurors carrying Crockett into a clearing in a snow-plastered forest. Crockett looked at the camera and broke down, saying, "Lydia, for God's sake, help me! Anyone out there! Help me and I'll give you a billion dollars!"

"Where are they?" Kane demanded.

"In the rookery," Hennessy said, a sense of dread coming over him as the phone rang on the other end. He asked for Terry Japrudi and Nick Faber, the men who'd designed the fence, and was told they were still on vacation. He finally got through to one of the vice presidents at White Hawk that he knew from his days working at the firm and was promised calls from either Japrudi or Faber within the hour.

Hennessy hung up, his attention leaping to the

computer screen again. A shaft of winter light showed in the glen and on a wooden four-poster bed with a plywood sheet for a mattress. The plywood was strewn with powdery snow that wisped in the breeze and took with it several black feathers.

A raven started to croak, gurgle, and then caw when the jurors cut free Crockett's wrists and ankles and attempted to tie him to the bed. The septuagenarian elbowed one jury member in the face and got his knee into the groin of another before punching a third in the head. They tackled the billionaire and threw him flat on his back. He tried to bite the thigh of the hooded juror who sat on his chest before he was choked into submission and tied spread-eagled to the bedposts.

All the while the rookery above had turned frenzied as one cawing raven on its roost became two and then four and were joined by a troop of raucous magpies. The cacophony of it continued as one of the jurors tore open Crockett's tuxedo shirt and yanked up his undershirt to reveal his paunchy old man's belly.

General Anarchy looked into the camera. "We considered smearing him in bacon grease and turning him loose near a grizzly or wolf den. But then we learned a little about the Jefferson Club's famous raven's roost on the hill above the lodge and, well . . ."

Two of the jury men came up with cans that they dipped their fingers into and came up with a thick white substance that they smeared over Crockett's belly.

"What is that stuff?" Cheyenne asked, watching from behind him.

"Looks like Crisco or lard," Hennessy said.

Another hooded juror came in carrying a bucket. He dumped the contents on Crockett's stomach and the other two jurors spread the mixture across the lard.

"And that's birdseed and scrap meat," Cheyenne said.

Hennessy's hand went to his mouth in gruesome awareness when the jurors left Crockett. The billionaire shivered violently. General Anarchy and Judge Truth, Citizen's Defender Emilia, and Bailiff Mouse came in around the bed.

"So, what?" Crockett said, bewildered. "You leave me here? I die of exposure?"

Hennessy felt sick. "Jesus, he doesn't get it."

Cheyenne turned away. "I can't watch this."

CHAPTER THIRTY-THREE

Hailey Hennessy stood halfway behind the bookcase, gaping in horror at the computer screen and the squawking coming from it.

"Will they? The birds?" she asked, horrified.

"I don't know," Bridger said, but his hand was shaking.

On the screen, Judge Truth grinned at the magnate's question about dying from exposure. "You might," he replied. "Depends upon your inner constitution. But I expect you'll be asking to die of anything before this is over. Albert Crockett, for enriching yourself through vultury and wanton disregard for human life, scavengers will be your punishment. May God have mercy on your soul."

Truth left the corporate raider's side. General Anarchy came to the camera and said in a simpering tone, "Coming up at eight eastern: the trial of Chin Hoc Pan.

He's a real-estate tycoon and commodities trader from Hong Kong, with a naughty, naughty side. You won't believe what he does with *his* profits. Coming up next in the Court of Public Opinion!"

The screen jumped to a horizontal split screen. The bottom frame featured a static long shot of the clearing with Crockett laid out on the bed. The tycoon was struggling against his lashes and shivering violently. The top frame showed Crockett from the biceps up, looking at him straight on and steeply elevated. Hailey figured the camera was fixed to one of the trees closest to the foot of the bed. The billionaire's teeth chattered. He raised his head and looked straight into the camera.

"Someone help!" he yelled. "Anyone! I will pay you two billion. No, five billion if you come to help me. Lydia! Please, tell them I will. Help me!"

"Whoa," Connor said. "That'll pull someone in here, right? Five billion bucks."

"Yeah," Bridger said. "I kinda like that number myself."

Connor looked at his brother, blinking. "Me too, and we're closest."

Hailey stepped back out into the library. "Don't even think about it," she said. "It's bad enough we're not in the passage right now with the door shut like you told Dad we were. Liars."

Her brothers didn't respond because, on-screen, the first magpie swooped from its roost. It made a lazy dive over Crockett. The billionaire saw the charcoal-and-ivory-breasted bird and stopped yelling. He watched the magpie swoop, loop, and then land on the snow between the camera and the bed. It hopped closer, head craning around as it flitted its dark tail. It spied a shred of the meat. The magpie cried clownishly, snatched up the meat, and flew away, warbling his victory. Two other magpies flushed from the trees to the right of the billionaire's head and gave chase. The first raven flapped and spiraled above Crockett, who watched it, tracking its glide.

A second raven flushed, swooped, and plucked meat from the snow. The third fluttered down to land on the top of the bed's headboard. The bird split its beak, crowed, and ruffled its black feathers, watching as its brethren wolfed down the meat scraps. Magpies, nearly a dozen of them, circled above the clearing.

Bridger said, "We could get to him through the woods out back."

"You'll set off the alarm leaving," Hailey pleaded. "They'll know."

"I already did set off an alarm," Connor said.

Hailey started to protest, but then stopped when she saw on the screen that Crocket was arching to see the raven on the headboard. "Get the hell away!" he cried.

Another raven landed on the snow beside the bed. Several magpies joined it, pecking at the grain. But the raven on the bedstead stayed where it was.

"Maybe they won't land on him," Connor said.

"That one landed right on Chef Giulio's arm," Bridger reminded him. "Ate from his hand. He said they're hungry, they'll eat anything, from anyone."

The raven leaped onto Crockett's chest. It snatched a beakful of suet and meat before the billionaire could buck it off.

Hailey turned away and went into the passage, saying, "This is worse than what they did to Sir Lawrence."

"Yeah, it is," Bridger agreed, picking up the machine gun.

A second raven landed on Crockett's upper thighs. He heaved his hips trying to flush it. But the bird snapped its head forward, clamping its beak and tearing. Crockett started screaming. The bird had ripped open his skin. He was bleeding.

"But what if they're—" Connor began.

He was cut off by a booming and splintering noise out in the hallway. He heard it again and then the alarm went off: whooping sirens and a female's electronic voice braying, *"Forced entry! Intrusion! Authorities are being notified! Forced entry!"*

"Team two's on the ground," Special Agent Phelps announced with relief inside the CIRG Command Center. "ETA here: twenty minutes. National Guard chopper's there at Bozeman waiting for them."

"Okay," Kane said. "Your men good to go?"

"Been practicing the entry according to that video simulation all morning," he replied. "We get to the Burnses' house. Use the same tunnel the kids used to get into the lodge. One guard on the hostages. We've got a real chance of this working if we can get by the fence without alerting them."

Hennessy winced. The satellite phone he'd been using rang. He snatched it up.

"Mickey," a gruff voice said. *"Terry Japrudi."*

"Terry, we have to beat the fence."

"How'd they do it?"

Hennessy explained while keeping one eye on the computer screens inside the command center where ravens and magpies had formed a conical whirling flock above Albert Crockett. The birds near the bottom landed on the billionaire, snapped at his abdomen, and retreated. He bled in several places.

"Help me!" Crocket squawked.

The birds landed on him with impunity now and had begun to squabble on his chest. On the upper split screen, the billionaire looked as if he were wearing a living black brilliantine scarf woven of the ravens' and magpies' ever-shifting tailfeathers.

"Please," Crockett croaked to the overhead camera, struggling weakly and crying. "Please. Someone help me! This isn't right! I don't deserve this torture."

"This is beyond barbaric," Cheyenne said, turning away. "It's obscene."

"How do they think anyone's going to follow their twisted revolution?" Kane wondered. "I mean, what are they offering here: sick political theater, a beef with global corporations, and public executions live on the Web? I don't think they'll attract anyone with this message. It's impossible to think of revolution as the point. What the hell are they after? It's not a third way, that's for sure."

Unable to watch anymore, Hennessy turned around

and finished telling Terry Japrudi how the Third Position Army got inside the Jefferson Club grounds.

"I always thought that two-point-two-second gap might come back to haunt us," the fence designer responded.

"It didn't have to be that long a gap?" Hennessy asked.

"It's well within code," Japrudi replied. *"With another eighty-K in upgrades, we could have had it under a second. But there were big cost overruns on everything at the lodge by that time and someone decided to leave it at two-point-two."*

"Well, somehow the Third Position knew," Hennessy said, his tired brain unable to fully process all this. "What I need is another way to beat it."

"There isn't," Japrudi said, somewhat defensively. *"When it's on, it's flawless."*

"There's got to be a way," Hennessy snapped. "My kids' lives depend on it."

"Well, unless you want to impersonate an elk, there isn't," Japrudi shot back.

Hennessy thought about that, then he arched an eyebrow and smiled. "No," he said. "That will do it. Thanks, Terry. Thanks a lot."

He punched off the phone and turned to find most of the FBI agents in the command center looking not at Crockett's plight, but at the Bloomberg broadcast. The banner playing across the lower part of the screen said, *Futures trading suspended. DOW down more than 800 points on murders of world's wealthiest. S&P and NASDAQ post similar losses.*

Several traders were being interviewed live on Wall Street, outside the New York Stock Exchange.

"If these trials go on without government intervention, you could see the market lose another five to ten percent tomorrow," one trader warned.

Another chimed in, "They're killing our best and brightest. The companies of every one of those men is in chaos. Who knows their value now?"

A third said, "Why doesn't the government go in there and stop this?"

"We're about to," Kane said, hardening and muting the television. He looked at Hennessy. "Right?"

Hennessy nodded. "I think I've got a way through the fence."

Suddenly, outside the command center, they heard the chug-chug of a helicopter.

Out the front window, Hennessy spotted a dark green helicopter, one hundred feet in the air, heading for the Jefferson Club. The side door of the bird was open. Men dressed in green SWAT gear sat in the doorway holding submachine guns. A second chopper followed, equally manned and armed.

"Contact them!" Kane yelled at Pritoni. "Find out who they are and what the hell they're doing!"

Pritoni used his keyboard to call up a broadband military frequency, then said, "Unidentified helicopter, this is FBI base, do you copy?"

There was a long crackling silence, then a drawling voice came back, *This is Greenwater flight commander, come back FBI base.*

Kane grabbed up his headset and barked into it,

"Mann, this is Willis Kane of CIRG. Turn back. The club has radar. You are endangering the hostages."

"Sorry, Agent Kane, but my client wants her husband out of there."

Watching the choppers disappear over the hill toward the lodge, Kane shouted, "Mann, I am ordering you to pull back. You have no authority and no experience at hostage rescue. Turn back."

"Agent Kane," Mann came back disdainfully. *"With all due fucking respect, my men have cleared more hellholes than you could come up with in a nightmare. Besides, there's five billion on the table."*

"Forced entry! Intrusion!" the alarm voice brayed.

Hailey jumped into the secret passage. Bridger ran in behind her, holding the machine gun. Connor came third, carrying the shotgun and flinching at the sound of a second kick splintering the front door. The second he was in, Hailey pushed the false bookcase shut and heard it click and engage. Over the alarm's wail came a final booming crash.

Connor stepped to the small two-way mirror, peered out into Horatio Burns's office, panting and swallowing softly at the bile in his throat. Then he soared into full-fledged panic. The computer was still on, still showing the split-screen shots of Albert Crockett, who had gone into a palsy of chattering and squirming, still trying to get the birds off him while his body lost blood and temperature.

"I screwed up!" Connor whispered. "They'll know we were in here!"

"Idiot!" Bridger said and punched him in the arm.

Before Connor could punch his brother back, the office door flew open.

"It's him!" Hailey whispered ever so softly.

Cobb stood in the doorway, sweeping the barrel of his machine gun around the room. A second Third Position soldier moved past him in a crouch. He peered forward under the desk and said, "Clear."

Cobb took several steps inside. His face was clean of the green paint, but his skin looked raw and his eyes were bloodshot and hard. He barked into his headset, "Radio, can you shut the damn alarm down or not?"

The alarm and the woman's warning suddenly died. So did the computer.

"Kid, they cut the power," Bridger whispered with relief.

Cobb grimaced as he walked to the gun case. He tried the doors. Locked. Dalton, the other Third Position soldier, came up beside Cobb and looked inside.

"Doesn't look like anything's missing," he said. "Gun in every slot. False alarm. Let's get the hell out of here."

Cobb just stood there with his back to the Hennessys, looking through the glass at the guns. After what seemed like an eternity, he shook his head. "Uh-uh. Look at the guns. Which one sticks out? Which one doesn't look like it belongs to the bazillionaire?"

Dalton craned his head forward to inspect the guns inside the case. There were twenty. The triplets saw him cup his hands and peer through the glass.

"See the shitty little .22?" Cobb said. "I seen that gun. They had that gun. Little fucks are in here. Or have been."

"C'mon," Dalton said, unconvinced. "There's no tracks outside. What'd they do, swing from tree to tree? Maybe it's Burns's gun. Maybe he uses it to shoot varmints."

"Uh-uh," Cobb said. "That gun couldn't cost more than a hundred bucks. Every other gun in there's a big-coin job. Purdys, Krieghoffs, the best."

Cobb began to pace around the room. He disappeared from view to the triplets' left. Connor was about to suggest they retreat back down the secret passage toward the wine cellar when Bridger grabbed his arm.

Cobb's face appeared in front of them. He was looking into the two-way mirror, not six inches away. The triplets held their collective breath while Cobb leaned in skeptically. Then he used a finger to raise his right eyelid.

"I got something in it, but I can't see a damn thing," Cobb said. "Paint or something." He turned away and growled, "You take the upstairs. I'll take down. Don't kill 'em. I want that for myself."

His back was no more than a foot or two away. Connor and Hailey glanced at Bridger. Their brother had taken a step back and raised the machine gun. He had it aimed at Cobb's neck. Bridger flipped the safety. Cobb cocked his head as if he'd heard something.

Bridger's finger moved to the trigger. Connor grabbed Bridger by the wrist. He shook his head and mouthed, *Please!*

Then the lights went on again in the house. Cobb's hand shot to the earphone of his headset and his shoulders tensed.

"Incoming!" Cobb shouted. He turned and ran. "Dalton! We've got incoming!"

At the rear of the Jefferson Club's ballroom, General Anarchy threw on his snow camouflage, barking into his headset, "How far?"

"Four-point-six miles out and closing," Radio replied. *"The men watching the gate spotted two of them. Nonmilitary. I repeat, nonmilitary."*

"Truth, you and your men on the roof," Anarchy barked. "Cristoph and Emilia, outside in the forest with the others."

Rose ran up to him. "You want us to webcast?"

General Anarchy paused, then said, "Yes. Take us live."

The director spun and raced to her station, snapping orders to her crew. The ballroom turned frenzied as men tugged on hoods and got rifles, heading toward the roof or out the doors that flanked the ballroom.

Cobb and Dalton rushed in gasping for breath after sprinting the two hundred yards from the Burnses' house to the lodge. General Anarchy spotted the men and yelled, "Use them! Now!"

The two men reacted immediately, sprinting into a corner of the ballroom where two hard-sided packs lay. They grabbed the packs, split up, and sprinted out the doors at either side of the ballroom.

"Take them down!" General Anarchy roared after them and to the camera now streaming his every word to the Web site. "Make them mourn the day they ever challenged the Third Position Army!"

"I have a visual, General," Truth said over the radio. *"I confirm birds are nonmilitary. Green. No markings. Looks like a corporate force."*

"When they pass."

"Roger that."

The helicopters came pulsing in over the top of the Jefferson Club Lodge. Outside, on either side of the ballroom, Cobb and Dalton pressed themselves tight against the snowy hedge that ringed it, their white camouflage making them blend in nearly perfectly.

The first chopper flew out over the terrace and ski lift, then buttonhooked and came around broadside to land on the flat above the lodge. The second swung out toward the stables, then turned as well.

Inside the ballroom General Anarchy watched the airships hover to land. Mirth crept to his real lips, turning his painted ones into sharp tusks.

Truth and his men rose up from the snowy roof and opened fire on the helicopters. The windshield of the airship closest to the ski lift shattered. The chopper swung violently. The Greenwater men in the belly began to shoot back, blasting wildly, jumping free of the chopper, several of them running toward the woods where Crockett lay. Harry Mann was leading.

The other Greenwater helicopter tried to retreat to a safer landing zone. But Cobb had already eased his body from the hedge and aimed a rocket-propelled grenade launcher at the gaping belly of the bird.

Cobb's finger brushed the trigger. The rocket-grenade covered the 450 feet in less than a hundredth of a second. It left a vapor trail flying into the open bay of the Greenwater chopper, right between two men firing at the door. When the ballistic tip struck the interior bell housing of the main rotor assembly, the blast was harsh, metallic, and blinding.

The gunship lurched hard to port, flinging out crew members riddled with shrapnel. Dalton fired from the opposite side of the ballroom. The rocket grenade left an orange slash in the night sky and a rank odor that turned scorched when the missile exploded against the landed chopper's rear rotor. The blades were still spinning when it hit. They snapped off and spun through the air like giant scythes that clipped the tops off several trees and slashed and severed the ski lift cables, which buckled, whipped, and coiled with a sound like a freight train hitting the brakes.

The chopper still in the air belched oily smoke, lurched, and swung, throwing up a terrible clanking. The Third Position soldiers on the roof and in the woods fired mercilessly at the wounded bird and at the Greenwater men led by Harry Mann trying to reach the rookery and Albert Crockett.

They were all cut down ten yards shy of the trees. The airborne chopper made shearing and seizing sounds. The bird looped through a 210-degree spiral, and then augured into Fortune's Alley ski run, where it blew and hemorrhaged great gouts of flame above the snowpack.

CHAPTER THIRTY-FOUR

Hennessy couldn't take in what he'd just seen on the computers inside the FBI command center. From their expression, neither could Cheyenne O'Neil or Willis Kane. The screens showed the Jefferson Club Lodge's heated terrace and the chairlift and the stables and in the distance the helicopters burning. Hooded soldiers of the Third Position Army appeared from the woods, weapons thrust overhead in victory.

Then the camera cut to General Anarchy. "You are lucky I am an understanding man. Any further aggression, corporate or governmental, will result in the immediate execution of the remaining hostages. We are ready to die for our cause. Are you?"

The screen returned to the wide shot of Albert Crockett on the bed in the woods. He had stopped moving. There were magpies pecking at his eyes.

"Turn that goddamn thing off!" Kane shouted before turning to Hennessy. "How are we getting in there?"

Hennessy startled, and then said, "We're going to need horses. Forty or fifty."

Bridger, Connor, and Hailey saw the helicopters shot down from Horatio Burns's office window. The place was freezing now that Cobb had kicked down the door. There was snow drifting into the foyer. They had all put their heavy snowboarding gear back on to stay warm. Bridger went to the computer and rebooted it.

"What are you doing?" Hailey asked. "We should be back in the tunnel until Dad and the FBI come."

"And I'm thinking he would want to know if we're all right and that Cobb knows we're in here," Bridger replied.

"Maybe we should get out now," Hailey said. "They're not thinking about us. They've just been attacked. The alarm's off, let's go."

"Let's let Dad decide," Bridger said, dismissing her.

Connor couldn't argue with the logic of either of their positions, so he went to the office door and stood guard where he could see out the front door and down the walkway toward the lodge.

Three minutes later, Bridger had the VOIP line up and was dialing his father's cell phone. When Mickey answered, Bridger told him everything that had happened. After several moments' discussion off the phone with Willis Kane, his father came back on and said, *"We don't know where their sentries and patrols are. By moving you increase the chances of being caught.*

Stay put. This Cobb character doesn't know about the passage. If he'd known, he would not have checked his eye in the two-way mirror. You're safe in there. Having the alarm at the house already deactivated gets us to you even quicker. Sometime between six and seven."

"How are you getting past the fence?" Bridger asked.

"I've got a plan," his father said.

"You coming with the hostage rescuers, Dad?"

"You know it, son."

Flush with triumph, standing like a maestro on a chair in the ballroom with his men arrayed around him, General Anarchy clapped and cried, "Well done, Cobb, Dalton. Well done. Worthy of a bonus. Say, another half million?"

"Just like duck hunting," Dalton boasted.

Cobb allowed himself a rare smile. "Slam-dunk shot."

"Not bad for a guy three fourteen-year-olds take prisoner," Truth said.

Cobb's lip curled. "I know where they're at."

"Go get them, then," General Anarchy said. "Don't kill them. Bring them to me."

"Your order was to eliminate," Cobb protested.

"They offer more leverage now alive than dead," the general said before directing his attention to everyone gathered. "Don't think we've won. We've won when we've put on as many of the trials as we are able before the real attack comes, which will be soon. A matter of hours. At that point it's every man for himself. Agreed?"

As one, the soldiers nodded. "Agreed."

General Anarchy let his gaze travel to the faces assembled before him. "You have changed the world more than you know," he said. "You have raised yourself up in protest and created the possibility of a new future. If you survive, as I have promised, you will be prosperous beyond your wildest dreams, free to carve out your own visions and dreams of the new order. If we die, comrades, we do so for a greater cause."

FBI hostage rescue team two landed on the sage flat a half mile east of the club's main gate. The media cameras caught them disembarking, hustling past Sheriff Lacey's fire toward the growing FBI encampment, where ten more outfitter's tents had been erected. Cheyenne O'Neil watched them coming toward her on the Bloomberg channel, where many of the commentators had been talking about the threat anti-globalists posed. They said the great aim of the movement was the dismantling of the world's capitalist system and a redistribution of wealth. Several prominent businessmen interviewed were demanding a government crackdown on the very idea.

A professor from Georgetown had been shown defending anti-globalists, saying that the majority were peaceful but wary of government and corporate control, not cold-blooded killers like the Third Position Army. But he'd been shouted down.

Cheyenne heard a woman pick up on the other end of the phone. Isabel Burns's secretary again. The secretary said she'd called Mrs. Burns three times and she wasn't answering her cell. Cheyenne got the number from her, hung up, dialed it, and got a message that her message box was full.

The door to the command center opened, Agent Phelps entered, followed by Jim Johansson, a wiry man in his early forties with a jaw that looked like the rear end of an anvil. Johansson was the special agent in charge of hostage rescue team two. Frustrated, Cheyenne stood up to find Hennessy in the conference room, shaking Johansson's hand. She listened as Hennessy went over his plan to beat the fence.

"As soon as darkness falls," he said, "Agent Johansson's team will enter from the southeast. Phelps's team will breach the fence from the northwest."

"How?" Kane said.

"Okay," Hennessy said. "Since I moved to Montana, I've gotten to be something of an American Indian buff. We're going to have to learn a trick the Plains Indians, the Sioux and the Comanche, used in battle. Approaching the fence on horseback, you'll hold on tight to the saddle pommel, release one boot from its stirrup, and hang down off the side of the horse. The Sioux did it to use the horse as a shield from U.S. Cavalry snipers. You'll do it because the fence is programmed to ignore elk, horses, and cows based on the head profiles. If you press yourselves tight to the horses, you should get through clean."

When he finished, Johansson snorted. "We gonna learn that move in two hours?"

"I thought you guys were the best," Hennessy retorted.

Johansson clouded. "We'll learn. Where do we do it?"

"This creek bottom and that cliff," Hennessy said, tapping on the map. "Jefferson's Nose. Your team rappels in from there."

"Tough to find in the dark?" Phelps asked.

"The Nose sticks out," Hennessy said. "Your men up on the ridges have seen it, I'm sure. Creek bottom's tougher to find, even with GPS coordinates. But I'll guide you."

Kane shook his head. "You're not an agent, Mick. Not going to happen."

"Once we get past the fence, I can take them the surest and safest route to the Burnses' house," Hennessy insisted. "After that it's your game, Willis. I'm out of it. I'm only there to make sure my kids are okay."

In early January, certainly on an overcast day in the late afternoon, the light in southwest Montana is a dull pewter that foretells the coming of night. It's the time that deer and elk start moving in anticipation of dusk and feed. Connor's father had also told him it was the time of predators. And so the teen was on extra-high alert, and spotted Cobb from way down the hill toward the lodge, coming back with Dalton in tow. He sprinted back toward his brother and sister, hissing, "Psycho's here again."

"This guy doesn't give up," Bridger said, flicking off the computer monitor and darting into the passage after his brother, who pushed shut the door.

Struggling to control their breath, they all squeezed in behind the two-way mirror again. A minute passed. Cobb pushed open the office door.

"This was open when we left," Cobb said.

"Wind," Dalton said.

Cobb seemed unconvinced. He looked all around, studying everything before fixing on something below the desk. "I don't remember the computer being on."

Dalton looked at Cobb like he was some alien creature. "You remember that?"

"I remember everything," Cobb said. "Everything I've ever seen."

"So what's it mean?"

"It means those little evil bastards *are* in here." With that he made for the door to the office, saying, "Where's the kitchen? They had to have eaten."

Both men disappeared into the residence's outer hallway. It was the last they heard or saw of either man for nearly half an hour. At 4:32 p.m., only Bridger was standing watch at the two-way mirror. Connor and Hailey sat beside each other on the floor, their backs to the passage wall.

"They're in here, I'm telling you!" Cobb insisted angrily as he knocked open the door to the office with the muzzle of his gun.

Hailey made to get up from the floor, but Connor shook his head and put a finger to his lips.

"I checked everywhere upstairs," Dalton said.

"And I checked everything on this level and down," Cobb said. "So maybe they're someplace hidden. Like one of those panic rooms in the movies."

He stopped, pressed his hand to his headset receiver, and scowled.

"The general's orders are a complete fucking waste of time," he snarled into the microphone. "We've been all through the basement. They're here somewhere."

He listened again, shouted, "Shit, fine. Fucking waste of time, Radio."

Dalton, however, seemed to think it was a good idea. He started heading for the office door again. Cobb stomped after him, raging, "Those little fucks are here!"

As he passed the leather couch, Cobb stopped. He flipped off the safety on his machine gun and raised it. He yanked on the trigger. The gun rattled and boomed fire and bullets. He swept the gun around the room, shooting. Vases and sculptures disintegrated. Wood splintered. The computer screen blew up. Books and framed photographs were riddled with holes.

Connor threw himself on top of his sister. He heard Cobb chuckling after the shooting stopped.

"That make you feel soft and fuzzy inside?" Dalton asked.

"As a matter of fact, yeah," he heard Cobb say.

Then their voices faded away. Connor was finally willing to rise up from the floor. He looked back toward the secret doorway. Bridger wasn't there at the two-way mirror. Several thin beams of light shone through holes in the wood below the mirror. The beams of light played on his brother, who was lying on the passage floor several feet back toward the wine cellar, biting his right arm so he wouldn't cry out, while his left gripped his shaking thigh.

Connor lurched off his sister and over to his brother. "You okay, kid?"

Hailey was getting to her knees when Bridger started whimpering, "No, cartoon idiot, I'm not. I'm hit. Real bad. Dying bad!"

CHAPTER THIRTY-FIVE

Cheyenne O'Neil watched in admiration as Hennessy answered all of Johansson's and Phelps's concerns with strong, logical answers. *He must have been good when he was with State,* she thought. *Real good.* Her cell phone rang. She turned away from the counterattack planning. Her partner John Ikeda was on the line. He'd spent the last eighteen hours working with government banking officials all over the world, trying to plot more of the route taken by the billion dollars transferred into Third Position accounts.

"*I've managed to unravel three of the transfer strings that Doore's money went through,*" Ikeda said, sounding weary. "*You won't believe where seventy-five million landed.*"

"Tell me," Cheyenne said.

"*Twenty-five in the account of the American Civil Liberties Union,*" Ikeda said.

"What? C'mon."

"Serious. And twenty-five million in the account of People For the American Way."

"Not a chance."

"Honest to God. The third twenty-five went to MoveOn.org."

"What are you saying?"

"I'm just telling you where the money went. Who should I report this to?"

Cheyenne told him to hold on, then went into the conference area and relayed Ikeda's discoveries to Kane. In return she received the number of the FBI director's private line. When she repeated that to Ikeda, he began to stammer.

"What do I say? Hi, is this the director?"

"I'd imagine you'd use his name," Cheyenne said. "Just identify yourself and tell him. Let him figure it out, but I say it feels strange. Like a false trail."

"This dawg's not done digging yet," Ikeda said and hung up.

Bridger Hennessy never understood there could be this much pain, no idea that such hurt could grow worse with every rip of his breath. His head spun at the torch cutting through his leg. A wave of searing agony crested through him. He arched his spine at it, gasping.

Kneeling beside him, her hands acting like they were searching for something, Hailey mumbled, "Oh, God. Oh, God, God, God."

She'd cut Bridger's snowboard pants open with scissors from Burns's desk. She was looking at the wound.

The bullet had hit her brother in the midthigh. There was blood everywhere and the flesh around the entry looked ground. The exit wound was worse.

"We've got to tourniquet him," Hailey said. "Gimme his belt."

Bridger gripped his brother's hand while Hailey knelt beside him, cinching the belt around her brother's upper thigh. She felt like part of herself was mortally wounded. Connor felt the same way. He held Bridger's hand tight and said, "Hold on, kid."

Bridger started seizing and spasming. "Mom," he whimpered. "Please, Mom. Help."

Hailey whispered through her tears, "Mom's not here, kid. It's just me and C. We'll get you help, just as soon as Dad comes."

"How long?" Bridger asked in a quaking voice.

Connor checked his watch. "They'll be coming soon." He stood up. "Stay with him," he told Hailey. "I'm gonna go find bandages and stuff to clean the wound and kill the pain."

Hailey looked after him in a daze, wondering why time had slowed and become the beating of her wounded brother's heart.

Connor ran out into the hallway and up the staircase into the master suite. The bed looked big enough for a wrestling match. The tub in the bathroom was more like a pool.

But he found a first-aid kit in one of the counter drawers on Isabel Burns's side of the bathroom. Even better, he found seven tabs of painkillers in a prescription bottle on Horatio Burns's side. He gathered them up, then leaped down the staircase, through the foyer, and into the office, not seeing the bloody shoe prints he'd left passing through minutes before.

Bridger was shivering and moaning when Connor got to him. He told his brother to eat three of the painkillers then started tearing open gauze rolls. Hailey released the tourniquet a second, then tightened it. Connor grimaced at the wound and did the only thing he could think to do. He coated pieces of the gauze in antibiotic cream and pushed them into the entry and exit holes.

Bridger cried out, "What're you doing? Ahh, that hurts! Ahh, that hurts!"

"Shhhh! You gotta stop moving, kid," Hailey said, holding on to her brother.

"I'm shot, Hailey," Bridger said. Tears poured down his face. "I'm shot."

"I know, Bridge," Hailey said. "Just hang on."

The sun finally set over southwest Montana at four forty-five. Looking out through the ballroom windows, General Anarchy watched the last blue glow of it shrouding Jefferson Peak. Truth stood beside him.

"Soon?" Truth asked.

General Anarchy nodded. "The tipping point's been reached. They won't tolerate any more. Is Radio monitoring the fence?"

"Constantly. Nothing so far."

"Tonight we risk it all, my friend. If we emerge, we emerge victorious."

"Then we emerge victorious. There's no middle

ground. All or nothing. You called it that way from the beginning, General."

"And now we are upon that decisive moment."

"It's been an honor to serve with you," Truth said. "No matter how it plays out."

General Anarchy nodded and clapped his hand on Truth's shoulder. "You too, Truth. Bring Chin Hoc Pan up for trial. Warn Carpenter his time will soon be at hand."

Sheriff Lacey arranged for fifty saddled horses to be brought up in trailers right after dark. Ranchers from all around the Jefferson Range came at his call to bring the animals and unloaded them swiftly. The smell of horse was everywhere in the bitter cold air. The animals coughed and puttered their lips against the sounds of men laying blankets, cinching saddles, and putting on bits and reins.

Sitting up on the back of a big roan gelding, Hennessy felt suddenly weakened, as if his arm wound was flaring up again. He had to hold on to the saddle pommel to keep from falling off the horse. Hennessy moved his bad arm. He had range in most directions. But it throbbed terribly and his anxiety about the kids was worse than ever. He felt someone tug at his boot in the stirrup.

"Hey," Cheyenne O'Neil said. She wore a tiny headlamp that gave out just enough red light to reveal her loveliness.

Seeing her, he felt strengthened. "Hey, yourself."

"You all right?"

"I will be soon."

"You'll have to introduce me to your kids."

He smiled. "I think they'd like that."

She patted his boot and then moved off. Hennessy watched her go. Willis Kane spoke in the headset Hennessy wore. *"You ready to lead there, scout?"*

"Here we go," Hennessy said. He switched his own headlamp to its red bulb, and then spun it around to face off the back of his hood.

"Follow the beacon," he said into the microphone, kicking up his horse.

He led them in a quick trot south across the darkened sage flat. Some eight hundred yards east of the fence he took a pack trail into the timber. They rode single file for two miles to a marshy swale of reeds and cattails all droopy and frozen.

Hennessy stopped and motioned Agent Phelps forward. He turned his bright headlamp on the marshy area. "Fence crosses about a hundred and fifty feet ahead. I'll hang my beacon a foot from it. Everyone goes in a bunch. The cattails will give you some cover. All the fence should see is horses passing."

The hostage rescue leader organized his men into three herds while Hennessy went forward and found the fence. Its many-twisting laser arms glowed violet in the light cast from his headlamp bulb. He hung the headlamp on the branch of a blue spruce that grew in the swale, then stood back as the FBI hostage rescuers hung themselves off the sides of their horses, one leg over the saddle, one gripping the belly, while their hands clutched the pommel and breast strap. The horses were agitated at the sudden shifting in loads, but walked through one after the other. Hennessy watched as the lasers found the animals and tried to probe them as they passed.

Hennessy crossed onto Jefferson Club grounds with the third group, holding on to the pommel for dear life with his good arm, gritting his teeth, squeezing his inner thigh muscles, and pressing his chest and head to the side of the horse, which shied and bucked as it passed through the fence. He was thrown and landed with a thud several feet beyond.

But exuberance bubbled up in Hennessy as he got to his feet and waded forward through the high grass, smelling the horses and the snow and the forest in the cold pitch-darkness. He was inside. After all the waiting, after all those feelings of helplessness, he was inside and on the offensive, fighting back, going to get his kids.

Inside the Jefferson Club's security center, Radio replayed the record of the intrusion, watching a screen that had jumped to a pale blue color and showed the yellow outlines of what looked like several herds of elk or horses swimming their way past the fence. He replayed it a third time, trying to figure out if he agreed with the computer, which kept flashing, *Animal crossing. Animal crossing.*

The second hostage rescue team rode north across the sage flat toward the trees several hundred yards east of the gate. Cheyenne O'Neil was with them. She would watch the assault by binoculars from the cliff and relay her perspective to Kane in the CIRG command center.

Later she would lead the horses back down the mountain. She had volunteered for the duty. As they passed the media encampment, she could see fires burning and the stage lights still glowing. No one spoke. To anyone not right on top of them, they were a herd of animals passing in the night.

They climbed a steep foothill trail paralleling the fence north for three miles before swinging west along the ridge top, with the Jefferson Club grounds to their left. Many of the lights had been turned out in the lodge. But even from miles away, she could tell how big the structure was and where it was. The wind blew harder. She had to duck her head and urge her horse forward up the mountain through the snow past the FBI snipers who'd been watching the lodge, heading for the northeast flank of Jefferson Peak.

At 5:47 p.m. they were still six hundred yards short of their destination. *Mickey has to be inside by now,* she thought. *Probably moving toward the lodge.* She thought of Hennessy reunited with his children and it brought a tightening in her throat. She didn't even know them, but she could imagine how happy he would be. That made her happy.

She flashed on Hennessy looking down at her from up on his horse, and her smile never left her as she crossed the last quarter mile of the frozen subalpine terrain.

Down in the Jefferson Club Lodge, in the Court of Public Opinion, General Anarchy stood behind the prosecution table, ignoring the form of Chin Hoc Pan slumped and sleeping in the witness chair. He checked his watch. Two minutes to six.

He adjusted his headset. "Radio?"

"Right here, General."

"Where are Cobb and Dalton?"

"They rechecked every inch of the basement. They're going back to the Burnses'. We had a herd of elk come onto the grounds from the southeast a few minutes ago."

The Third Position leader thought about that. "Tell me if we get any other herds coming through the fence from the north."

"Roger that," Radio said.

General Anarchy glanced down at the machine gun he'd stowed under the prosecution table, then over at Citizen's Defender Emilia and the gun beneath her desk. She pushed back the veil. Their eyes met. She smiled and whispered, "I love you."

He nodded and said, "The final act, my sweet. All or nothing now." Their eyes lingered on each other, then Anarchy hardened, turned, stood, and looked past the hooded figure in the witness stand, past the Gauguin panting on the easel, and nodded to Bailiff Mouse, who waited offstage.

Mouse stepped out and pounded her staff on the ballroom floor. *"The Third Position versus Chin Hoc Pan.* The Court of Public Opinion is now open. Judge Truth presiding, all rise!"

Truth ordered Chin Hoc Pan's hood removed. The Hong Kong developer squinted at the lights, his eyes barely visible as he took in the room scornfully.

"You do not scare me," he snarled after spotting General Anarchy. "You make me watch others die, but you don't scare me."

Judge Truth said, "General Anarchy, the charges?"

"Depraved indifference, perversion, and willful destruction of life."

"What this depraved indifference?" Chin Hoc Pan said with the slouched bluster of a poker player. "I no pervert. I no destroy life."

"Guilty or not guilty?' Judge Truth demanded.

"Not guilty," the Hong Kong developer said. "Hoc Pan not guilty."

General Anarchy crossed to Gauguin's painting. "You enjoy art?"

The tycoon rolled his jaw as if deciding to answer before replying, "I have one of finest private collections in the world."

"Would you say this is your favorite painting?"

He shrugged. "It is my most recent acquisition, so it is favored."

"But not more than any of the others?"

Chin Hoc Pan hesitated, then said, "No, it is my favorite."

"Why do you like it so much? I'm just interested."

The developer glanced over at his beloved painting, struggling to explain. "With the jungle and the palm tree and the ocean beyond her, whole stories are suggested in questions: Who was she? Where did she come from? Who is her lover? I think in many ways it is a haunted thing, you know? More than it seems."

General Anarchy bobbed his head agreeably. "You

love her beauty and yet you have no wife and no known homosexual proclivities. Are you gay?"

The billionaire took that as a slap. "I am no gay. I just have little time for wife, family. For record, I like women."

"I don't think so," General Anarchy replied, wagging a gloved finger in the air as he walked to the jury box. "Mr. Hoc Pan, how did you make your money?"

He fielded the question easily. "Real estate development and various industries. All over Asia. I am very active in Shanghai these days. And I do like women."

"And Cambodia and Thailand?"

Chin Hoc Pan missed a beat before settling back into his poker face. "I have interests there, yes."

"Rantoon Beach?"

"Yes, I build oceanside resort there. Already sold out."

"How wonderful for you. And what of the people who lived near Rantoon Beach before you bought the land out from under them and built your exclusive resort?"

"Most work at resort."

Before General Anarchy could reply, Radio muttered in his headset, *"Second set of elk just entered, General. Northwest. Up on that cliff we crossed."*

Cheyenne O'Neil stood in thigh-deep snow, watching the last of the hostage rescuers go over the side of Jefferson's Nose. She was back from the rim twenty feet, on the edge of the woods where they'd tied up the horses. She shivered in the frigid night air and pulled up the hood on her parka. Then she stomped down the snow to give herself some room and lifted up the night-vision binoculars Kane had given her and peered around, seeing that the cliff ran on for several hundred yards before joining a ridge that ran down off Mount Jefferson to a saddle. The saddle gave way to Hellroaring Peak and the ski slopes, no more than a mile away. She put down the binoculars, frowned, and lifted them again to examine the saddle one more time.

Cheyenne recognized it for what it was, a likely escape route. She lowered the binoculars and made to turn on her radio headset to tell Kane, but then stopped. He'd ordered radio silence until the counterattack was sprung.

She stood there, stomping her feet, feeling increasingly anxious about the situation. Finally, she went with her gut and turned into the woods to find her horse. She'd ride to that saddle. The view of the lodge had to be at least as good.

It had taken six tablets of painkiller before Bridger stopped moaning. But the drugs turned him incoherent. He kept talking about things that had happened years ago when they were little kids, how Connor was always looking for Goldfish crackers and never shared.

Kneeling beside him, Connor grinned. It was true. But then Bridger began to sweat and shiver. "I'm cold and thirsty, Hailey. Cold and thirsty."

"I'll get him water and blankets," Connor said.

"You've gone the past two times, I'll do it," Hailey said. She stood up and took Cobb's pistol. "Dad's got to be here soon, doesn't he?"

Connor nodded. "He's probably right outside."

Hailey peeked out the two-way mirror into the office partially lit by the chandelier still blazing in the foyer. Empty. She eased the bookcase door open. She stepped out, then pushed it back, almost shut. She sniffed the air still tainted by the burnt fuel from the helicopters. She crossed the office in a trot toward the foyer. She stopped at the door and looked out at the tile floor. She saw Connor's bloody footprints and froze. Her heart beat faster. *How long have those been there? An hour at least.*

She leaned out and gazed left through the busted front door. She could see the lit walkway, empty. She almost moved, then noticed boot prints in the snow that had blown in the front door. Were they fresh? She didn't know. What should she do? She wished to God her father were there to help her. *Please,* she prayed, *please get him here in time.*

Hailey hesitated, telling herself to move, to get what Bridger needed. But something held her there a long moment. At last she took a breath and darted right around the doorjamb into the hallway.

Her wrist instantly felt as if a claw had clamped down on it. In one swift fluid movement, Cobb stripped her of the pistol and slammed his forearm across her mouth. He rammed her against the wall.

"You honestly thought you could keep me from finding you, little bitch?" Cobb laughed softly, throwing the pistol to Dalton and drawing his combat knife.

Hailey was rigid with fear, then got angry and started to struggle. Cobb's smile disappeared, replaced with homicidal fury. He wrenched on the girl's hair and put the knife to her neck. "You and your brothers like to play with razors, don't you, little bitch? Like to put 'em between toes. Know where I like to put 'em? All the way through the windpipe back to the spine. Pretty young neck like yours, I could take your head off in one cut. Iraqis taught me. They got a talent for it."

Hailey saw the pleasure pooling in Cobb's eyes, and felt it hack into her like the cold blade of a dull sword. Tears welled and dripped down her cheeks and she thought she'd pee her pants.

Dalton said, "General said he wants them alive, Cobb."

Cobb pressed the knife tip to Hailey's Adam's apple and whispered, "Only reason I'm not carrying your fucking head out of here."

He grabbed Hailey by the neck and marched her toward the front door. "By the blood that's all over her, one of her brothers is hit good," Cobb called over his shoulder to Dalton as he left the house. "Track the blood. Find 'em. Bring 'em to the ballroom."

Cobb dragged Hailey out the door and down the walkway. Hailey was shocked by the bitterness in the air, by the snow falling, by everything that had happened to her in the last fifteen seconds. Her father was supposed to be coming. It was supposed to be over. What about Bridger? They couldn't move him. They'd kill him. They'd kill Connor. He wouldn't give up without a fight. She had to get away and help.

She tried to squirm from Cobb's grasp as they went down the walkway to the lodge. She got her head around and bit his right forearm. Cobb howled in pain and she got free. But only for an instant before the Third Position soldier grabbed her vicelike and expertly with his left hand at the base of her neck, igniting nerves and rendering her helpless. She felt like he could snap her neck with a twist and she got up on tiptoe, dancing after him, feeling his fingers like hot tongs.

"Better," Cobb grunted, hustling her along. "Maybe you'll live awhile. Maybe I'll bite you somewhere before you die."

CHAPTER THIRTY-SIX

Inside the Court of Public Opinion, General Anarchy showed no physical reaction to the news that another herd of animals had crossed into the Jefferson Club grounds.

Instead, he glared at Chin Hoc Pan and growled, "Before you arrived, Rantoon was a virtual paradise. The people were dirt poor from a globalist's accumulated-wealth perspective. But the jungle along the beach there teemed with fruits and animals. And the sea held schools of fish. The people lived in a subsistence economy that functioned perfectly well enough to support generations going back thousands of years. You managed to destroyed Rantoon in two years."

Chin Hoc Pan rolled his eyes. "This is progress. World economy coming whether you like it or not. These people have no medical care. I give it. They have poor shelter. I give building supplies. They have no money. I give them jobs."

"Stole their lives, and gave them jobs," General Anarchy said coldly. "You like that, don't you, stealing lives, stealing spirits?"

The billionaire scrunched up his face. "I do not know what you talk about."

General Anarchy sat back against the prosecution table with his arms folded. "We figure you must lie there at night in one of your thirteen homes around the world or in your big jet, and you must think about the lives you've stolen, the innocents you've shattered. We figure it must please you. Otherwise, why do it?"

Chin Hoc Pan sputtered with uneasy laughter. "You make no sense."

"I make perfect sense," General Anarchy informed the jury, before returning to the painting. "Do you know why you really love this Gauguin?"

"You read my mind now?" Chin Hoc Pan said, and his laughter grew caustic. "Many men try to read Hoc Pan's mind and fail. Go. You try."

General Anarchy pointed his crème-colored glove at the girl in the painting. "You love the painting because of her. She represents something to you, doesn't she?"

"Gauguin at height of his powers."

"No," General Anarchy said. "We believe it's her girlish waist and her breasts just pouting. Or is it the smoothness of her skin? Not womanly at all."

Chin Hoc Pan said nothing, but his eyes darted to the girl.

"You love looking at this painting because this is the

age you like them," General Anarchy said. "Fourteen, maybe thirteen, twelve on occasion. All blushed with their first femininity as you take their virginity. That's your specialty and your obsession."

"I do nothing like this!" the billionaire shouted. "These are lies. Not true!"

Inside the darkened passage off Burns's office, Connor heard Cobb order Dalton to find him and Bridger. *Hailey!* He sprang from his wounded brother's side, grabbed the nearest gun, the shotgun, and got to the two-way mirror in time to see Cobb taking Hailey out.

His immediate reaction was to barrel out the secret-passage door and go after her. But then Dalton stepped into the office, his machine gun up. Connor froze and realized that the bookcase door was slightly ajar.

Dalton flipped on the light and strolled in, the gun sweeping the room. Connor's stomach dropped when he saw the Third Position soldier following bloody foot-prints on the rug. Dalton's eyes came up and he looked right at the two-way mirror. Connor took a step back. Bridger started muttering, his eyes closed.

"Shhhh, kid," Connor whispered, taking a soft step back and lying down quick on his belly in the prone shooting position his father had taught them. He pressed off the safety and looked down the barrel at the beam of light shining through the gap in the door, knowing what he had to do, and wondering if he could.

The door started to push open. Connor rolled his shoulders and got low over the shotgun's rib. The machine gun barrel appeared first. Dalton pushed the door open more, revealing his shoulder. Connor's finger twitched, then he saw the side of the Third Position soldier's face. He slapped the trigger.

The report was deafening in that enclosed place as the gun bucked against his shoulder. But he saw Dalton spin sideways from view and there was a crash. Connor suddenly felt sick and wanted to cry.

"Think I killed him," he choked at his delirious brother. "I killed him, Bridge."

Connor stood up, wobbly, his mind tilting, telling himself he'd done it to protect Bridger. But he'd killed someone. Really killed someone. The shroud of that enveloped him as he got to his feet, reeled over, and pushed the door open wider, expecting to see Dalton lying dead behind Burns's desk.

But he wasn't there. Just smears of blood on the wood floor.

Connor's adrenal glands gushed a wanting to flee and he remembered he hadn't pumped the shotgun. His arm shot out for the pump.

Dalton got up from the other side of the desk. His left cheek was stripped of skin. His lips looked minced. Blood dripped from his mouth. His left ear looked like cauliflower dipped in ketchup. His left eye was deflated and bleeding down on the exposed muscle of his face.

"Mutherfuck," he said in a garbled tongue. "Mutherfuck kill you, kid."

Connor struggled with the action. It felt jammed. When Dalton swung the machine gun at him, he started to scream.

* * *

At the same time, General Anarchy was ranting at Chin Hoc Pan in that weird, electrically altered voice.

"You destroy cultures, impoverishing the people so they'll give up their virgin daughters to you for payment," he thundered. "Sometimes three a day. We spoke to one madam in Laos who says you had four in one afternoon last year. You're a pure sexual predator, a serial pedophile, who knows no boundaries to his cravings. By our incomplete count, you've forcibly taken the innocence of more than three hundred girls in the last five years. Before you came here to the Jefferson Club, you had your personal jet land in Phnom Penh, Cambodia, just so you could break the hymen of an eleven-year-old."

Chin Hoc Pan shook his head and spat. "You no destroy me with stories."

General Anarchy snatched up the television remote and hit PLAY. The screen illuminated with a home video shot of the billionaire wearing a black silk robe hanging open, revealing his rolling flesh. The young girl on the bed was naked too. Her eyes were shut. Her head hung and she was whining in shame. Chin Hoc Pan seemed pleased as he stood beside her, stroking himself while rhythmically pushing his finger in her vagina.

General Anarchy went to the rear of the courtroom and took a black crocodile leather briefcase from one of his soldiers. When Chin Hoc Pan saw it, he began to shake. "How you get that?" he demanded, growing anxious.

"We employ safecrackers," Judge Truth replied.

The Hong Kong billionaire stared at the briefcase in

General Anarchy's hands as if looking at the book that told his life and sealed his fate. He cringed and strained away when the briefcase was opened to reveal hundreds of DVD disks.

"Filmed every one of his deflowering sessions for the past twenty-six years," Anarchy told the cameras. "He takes these disks everywhere he goes. All categorized by name, nationality, and age."

General Anarchy shook his head. "The fourth-richest man in the world, and these are his most valuable possessions—the digital balance sheet of the innocence he's stolen. Your Honor, the Third Position rests."

Inside Horatio Burns's office, Connor saw the machine gun coming for him and his world went slow-motion as he yanked fruitlessly on the shotgun's action. Dalton's good eye gleamed with brutal hatred as he made to press the trigger.

The first shot hit the Third Position soldier square in the back. His armored vest stopped the round. But the impact threw him forward and he triggered the machine gun, blasting the open door of the secret passage and blowing out the two-way mirror. The second shot caught Dalton at the nape of his neck, severing his spinal cord and blowing out the front of his throat, spraying Connor with blood before he collapsed like a rag doll, the machine gun falling from his hands.

Connor's whole being turned upside down and he started to faint. But before he lost consciousness, he swore he saw his father in the office doorway, rising from a combat shooting position.

Mickey Hennessy saw his son drop and sprinted to his side, fearing he'd been hit. Connor lay in a heap next to Horatio Burns's desk chair. He rolled the boy over, seeing that he was still breathing. Tears welled in his eyes.

"Connor," he said as Phelps and the rest of the hostage rescue team fanned out inside the office, some of them already moving to the passageway door. "Connor, can you hear me?"

Connor felt like someone was drawing him up from a well. "Dad?"

Hennessy saw that his son wasn't wounded and grabbed him up in his arms and hugged him, the tears flowing freely. "Oh, my God, I thought he'd shot you," he cried. "I thought I shot you."

"Dad," Connor managed. "Bridger's been hit bad. And they took Hailey."

His sister heard the dull bump of the shotgun blast as Cobb hauled her toward the open door to the snowmobile garage. The Third Position soldier heard it too and halted, looking back toward the Burnses' house, expressionless. Several moments passed, and then they heard a shot that swelled into a burst of machine gun fire.

Cobb grinned. "Maybe your brothers won't be coming after all."

"Or maybe your buddy's dead," she snarled.

Cobb pushed her roughly inside the garage, past the snowmobiles, and up the metal staircase and into the lodge down the hall from the Dirty Shame Saloon. Hailey moved numbly while her brain screamed for answers.

Where's Dad? Where's the FBI? What were those shots? Are Bridger and Connor dead? Am I going to die?

Cobb marched her into the atrium and down the stairs into the ballroom just as General Anarchy was finishing his tirade against Chin Hoc Pan.

"Filmed every one of his deflowering sessions for the past twenty-six years," she heard him say as Cobb threw her into a straddle position on a chair between Cristoph and Rose. He used plastic restraints to lash her wrists to the back of the chair.

"Don't move," Cobb growled in her ear.

She caught Anarchy's image on one of Rose's monitors. "He takes these disks everywhere he goes," he was saying. "All categorized by name, nationality, and age."

General Anarchy shook his head. "The fourth-richest man in the world, and these are his most valuable possessions—the digital balance sheet of the innocence he's stolen. Your Honor, the Third Position rests."

Hailey swiveled her head. Cobb was leaning up against a timber post that supported the ballroom ceiling, still decorated with the tattered remnants of the New Year's Eve ball. Cobb had his knife in his hand and was sharpening it on a stone. With every pass of the blade, Hailey's terror grew. It multiplied when she realized that neither he nor Rose nor Cristoph were wearing hoods.

I've seen them, she thought. *They'll definitely kill me.*

Her insides turned jittery and she forced herself not to look at Cobb, but at the screens Rose was watching. On the largest screen, Truth gave the jury their instructions. "Chin Hoc Pan, guilty or not guilty. You decide.

Fifteen minutes. Start voting now on www.thirdposi tionjustice.net."

"And we're down," Rose said into her headset. The screens went blank.

Hailey heard Chin Hoc Pan yell, "I speak in my defense! I speak in my defense!"

General Anarchy walked in off the set of the Court of Public Opinion with Truth behind him and Citizen's Defender Emilia trailing.

"Get your men ready to fight," Anarchy said. "They're inside the grounds."

Rose panicked. "General?"

"Leave one camera on, high rear," he ordered as the room descended toward chaos. The jury members and other Third Position soldiers lunged for their weapons and put on their camouflage clothing and hoods.

General Anarchy noticed Cobb and then Hailey. He walked up to her and backhanded her across the face so hard she and the chair fell to the floor. Everything in Hailey reduced to a blur of searing pain in her face. She'd never been hit like that. She couldn't even imagine it. And in that stunned and imbalanced state, she heard Anarchy shouting at her in this strange voice, this non–electrically altered voice, "You honestly think you can stop the inevitable?"

She rotated her head and saw Anarchy draw back his boot to kick her.

Cobb stepped in. "Uh-uh, General. You promised her to me."

General Anarchy glared at Cobb, then at Hailey, and back again. He relaxed. "Where are the other two?"

"One's hit," Cobb said. "Dalton's after them in the Burnses' house."

"Radio, call Dalton," Anarchy said into his headset. "Tell him the government's coming."

The Third Position leader hesitated, then went straight to Cristoph, who was standing, frantically typing on his keyboard. "How many?" he demanded.

"Couple hundred over thirty million," Cristoph replied. "*American Idol* numbers."

"You've done your job, then," General Anarchy said. "Get your gun."

"Don't you want the vote?" Cristoph asked.

"I already know the verdict," General Anarchy replied. "Cobb? I need you to take care of Mr. Pan before you go."

"And the girl?" Cobb demanded.

"She's yours when I'm done with her," General Anarchy said, adjusting his headset. "Radio?"

"*Nothing from Dalton, General.*"

The Third Position leader seemed to factor that, then said, "Tell Carpenter it's time. The moment he hears shooting, kill them all."

CHAPTER THIRTY-SEVEN

Phelps, the hostage rescue leader, put out a hand and stopped Mickey Hennessy as he attempted to leave the office.

"Where do you think you're going?" Phelps demanded in a hushed voice.

"To get my daughter," Hennessy said.

"That's my job," Phelps said. "And Johansson's. You've got a wounded boy here who needs you. We'll find her."

Hennessy wanted to fight, but then realized if he went in there half-cocked he'd probably hurt Hailey's chances of survival. He swallowed his wanting to attack the lodge and hurried back to the secret passageway, where Connor watched the medic on Phelps's team put a morphine drip line into Bridger's arm.

"Promise me you won't go in there," Phelps said,

turning on the switch that activated the small camera mounted to his helmet.

"Promise," Hennessy said, then watched with mixed emotions as the hostage rescue leader took off down the passage toward the wine cellar.

Hennessy knelt in the doorway to the passage, feeling battered and helpless again.

"The tourniquet saved him," the medic said.

Connor's lip started to tremble. "It was Hailey's idea, Dad."

A mile west and three thousand feet above the lodge, Cheyenne O'Neil dismounted her horse a second time, dropping into thigh-deep snow. She tied the horse to a tree and pulled out her binoculars. She trained them on the lodge and spotted armed men in white camouflage slipping out various doors.

She reached to her waist and triggered the radio. "This is O'Neil."

Kane's voice came back immediately. *"Shut down. Now."*

She winced, pursed her lips, then triggered the radio again. "They know, SAC."

A second later, she heard the unmistakable rattle of gunfire and spotted tracers zipping across the canyon floor in front of the lodge.

"We're engaged!" came Johansson's voice over her headset.

"Team one, go!" Kane ordered.

* * *

At the sound of the shooting, General Anarchy began barking into his headset so all in his army could hear. "Resist, then escape. Live a low-profile life. Await my contact. If you are caught, tell them your cover story. Confusion is everything. Never forget, confusion is everything!"

Jury members grabbed their weapons and fanned out. Citizen's Defender Emilia yanked off her veil, revealing her blackened face. She passed so close that Hailey could smell the woman and her scent: jasmine, like her mother wore.

General Anarchy yelled at Rose, "Take us live!" And then he took off into the courtroom while the gunfire began to build outside. "Cobb!" he yelled. "Cobb!"

Cobb looked at Hailey. "You wait right here for me, little bitch." Then he drew his pistol, pulled on his white hood, and followed.

The computer screens lit up on Rose's table. Truth stood behind the bench looking down at Chin Hoc Pan, who'd been gagged. General Anarchy's face appeared on the screen closest to Hailey. "I warned what would happen if those loyal to the corporate kings attempted another rescue attempt."

Rose typed on her keyboard. The screen changed to that high rear long shot of the courtroom. Truth stood behind the bench. "We the people of the Third Position find Chin Hoc Pan guilty of serial child rape and perversion," he roared. "The penalty is death by an appropriate method!"

Cobb entered from behind the jury box, hood on. He

carried a pistol. The Hong Kong developer went wall-eyed with fear when Cobb began to raise the gun. But then Mouse stepped out and put her hand on Cobb's weapon.

"Let me," she said, then took the pistol and aimed it savagely at Chin Hoc Pan's groin and said, "This is how it feels to be raped." She fired three times.

The billionaire screamed and writhed in misery while Truth pounded on his gavel. "The Court of Public Opinion is in recess. Check this Web site for further broadcasts."

"That's it," Rose said, standing from her post. She yanked on her white hood, picked up her machine gun, then stuck a cigarette in her mouth. She lit it walking away.

Cristoph was still typing furiously. It looked to Hailey like he was uploading something. She struggled to maneuver her chair so she could get free of the plastic restraints. But then Cobb exited the courtroom, coming right at her with his knife drawn.

"Nighty-night, little nightmare," he called.

Hennessy knelt in the mouth of the secret passageway watching the medic continue to work on Bridger, who had not regained consciousness. He heard Cheyenne O'Neil's warning through his headset, followed quickly by the first chatter of gunfire, and then Kane's order for hostage rescue team one to attack.

He knew Phelps and the eight men who'd entered the lodge through the wine cellar were now in full assault mode. He spun around in time to see the rest of Phelps's men sprinting out the front door to the Burnses' house, heading toward the lodge. In an instant, he decided to break his promise to Phelps.

He got up, grabbed Dalton's machine gun, and started across the office after them.

"Dad!" Connor called.

"Stay with Bridger," he ordered. "Help the medic. I'm going to get Hailey."

Hennessy didn't hesitate when the medic yelled at him to stop. He broke into a trot down the hill away from the house, seeing the band of hostage rescuers sweep left down the south wing of the lodge, heading toward the kitchen door. He went the opposite way, and climbed up onto the loading docks, seeing the bodies of many of his men lying there alongside the corpses of the Capitol Police officer and Chef Giulio. Lerner was facing up.

He stared in disbelief and sorrow. They had wives. Kids. At the sound of more shooting on the other side of the lodge, Hennessy felt himself turn ruthless, violent, and vengeful. Any thought of the pain in his wounded arm was gone as he called up all the counterassault training he'd gotten with DSS and became someone else, a ruthless person who would not hesitate to kill in pursuit of his goal. *Hailey.* He moved into the laundry. Empty. He quickly climbed the short flight of stairs to the dead-bolted door that blocked access to the utility stairwell.

He twisted the bolt and threw the door open. *Clear.* Hennessy took ten steps to the door that led to the first floor south hallway. He hesitated, then heard more shots and kicked the door open. He came into the hallway in a crouch. Out of his peripheral vision he caught a Third Position soldier coming right at him.

Phelps and his men stormed into the basement storage area from the hallway off the bakery. Two Third Position soldiers guarded the stairway. The one they called Carpenter stood in the open doorway of the storage unit closest to the staircase. He was aiming a pistol inside.

Carpenter got off two shots before Phelps opened up, killing him. The Third Position soldiers near the stairs returned fire. Phelps rolled behind a stack of canned goods, and rolled again into the next opening, spraying both men. One crashed down the staircase. The other hung up on the railing. Dead.

"Take that staircase!" Phelps shouted. Two of his men ran forward and climbed up over the anti-globalist toward the kitchen, Heckler & Koch 9mm machine guns tight to their shoulders.

Phelps went to the open cell, stepped over the body of Carpenter, and found a corpse in a tuxedo and hood. The victim was lying on his side, blood seeping from the hood and puddling on the storage room floor. The hostage rescue leader cursed and took the hood off.

Back inside the CIRG command center, on the monitor broadcasting the hostage rescue leader's camera, Willis Kane saw what Phelps saw and hung his head. Jack Doore, the visionary genius behind YES!, lay dead on the floor of the storage unit with two bullets through the back of his head.

"Oh, God, no," Kane said, crumpling into a chair

next to Agent Pritoni, who watched the scene in stunned silence.

Gunfire erupted from somewhere behind Phelps. The hostage rescue leader whirled, leaving a blur on the screen as he exited the storage unit and looked up the stairs toward the kitchen.

"Phelps, this is CIRG Commander," Kane called into his headset. "Do you have survivors?"

Before Phelps could reply, another voice broke in. *"SAC, we're taking heavy fire up here. Four, maybe five in the hallway beyond the kitchen."*

Kane grew angrier. "This is CIRG Commander. I repeat. Are there survivors?"

Hennessy threw himself sideways, triggering the machine gun as he crashed to the hallway floor. The Third Position soldier danced at the impacts, hit the wall, and crumpled. Hennessy reacted in an instant, springing up and taking the spare clips off the dead anti-globalist. And something better: two hand grenades.

He snatched them up too, stuffed them in his jacket pocket, and almost headed straight toward the grand atrium, meaning to fight his way into the ballroom. Then he thought better of it. He had no way of knowing where she was. If she wasn't in the ballroom, he wouldn't find her.

So he charged back into the utility stairwell and climbed the stairs two at time to the second floor of the lodge. He entered the hallway and found it clear. The gunfire elsewhere in the building sounded intense as he ran toward the north wing of the lodge.

He rounded the corner. The hallway was empty as well save a room service cart turned over at the far end, near the door with a camera bubble mounted above it. He went straight at the security center with the machine gun up, ready, knowing that if it was still manned, the Third Position soldier inside was seeing him coming.

Radio did see Hennessy coming. He picked up his machine gun, keeping an eye on the hallway camera and the one above the door. Hennessy was moving at a deliberate pace ten feet from the door. Radio smiled and flipped off his safety.

But Hennessy suddenly broke into a sprint. For an instant the Third Position soldier lost sight of him on the monitors. Then he caught him diving right beneath the camera mounted above the door. Something thumped the door. The hallway monitor showed Hennessy scrambling to his feet and hauling ass toward the landing and the atrium staircase.

Radio frowned. He spun and grabbed a joystick mounted in the console. He toggled it so the door camera aimed straight down. He saw what had thumped the door and instantly felt bile rise up in his throat.

A live grenade lay on the transom.

Cobb's beefy left paw reached for Hailey's hair. His right hand clutched the knife like a hatchet. Hailey swung the chair diagonally upward and smashed the legs against Cobb's knees. He buckled. She wrenched her body around, then struck the chair against his head. He reeled to one side and she thought she had her freedom.

But when she tried to hit his head a second time and put him out for good, he grabbed the leg of the chair and held it with his left hand. He yanked the chair toward him, bringing Hailey with it. He brought the tip of his knife to his left shoulder, meaning to slash her across the throat.

Hailey screamed, "No!"

Cobb never got the chance. General Anarchy stepped up and grabbed his wrist. "I still need her." Cobb gritted his teeth, struggled, then thought better of it and relaxed.

Hailey started sobbing.

"Cut her free," Anarchy said, and released his hand. The Third Position soldier glared at Hailey as he sliced the plastic restraints.

A firefight erupted right outside the ballroom windows. Anarchy grabbed her by the hair. "No!" she screamed as he began to drag her. "No! No!"

Floor-to-ceiling windows at either end of the ballroom exploded inward with concussive booms that stunned everyone. To Hailey it felt like jackhammers had chiseled through her ear to ear. Hailey's hysteria turned delirious. The whole room seemed to sway. Two more flash-bang grenades exploded, throwing a brilliant, blinding aluminum light, thundering through Hailey's skull and vibrating through every bone in her body. For a moment she knew only that she felt cold and the air smelled poisonous.

Then she felt Anarchy tugging on her hair again. She peered up at him, seeing that his painted lips were contorting and popping wickedly. But she heard nothing except the hollow roar of the stun grenades echoing in her rattled brain. She noticed the Third Position leader had a machine gun now and he wrenched her along beside him, throwing the barrel of the gun over her shoulder.

"I repeat, are there survivors?"

Phelps twisted from the staircase and spotted one of his men emerging from the far storage unit leading Horatio Burns, who was bent over in his tuxedo, looking terribly aged, bewildered, and scarred by his ordeal.

"We have survivors, CIRG Commander," Phelps said, smiling and training his camera on the billionaire.

"Am I the only one left?" Burns asked in a wavering, weak voice. "Please don't tell me I'm the only one left."

A second hostage rescuer emerged from the adjoining locker, helping a shattered Aaron Grant, whose face was smeared with grime.

Burns stared at him and then broke into tears. "Yes. At least there's another."

"Get them out of there," Kane ordered in Phelps's headset. *"Now!"*

The hostages rescuers made to lead the industrialist away. But Aaron Grant saw the open door to Doore's cell and asked, "Where's Jack?"

Phelps shook his head. "I'm sorry, sir. He's dead."

"Jack?" Grant said, staggered. "No. Not Jack! Jack?"

He tried to lunge past Phelps to see, but the hostage rescue leader blocked him. "Mr. Grant, you don't want to remember him that way."

Grant gazed at Phelps in disbelief before doubling

over and breaking down. "Oh, my God. Why? Jack Doore never hurt anyone in his entire life. All he did was give to people. An honest-to-God visionary genius and they've killed him. Why?"

"I don't know, sir," Phelps replied, helping Grant up and moving him after Burns. "I honestly can't imagine what goes through some people's minds."

CHAPTER THIRTY-EIGHT

Hennessy dodged around the corner onto the staircase landing and threw his back up against the wall. He heard the flash-bang grenades go off two stories below him in the ballroom a split second before the real grenade detonated at the door to the security center. Smoke and dust from the blast blew down the hallway and out into the atrium. Downstairs the sound of gunfire swelled as Johansson's men stormed the lodge.

Hennessy waited a count of three before dodging back into the hallway. He squinted and choked against the explosive dust. The security room door was perforated and half off its hinges. He kicked it in and found Radio sprawled backward across the monitor console. The Third Position soldier had gaping chest wounds, and struggled for air. Most of the monitors were shattered. Only three glowed.

Hennessy grabbed Radio by the throat. "Where's my daughter?"

Radio looked at him and smiled. "In the hands of Anarchy."

Hennessy squeezed. "Where?"

Radio shrugged and coughed up blood. Hennessy wanted to throttle the man. "Why did you do this?" he shouted in rage.

That made Radio laugh a gargling laugh. "The money," he said. "What else?"

Radio choked on his laugh and then seized up, straining and bug-eyed, before a clot of blood was expelled from his lips and he died.

Hennessy threw Radio's body aside and found five monitors still glowing. One displayed the rear of the lodge. Another the relics of the Greenwater helicopters. The last three showed the ballroom lit only by the tracer rounds ripping through it, and the atrium staircase from both sides.

Hennessy typed furiously. The monitors split into grids of twelve. Each slot showed a different camera angle in the lodge. He leaned over the panels, trying to study them, desperate to find her. *Where is she?*

General Anarchy kneed Hailey roughly in the butt, urging her toward the back wall of the ballroom. Johansson's men stormed the ballroom through the shattered window frames. It had started to snow again and the fury of a building storm swirled in behind them.

Another flash-bang grenade went off. Windows on

the ballroom's west side disintegrated and threw shards through the room like daggers. The Third Position soldiers inside the ballroom opened up with machine guns. The real pitched battle began.

Hailey felt her entire upper body being jerked around. Blue flames burst out the end of General Anarchy's machine gun. She heard what sounded like bells pealing over the roar of a stormy ocean, saw FBI agents ducking for cover, and realized Anarchy was shooting at them. The smell was like burnt oil. She reached up and slapped at the barrel, crying out at the way it singed her, but knowing that his bullets were missing the hostage rescuers.

General Anarchy smashed the gun against her face, then grabbed her tightly by the collar of her sweatshirt and hauled her in close to his body, using her as a shield.

"Kill him!" she screamed at the hostage rescuers. "Kill him!"

Bullets hammered the wall right next to her. Then she felt herself dragged backward. And suddenly Cobb, Truth, and Citizen's Defender Emilia were there with their backs to her, covering General Anarchy's retreat through the doors to the kitchen.

Inside, General Anarchy spun Hailey around and marched her alongside him, keeping her between himself and six other Third Position soldiers fighting at the other end of the kitchen, where a staircase gave way to the storage basement. She and Anarchy went toward a door that led to a hallway off the kitchen where the banquet-ware was stored. Hailey had gone all over the lodge with her father and vaguely remembered that it ultimately led to a bank of service elevators between the Dirty Shame Saloon and the snowmobile garage.

Anarchy dragged her past a stainless steel prep table ten feet from the doorway. Hailey spotted a butcher knife on it.

Up on one of the security room monitors, in one of those tiny square displays, Hennessy spotted Anarchy dragging his daughter into the kitchen. His hope soared and he double-clicked on the thumbnail. The feed filled the screen, revealing Truth and Citizen's Defender Emilia guarding their leader's rear as they passed a prep table. Hennessy saw the knife at the same time his daughter did.

"Jesus, Hailey, don't!" Hennessy cried.

But she reached out, snagged the knife, and tried to hook around and stab General Anarchy. Truth had seen the knife too, and stepped in before she could. He struck her wrist a vicious blow, sending the weapon spinning. Hailey hunched up and held her wrist like it was broken. General Anarchy released her a second, then slapped her across the face. She fell to one knee. He wrenched her back upright and forced her through the swinging doorway.

At the sight of his daughter's courage and mistreatment, Hennessy felt something primal rise in him, something so deep in his DNA that it was impossible to name, let alone contain. On the screen, Hailey and Anarchy disappeared into the hallway off the back of the kitchen. In an instant, he knew where they were going and why. Hennessy spun around, grabbed his gun, and ran back to the staircase landing. He crossed the landing to the south wing, raced to the bank of service elevators, and hit the DOWN button.

One pinged and opened. He jumped in and hit the button that said 1ST FLOOR, DIRTY SHAME SALOON. The doors closed. Hennessy threw himself up against the operating panel, feeling himself drop two stories and then settle to a stop. He moved with the sound of the door opening, swinging around with the Sterling in the lead.

Truth and Cobb were already past him, heading into the hallway opposite the saloon and the entrance to the snowmobile garage. Hennessy was about to step out of the elevator when General Anarchy appeared, pushing Hailey in front of him. Hailey spotted him first. "Daddy!" she shrieked.

Hennessy saw the gun barrel over her shoulder and twisted back behind the control panel and to the floor just as General Anarchy and Citizen's Defender Emilia opened fire. The mirror on the elevator's back wall shattered. Bullets stung and whined around Hennessy, who held his hands over his head until the shooting stopped.

He rolled over onto his belly. They were gone, replaced by Cristoph. Hennessy cut him down in his tracks. Hennessy then leaped to his feet and sprinted across the opening, firing over Cristoph's body back down the hallway toward the kitchen.

"Daddy!" he heard Hailey scream from the other side of the garage doorway. "Daddy, please!"

Hennessy slammed in a new clip, then kicked open

the door and stepped out onto the metal staircase landing above the garage floor. A Third Position soldier was waiting and tried to hit him from behind with the butt of his gun. But Hennessy caught the motion and spun with it, using the soldier's forward momentum to heave his attacker over the railing. The man hit the cement and didn't move.

Hennessy saw at least fifteen Third Position soldiers in the garage. Seven or eight were trying to get snowmobiles started. Seven or eight were already squealing the machines across the cement floor toward the open garage door and the snowy night.

General Anarchy had Hailey in front of him on one. Citizen's Defender Emilia rode behind Truth on another. Cobb rode alone. Hailey was looking wildly back at her father as they accelerated. The other five sleds with them blocked his ability to shoot as they fled the garage and disappeared into the night.

Hennessy went insane when another sled started up. It was a heavy-duty Polaris, one of the ski patrol's, and had several pairs of skis strapped into a basket on the back. The soldier hit the throttle. The tractor treads spun and threw up sparks crossing the concrete floor. Hennessy shot him as the machine hit the edge of the snow. The Third Position soldier flipped off. His machine flew out the door and crashed.

Hennessy raked the rest of the garage, sending the other Third Position soldiers who were trying to escape scurrying for cover. He jumped down the stairs firing back and forth, oblivious to the danger. He burst out the door into the snowstorm, seeing the headlights of the escaping snowmobiles bobbing and weaving toward the ski lift and Fortune's Alley. He wrenched up the crashed snowmobile, which was still running, and got on.

He went skidding through the snow as he tried to jam the machine gun barrel between the brake lines and the handlebars. The muzzle finally slid through and wedged. Hennessy braced the butt of the gun against his chest, got hold of both handles, and twisted the throttle.

The snowmobile floundered in the powder snow, then gained speed and began to plane as he passed the door to the kitchen. He was going forty when he roared past the ballroom where the firefight still raged. A Third Position soldier burst out of a side door, heading toward the woods. Hennessy aimed at him, released his right hand from the steering column, and found the trigger of his gun.

The soldier tried to turn to shoot at the headlight, but Hennessy's fire dropped him. He peered ahead through the falling snow, seeing the beams of light that represented his captive daughter passing one of the downed Greenwater helicopters, heading up the face of Hellroaring Peak.

In the saddle that joined Hellroaring and Mount Jefferson, Cheyenne O'Neil watched the lodge through the night-vision binoculars, hearing the shots and explosions from nearly a mile away. She felt frozen and useless. The fight was inside and she couldn't see a thing. She was almost going to ask permission from Kane to return to the horses and start the ride back down to the command center when she spotted the first snowmobiles clearing the lodge base area and starting the climb toward her.

She pressed the transmit on her radio and spoke into her headset. "CIRG Commander, this is O'Neil."

There was a moment's pause before Willis Kane's voice came back with slight exasperation in his staticky voice. *"Go ahead, O'Neil."*

"I've got eight, repeat eight snowmobiles leaving the lodge area, heading west-northwest up the face of Hellroaring Mountain," she said, raising the binoculars again.

"How far . . . your location?" Kane asked.

"I changed location, SAC," she said. "I'm a mile west-southwest of where I left Johansson's men. They're coming right at me."

". . . far?"

"Thousand yards, maybe less," she said, then spotted another snowmobile blazing out of the base area. "Make that nine snowmobiles now."

Mickey Hennessy's anxious voice came over her headset blurred by wind. *"This is Hennessy, I'm on that ninth snowmobile. Anarchy's got Hailey. I repeat, my daughter Hailey is with them."*

Hailey shivered uncontrollably in the frigid wind that seeped around the windshield of the snowmobile as it climbed Hellroaring Peak. Anarchy sat right behind her. She could feel the power of his body through his heavy snow camouflage. She heard him say something and the whole escape party slowed. She trembled violently, watching them put on night-vision goggles. They turned off the snowmobile headlights and took off again. She couldn't see a thing, and the snow stung her eyes. She ducked down behind the windshield again, trying to stay warm.

She kept looking at the shadows of Anarchy's arms to either side of her. Biting him was impossible with the insulation he wore. And there were sleds all around her. If she tried to escape, they'd catch her or run her over. But the truth was she didn't have the strength to try. With every passing second in the terrible cold she felt weaker. She dropped her head, praying to God that her father was coming, that he would save her.

Something compelled her to look back as they crossed a traverse on the ski trail. Far behind the seven other snowmobiles, she caught sight of a single slashing beam of light. *It's him!* she thought. *He's coming!*

She'd no sooner had that hopeful reaction when she saw the beam of light veer off to the north and disappear. *It's not him. It's another Third Position soldier.* She felt crushed and forsaken. Her tears dripped to icy streaks on her numbing face.

Hennessy was just below the low traverse to Platinum Bowl, the farthest northern ski terrain on the mountain, when the escaping Third Position Army leaders extinguished their headlights. He slowed and stopped his machine. He heard them still churning up Fortune's Alley, and in a split second he understood why General Anarchy and his men were taking Hailey toward Cheyenne. They were going to cross the saddle, heading toward Wolverine Pass. If they made it through the pass, they'd be heading down the Jefferson Range's west flank. The valley beyond stretched toward Idaho and was one of the most remote in the state of Montana.

Hennessy looked at the lights one last time, then veered off. He yelled into his microphone, "CIRG Commander, do you copy?"

Kane's voice came back garbled.

"Repeat?" Hennessy yelled. Nothing. His radio was dying and he knew it. "Cheyenne, can you hear me?"

"Barely," she said.

"I'm coming toward the saddle from your north," he said. "Do not shoot. Repeat, do not shoot!"

"I copy," Cheyenne said. He tore up a trail between stands of pine trees, ducking at the deep powder snow that burst all around his head and muted the glow of his headlight.

Three minutes later, Hennessy killed the headlights and relied on his headlamp as he approached the top of Platinum Bowl. He eased the sled forward until he spotted a small red light flashing twenty yards away. He shut down the snowmobile, wrestled his machine gun free of the brake cables, and jumped off into the deep snow. He waded his way to Cheyenne, who stood at the triangular tip of a stand of bare aspen trees that separated Platinum Bowl from Fortune's Alley and the saddle between Hellroaring Peak and Mount Jefferson.

"My radio's dying," he said. "Tell Kane they're heading for Wolverine Pass and the western side of the Jeffersons, Anarchy, Truth, Citizen's Defender Emilia, all of them. Tell him to get helicopters up there."

Cheyenne handed him the night-vision binoculars. Hennessy rammed the glasses to his eyes, seeing the world take on that peculiar green hue. One hundred yards below him and closing fast in the howling storm, General Anarchy drove the fourth sled from the front. Hennessy had a moment's panic not seeing Hailey and dreaded what had become of her. But then she raised her head behind the windshield as the column slowed.

"Fourth from the front's Anarchy and Hailey," he whispered to Cheyenne. Cheyenne saw how close they were and put down the radio before she could call Kane.

"We'll take out the first three and the last four," she said, unholstering her pistol. She held it balanced over her left hand, which now grasped a powerful SureFire flashlight.

Hennessy got his gun. Fearing what might happen if he sprayed the escape party with machine gun fire, he flipped the switch from automatic to semiautomatic, hoping to reduce the chance that Hailey might get hit.

"First guy's mine," he whispered.

"I'll hit your guy in the goggles with the SureFire, then take the second," she said.

CHAPTER THIRTY-NINE

The first sled closed ground, grinding its way up the last vertical of Fortune's Alley. Cheyenne waited until they were almost upon them before she thumbed the SureFire LumaMax light on full, blinding power. The beam hit the lead soldier in the night-vision goggles. He twisted as if shot and threw up his hands.

Hennessy's gun barked. The Third Position soldier flipped sideways off the sled, right in front of the second rider, who slowed to avoid him.

That was all Cheyenne needed. She hit the second rider in the goggles with the SureFire and shot at the same time. Her bullet shattered the windshield and hit him in the throat. The second rider rocked backward off his sled, right in the path of Mouse.

But Mouse had torn down her goggles after the first shot. She drove her sled straight over her dead comrade, machine gun up and over the windshield, firing at the woods where Hennessy and Cheyenne hid.

The bullets cracked in the aspen branches above them as they dove for cover, landing right next to each other behind a snowed-in log. Hennessy threw his body over Cheyenne's as other members of the escaping party opened up, adding to the deadly barrage that bit and gouged the trees around them.

Even over the sound of gunfire, Hennessy heard snowmobiles accelerating away. The shooting stopped. His heart was pounding. Cheyenne made to move beneath him.

"Don't," he hissed softly as he heard the sled engine noises fade. "Some of them are still here."

He huddled there, tense, listening. After a long moment, he heard the swish of fabric against fabric. One of the Third Position soldiers was close, easing into the thicket where they lay. He heard that swish again and flipped his gun back to full automatic. Then he reached down into his pocket and found the second grenade. He thumbed out the pin and lobbed it up and over the log.

At the explosion he heard screaming. Hennessy lurched upright, spraying the area with bursts of gunfire. In the light of the flames flaring out the gun's muzzle, he saw Rose, the Third Position's Web broadcast director, already on her knees, wounded. He caught motion to his left and realized one of the other soldiers had flanked them.

He tried to get turned, but knew it was too late. Then Cheyenne thumbed on the flashlight, revealing Mouse in that mime's makeup she'd worn during the trials.

The anti-globalist staggered back at the piercing light in her eyes and opened fire.

Cheyenne pumped three shots at Mouse. They hit her in the combat vest and drove her backward against the trunk of a pine tree. The back of Mouse's head smashed into the tree and she crumpled.

Hennessy heard Rose groaning. He flipped on his headlamp and found her, lying on her side in the snow, struggling for breath. He squatted and wrenched the night-vision goggles off her head.

"Where are they taking my daughter?" he demanded, putting the goggles on.

"Daughter?" Rose said blearily.

He put the machine gun barrel between her eyes. "Where?"

She mumbled, "Pickup points."

"What pickup point?" he shouted.

But she lost consciousness.

"We'll have to track them," he shouted at Cheyenne.

She'd followed his lead and taken Mouse's night-vision goggles and was already wading through the deep snow toward the snowmobile. Hennessy fired it up and Cheyenne got on behind him.

It took several seconds for the machine to stop bogging, but then the going was easier than before, even without the headlight on and with the added weight. The night-vision goggles kept snow from Hennessy's eyes and the green tint made it easier to see the tracks of Hailey, Anarchy, and his crew.

For many minutes, he refused to think about anything else but those tracks and the fact that Hailey lay at the end of them somewhere, waiting for him. He was barely aware of Cheyenne behind him, ducking her head behind his back to avoid the wind. That single-mindedness allowed him to wrestle the sled through the saddle and out onto the long ridge that climbed toward Wolverine Pass. He figured they were no more than four minutes ahead of him and now that he could see, his superior knowledge of the terrain gave him the advantage. The ridge dropped south at a gentle angle from the saddle between Hellroaring Peak and Mount Jefferson. The wind had been at it and the snow was shallower. They picked up speed.

"What did she say to you?" Cheyenne yelled in his ear. "The wounded one?"

Hennessy startled at her voice so close, but replied, "That they were going to pickup points."

"Up here?"

"Or the other side of the pass."

"Got to be helicopters, then," she said, reaching inside her coat to trigger her radio. "CIRG commander?"

She heard nothing but static in her headset.

"SAC Kane?" she called. Nothing but hiss.

"We're out of range," Hennessy yelled. "There's an entire mountain between us."

"He needs to know," she yelled.

"I don't know what he can do. Helicopters can't fly in this."

"Then maybe their helicopters can't fly. They might be stranded ahead of us."

"I know," Hennessy said and twisted the throttle harder.

* * *

Down the ridge a mile to the south, huddled behind the windshield of General Anarchy's snowmobile, Hailey was racked with shivers. *Was that my father shooting back there? Or the FBI? Where's Anarchy taking me?*

Suddenly the sleds slowed and then stopped. She pushed herself up and looked around, unable to see that they'd reached the low point of the ridge where it met another that climbed west toward Wolverine Pass. She felt Anarchy kill the engine and get off. The other machines shut down too. Even with the wind, Hailey could make out the sound of another snowmobile in the distance. *Dad?*

"Cobb, take her," General Anarchy said, getting off the snowmobile. "We're splitting up from here. You and Truth take the girl to our drop-off point. Emilia and I will go on through the pass to the other landing zone. If the chopper comes to us first, we'll come back for you. If the chopper finds you first, come for us."

"How do we know you'll come?" she heard Cobb ask.

"I'm a man of my word," the Third Position leader snarled.

She heard one of the snowmobiles start up and leave just before a gloved hand wrenched her from her seat. Colder than she'd ever been, blind to the force that held her, Hailey felt like a marionette about to have its strings slashed.

"Hello, little bitch," Cobb muttered in her ear. He wrenched her along after Truth and she felt herself dropping down the side of a steep hillside. The snow deepened. She slid and crashed through tree branches and then into what felt nearly like free fall before landing again in a heap against Cobb.

Hailey was disoriented in the darkness and the storm, terrorized by the whirlwind of forces that seemed arrayed against her. But her hatred of Cobb would not let her succumb to them. She and her brothers had defeated him before. She could do it again. She would do it again. She began to try everything she could think of to slow Cobb down. She dragged her feet and kept stumbling, forcing him to pull her upright, to use up his strength. When she felt branches, she pushed into them, so it was harder to force her through. Whenever she could, she fell.

Cobb knew. He started to choke her. "Trying to slow yourself down for Daddy?" he asked. "Or whoever the hell's back there? Not happening. I got a date with a bird."

Cobb dragged her choking and gagging down another hill. When the ground leveled he eased the pressure on her throat. She gasped, "Just leave me. Please. Just leave me."

"Uh-uh," he said. "If that is your old man back there, then you're my insurance for getting out of here. Besides, you and I got a score to settle."

Five hundred yards above Hailey, her father caught up to the three abandoned snowmobiles and slowed. The snow had tapered to flurries. The wind had died too. He looked all around at the tracks.

"Three went downhill on foot," he said. "The rest went on."

Cheyenne was already using the night-vision binoculars to scan the slope above them. She couldn't make out anything but two pinnacles of rock. Then the near-full moon showed through a sudden break in the clouds and she saw the vast alpine cirque around them as if it were midday.

"I see two of them on a snowmobile, climbing toward those pinnacles up there," she said. "I think they're both wearing camouflage."

"Then Hailey went down," Hennessy said. "Why would they split up?"

Then he heard an echo of what Rose had told him. *The pickup points.* If the weather cooperated you could land a helicopter at the head of Wolverine Pass even at night. *Then where were the others taking Hailey?*

He racked his brain, trying to remember the area he was in. He'd hiked much of it. Hiking in the wilderness had been part of his recovery, where he'd found himself again. He flashed on a favorite spot he'd found to meditate.

"I know where they're going," Hennessy said.

"Where?" Cheyenne asked, dropping the binoculars to see him going around the back of the snowmobile to the skis.

"There's a balcony of stone down there around fifteen hundred vertical feet. It sticks out off a cliff above Wolverine Gorge," he replied, seeing that one of the skis strapped to the sled carried telemark bindings. He didn't have telemark boots on. But the heavy winter boots he wore just might work. He grabbed the skis.

"You're going to ski down?" she asked.

"Much faster," he said, kicking his boot into the binding. "I should get there before they do."

He knelt and adjusted the binding so the cable held his heel and toe somewhat in place. He snapped the lever that held it tight. He quickly did the other ski, then stood up to sling his machine gun over his head and shoulder. The snowmobile fired up beside him.

He looked at Cheyenne. "Where are you going?"

"After the other two," she said.

"You can't go alone."

"And neither can you," she said. "But it's got to be done."

Hennessy nodded finally. "They're heading to those pinnacles up there."

She leaned over and kissed him. "Please come back," she said.

Hennessy was flummoxed, then he kissed her back and said, "You too."

Cheyenne lowered her goggles and twisted the throttle. He felt sick watching her go away. But he picked up the ski poles and kicked off. The moon now showed cleanly through a huge vent in the cloud cover. Hennessy had skied on moonlit nights dozens of times. But with the night-vision goggles, he could see everything plain as day. He didn't bother following the tracks and instead dropped off to the southwest, intending to loop ahead of them.

It had been years since he'd telemark-skied in boots as soft as these, and it took him several turns before he figured out the stance and the amount of knee angle necessary to turn and absorb the snow and the slope. But then he caught the rhythm and went with it, flying through the powder, growing righteous and angry like some kind of winter war bird swooping to defend his own.

Above him, Cheyenne fought to drive the snowmobile. It had looked easy when Hennessy did it, but she felt like her arms were being pulled out of their sockets as the machine pitched and rolled up over the mounds of snow. Even from hundreds of yards away, Cheyenne spotted the headlights of her quarry blink on. She slowed to a stop, wondering why. She raised her binoculars and saw one of the two people standing in the headlight beams. Then, off to her southwest, she saw blinking red lights. She swung the binoculars around and spotted a helicopter rising over the top of Wolverine Pass between the pinnacles of rock.

"Shit," she cried and cranked the gas, shooting up and across the slope at a steep diagonal angle, struggling to keep the sled upright in the deep snow.

The helicopter banked and rolled toward the snowmobile headlight. She did the only thing she could think of. She turned on her own headlight, trying to confuse the helicopter. When she did, she saw one of the Third Position soldiers up the slope step into his own headlight beam, facing in her direction.

"You see me coming, don't you?" she said, gritting her teeth. "You know I'm going to get to you before they do."

But then she saw the anti-globalist step, raise his arm, and hurl something in her direction. Or at least he'd made that motion. And now he was running the opposite way. She slowed just in time to hear the grenade go off with a dull grunt, like a bear awakening. Then she heard what sounded like a giant exhalation of air, like a *huh* sound. High above her a fracture line scribbled across the slope. A hundred yards of snowpack settled and then started to slide.

Hennessy saw the red blinking lights of the helicopter rising over Wolverine Pass as he prepared to make a giant arc that would bring him hard to the south toward the promontory of rock where he believed Hailey was being taken.

Then he heard the *KA-THUD!* of the grenade go off, followed by the huffing of the snowpack as it expelled its air. Hennessy had been living in the Rockies for years now. He knew what that sound was. Avalanche! And it was coming right down the mountain at him.

Moving down an open sage slope, Hailey saw the helicopter swoop toward the high pickup zone. She heard the distant rumble of the grenade going off, but not the avalanche picking up speed toward Cheyenne O'Neil and her father.

"Let's move it, Cobb," Truth said. "They won't wait."

"How far?" Cobb demanded.

"No more than a quarter mile," Truth grunted and picked up the pace in the knee-deep snow, his long legs chewing up the terrain.

Cobb was shorter and could not keep up with Truth, especially since Hailey was still doing her best to trip over every sage bush buried in the snow. In the moonlight, she could see better now, and she kept looking back the way they'd come for her father, telling herself over and over again that he had to be back there somewhere, not far, and coming to her rescue.

Cheyenne peeled the sled around, then pointed the snowmobile down and across the mountain at a forty-five-degree angle. She wrenched the throttle and felt herself leap and tear down the side of the slope, headlight on, crouching down, desperately trying to keep control of the accelerating snow machine. But behind her she heard the building roar of the avalanche gathering speed and mass, snapping trees, hurling up rock and boulders as it bore down the mountain after her.

CHAPTER FORTY

High above the rim of Wolverine Gorge, Mickey Hennessy heard the avalanche coming. He felt it too, shaking the snowpack beneath him. He didn't wait around to see it. He skied off the shoulder of a slope that dropped away to the southeast, heading dead downhill, waiting until he'd reached the point where the slope no longer registered above thirty degrees, then shifted his weight and arced into a steep traverse that led him toward a pine glen near the rim of the gorge and a balcony of stone that jutted off the side of the drainage.

One hundred and fifty yards away, Hailey stumbled along as Cobb dragged her through a meadow of snow toward a pine glen. Truth was almost to them. Hailey caught Cobb's expectant expression in the moonlight.

Wherever they were going, they were close. With every footstep she felt more expendable.

Then she heard the rumble of the avalanche.

Upslope, the slide exploded after Cheyenne O'Neil. The edge of it caught the rear of her snowmobile and flung it downhill. For a second she swore she'd be taken. But then it just let her go and blew down the mountain toward the gorge. She stopped the sled, pointed straight uphill. She collapsed over the handlebars, her heart punching her throat like a speed bag. Tremoring, Cheyenne got turned around in time to see the slide roll over the shoulder of a ridge far down the slope where she'd last spotted Hennessy skiing.

All around her she heard the groaning and cracking of the avalanche rubble settling, and now the distant *thud-thud-thud* of the Third Position helicopter rising from the snowpack high on Wolverine Pass.

Two of them have escaped. Kane has to know.

Cobb stopped at the sound of the avalanche. So did Truth. Hailey peered through the dim light, seeing the slide burst over the shoulder of a slope to their west. To Hailey it looked eighty feet high, like a tsunami on the hillside. She had the sudden, horrible thought that it was swallowing her father.

"Daddy!" she screamed and shook with sobs. "Daddy!"

Hennessy felt the gale the avalanche created as it swept past the tails of his skis. He heard it erupt off the edge of the gorge and clatter and smash deep into the sheer-sided ravine. After the bulk of the debris passed, a cloud of fine snow lingered in the air. Even with the night-vision goggles, he skied blind, hands up, praying he didn't undershoot the glen and fly off the rim of the gorge. In the shimmering greenish glow around him he caught the suggestion of trees and skidded to a stop. He froze, listening, as the snow whirling around him began to settle and offer more distinct views of the trees. He was right where he wanted to be.

"Daddy!" he heard Hailey scream. She was close. She was crying. *"Daddy!"*

Hennessy turned grim as he squatted to release the telemark bindings. He stepped off them and into deep snow, peering ahead through the scattered woods, trying to spot the men who had his daughter.

"Heh, heh," he heard Cobb laugh. *"Who do you think set off that avalanche? He's gone over the side, little bitch."*

"No!" she yelled. *"No! Daddy!"*

Hennessy purged himself of all emotion. In his mind, he saw his daughter the way a professional bodyguard does, as a precious object to be protected at all costs. He slid to his right, angling through the snowy trees toward the rim of the gorge and that balcony of rock.

Chug, chug, chug, chug. He heard the helicopter coming.

"See?" he heard Truth say. *"General's a man of honor."*

"And we're about to be rich men," Cobb said, glee in his voice. *"Very rich."*

That's when Hennessy saw them, or Hailey, actually, moving laterally to him about twenty yards away. At first he had to strain to make out Cobb and Truth in their snow camouflage, but then he did. Truth was leading. Cobb trailed, pushing Hailey in front of him, his head not craning about as Hennessy would have expected.

He's got other things on his mind, Hennessy thought. *He thinks he's home free. Already rich. Counting his money.*

Hennessy waited until Cobb had gotten ahead of him, then laid down his machine gun. He couldn't risk hitting Hailey. He'd have to do this with his hands. He slid forward, moving in and out of the trees as if they were slalom gates, quickening his pace when he could not see them. Ahead of him he could make out the thinning of the trees and then the balcony of rock above the black maw of the gorge. Hennessy moved carefully but quickly into position directly behind Cobb.

Truth reached the pinnacle just as the helicopter's engines went from a chugging to a pounding due west. The bird was flying right up the middle of the gorge. Hennessy sprang forward at Cobb's back. His sleeve brushed a pine branch, dumping snow. It was enough to alert the Third Position soldier, who flung Hailey forward after Truth and twisted, trying to get his gun around.

Hennessy's forearm pounded the side of Cobb's neck. Cobb toppled as he triggered his machine gun. Bullets blazed into the trees, cutting down limbs. Hennessy kneed Cobb in the side of the hip below his bulletproof

vest. The Third Position soldier grunted in pain and let
go of the gun. He sprawled on his side.

Hennessy pounced on him and struck him with the
butt of his palm under the jaw line. He heard crunching
noises.

"Dad!"

Hennessy looked up to see the balcony illuminated
by the searchlight of the helicopter, which was no more
than a hundred yards out now and closing. In the brightest part of the searchlight beam, he saw Truth backing up
toward that snaggle of a tree out on the end of the pinnacle. Hailey was in front of Truth, backing up as well. He
held a pistol to her head. She was screeching, "Daddy!
Daddy, please!"

Hennessy didn't see Cobb's backhand blow coming.
Cobb's fist struck the side of Hennessy's face, breaking
his nose and throwing him off balance backward. Cobb
bucked and dislodged him, then twisted around in the
snow. Hennessy landed on his side, and came to his
senses in time to see a knife blade coming at him and to
hear Cobb saying, "Coming to rescue my little bitch? I
don't think so."

Hennessy shot up his left elbow, connecting with
Cobb's forearm, stopping the knife. He twisted onto his
back and threw up both hands when Cobb tried to stab
him a second time. He trapped Cobb's wrist inches
from his throat. Even through the insulation that surrounded his fingers, he could feel the steel-like strength
in the Third Position soldier's hands and arms. For a
heartbeat he didn't know if he could hold the man off.

"Daddy! Daddy, he's taking me!"

That primal rage boiled and exploded through Hennessy again. His arms stiffened. His fingers probed the cuff of Cobb's jacket, finding the thinnest fabric before digging and ripping at his ulnar nerve. He heard Cobb grunt with pain and knew he had the man in the right place. He dug at the nerve savagely, feeling Cobb's strength weaken and his hand begin to palsy before the knife slipped from his grasp and fell in the snow.

Hennessy swung his forehead up. It cracked hard against Cobb's chin. He swung it a second time, harder, and felt and heard teeth giving way. The Third Position soldier's weight came off him as Cobb fell to his right. Hennessy's gloved hand groped for the knife. But then Cobb hurled himself back at Hennessy. He kicked at Cobb with his right boot. The Third Position soldier caught the kick and twisted, trying to break Hennessy's ankle. Hennessy felt the move and went with the motion, rolling over his right knee and ankle, and then continuing the momentum. When his left leg came free of the snow, he mule-kicked Cobb in the cheek with the heel of his boot. Cobb let go and staggered to his left.

Suddenly the helicopter's whining roar was everywhere. Snow came like buckshot on the blast of rotor wind. Chunks of it lashed Hennessy's face. But through the snowy haze, he saw Truth and Hailey almost to the end of the pinnacle, out there right above the black maw of the gorge. Her mouth was open. She must have been screaming, but he couldn't hear a thing.

The helicopter turned counterclockwise in space. The side door was open. A red light lit the interior. General Anarchy sat in the doorway, attached to some kind of harness. He threw a rope out. He shouted something to Truth. Hennessy forced himself to his feet, feeling himself surge once again with that killing force. He spotted Cobb's machine gun, lying where the rim of the gorge gave way to the balcony of stone.

He ran for it. He bent to snatch it up when he caught a blur of motion in his peripheral vision. Cobb had found his knife. He was bleeding from the nose and mouth and coming for him again. Ahead, he saw Truth aim his pistol at him. Hailey threw her hand up and hit the pistol. Hennessy went flat. The bullet cracked right over his head. Cobb tripped over him, then found his footing and twisted back.

Hennessy threw snow up into Cobb's face, then lurched to his feet. Cobb swung the knife wildly at him. Hennessy leaned back and brushed it aside. Cobb stabbed at him backhanded. Hennessy slid off the line of his attack, redirected the blow downward with his right hand, and then hit Cobb on the bridge of his broken nose with his left. Cobb grunted in pain as more blood spewed from his nostrils. But then Cobb shifted the grip he had on the knife, holding the weapon by the butt between his thumb and index finger, blade sticking out below the pinkie, chopping-style.

Hennessy saw the switch and knew Cobb meant to strike him overhand or diagonally, with a hatchet motion. Rather than panic, everything went calm in Hennessy's mind. Rather than retreat, he watched as Cobb raised his hand overhead. At the instant the Third Position soldier rushed him, Hennessy stepped forward to meet him.

In a split instant, his hands caught Cobb by the wrist and elbow and lifted him even as he pivoted and slid tighter to the man. The action blended him to Cobb's forward motion. It also lifted Cobb up behind Hennessy. He felt the load and extended his arms so Cobb's mass and momentum continued straight ahead. Then he dropped to his knees beneath the man and wrenched Cobb's arm backwards.

Cobb flipped in space over Hennessy's head. His night goggles flew off. Cobb looked back blindly. Hennessy caught the instant of horrible understanding in the anti-globalist's mind before he released his grip on Cobb's arm. The Third Position soldier sailed over the side of the balcony of stone, and dropped into the gorge.

As Cobb's screams faded into the night air, Hennessy heard a burst of gunfire. The icy rocks right next to him exploded. He rolled over out of the way, seeing that Hailey was still fighting, throwing punches up at Truth's face as he reached to clip the harness he wore to the rope. Above them forty feet in the helicopter, General Anarchy was shooting at Hennessy.

Hennessy dove behind a rock as more bullets cracked and whined around him. He peeked out in time to see Truth make some kind of decision. Then, as if he were swatting at a mosquito, the huge Third Position soldier grasped Hailey by her chin and spun her around to his left. She twisted, toppled, and fell over the side of the gorge.

She was gone.

"Hailey!" Hennessy screamed. "Hailey!"

General Anarchy laid down another burst of fire as

Truth clipped onto the rope. Shock and disbelief at the loss of his daughter gave way to suicidal rage. Hennessy threw himself out into the open toward Cobb's machine gun and got it just as the chopper began to lift up and away, with Truth dangling from the rope.

Hennessy got to his knees, threw the gun to his shoulder, and opened fire maniacally, screaming incomprehensible fury at the men who'd taken his daughter from him, who'd thrown her life so casually aside.

Hennessy's bullets riddled Truth's legs from his calves to his pelvis. Through his tears, Hennessy saw Truth's core give way and the massive Third Position soldier dangle helplessly from the rope. Hennessy tried to raise his line of fire up the rope toward Truth's head, Anarchy, and the helicopter. But the bolt of the gun slammed open. Empty.

"No!" Hennessy screamed. "No!"

He wanted to kill them all for what they'd done. He found the spare clip duct-taped to the gun and almost reached for it before seeing it was hopeless.

The helicopter had started to accelerate away. Truth's hands were raised up on the rope, as if he were trying to climb it with his arms. Hennessy watched Anarchy silhouetted in the helicopter's hold as the bird moved west. He was working on the rope. For a second Hennessy thought the Third Position leader was trying to bring Truth in.

Then he saw Truth's head snap back in realization of what Anarchy was really doing. The rope severed free of the helicopter and whipsawed against the full moon before straightening and trailing after Truth as he plunged into the gorge. The last thing Hennessy saw before the lights in the helicopter died was Anarchy looking back at him.

Hennessy dropped the gun and fell forward on his knees in the snow, crying up at the night sky. "Hailey!"

For a long moment there was only the frigid, hollow howl of the wind rising over the fading chug of the helicopter. The arctic wind burrowed straight into Hennessy's gut, emptied him out, and made him waver like a dry cornstalk in the snow. His mind felt torched to embers.

The sound didn't register the first time. The noise was just part of the wind that wanted to take him off the side of the balcony of rock after Hailey.

But the second time, the noise took form and became a faint cry.

His head jerked up in disbelief. He strained, sure he'd heard something.

"Daddy!"

Hennessy ignored the sheer cliff to either side of him, bolted up onto his feet and straight out onto the narrow point, buffeted by the gusting wind, screaming, "Hailey!"

"Here! Dad!"

He threw himself on his stomach, scrambled to the edge, and peered over. Through the goggles he could make her out, seven or eight feet below him, holding tight to the root system of an ancient white-bark pine tree that grew from a crack in the rock on the side of the balcony of stone.

"I'm here!" Hennessy shouted. "Hold on!"

"It's moving, Dad!" she shrieked. "It's going to break! I can hear it!"

He tore the night-vision goggles off, dug in his pocket, found his headlamp, and turned it on. Filthy, bruised, and petrified, Hailey's fingers were woven in the roots. Her body straddled the pine's thin, gnarled trunk. Below her, rocks and ice broke free and fell.

"The roots are tearing," she said, starting to weep.

She had minutes, maybe less, before the whole thing broke free and she was gone for good.

"Don't move!" he shouted. "I'm coming right back."

"No, Dad!" she screeched behind him. "Don't leave! Don't leave!"

But Hennessy was already dancing back across the pinnacle like a high-wire artist. He grabbed Cobb's machine gun, released the clip, flipped it, and slammed in the other. He ran into the trees, looking for a suitable limb. When he spotted one that looked about the right length, he aimed where it left the trunk and opened up, severing it.

He grabbed the limb and dragged it back toward the balcony of rock.

"Hailey?" he yelled.

"Hurry!" she screamed. "Hurry!"

Hennessy let go of the branch, reached down, and took off his leather pants belt. He wrapped and buckled it around the limb's first side branch, then took hold of the belt and swung the bough off the side of the gorge.

"Grab it," he yelled. "Can you get it?"

"You've got to lower it!" she shouted.

Hennessy lowered it, and as he did, he heard a snapping and splintering noise.

"Lower! It's going! Lower!"

Hennessy knew how dangerously close he was to going over the side of the cliff himself. But he didn't care. He was either going to save her or die trying.

Hennessy jammed his feet against an outcropping of rock and shifted his hips forward so the limb dropped several more inches down the side of the cliff. Three sharp cracks sounded over the wind. For a moment, he heard and felt nothing. Then he felt weight come onto the limb, pulling him forward, and heard Hailey scream, "Got it!"

Hennessy sensed her full weight come onto the tree limb. It almost jerked him forward and over the side. But he threw himself backward, straining to keep his heels locked down tight against the nubs of rock that kept him on the cliff, straining to hold on to the strap of leather that connected him to the tree limb and his daughter. The moon disappeared behind a cloud, and for a terrible moment he imagined himself forever trapped in night.

Then he felt tugs and shakes on the tree limb as Hailey pulled herself up the side of the cliff. Seconds later, he saw her face pop up over the rim. She was grinning fiercely at him.

The branch that connected them began to snap with their combined weight levered across the rim of the cliff. As it broke free, Hennessy released one hand from the belt, shot it forward, and caught Hailey by the wrist.

He dragged his daughter up over the side of the cliff and into his arms. Hennessy held his daughter so tight he thought he'd break her.

CHAPTER FORTY-ONE

At one the next afternoon, Mickey Hennessy felt every sore and torn muscle in his body as he walked down a hallway in Bozeman Deaconess Hospital. His nose was taped. He was dressed in jeans, boots, turtleneck, and a wool jacket and was somewhat baffled to realize he was heading for the same room where he'd recovered from his shooting. *Has it only been sixty hours since the attack? Only fourteen since the Guard helicopter rescued us?*

The whole incident at the Jefferson Club had unfolded in less than three days, but the memories of it flashing by his eyes seemed like weeks, even months long. His entire sense of time, his entire sense of self felt thrown to a hurricane until he rounded the corner, looked into the room, and felt instantly at peace and in a state of complete gratitude.

Bridger slept in the bed closest to the door. His leg

was in a cast from hip to toe and hung from a pulley system above the bed. Cobb's bullet had broken his femur and cut his femoral artery. Connor and Hailey's actions had undoubtedly saved their brother's life.

Connor was slouching in a chair between Bridger's bed and Hailey's. His eyes were closed. His mouth hung open. Hailey was sleeping too. Her feet and left hand were bandaged from frostbite. She had salved patches of it on her cheeks and forehead as well.

Hennessy could feel the burn of his own frostbite patches on his face and neck as he stepped across the transom into the hospital room. The nurse stood up and bumped Hailey's bed.

His daughter roused and looked around before spotting him and smiling. "Hi, Dad."

"Shhhh," he said, crossing to her. "Let them sleep."

Connor cranked his head around, saying, "I'm awake." He raised himself up and embraced his father. Hailey reached out and put her bandaged hand on Hennessy's arm.

Before the attack, Hennessy could barely get a hug out of them. Ever since they'd been reunited at the hospital, the kids had been holding on to him whenever they could. Feeling tears well again, he raised his eyes to the ceiling and thanked God for saving them. They were his anchors. Without them . . .

"Hi, Dad," Bridger slurred behind him.

Hennessy broke from Connor's embrace. "You're awake, kiddo!" he said, leaning over and kissing his son on the cheek.

"Sort of," Bridger said. Then his face contorted in pain. "It hurts, Dad. Real bad."

Hennessy hesitated before asking the nurse, "Can he have something?"

"Absolutely," the nurse said, then went to the IV sticking out of his son and injected a drug into the line.

In seconds, Bridger got bleary-eyed, nodded, and licked his lips. "Better."

Hennessy felt buffeted by his own sad story of narcotics and his son's real need for relief from suffering. "Good," he said at last. "Good."

"You'll never be able to keep up with me on a board again," Connor told Bridger.

"No way, dude," Bridger protested. "I got titanium rods in my leg now. I'm coming back stronger and faster."

Hennessy put his arm around Connor's shoulders. "That's enough. No bitching. Not when we've all come out of this alive."

Bridger gazed at his dad like he was speaking another language. "We're not bitching. It's how we talk, Dad. I'm happy we're alive. Believe me."

"Me, too," Hailey said.

"And me," Connor said, clinging to his dad.

Cheyenne O'Neil knocked on the doorjamb behind them. She'd had a shower, a few hours' sleep, and had changed into jeans, a ski sweater, and a red down vest. Hennessy thought once again that she looked incredibly beautiful. She smiled nervously. "Are they taking visitors?"

"You're a VIP in this room," Hennessy said, letting go of Connor and going to greet her. "Agent O'Neil was the one who called in the helicopter for us, Hailey."

"How about me?" Willis Kane said, coming in behind Cheyenne.

Hennessy shook Kane's hand. "Always, Willis. Always."

After a few minutes of small talk, Kane brought them up to speed on what had transpired after Hennessy, Cheyenne, and Hailey disappeared into the wilderness behind Hellroaring Peak. He described the intense battle between his men and the Third Position. The antiglobalists fought like professionals. Highly trained professionals. The FBI lost five agents. Six others were wounded. Fourteen Third Position soldiers had died. The rest had fled, some on foot, some on snowmobile. The construction helicopter General Anarchy and Citizen's Defender Emilia used to make their escape was found in a potato field near Rexburg, Idaho. The pilot was shot through the temple. Only one member of the Third Position Army had been taken alive: Mouse. She'd revealed little other than proclaiming herself a member of a rebel uprising with rights under the Geneva Convention.

Teams of FBI agents and Montana State Police were trying to pick up the tracks of anyone leaving the perimeter of the club. But it was snowing again, with blizzard conditions forecast. Many trails had already disappeared.

Roadblocks had been set up on all roads out of the Jefferson Range. But so far their efforts had yielded nothing. The FBI director had ordered in the Bureau's top criminologists to oversee the gathering of evidence inside the lodge. The process of identifying the Third Position soldiers, alive and dead, could take days if not weeks.

"So Anarchy's still out there?" Hailey asked, pulling up her covers.

Hennessy went and sat with her. "They'll find him. Don't worry."

Cheyenne went to the television. "Do you mind if I turn it on? Horatio Burns is going to talk to the press at one-thirty. You should be able to see them out there in the parking lot."

Hennessy had seen the satellite vans and television cameras and managed to avoid them by entering the hospital from the rear. He'd heard Burns had been brought here for observation. Aaron Grant too. He was leery of the kids watching too much of the coverage. He'd watched a bit after sleeping six hours and feared the attention being paid to them. But he was curious to hear what Horatio had to say, so he nodded and said, "Go ahead."

Cheyenne clicked on the television and found MS-NBC. Six hours into trading, the Dow was down almost two hundred points. Nearly seven percent of the stock index's value had been lost since the opening bell the day before. Hundreds of billions of dollars.

Maria Bartiromo looked earnestly into the cameras. "Now we go live to Bozeman, Montana, where Horatio Burns is leaving a local hospital after being rescued from anti-globalists late last night in a daring, bloody raid by FBI counterterrorists."

The screen jumped to an exterior shot of the entrance to Bozeman Deaconess. Horatio Burns walked out the front door of the hospital looking worn, weakened, and savaged by grief. His wife, Isabel, trailed him, also wearing dark sunglasses. For all she'd been through she still radiated beauty through the camera. Beside her stood a solidly built man in his early forties, with a rocky face and brown hair cut military-close to his scalp. He wore sunglasses too, and an earphone. His attention roamed everywhere.

"That's my boss," Hennessy said. "Former boss, anyway. Gregg Foster. He got here quick from South America."

Horatio Burns stepped to the microphones. He cleared his throat, and began in a slow, somber tone, "The world suffers today a devastating loss of vision, intellect, and entrepreneurship as a result of the death of my friends and colleagues, Albert Crockett, Friedrich Klinefelter, Sir Lawrence Treadwell, Chin Hoc Pan, and Jack Doore."

Burns straightened and stared into the cameras with that Horatio look Hennessy knew so well, the one that made lesser mortals quake, and said, "But I wish to make one thing perfectly clear to the markets and to the world. I refuse to be intimidated by the Third Position Army and their leader, General Anarchy. I continue to believe in America, the global economy, and the inherent strength of capitalism and democracy. I pray that other investors think the same and step back into the markets. There is nothing wrong with the U.S. economy. Nothing fundamentally. My decision to cash out of equities in December was based on logic no longer valid in the wake of these attacks."

He looked around at the reporters, then directly into the camera in close-up. "An hour ago, I ordered my brokers to buy equities across the full spectrum of the world economy, especially in the well-run global corporations that are its backbone, especially in the companies of the visionary men who died at the hands of the Third Position. I am also demanding that world leaders work together to stamp out these anti-global terrorists before they can do more evil in the name of their progressiveness. And I pledge my fortune to tracking down the twisted individuals who perpetrated the mass murder at the Jefferson Club."

He stepped back from the microphones and the reporters began to shout questions: *How does it feel to be one of the survivors? Will the Jefferson Club go on? Tell us how you escaped!*

Hennessy's cell phone rang before he could hear any of Burns's answers. He answered and heard, *"What the fuck? I hear you're alive?"*

Hennessy smiled, went out to the hall, and said, "I am, thanks for asking, Jerry."

"Least I could do for a guy who's just made a bundle," Jerry said, glee in his voice. *"And by the way, I'm taking one percent for my brilliant fucking efforts."*

Hennessy raised an eyebrow. "How much have I made?"

"It's not over yet," Jerry said. *"Just a couple more instruments to unwind. A couple more to move. I'll let you know at the close."*

"But I've made money, right?"

Jerry's laugh was more a snort. *"I'll call you when everything settles so I'm giving you hard, bankable numbers."*

"Jerry—" Hennessy began.

But the line went dead. Frustrated, Hennessy snapped shut his cell phone. *So how much? A couple hundred thousand? Double my money?* He was still not quite sure how shorting a market worked and what its exact ramifications were if successful. But there was no mistaking the happy tenor in Jerry's voice.

For the fourth time since the shots rang out at midnight on New Year's Eve, Hennessy allowed himself to feel good about his life. Yes, horrible things had happened on his watch. Good and decent people had been murdered in cold blood. But his own children had been saved. He had been saved. And now he'd made money.

He flashed on Horatio Burns in the ballroom the afternoon before the party, telling him that shorting a market was for someone with a lot of financial balls. Hennessy smiled. *Guess I have a capacity for balls after all.*

"Where are they?" a woman's unmistakable voice called.

Hennessy looked up to find Patricia, his ex-wife, barreling down the hallway at him. She'd dyed her hair sawgrass-blond and had it tied in cornrows. Her tan was incredible. A short, balding, tubby, forty-something, equally tanned man followed her. *That's Ted?* Hennessy thought. He'd imagined someone more formidable.

"In there," Hennessy said, pointing to the doorway. "Nice tan."

Patricia blew past him into the room, shaking a finger. "I'm not talking to you."

She took one look at Bridger and Hailey, and bawled her way into Connor's arms. Years ago, Hennessy would have been embarrassed by her histrionics. But watching her hug and kiss each of their children, he understood the feeling completely.

Ted came over, pushing his glasses up his nose. "I'm Ted Watkins," he said and shook Hennessy's hand. "You look like you've been through hell."

"I have."

"Thank you," Ted said.

"For what?"

"For saving them. Patricia would never have survived if you hadn't."

"Me neither, Ted."

Inside the hospital room, Patricia stopped kissing Hailey, who was squirming and saying, "I told you she'd be like this."

Patricia stood and saw Kane. She dried her eyes and hugged him. "You're always in hospital rooms when I am," she said.

"Let's break the habit," Kane said, hugging her.

Patricia noticed Cheyenne for the first time. "Who are you?"

"FBI agent Cheyenne O'Neil," she said, shaking Patricia's hand.

"She helped save Hailey's life," Hennessy said a little too forcefully from the doorway.

Patricia studied Hennessy, then bobbed her head at Cheyenne. "Thank you, Agent O'Neil. For whatever you did, thank you."

"You have very brave children," Cheyenne said.

"So I understand. Could I have some time with them?" Patricia asked. "Mom time? I think there's been quite enough of dad time lately. Everyone. Scoot."

Out in the hallway, Ted wandered off in search of a Coke machine. Kane shook Hennessy's hand. "Good to see you back on your game."

"Like old times," Hennessy said.

"I'm married now, Mick. I'd like to introduce you two sometime."

"The woman who tamed Willis Kane," Hennessy said. "I wouldn't miss it."

"I've got to head back to the Jefferson Club," Kane said. "Agent O'Neil?"

Cheyenne blushed, then said, "I'm supposed to have a conference call with my partner back in New York, SAC. I'll follow you up in my car when we're through."

Kane hesitated, glancing at Hennessy. "Fine," he said. "Keep me posted."

He slapped Hennessy on the back and walked toward the elevators. Cheyenne had her hands in the back pockets of her jeans. She grinned at Hennessy. "I wanted to say how happy I am for you," she said, her eyes glistening. She brushed back her auburn hair with her fingers. "Your kids and all."

"You had a lot to do with it," he said, remembering their kiss the night before.

"I just rode back into radio range," she said. "Kane took it from there."

"If it wasn't for you, we'd have froze," he insisted. "Can I buy you dinner?"

"Kind of early for dinner."

"A late lunch, then."

She smiled and her cheeks reddened. "I'd like that."

"So would I."

CHAPTER FORTY-TWO

Twenty minutes later, they walked into Boodles restaurant on Main Street in downtown Bozeman. The air smelled of garlic. The lunch crowd had already thinned out. But several people seemed to recognize Hennessy and Cheyenne from the television coverage and they stared after them as they took a booth in the corner and ordered.

"Have you had time to think?" Cheyenne asked when the waiter left.

"About?"

"Any of it," she said. "All of it."

He shook his head and yawned. "It's like a blur. I don't even know if the anesthesia from my surgery's totally left my body yet."

"I know," she said. "It happened so fast that I still haven't had time to get my head around everything that's—"

Her cell phone rang. She hesitated, then grabbed it. "O'Neil."

"I got more strands of those transfers unwound," her partner grumbled. *"I've been up most of the night."*

"Join the club," Cheyenne replied. "Where'd the money go this time?"

"Some of Sir Lawrence Treadwell's money ended up in accounts belonging to the Sierra Club, Natural Resources Defense Council, NOW, ACLU, and the NAACP," Ikeda said. *"Ten million each."*

"Come on," she protested. "You don't think they're actually involved, do you?"

"Don't know, but when I told the director a few minutes ago, he was talking about seeking court orders to raid their offices," he said.

"ACLU will flip if he does."

"I'd expect so," Ikeda said. *"But what if they are part of it?"*

"Some vast leftist anti-globalist conspiracy?" she replied skeptically. "I don't buy it. What would be the point and benefit of participating in kidnapping, extortion, and murder, especially if they're going to leave a money trail we can follow?"

"It wasn't an easy trail," Ikeda reminded her.

"No, I know it wasn't," she said. "You've done great. Anything on ownership of the accounts the transfers moved through?"

"Dummy corporations set up in the Caymans, Hong Kong, Macau, Panama," he said. *"Interpol's digging for us."*

"No common names associated with the companies?"

"Just an attorney in Liechtenstein who set up an- other six of them on behalf of Gilbert Tepper. And an attorney in the Caymans who did the same for Gil Tran Tepp."

"Can you PDF the documents to me so I can check them from here?"

"Sure, before I leave anyway," he said, stifling a yawn.

"Sounds like you should leave now."

"Another hour or so won't kill me."

Cheyenne hung up the phone, apologized, and gave Hennessy the update. He shook his head. "Why would the money end up with those kinds of organizations?"

"Same thing I asked," she said, drinking from her Diet Coke. "They're hardly radical anti-globalists."

"Depends on your perspective, I suppose," he said. "Doesn't someone have to have an ID picture for Tepp or Tepper or whatever his name is?"

Cheyenne shrugged. "A lot of these dummy corpo- rations can be set up with a letter and a check. If we're lucky, we'll find a picture of someone. But who knows if Tepp's just some other attorney operating on Anar- chy's behalf?"

"Ruthless bastard, whoever he is," Hennessy said, then sat back when the waiter brought their pizza.

"He can't stay hidden forever," she said. "Someone will out him."

"If the reward's big enough," he agreed.

"Think Burns will post one?"

Hennessy considered it, then nodded. "He looked like he meant business."

"Too bad his wife didn't," Cheyenne said, then took a bite of her sandwich and grinned. "That's good."

"What didn't Isabel do?" he asked.

"Call us with the security code to the house," Cheyenne replied. "I called and called. We never heard back."

Hennessy shrugged. "She had a lot on her mind. Besides, after Cobb kicked in the door, we didn't need it anymore."

"True," she said, then took another bite.

The conversation drifted. Hennessy confessed his fear that his ex-wife would use the crisis as a pretext to keep his visitation rights limited. Cheyenne told him about her childhood growing up in Colorado, and her switchbacked road into the FBI.

"Well, I'm damn sure they're happy to have you," Hennessy said.

"Make sure you tell that to Kane the next time you see him," she replied.

"You going to stay out here awhile?" he asked, hoping it sounded nonchalant. "Working the case, I mean."

She smiled. "As long as I'm wanted."

"I have a feeling you'd stay even if you weren't wanted."

Cheyenne frowned and Hennessy quickly added, "Not that you aren't wanted. You are . . . uh, wanted."

Her frown twisted back toward a smile. "Thanks. I think."

An awkward silence enveloped them. Hennessy glanced away. When he looked back she had glanced away. When her attention returned to him, their eyes locked.

"Would you—" Hennessy began, but now his cell phone rang. "Ugggg."

He grabbed for his cell phone and flipped it open. "Hennessy."

"What the fuck?" Jerry said.

"Hold on," Hennessy said. He cupped the mike on his cell and started to slide out of the booth, saying, "Sorry, Cheyenne. I have to take this."

"I can't promise you there'll be any food left when you get back."

She looked so damn adorable saying that, Hennessy wanted to kiss her again. But he walked back toward the kitchen and said, "Okay, I can talk."

"I should fucking hope so," Jerry said. *"Everything we did Monday has now been settled and I've got your profits redistributed across the board in your old portfolio, setting aside twenty percent for cash."*

"How much?

Jerry told him and Hennessy thought he'd just dropped an OxyContin with a double chaser of Old Bushmills. He leaned up against the wall of the restaurant, watching the pizza chef spread dough. "That's not possible."

"It's not only possible, it's for real," Jerry said.

"The cabin on the Big Hole?" he said in shock.

"Whatever you want," Jerry said. *"I mean within reason. Don't be a moron."*

"No. No, of course not."

"You don't sound happy. I'd be jumping-up-and-down happy."

"No," Hennessy said, bringing his free hand up to

his brow and finding it sweaty. "I am. I just . . . After everything. It's surreal, that's all."

"Welcome to your new reality, Salvador Dalí. Go out. Celebrate."

When Hennessy returned to the booth, Cheyenne noticed the shock on his face. "Is something wrong, Mickey?"

He felt more upended than he had riding in the National Guard helicopter to the Bozeman hospital with Hailey the night before. Hennessy wanted to tell Cheyenne about the call. But then something inside him told him otherwise. Telling her would change things. He wanted to know what she thought of him irrespective of this turn of events.

"No," he said. "Everything's good."

"You look like you saw a ghost."

"I'm forty-something," he said.

"I said you look like you saw a ghost, not are a ghost," she said. "Besides, I would have said you were thirty-seven."

"Does it matter?" Hennessy asked.

"What?"

"My age."

"Age is a state of mind," Cheyenne said. "Why?"

Hennessy balked. It had been so long since he'd felt this way, churned up and giddy, and he couldn't tell if it was from the exhilaration and relief of having rescued his children from the clutches of Anarchy, or the phone call he'd just had with his investment advisor, or the incredible way Cheyenne smelled and the coy look she was giving him.

Whatever the cause of the feeling, he gave in to it and said, "Because I hope I'm not off base here, but Agent O'Neil, I find you incredibly attractive and brilliant and I want to know if I have any kind of a shot with you, given the fact I live here and you live in New York City."

Cheyenne's lips pursed and for a heartbeat he didn't know if they were heading up or down before she smiled and said, "I was wondering the same thing about you."

Hennessy's hand slid across the table and took hers. She drew it back quickly and whispered, "I don't think, given your high profile these days, that public displays of affection are appropriate just yet."

Hennessy glanced around at the other parties eating in the restaurant. He touched the bandages on his nose self-consciously. "Oh, I'm sorry, you're right."

Another silence hung between them before he muttered, "How about a nonpublic display of affection, Agent O'Neil?"

Now it was Cheyenne's turn to hesitate before she looked up from the tabletop with lazy eyes and murmured, "I think a nonpublic display of affection would be wonderful, Mr. Hennessy."

CHAPTER FORTY-THREE

Several hours later, Hennessy roused from a doze, rolled over on his back in his room at an inn around the corner from the hospital, and stared up at the ceiling. Cheyenne rested her head on his chest. Hennessy felt more befuddled now than he'd been after his conversation with Jerry. Here he was, a moderately wealthy man with three wonderful, gutsy, safe kids, lying in the arms of a beautiful, sensitive, intelligent FBI agent. *How did that happen?*

Tears began to form in his eyes and they dripped down his cheeks. Cheyenne saw them and became concerned. "Hey, I wasn't that bad, was I?"

He grinned. "No, no, you were . . . you are amazing." He held her tight to him and pulled the sheets and blankets up around her shoulders. "People are saying I'm responsible for the security breach at the club, responsible for the deaths of all those innocent people. I should be blue and wanting to drink and drug. But I don't feel like that at all. I feel like anything's possible now. No limits."

Cheyenne rested her chin on his chest and said, "Tell me what that's like."

But before he could begin to tell her the facts, ideas, and emotions whirling in his exhausted head, her cell phone rang.

"Don't," he said.

"Got to, you know that," she said, throwing him a pout. "Part of the badge."

Cheyenne rolled out of bed, taking the cover with her around her shoulders. She got her cell phone from her jeans and answered, "O'Neil."

"Did you fly out here on New Year's Day against the direct orders of your supervisor?" It was Kane.

For a second Cheyenne was flustered, then she replied, "Yes, sir. But I paid my own way. It was a national holiday. I wasn't on the job."

There was silence on the line, then she heard Kane chuckle. *"Your boss has his undershorts all twisted up over you."*

Cheyenne didn't know what to say at first. "Does this mean I will stay on here?"

"It means you'll stay on the money," he replied. *"You and Ikeda."*

She told him about the various special interest groups that received ransom monies and the mysterious Gilbert Tepper and Gil Tran Tepp.

"I got the report on that about a half hour ago. Where are you?"

She looked over at Hennessy, who was watching her with drowsy, happy eyes. "A hotel in Bozeman, SAC. I'm going to try to get some sleep and come up in the morning."

After another silence, Kane agreed, but told her to make it early. The computer experts were arriving from Quantico and he wanted her to help find the machines that made the ransom transfers. He also told her that when confronted with the fact that she was the only Third Position soldier in captivity and therefore the only person who could possibly be held responsible for the attack, Mouse had begun to talk.

Cheyenne put her cell on speakerphone, made a signal to Hennessy to remain quiet, then sat in the hotel room chair, wrapped in the bedcover, and listened as Kane gave her a brief overview of what Mouse had told investigators.

Her real name was Mary Ann Chisholm. She was a native of Bremerton, Washington, an honors graduate in economics and political science from the University of Oregon, and a passionate anti-globalist.

She was arrested at nineteen for protesting in the streets of Seattle during the 1999 uprising against the WTO. After Seattle, she devoted much of her life to the movement, teaching, giving speeches, and participating in rallies. But in recent years, she said she had grown increasingly frustrated. Globalization wasn't slowing. It was accelerating.

Then one day about sixteen months before the attack, she said a big African-American man approached after a meeting of fellow anti-globalists in Eugene. He introduced himself as Truth. He told her that he believed the anti-global movement should be taking bolder steps to wake the world up to the problem of unchecked corporatization. He told her the time had come to take up arms against the corporations. But it wasn't until their fourth meeting that he told her about the Third Position Army, and not until the fifth that she met General Anarchy in a park at night in Salem, Oregon. He sat in shadows and told her he had served in the Middle East as part of the military-industrial complex and seen firsthand the power and greed of corporations in war. He told her the government had become a mouthpiece for the corporations no matter what political party held power.

Kane said, *"Anarchy told her the future lies in a third direction through a dangerous crossroads where global corporate power had to be challenged, held accountable, and defeated. He said he had the backing of someone he called 'the Benefactor,' who he described as a wealthy renegade from capitalism who saw the corporate gluttony in the Middle East and was so sickened and angry that he was paying for the training of an elite force that would fight for the anti-global movement."*

"She know who the Benefactor is?" Cheyenne asked.

"She claims she doesn't even know who Anarchy is."

After Mouse agreed to join the Third Position Army, Kane said, General Anarchy told Mouse she should chose a nom de guerre and from that point on only those war names would be used among them. He told her that Truth would train her and left.

Truth took her to a house in Vancouver, British Columbia, where she met Cristoph, Rose, and twelve other recruits. They left the next day in vans and drove twelve hours into the northern interior of British Columbia, where they boarded helicopters in the middle of nowhere, bound for an abandoned gold mining operation southwest of Atlin, British Columbia, that had been transformed into a training facility.

Mouse lived there eight months, steeping herself in Third Position dogma and training to be part of General Anarchy's army. Seven months before the attack, she saw their forces nearly double with the arrival of twenty new recruits, all of whom seemed more familiar with combat than the first wave. General Anarchy came with them and she saw him in daylight for the first time: handsome, early forties, fit, with long brown hair that was always falling across his slate-colored eyes. He told Mouse and the other recruits that he had discovered that many powerful globalists were going to gather in one remote place later in the year.

"Mouse claims that the original plan only called for attacking and holding them for ransom to fund the Third Position Army and other organizations that were their natural allies against corporate aggression," Kane said. *"A month later, General Anarchy told them all that the Benefactor had paid for private investigators who'd turned up damning evidence against the tycoons. He said they were going to have trials and they were going to webcast them to the world. Anarchy supposedly said he believed the trials would come as a shock that would awaken people to the Third Position's cause."*

"Killing them on the Web was supposed to do that?"

"We're not exactly dealing with logical minds, are we?" Kane asked.

"I suppose not, SAC," Cheyenne said doubtfully. "Did she think of it as a suicide mission?"

"What's that?"

"They couldn't have expected to come back, could they?"

Kane mulled that over before saying, *"I guess not. At least if they had half a brain. But I know she did say that General Anarchy promised them ten million dollars apiece if they succeeded and survived."*

"She didn't see the irony in that, I suppose."

"Evidently not," Kane said. *"Get some sleep. I'll see you tomorrow."*

"Bright and early," Cheyenne promised, then ended the call and snuggled back under the covers with Hennessy. "What do you think?"

"I think they were all insane to think they'd get away with it."

"Anarchy has," she said.

"So far," he said. "But he'll be caught."

"That's what they said about Bin Laden."

"Coming from an FBI agent?"

She shrugged. "The truth's the truth."

Hennessy put his finger under her chin. "I need to tell you the truth about—" The phone in the room rang. Hennessy startled and reached for it, saying, "It's probably my kids. They're the only ones who know I'm here." He picked it up. "Hello?"

"Michael?"

It was Patricia. She was the only person left on earth who called him Michael. And she usually did so when she was in high dudgeon about his shortcomings. He braced himself, then said, "Right here, Patricia."

"We're leaving in the morning," she said. "Aaron Grant's wife, Margaret, stopped by to see the children. She's offered to charter a jet to get Bridger back to Boston and a qualified orthopedic surgeon."

"He's had surgery already," Hennessy said, sitting up, concerned.

"And the doctors say he'll have at least two more," she replied. "So it's settled. The kids will ride on the jet with a doctor and a nurse. Ted and I will take the first Northwest flight out of here in the morning. Six a.m. so we can be at Logan to meet them. You'll have to arrange to get the kids from the hospital to the jetport at Gallatin Field. I've already got a surgeon at Mass General waiting to examine Bridger."

"Okay," he said, though he was perturbed that she'd made these arrangements without consulting him at all. "What time?"

"The medevac flight arrives at nine a.m. from Seattle," she said. "Turnaround is half an hour."

"I'll have them there at ten of nine," Hennessy promised.

"Good," she said. Then her voice softened. "And thank you, Mickey. They've told me what you did. With Hailey."

"You'd have done the same, Pat," he said and hung up.

Hennessy looked at the clock. It was past six in the evening. "You hungry?"

Cheyenne yawned. "I could go for something after another nap."

He shut off the lights, got back under the covers, and held her in his arms. "Another nap sounds wonderful."

"You were going to tell me the truth about something," she murmured.

He nuzzled into her hair. "That was my broker calling me at the restaurant. I made a lot of money in the stock market the past couple of days."

There was a pause before she murmured, "How much?"

"Almost three-point-nine million," he mumbled, feeling once again that sense of incomprehensibility coupled with fatigue, dragging him toward unconsciousness.

The bed shook. A light shone in his eyes. Hennessy groaned, surfacing enough to crack an eyelid. Cheyenne was sitting up beside him, looking at him intently. "You made three-point-nine million dollars in the last two days?"

"Yeah," he said, holding his hand up to block the light. "I hope it doesn't change things between us."

She frowned. "Why would it?"

"I don't know. I've heard it does. And never having had any money before to speak of, I wondered. Can we talk about this later? I am tired. You wore an old man out."

"How did you make that kind of money in just two days?" she asked.

Hennessy saw that she wasn't going to let him sleep until he explained. He reminded her about overhearing

Albert Crockett and Friedrich Klinefelter talking about the high volume of shorts on the markets on December 31, and how they suspected Sir Lawrence Treadwell was one of the major players. He told her how after overhearing Horatio Burns shorting the market, he decided to do the same.

"I told Jerry to do exactly what Horatio was doing," he recalled. "I bought puts on the NASDAQ, DOW, and AMEX Spyders at the money, January expiration with a fifteen to eighteen percent fix. Whatever that means."

Cheyenne seemed to be doing numbers in her head. "It means you were betting that the entire market would drop so you could sell the puts at a lower price and pocket the difference. The lower the market went, the more money you made. Why would you take that kind of risk?"

"I was frankly ticked off at Horatio because he said I didn't have the balls to make that kind of play. That afternoon, he looked right. I lost twenty-three thousand in the last two minutes of trading before the holiday. God only knows what he lost. He had to have known at the New Year's Eve party, but he acted like it didn't matter."

"How much did Burns put in?"

"I think I heard him place orders for another hundred million in puts each on the NASDAQ, DOW, and AMEX Spyders."

Cheyenne began to bite on her lower lip. "*Another* hundred million each? That means, what, he'd already bought puts on those Spyders?"

Hennessy shrugged again. "Yeah, I guess. He probably made billions. Some guys are just like that, the Midas touch."

Cheyenne sat there quietly, lost in thought. Hennessy rolled onto his side, watching her, feeling drowsy again. His last words before his eyes fluttered and closed were, "But being here, with you, Cheyenne, I think I may be the richest man alive."

Cheyenne heard Mickey's breathing become deep and rhythmic. She gazed at him for a long while, wanting nothing more than to lie next to him and sleep. He was the kind of man she hadn't realized she'd been looking for her entire life, solid, mature, resourceful, heroic, flawed but trying to be better.

Still, something about his story nagged at her and wouldn't let her mind do what her body longed for. She reached across Hennessy and turned out the light. Then she eased from the bed, found her clothes, and went into the bathroom to shower and dress.

She left Hennessy a note, saying that she couldn't sleep and had gone back to the motel desk to get a room where she could work.

Come find me when you wake up, she wrote, then slipped out the door.

They gave her a room with a high-speed Internet connection across the parking lot from Hennessy's room. Cheyenne made coffee in the drip machine, booted her computer, and sat at the desk. She didn't know what she was looking for, other than an explanation for all the shorts on the market on December 31.

She started by putting in a call to Scott Timmons, an investigator with the Securities and Exchange Commission in Washington, D.C. She and Ikeda had worked with Timmons several times on joint task forces looking into white-collar corruption. She got no answer at his office and left a message that she was involved in the Jefferson Club case and needed some advice.

Before she could think of sleep again, she opened up the PDF files Ikeda had sent. She scanned through documents from banks in sixteen different countries, Interpol, the U.S. Treasury, SWIFT, and a half dozen other banking regulatory agencies overseas.

It was like looking at a financial jigsaw puzzle with many of the pieces missing. She had account numbers, and the supposed names of ownership. But most were dummy corporations set up in money-laundering havens around the world.

She noticed the names Gil Tepper and Gil Tran Tepp cited as officers of eight or nine of the shell companies. In three cases, Tepper was listed as president of the company with "Ludwig Meyer" named as the attorney of record in the formation of the corporations. Meyer's address was in Liechtenstein, in the city of Vaduz. The accounts the money passed through were all at the same private bank in Zurich.

Cheyenne Googled Meyer and found his Web site. The barrister offered quick, confidential work specializing in the organizing of "Anstalts," essentially dummy corporations that could be used to open accounts at private banks. To her surprise, Meyer listed his office, home, and cell phone numbers.

"Ready for corruption at all hours," she muttered. On a whim, she picked up the phone, got an international line, and punched his home number. It had to be early, early morning in Europe. She was surprised when the line clicked and she heard a gravelly, befuddled voice say, "Meyer."

She identified herself and told him she was looking for information about Tepper. The attorney tried to claim client privilege, but yielded when she said it was related to the attack on the Jefferson Club. Meyer told her he'd never met Tepper. They had conducted their business by phone, letter, and e-mail. Reluctantly, Meyer agreed to send her copies of everything he had on Tepper when he got to his office.

It was nearly eight p.m. now in Montana. She wondered whether she should go back to wake Mickey so they could have dinner. Her cell phone rang. "O'Neil."

"Scott Timmons, Cheyenne," a familiar smooth baritone voice said. *"How did you get involved in the Jefferson Club?"*

"Long story," Cheyenne said, trying to shift gears in her tired brain. "But one of the things we're digging into is the volume of shorts on the market on December thirty-first. How would I figure out how big a short position certain people may have held?"

"There's no reporting requirement, if that's what you mean," Timmons said. *"We usually get tipped about big bets by brokers and I haven't heard anything about this yet. Then again, if someone was clever, we might not get wind of it at all."*

"How's that possible?" she asked.

"If they were using many different accounts, building up short positions over time, say a month, suspicions would not be raised, and we might not see it," Timmons replied.

"What if I was looking for short positions being held under specific names?"

"Again, no reporting requirement," Timmons said. *"IRS does for profit and loss, but they're part of the April tax package. I don't know. Subpoena their accounts?"*

"I can't get a subpoena at this point," she admitted.

"Talk to their brokers, then," he said. *"They won't like it, but they'll talk."*

It wasn't a bad idea and she knew just the person to help her track those men or women down. "Thanks, Scott, I appreciate it."

"You get on to something let us know."

Cheyenne promised she would, hung up, yawned, and drank more coffee. It didn't seem to be helping. She felt woozy. She got up and splashed water on her face, then called up her personal telephone directory and found the name Richard Oglethorpe. Mr. Oglethorpe was the senior vice president at one of the world's most distinguished money management firms. He was seventy-five, but still had a startling memory for names, faces, and connections. He had helped her on several cases a few years back and they kept in touch.

She called him at his home. When she told Oglethorpe she was looking for the names of the brokers in New York representing the seven men taken hostage at the Jefferson Club, Oglethorpe paused and then rattled off a list of names and phone numbers before abruptly excusing himself. He and his wife were entertaining old friends from Princeton.

It was past nine when she finished calling all the

numbers and leaving messages. For several minutes she racked her brain, trying to come up with some other angle she could work. Finally she surrendered, closed her laptop, and stumbled onto the bed. She set the alarm for five a.m. and flipped off the light.

CHAPTER FORTY-FOUR

Hennessy woke up in the pitch-black room, sure he'd only been out for twenty minutes. He stared around, unsure where he was, and then reached for Cheyenne. She was gone. He wondered if she'd thought better of their impulsive tryst and had escaped to avoid an ugly scene. He checked the clock. It was four a.m. He'd been asleep nine hours.

Hennessy lay back and dozed in and out of consciousness, the memories of the attack, siege, and counterattack playing out of sequence, mutating into a nightmare where General Anarchy had become his terrible, vengeful foe in a dark house he did not recognize. He jolted awake, drenched and gasping. He lurched out of bed and went into the bathroom. He turned on the light, saw Cheyenne's note, read it, and felt better.

He showered, then watched the television coverage documenting the manhunt for General Anarchy,

Citizen's Defender Emilia, and the remaining fourteen Third Position Army soldiers believed at large. The dragnet was huge, from the Canadian border west to Spokane, south to Boise, and across the Utah state line into Wyoming. Hennessy's children were being hailed as heroes, which made him proud and also anxious about the kinds of people who would be sure to try and exploit them in the future.

He went to Cheyenne's door around six. She answered immediately at his soft knocking. She looked rumpled but awake. "Kind of early for dinner, isn't it?"

"Or late, depending on your perspective," he said.

"I'd offer you delicious motel-brewed coffee, but I'm out."

"I've got some at my place," he said. "I'll be right back."

Hennessy got the coffee filters and found her door ajar. When he pushed it open, Cheyenne was scrolling down through documents in what appeared to be German and some other language he didn't recognize. She was looking at the documents so intently that he slid around her and got the coffee machine going.

When he turned back, he found Cheyenne closely studying something on the screen. She threw her hands overhead and cried. "He's broken pattern!"

"Who's broken pattern?" he asked.

"Gilbert Tepper, the president of several of the companies the ransom money moved through," she explained excitedly. "I got these documents from the attorney who helped organize them. They did business entirely by phone and wire transfers." She clicked her fingernail on her computer screen. "Except in this case."

Hennessy leaned forward to see a photocopy of a cashier's check drawn on the Bank of Netherlands for fifteen thousand dollars. It was signed Gilbert Tepper.

"Okay?" he said, not understanding.

"Cashier's check for an amount over ten thousand dollars exceeds international currency limits. Even if he paid for the check in cash it triggers a report and a demand for a photo ID. He'd have to have shown his passport."

"Or his forged one," Hennessy said.

Cheyenne frowned. "I hadn't thought of that."

"Still worth pursuing," Hennessy said.

She sipped from her coffee. "I think so too."

"I have to go soon," he said. "I'm responsible for getting the kids to the jetport."

"You'll probably need to rent an ambulance."

"My ex is one step ahead of you," he said. "I'm just along for the ride."

"So maybe you don't have to go so soon."

She had a sly grin on her face. Hennessy smiled and pulled her into his arms.

Hennessy left Cheyenne's motel room happily an hour later with a kiss and a promise to call after the kids were off.

When he was gone, Cheyenne sighed and leaned against the door a moment, savoring what they'd shared, what they'd become in so short a time. Then she compartmentalized and used the Internet to find a number for the bank in Amsterdam where Tepper bought the check. The manager spoke perfect English and said she would check her files regarding the cashier's check. Five minutes later, she came back on the line and confirmed that the bank teller made a copy of Gilbert M. Tepper's Canadian passport. She promised to send over a PDF copy of it within the hour.

Cheyenne hung up, threw her arms over her head, and did a little dance. "He screwed up! He screwed up!"

Something was breaking. She could feel it. If they had Tepper's face, they could broadcast it everywhere. Sooner or later someone would recognize him and turn him in. Sooner or later the plot would begin to unravel. It always did.

At 7:40 her cell phone rang. The late Sir Lawrence Treadwell's broker at UBS was on the line. When the broker heard what she was looking for, he balked at first before reluctantly confirming that Sir Lawrence had a heavy short position heading into the holiday, three hundred million worth on the U.S. markets alone. Cheyenne asked if Sir Lawrence had shorted the market using puts. The broker replied that he had not. He'd done it using the futures markets and options contracts.

Cheyenne hung up, not knowing where any of this was going and whether she should continue to pursue this arcane angle of the investigation. She was feeling hungry. She programmed her computer to forward her e-mail to her BlackBerry and walked to a breakfast diner at the east end of town.

She had eggs, bacon, and toast and read the coverage of the attack in the local Bozeman paper. She was leaving when her phone rang again.

"Agent O'Neil, this is Bill Murphy at Goldman Sachs. You called?"

Murphy was Horatio Burns's broker.

"Oh, thank you, Mr. Murphy, for calling back," she said before explaining that she was looking into the short positions that appeared on the market on December 31.

"They always do," Murphy said.

"Right," she said. "But from what I can gather, the volume was heavier than usual."

"I couldn't speak for the market," Murphy said.

"We were told Horatio Burns bought several hundred million dollars in puts on December thirty-first."

Silence. *"Some on the thirty-first, more before."*

"I thought he told everyone he'd gone to cash," she said.

"He did, in mid-November," Murphy said. *"But in the first week of December he grew more pessimistic about the markets, told me they were out of whack and due for a serious correction. He went short."*

"How big a position?" she asked.

Silence. *"Substantial enough that he lost hundreds of millions in the middle of the month and right through Christmas week, I can tell you. Substantial enough that I told him to cut his losses. But he didn't. That's why he's a genius and I'm just a broker."*

"So he did make money when the market tanked, is that correct?" she asked, then waited through a silence that lasted so long she had to say, "Mr. Murphy?"

"He did make money when the market corrected. Yes. A substantial amount."

"Are we talking hundreds of millions?"

"More like nine billion," Murphy said, sounding irritated.

"Nine billion?" she said, awed. "Is that possible?"

"Of course it's possible," Murphy said, *"at least for someone as visionary as Horatio. He's horrified by the forces that corrected the market, but he's putting his profits to good use by reinvesting his money across the board in equities, calming the markets. We opened an hour ago and the Dow's up."*

"I'll bet it is," she said softly before something occurred to her. "Did Mr. Burns have any position on the markets other than the puts on December thirty-first?"

"He shorted the dollar and bought gold," Murphy said curtly.

"Traditional defensive positions," she said. "No equities?"

"No," Murphy replied.

"He went in naked on the puts?"

"If you mean he had no equity holdings to offset the puts, that's correct."

Cheyenne shook her head, baffled. "Why would he short a market naked?"

"You'd have to ask him that," Murphy said curtly. *"I don't begin to understand the complexities of Mr. Burns's mind."*

"Okay," she allowed. "Know where I might find him?"

"I'm not his secretary, Agent O'Neil, but as a matter of fact, yes," Murphy said. *"I just spoke with him.*

He's on his way to the Bozeman airport from the Jefferson Club. He's taking the HB1 jet to New York in about an hour."

HB1 Financial built the jetport at the east end of Gallatin Field so members of the Jefferson Club could land and store their jets and avoid the commoners in the commercial terminal down the road. The port featured two large hangars, a broad tarmac, and a private luxury lounge where club members could wait for their flights to depart, or find a cold Pellegrino after the long trip into Montana.

It was overcast and snowing lightly when ambulance workers wheeled Bridger Hennessy and the medical machinery surrounding him through the jetport doors. His father trailed, tired, but appreciative that Patricia had arranged everything and gone ahead on the early Northwest flight to Boston. A welcoming older Japanese woman in a Jefferson Club uniform came out from behind the counter, spotting Hennessy coming in followed by Hailey and Connor.

"Oh, Mr. Hennessy," she fussed. "I'm so glad you are all right. That your children are all right."

Lee Chiba was concierge at the jetport. Hennessy had vetted her during the hiring process and saw her almost every time he flew in and out of the facility.

"Thank you, Lee," he said, then introduced the kids.

On the ride over from the hospital, Hailey had complained that her hands burned beneath her bandages and had acted surly. Connor was only half awake. They grunted their hellos with little enthusiasm. Bridger, however, had just had a shot of his medicine. He was lively and greeted the concierge like they were old friends.

"Hi, Lee," he said. "Got any caviar?"

"Caviar?" Hennessy said.

"He got hooked on it when we were in the Burnses' house," Connor explained.

Lee Chiba grinned. "Of course we have caviar. Ms. Isabel loves caviar. It's in the cabinet over the refrigerator in the lounge. Why don't you all go in there? We just spoke to the pilot of the medevac flight. They're about twenty-five minutes out. Go on. You've got some admirers in there waiting for you."

The ambulance workers wheeled Bridger through a double door to the left of the concierge station. Hennessy and his other two kids followed into a spacious, richly appointed room with a plasma-screen television on one wall, as well as a bar, a kitchen area, and leather chairs and couches. Margaret and Aaron Grant were in the kitchen. Their daughters, Katherine and Sophie, were with them. Sophie, the youngest, was hanging on to her father's pants as if they were a lifeline.

When the wife of the cofounder of YES! spotted them, she hurried out, munching on a potato chip and crying, "I was worried I wouldn't get to see you before we left and Aaron wouldn't get to thank you himself!"

Aaron Grant followed his wife, rubbing his hands on a paper towel before dropping it in a trash basket. The big bear of a man that Hennessy remembered at the New Year's Eve party had shaved. His eyes were hollowed out, but he managed a smile moving toward the triplets. "I have you to thank for my rescue, I hear," he said.

"I wanted to rescue you first time we went through that basement," Bridger announced.

"We would have had to kill the guard," Hailey protested.

"We could have saved Mr. Doore, maybe," Bridger said, suddenly maudlin.

"You did the right thing at the time, and the right thing when you told Agent Kane where we were being held," Aaron Grant said, getting emotional. "I owe the three of you, and you, Mr. Hennessy, a great debt. I am your friend for life. I was the same way with Jack. I think he would have enjoyed knowing you."

"I got to ski with him one day," Hennessy said sympathetically. "A great guy."

"We knew his son, Ian," Hailey said. "Is he all right?"

Aaron Grant shook his head, his eyes welling. "Ian worshipped Jack. Stephanie said he's retreating into himself. She's devastated and has taken him home to her parents in Iowa."

"Sucks," Connor said.

Aaron Grant nodded at him. "It does suck, Connor. Jack was the smartest man I've ever known. A great creative genius, but unimpressed with himself. Funny and personal and caring. You would have liked to have known him."

"Yes, sir," Connor said. "I think I would have."

"Can we get you something to eat?"

"Caviar!" Bridger said. "In the cabinet above the fridge."

"Expensive taste," Margaret Grant said, heading into the kitchen alcove. "Do you know my daughters, Katherine and Sophie?"

The girls looked spooked, especially Katherine. Hailey realized she and Katherine were about the same age and brightened. She went over to talk to her.

"They put a gun to my head too," Hailey told her.

Tears welled in Katherine Grant's eyes as she nodded.

Hennessy realized he was paying the ambulance workers by the hour and told them they could leave. The medevac plane would be on the ground in fifteen minutes and Bridger's vitals had been excellent the past eighteen hours. After signing documents and handing over all of Bridger's medical documentation, the ambulance workers left.

Margaret Grant opened the cabinet door above the fridge, revealing boxes of expensive crackers and jars of caviar. She twisted the cover off one and spooned it out onto a plate with crackers.

"Lots of caviar," she said, bringing the plate to Bridger.

"Mrs. Burns likes caviar," Bridger explained. "If it wasn't for caviar I wouldn't have survived. There was like no food in their house, except caviar, crackers, and soup."

"In the fridge anyway," Hailey informed Katherine Grant. "Just water."

"Really?" Hennessy said, surprised. Isabel Burns loved to cook and entertain and usually stocked her refrigerator during extended stays.

"And they're like wicked cheap," Connor said as the

door to the lounge opened behind them. "They keep the house really cold and he uses Skype for long distance."

Hennessy looked over his shoulder to see who had entered and felt his stomach drop. Isabel and Horatio Burns were standing there watching them, listening.

CHAPTER FORTY-FIVE

Isabel Burns wore a black Armani ski jacket, a matching head scarf, and sunglasses. She was scowling. But Horatio, who wore jeans and cowboy boots, a sheepskin coat, and a cowboy hat, managed a sour smile.

"I *am* wicked cheap, young man," he said to Connor. "It's one of the foundations of my good fortune, never having to pay more for something than it is worth."

Burns took off his cowboy hat, came over, and shook Connor's hand. "I understand that you and your brother and sister saved my life."

"Sort of, I guess," Connor admitted.

"They did," Aaron Grant said. "It's why we're here, Horatio. To thank them."

The tycoon gazed hard at Connor. "How did you know about the passage between my house and the lodge?"

Connor glanced at his father. "Uh, my dad."

Burns spotted Hennessy, crossed to him, and

gripped his hand and pumped it hard. "A good thing you don't know how to keep a secret."

Hennessy didn't know what to say.

Burns gazed deep into Hennessy's eyes, making him feel probed. "I heard what you went through, Mickey, to save your daughter, and what she and your sons did for Aaron and me. The Third Position Army may have underestimated you. They certainly underestimated your family. I know I did."

Hennessy nodded, warmed by this rare praise from his former boss. "Thank you, Horatio. I just wish I could have prevented the attack in the first place."

Burns released his hand and glanced away somberly. "We all do," he said. "Gregg, too. He and I made the decision not to upgrade the generator link beyond two-point-two seconds because of huge cost overruns during the construction of the fence and the lodge. It was an Achilles' heel and we're taking responsibility."

"No, I'm taking responsibility," a man's voice said. "I made the call."

It was then that Hennessy noticed Gregg Foster, head of HB1 Financial security, was standing nearby, shaking his head bitterly. Foster was a hard-nosed ex–Navy SEAL and retired full-bird colonel with the Defense Intelligence Agency, a stern, authoritative man with military-cropped sandy hair, a bomber jacket, jeans, and hiking boots. He was deeply tanned from trekking in Patagonia, early forties, with a ramrod posture and penetrating sapphire eyes.

The few times Hennessy had met him in person, Foster had always seemed a cold son-of-a-bitch, who had only one way of thinking: his own. Thankfully, for most of Hennessy's tenure with HB1 Financial, Foster had been in Thailand overseeing the construction of the company's Celadon resort.

"I seconded the call," Burns insisted, wavering emotion in his voice.

Aaron Grant cocked his head. "How much faster could the fence have rebooted?"

The question seemed to throw Foster, but he recovered. "Maybe a second faster. They still would have probably gotten in."

"Even with YES! running the junction?"

"Diesel engines," Foster explained. "Coil's got to heat, then fire."

While Grant mulled this explanation, Burns clapped Hennessy on the shoulder where he'd been shot. Hennessy cringed as Burns said, "I understand Isabel fired you?"

"I believe so."

"Consider yourself unfired," Burns said. "How would you like to run Celadon security for me?"

"Thailand?" Hennessy said.

"I am so sorry, Mickey," Isabel said, removing her sunglasses and firing up the voltage on her smile. "I knew nothing of this gap thing in the generators. I hope you accept my apology. I say these things to you under the stress."

Hennessy sighed and nodded. "Of course, Isabel." Then he turned, puzzled, and looked to Foster. "I thought Celadon was your dream assignment, Gregg."

Foster shrugged and said, "On to bigger and better

things." A woman almost as beautiful as Isabel Burns had appeared at Foster's side. She was in her mid-thirties, with stunning dusky features and dark mahogany hair.

"My fiancé, Alana Escovar," Foster said. "Mickey Hennessy."

"Nice to meet you, *Meester* Hennessy," she said in a soft Latin accent. "I have read so much about you and your kids in the papers the past few days." She pointed around with a long fingernail. "Now, who is who?"

Hennessy pointed out his children and introduced them. The Grants did the same.

"One big family of survivors, then," Isabel Burns said, smiling plastically. "I think we've all gone through something horrible and survived, that's how you fight these kind of terrible men, you know, by surviving to make the world a better place."

"Amen, my dear," Horatio Burns said solemnly.

"It'll be a hard thing to do without Jack," Aaron Grant said.

His wife hugged him. "You'll push on in Jack's honor," Margaret Grant said insistently. "Take up his vision, add your own, and see it come to pass in Jack's memory."

Grant looked heartbroken, but he nodded and hugged his wife back. "We'll make YES! bigger and better than ever."

Hennessy noticed Horatio Burns harden for a moment, then cock his head when Bridger asked softly, "Could I have some more caviar and crackers?" His plate was empty. Margaret Grant made to return to the kitchen. But Gregg Foster's fiancé, Alana Escovar, broke from his side and beat her to it.

"I'll get it," she said.

Isabel Burns said, "So you like my caviar?"

Bridger nodded. "Yeah. It's good. Especially in chicken soup."

Alana cracked the lid on the jar and crossed the room to Bridger's gurney.

As Foster's fiancé passed Hailey, Hennessy saw his daughter sniff, frown, and look after the woman. Alana handed Bridger the whole jar. "Careful. It's heavy."

Foster pulled out a cigar. "If you'll excuse me, I think I have time for a quick smoke before the pilot calls us."

"Waste a perfectly good Havana for a few puffs?" Burns said disapprovingly.

"Man's got to have some vices, boss," Foster said, passing Connor, who was sitting on one of the couches, looking up from his Game Boy and appearing puzzled.

Hennessy only noted it because at the same time he heard Cheyenne O'Neil say, "Mr. Burns? Horatio Burns?"

Cheyenne was closing the door to the lounge. Foster's right hand moved behind his back where Hennessy knew he kept his pistol.

"Who are you?" Foster demanded. "How did you get in here?"

"Gregg—" Hennessy began.

Cheyenne already had her FBI badge out. "Agent Cheyenne O'Neil. FBI."

"She's working on the Jefferson Club case, Gregg," Hennessy explained. "She's been on it since the beginning."

Foster's hand left the butt of his pistol and he smiled unconvincingly. "Sorry, Agent O'Neil. We're all still a little jumpy. What can I do for you?"

Foster had moved slightly in her way. Cheyenne gave him a steady appraisal. "You can stand aside so I can ask Mr. Burns a few questions."

"About what?" Isabel Burns snapped. "We spent all yesterday afternoon giving Agent Kane our statements."

"He ask you why you didn't call with the security code to your house?"

Hennessy grimaced. *What the hell is she doing?*

"Dad?" Hailey said. He glanced at her and saw she looked frightened.

"It's okay," Hennessy said. "Just a second, kiddo."

Isabel Burns appeared taken aback at Cheyenne's question. "No one tells me about a call about the code."

"I talked to your secretary three times. I left five messages on your cell."

"Well," Isabel blustered, "my secretary, she is an imbecile. She's fired! And I was not listening to my messages. Everyone was calling. I was going crazy and turned it off."

Burns checked his watch. "Your other questions, Agent O'Neil?"

"You shorted the markets using puts on the exchange Spyders," Cheyenne said.

Burns showed little reaction from Hennessy's perspective. But Foster's lips thinned. Isabel Burns's polished fingernails sought the gold strand around her neck.

"In retrospect, it was HB1's best financial gamble ever," Burns said in a hoarse voice. "I'm just sorry it worked out for me under these circumstances. How did you know? We weren't going to make that public until the stockholders' meeting."

Cheyenne cocked her head. "When I heard Mickey made three-point-nine million shorting the market indexes, I asked him where he got the idea from. He said from you."

Burns glanced at Hennessy, reappraising him. "You shorted the market?"

"Three-point-nine million?" Bridger said. "Whoa. Way to go, Dad."

"Dad?" This time it was Connor, and he was looking frightened too.

Hennessy turned to Burns and shrugged. "Craziest thing I've ever done."

Burns looked angry. "You could have been ruined, Mickey."

"You too, sir."

"Hardly," Burns snapped. "I invested less than one-fortieth of my fortune. You must have bet everything."

"I always do."

Cheyenne said to Burns, "Your broker says you made in the neighborhood of nine billion on the play. Is that correct?"

Burns reddened when he realized everyone in the lounge was looking at him, jaws agape. "Well, yes," he said, "somewhere in that neighborhood."

Hennessy was shocked. *Nine billion dollars in two days?*

Cheyenne said, "Were you long on gold and gold futures too?"

Burns turned his full attention to her now and replied, "It's what you usually do when you believe the market is overheated and about to get some of the gas blown out of it. I've made this play five times in my career, Agent O'Neil. Twice I've lost my shirt. Three times I've made money: the oil crisis in 1972, Black Monday in 1987, and the recession in '92. I missed 9/11/2001. Then again, so did everyone."

"What were your reasons for shorting this time?" Cheyenne asked. "I mean, I know you went to cash in early December because you couldn't make sense out of the market. But shorting it is a whole other story."

Burns smiled condescendingly. "Do you understand business, Agent O'Neil?"

"MBA, Kellogg School," she replied. "I work financial crimes for the Bureau."

Burns's smile vanished. "Very well, Agent O'Neil. My reasons for going to cash were many and well publicized. I believed that the market had become grossly overinflated in mid-November. I didn't understand the price-to-earnings ratios or the debt-to-earnings ratio of most of the world's largest corporations, including my own. I said to myself, this doesn't make sense and I'm heading to the sidelines until I figure it out."

Cheyenne pressed, "But you didn't stay on the sidelines long. You shorted."

Burns nodded again. "Once I was free of the equities market, I became convinced that the markets were due for a major technical correction and I invested accordingly."

"But the markets didn't lose seven percent of their

value due to overvaluation or technical triggers. They dropped because of the attack on the Jefferson Club."

"Did they?" Burns asked. "Or were the markets just acknowledging their overheated state? That is what knocks markets back, Agent O'Neil, some fuse blowing that makes people come to their senses and see that the emperor has no clothes. It could have been bad news out of the Middle East like it was in 1975. It could have been the Latin American banking collapse, as it was in November 1986. It could have been the invasion of Kuwait, as it was in 1990–91."

"So you agree the attack triggered the decline?" she asked.

"I happen to believe the trials were what triggered the decline, not the attack," Burns said. "But it could have been any number of things. The market was bound to correct. I just wish it hadn't been under those awful circumstances."

"You mean circumstances that allowed you to benefit from misfortune and murder?" Cheyenne asked coldly.

Hennessy stiffened. She'd crossed a line. *What the hell's she doing?*

Burns's features hardened. "Agent O'Neil, since the beginning of money, one man's misfortune has created another's fortune. You may not like it. I did not like it once I'd learned that the markets had crashed. That's why I sold my puts and bought so heavily into the markets afterwards: I didn't want to see other lives ruined by this vicious attack. I made a statement in full support of capitalism, globalism, and the economy."

Isabel Burns looked insulted. "The President called his actions noble. He called us last night. It's in the paper this morning."

"It's in every paper in the country this morning," Foster added.

Cheyenne appeared to hesitate, but then stood her ground. "As you said, Mr. Burns, everything is open to interpretation in the global marketplace. And another, more conspiracy-minded person such as myself might speculate that it wasn't chance that caused the markets to fall. Another, more cynical person might speculate that somehow, in some way, you knew the club was going to be attacked and knew what putting capitalism on trial would do to the markets. So you shorted them and bought gold."

Burns looked like someone had spit in his face. His head cocked back and a snarl captured him. "How dare you? Who the hell do you think you're dealing with?"

Isabel Burns leaped to her feet and marched across the room at Cheyenne, wagging her finger in the agent's face. "That's the outrage. The slander!"

Foster looked to Hennessy. "Mickey?"

Hennessy looked at Foster and then Cheyenne. So did the boys and Hailey. Hennessy didn't know what to think. He didn't believe it.

Cheyenne said, "All I'm suggesting is that there could be another interpretation to what happened."

"You suggest it to a man who almost died in there!" Isabel Burns shouted, then waved her hand wildly at Aaron Grant. "At two men who almost died in there, tied up for days, forced to watch the trials, not knowing if they would be next. Think what this has done to him! Look! Look at what this has done to my poor husband!"

Isabel started to weep. Burns glared at Cheyenne as if this were the final indignity.

"What shred of evidence do you have to support that *interpretation*, Agent O'Neil?" he thundered. "None. Why? Because there is none. And if you repeat your bullshit accusations, I'll sue."

The billionaire was sweating now, red-faced and breathing shallowly and rubbing at his chest. He suddenly did not look like a well man, and for a second Hennessy feared he might be having a heart attack.

"Unless you have any more crap to hurl at me, Agent O'Neil, I'll ask you to leave," Burns said. "And you can be assured that I will be speaking to the President, who will be speaking to the FBI director about you. Get prepared for a call."

For the first time, Cheyenne looked uncertain. Then her cell phone jingled and she startled. She grabbed it and flipped it open. "Just a minute," she said and started hitting buttons.

"No," Burns seethed. "We're leaving, Agent O'Neil. We have a plane to catch!"

"Dad, we should get out of here too," Hailey said in a timorous voice. She was on her feet, pale.

"Yeah," Connor said, moving beside his sister. "In the hangar or out front, Dad. Bridger too."

Hennessy knitted his brows. "What's wrong with you guys?"

Gregg Foster and Alana Escovar led the way past

Cheyenne, who was staring at her cell phone. The Burnses were almost to the door when she snapped shut the phone, reached around the back of her waist, and drew her service pistol.

"You're under arrest!" Cheyenne shouted. "Get down or I'll shoot!

Hennessy was horrified. She'd gone completely off the deep end. He immediately started thinking how to get the gun away from her and slid toward her in a loop. Hailey and Connor moved in front of Bridger. Aaron and Margaret Grant grabbed their daughters and dragged them into the kitchen.

Frightened, Isabel Burns moved closer to her husband. Burns's hands were rising in surrender when Foster stepped in front of his boss. "You're making a big, big mistake, Agent O'Neil," he said, now coming toward her.

"Down on your knees," Cheyenne shouted, waving the pistol. "Hands behind your heads, all of you."

None of them moved. She thumbed off the safety. "Down!"

Isabel dropped to her knees, sobbing, "She's crazy. Why, Horatio?"

"I don't know," Burns said, shaking as he knelt beside her.

"Put the gun down, Agent O'Neil," Foster said, halfway to his knees. "This isn't right."

"Cheyenne," Hennessy said softly, slipping toward her. "What are you doing?

Hailey and Connor shouted over the top of each other, "No! She's right, Dad!"

"Tell him how Alana smells, Agent O'Neil!" Hailey called.

"Tell him about the cigars he smokes!" Connor cried, pointing at Foster.

Cheyenne glanced at them, confused, then shook her head, turned back to Burns, and demanded, "Where was the hedge, Mr. Burns?"

Burns looked at her like she was insane. "What?"

"The opposite side of the trade when you shorted the markets," Cheyenne insisted. "You went in naked on a billion bucks."

"And for that you're going to shoot us?" Burns asked in bewilderment.

"You didn't have any food in your refrigerator on New Year's Eve," Bridger said, trying to sit upright. "You knew you weren't coming back after the party."

Connor nodded. "And they turned down the heat for the same reason."

Foster, who was now on his knees, growled at Cheyenne, "You're inventing things. You're an FBI agent, for God's sake, Agent O'Neil. You have to have—"

"Shut up, Foster," Cheyenne said, taking a step toward him and pointing the pistol directly at his head. "Or should I say Gilbert Tepper?"

"Gilbert Tepper?" Connor cried. "No, that's—"

The silenced round hit Cheyenne in the right ring finger, blowing it off. Her service pistol spun across the floor. She twisted, crying out. Hennessy grabbed her as she went down. Foster dove across the floor and came up with the pistol in a military shooting stance and aimed it at Hennessy and Cheyenne, who was looking at her hand incredulously, making choking noises. Alana Escovar was moving toward them from the opposite side of the room, a silenced pistol sweeping before her.

"Are you crazy?" Hennessy yelled. "You just shot an FBI agent! Call 911!"

"That won't be necessary," Foster replied icily.

Isabel Burns was on her feet, anxious. "What are we going to do?"

"Shut up, Isabel," HB1's security chief said. "Leave this to the professionals."

Hennessy stared at them all, his mind whirling and filling in puzzle pieces.

Cheyenne gasped, "He's Gilbert Tepper, a Canadian businessman who set up the accounts that the ransom passed through."

"No, he's not," Connor said in a tremulous voice. "He's General Anarchy."

Hailey pointed at Alana Escovar. "And she's Citizen's Defender Emilia."

CHAPTER FORTY-SIX

Gregg Foster's smile was sharp and icy. He walked toward the Hennessy triplets with both guns up. "Nosy, prying little bastards," he said. "I'll have the pleasure of shooting the three of you myself. And don't think I'm going to end any of you mercifully."

"Don't hurt my kids," Hennessy said, taking a step toward Anarchy. "If you want to shoot anyone, shoot me."

Alana Escovar turned her pistol on him. "One more move, Mr. Hennessy, and I shoot you now."

Horatio Burns said, "You can't kill them here, Gregg."

Isabel Burns headed toward the door to the hangar, upset, waving her hands. "I don't want to know. What are we going to do, Horatio? They know! They all know!"

"Shut up, Isabel!" Foster commanded, then looked at Burns. "We tell them that Anarchy broke in here and finished the job. We miraculously escaped. So go to the jet. That's why you weren't in here when the Third Position Army came to finish the job. You were in the jet."

Aaron Grant's daughters began to cry. "Are they going to kill us, Mom?"

"No," Isabel protested, turning back. "This is not how we planned it. No more killing."

"Plans change, Isabel," Foster said. "Adapt or go to prison."

"Why?" Cheyenne asked Burns. "Why did you do this? For the money?"

Burns couldn't help himself. "Of course, for the money," he replied. "I deserved to have the most. No one's worked harder to be number one than I have and no one remembers who comes in second. First thing I learned in life. Number one or nothing." He looked to Aaron Grant. "The way the markets are rebounding, I'll soon be richer than you. The richest man in the world."

Aaron Grant shook his head with rage and disbelief. "You had Jack murdered just so you could be number one?"

"I think he was after more than that," Hennessy said, looking at Burns, disgusted. "If all you were interested in was being number one, you could have just killed everyone between you and the top. But you put on those sadistic trials. Why?"

Burns smirked. "You continue to surprise me, Hennessy. Stronger than I thought. More resourceful than I thought. And now smarter. Well, not smart enough. We held the trials to change the world."

"And how was that supposed to happen?" Hennessy retorted.

"It already has," Burns said, enjoying himself. "The anti-global movement was becoming too strong, becoming an impediment to my business, to the world's business, throwing up regulations designed to slow our destiny. For unbridled capitalism to continue, for people like me, an orphan boy from Wyoming, to go out and conquer the world, to thrive and reach his dreams, it was necessary to stamp out the threat once and for all, to make anti-globalism so radical a fringe that no one in their right mind would embrace it. Now governments, especially our government, as well as the people of the world, have seen the dangers of anti-global terrorism. Congress is already drafting legislation outlawing the movement. Politicians on both sides of the aisle are stampeding to sign it. Soon life will proceed in the way it should, for the good of commerce."

"That's how you came up with the idea for the attack?" Hennessy asked.

Burns and Foster exchanged glances before the HB1 security chief said, "The idea of the trials came first. When we decided to hold them at the Jefferson Club, a well-choreographed attack was inevitable."

"The whole operation was planned to the second," Hennessy said.

"Nothing was left to chance," Burns agreed. "I thought you'd have understood that about me, Mickey: I never leave anything to chance."

"Except you and your kids," Foster said, loathing laced through his voice. "You were supposed to die in the attack. Your children were supposed to leave with the other hostages and find their mother. You went off script, Hennessy, so now you all die."

Burns walked toward his wife. "Isabel? Shall we go?"

"Cover them," Foster told his fiancé. "I'll be right back and we'll finish business."

Alana Escovar nodded, training her pistol on them. "Sit," she commanded.

The office door opened. Lee Chiba entered, saying, "The medevac flight is—"

Alana swung the pistol and shot the jetport concierge between the eyes. The woman crashed backward into the office.

"No!" Katherine Grant screamed. "No! Please! Stop!"

"Shut up and get on the floor," Alana snarled.

As Connor and Hailey lowered themselves toward the floor, Bridger suddenly heaved himself upright on the gurney behind them and whipped the caviar jar as hard as he could. The jar struck Alana Escovar behind her ear. Her eyes rolled white. She pitched flat on her face. Her silenced pistol went off. The round shattered the glass on the microwave door.

Her gun skittered across the floor to Hennessy. He grabbed it and got to his knees to find Foster pivoting and raising his two pistols at him. Isabel and Horatio Burns were through the door, hurrying into the hangar. Hennessy threw himself forward toward Foster, firing. He slammed to the floor behind one of the lounge chairs just as a barrage of unmuffled shots thudded into it.

It started in the ringing silence that held the jetport after that first exchange of gunfire, a shrieking that no one who heard it would ever forget, female and so full of disbelief and fear that it tore like claws at those who heard it, making them feel pity for anyone to be in that much pain.

"Horatio!" Isabel sobbed. "It hangs from me. It hangs from me. Haaa. Haaa."

"Gregg!" Burns roared. "Gregg, she's hit."

"Mío Dio," Isabel screamed. *"Mío Jesús. Santa María, Madre di Dio. Horatio?"*

"Isabel! Isabel! No!"

Hennessy heard two more shots, one silenced, one not. He came up firing at the retreating form of Foster ducking into the hangar. His bullets chipped the floor around Horatio Burns, who held his dead wife in his arms. Blood drained from her lips.

Foster stuck a gun around the doorway and shot blindly. Hennessy ducked.

Then he heard Cheyenne behind him barking into her cell phone. "Nine-one-one, this is FBI Agent Cheyenne O'Neil, repeat FBI Agent O'Neil. I am working the Jefferson Club case. Shots fired at the jetport at Gallatin Field. We are engaged in a firefight with General Anarchy. I repeat, we are in a firefight with General Anarchy of the Third Position Army. His name is Gregg Foster, head of HB1 Financial security. They have a jet."

"C'mon!" Foster shouted.

Hennessy sprang up to fire again and saw Foster dragging Horatio Burns from his wife's corpse.

"I can't leave her!" Burns cried.

"You stay, they'll tear you apart," Foster shouted.

Hennessy crouched and drew a bead on Anarchy's back. But it was as if the man had a sixth sense for danger. He dodged just before the shot. Hennessy's round whistled harmlessly over Anarchy's head. Hennessy heard his pistol's breach clang open. Empty!

Foster twisted and opened fire again. Hennessy dropped and hit the rug behind the chair. Bullets thumped into the upholstery.

Cheyenne dug in her pocket with her good hand, came up with her spare clip and threw it to him.

Hennessy slammed it home, bolted upright, and took off after Foster and Burns.

"Dad! Don't!" Hailey screamed after him.

But Hennessy did not slow. He dove through the door into the hangar, rolled across the cement floor, and came onto his knees, gun up, sweeping, just in time to see the Gallatin County Sheriff's cruiser assigned to the airport blow through the jetport gates and skid out onto the tarmac to the left of Foster and Burns, who were running toward the HB1 Gulfstream jet.

Foster put four bullets into the cruiser's windshield at close range before the deputy at the wheel could get the cruiser stopped. It went rolling past them and crashed into the side of the hangar, blocking Hennessy's shot and view.

He scrambled to his feet and tore straight at the sheriff's cruiser. He spotted the deputy, wounded and trying to get to his radio. Hennessy brought his pistol up over the roof, and spotted Foster looking back at him from the bottom of the jet's staircase aiming in his direction. He opened fire. Hennessy dropped, hearing bullets ricochet off the roof of the cruiser and shattering more glass.

Hennessy wrenched open the front passenger door.

"Officer down," the deputy was calling weakly into his radio.

Hennessy grabbed the deputy by his collar and wrenched him sideways across the console and passenger seat and out onto the ground. "You'll be safer here," Hennessy said, hearing sirens already starting at a distance, and then the Gulfstream's idling jet engines rev and let loose a high-pitched roar as it began to pivot and taxi out of sight.

Hennessy crawled across the passenger seat, past the cruiser's shotgun rack, and spotted the deputy's pistol on the floor. He snatched it up and got the door behind him closed in time to see the jet pulling off the apron, picking up speed, and heading toward the runway. The cruiser was still running. Hennessy threw it in reverse, prayed, and slammed on the gas.

The cruiser came free of the wall with a screech and a crunch. Hennessy threw it in low and cranked on the wheel.

The jet was now accelerating toward the west end of the runway and was already several hundred yards ahead of the cruiser when Hennessy came onto the tarmac. The radio crackled with the alert from the 911 center. He grabbed up the microphone.

"This is Mickey Hennessy," he shouted. "I am in pursuit of General Anarchy. He's in the HB1 Financial jet with Horatio Burns. They are heading west on the airport runway."

Hennessy swung the cruiser out into the center of the runway and floored it. The police engine growled and took off, building speed on the slick surface. But the corporate jet was already at the far west end, turning around, preparing for takeoff.

Hennessy wrenched free the shotgun from its rack as the jet started to accelerate toward him. He gritted his teeth and kept the gas pedal mashed to the floor. The jet was closing. For an instant he did not know what to do, then he grinned maniacally and swung the wheel so the cruiser skidded sideways down the runway on a direct collision course with the screaming jet.

"This time you're mine," he muttered grimly as the cruiser skidded to a stop.

He threw open the door, took four steps toward the rear of the vehicle, and dropped to his side. The jet was just lifting off, nose in the air as it approached the sheriff's car. For a split second Hennessy saw through the windshield. He saw the pilot in the cockpit alone and looking frightened.

Behind the corporate jet, a Northwest Airlines 737 roared in out of the snow. The commercial jet's wheels were already down. Its wings were flared for landing. Hennessy aimed at the windshield of the HB1 jet and fired the shotgun at ten yards. The corporate jet's windshield spiderwebbed. He rolled over on his back, pumped, and fired again at the underbelly of the jet as its wheels struck the roof of the sheriff's cruiser with a sharp thump that threw the corporate plane off-kilter. The jet tilted and yawed. The left wing brushed the snowy runway.

The pilot almost righted the craft. But he overcountered in his steering. Burns's jet reeled back across the runway just as the commercial aircraft thundered in over Hennessy's head, causing him to throw his arms up to protect himself.

The right wing of the HB1 plane hit the snowy runway hard. The tail seemed to rise in a spiral, causing the entire aircraft to begin a series of whirling cartwheels. At the end of the first revolution Hennessy saw a slash of fire appear at the rear of the jet. During the second complete revolution, the fully fueled aircraft exploded in a red and terrible fireball that bounced and disintegrated down the runway.

The Northwest jet skidded on the runway, blew through the fiery debris of Burns's jet, and slid off the far end of the runway, shattering the approach lights before it stopped out near the east fence.

Hennessy stayed there on his knees on the runway until Connor and Aaron Grant and the police cars and fire trucks found him. He was frozen to the spot, blinking at the snowflakes, his mouth open and huffing clouds in the frigid air while he watched what was left of Horatio Burns's twisted plans burn up in flares as brilliant as an acetylene torch, throwing plumes of black smoke that billowed and spiraled into the falling snow.

CHAPTER FORTY-SEVEN

Mickey Hennessy could not remember ever feeling this happy. The morning was warm and bluebell clear. The leaves rustled in the light breeze blowing through the giant cottonwoods that surrounded his new cabin on the banks of the Big Hole River. The summer waters called behind him, but his constant attention was over the top of the fifty people gathered in rows of chairs between the porch and the front door. He was wearing a tuxedo and bolo tie. So were Connor and Bridger, who stood beside him. Bridger was fidgeting with the cane he still used.

"Stop that," Hennessy whispered out the side of his mouth.

"When's it gonna start?" Bridger whispered. "My leg hurts."

"When Cheyenne says so," Hennessy hissed back,

wondering himself what was taking so long. Even Cheyenne's mother, Evelyn, was looking over her shoulder.

Hennessy got his mind off the waiting by once again focusing on the aftermath of the attack. In the six months since the shoot-out at the airport, Cheyenne, Ikeda, and dozens of forensic accountants had been trying to dissect Burns's actions prior to the seizure of the Jefferson Club. But Burns's financial machinations remained murky. He'd formed literally thousands of corporations and partnerships and almost as many bank and stock accounts over all his years of business. As a result, little of his liquid wealth had been located despite federal efforts to freeze and seize his assets. Stockholders, creditors, and survivors of the siege were suing HB1 Financial from all sides as well and having as little success finding his money.

One thing was certain, however. According to documents found on Burns's and Foster's computers, the original plan had been to saddle Hennessy with the blame for the security breaches. Burns's investigators had discovered his secret past and meant to exploit it after his death, destroying his reputation as part of the cover-up. That fact had caused much angst and anxiety on Hennessy's part. So had the attention paid to him and his children. The press had been after them relentlessly in the months after the attack. He'd agreed to several interviews, as well as a book and movie deal which had guaranteed the funding of their education while still managing to avoid much of the direct media glare. Cheyenne would continue to work in New York.

They'd bought a place together in SoHo and he was entertaining offers to work as a security consultant.

All in all, life has been very, very good, he thought just as the violin and cello players put bow to string and played the Pachelbel Canon. Hailey stepped out first.

Hennessy's breath caught. He hadn't been allowed to see Cheyenne's dress or hers. His daughter held a summer bouquet and wore violets and baby's breath in her hair. Her dress was crème-colored and shoulderless, and for the first time, Hennessy saw Hailey as a woman. He felt proud and helpless in the same heartbeat.

Then Cheyenne appeared. She wore a simple crème-colored gown, a tiara of dried flowers woven in her auburn hair, and around her neck a string of pearls he'd given her as a wedding present. She was more beautiful than he could have imagined. She was the most beautiful woman he'd ever seen. *Why would someone like her choose me?*

"Whoa," Bridger whispered behind him. "We've got a hot stepmom."

"No kidding, cartoon idiot," Connor agreed in a murmur.

"Have some respect, knuckleheads," Hennessy muttered, but grinned.

Hailey was beaming when she came down the aisle past Willis Kane and his wife, Marie, and Agent John Ikeda and his wife, Sam. She passed Sheriff Lacey sitting on the left with Special Agents Phelps, Seitz, Pritoni, and Johansson; and then Jerry Martin, his broker; and finally Aaron Grant, Margaret, and their daughters, who had become Hailey's good friends. Hailey came up to her father and kissed him.

"I'm so happy for you, Dad," she said.

"You have no idea, noodle," he said and kissed her back.

As he turned back toward his bride, Hennessy felt positively euphoric. All thoughts of the attack were forgotten, turned to char and smoke and blown away on the wind just as the bodies of General Anarchy, Horatio Burns, and the pilot had on that cold January day, incinerated by the exploding jet fuel beyond all recognition, now the stuff of dark legends.

Cheyenne stepped off the porch and walked toward him down the aisle, smiling. Her eyes found his and glistened with joy.

Hennessy's own eyes watered, and inside he felt completely filled up by the certain understanding that all his future dreams and adventures would be lit brilliantly by Cheyenne's smile, warmed by her touch, and free of all conspiracy except their love.

Read on for an excerpt from
Mark T. Sullivan's next book

BROTHERHOOD OF THIEVES

Coming soon in hardcover from St. Martin's Press

Algiers

French and Arabic rap and reggae thudded from windows high over Monarch's head as he entered the warren of alleys that climbed into the Kasbah, the oldest part of the city, a maze on the steep hillside above the Grand Mosque and the Place of Martyrs. The air drifting in the Kasbah smelled of simmering garlic and lamb and tobacco and the sea. Fruit vendors called to Monarch. So did fishmongers, and rug and curio dealers, and restaurant owners, who stood outside their empty establishments, spitting, and praying for relief from the merciless sun.

It was Monarch's fourth day in Algiers, and the fifth day of the holy month of Ramadan, the fifth day of fasting from dawn until dusk. The hardship of the fast already showed in the faces and postures of the people he saw. He matched himself to their manner. He did not swallow his spit, and he acted on edge as he climbed deeper into the Kasbah, heading toward a familiar address. It was also Friday, the day of giving, and Monarch went out of his way to put coins in the jars of the beggars who sat in the doorways, crippled, or blind, or half crazed by the life Allah had given them.

In the fourteen days since leaving Istanbul, Monarch had let his beard grow. His skin was darker from long hours in the sun on the Greek cargo ship he'd taken across the Mediterranean. And he'd made sure he wore clothes that let him fit in: gray slacks, black lace-up shoes, and a white cotton dress shirt he'd bought on the docks in Tripoli. To the casual observer, Monarch could have been anybody from a merchant on break to a government *functionaire* out for a mid-afternoon stroll.

Monarch had the freedom to do whatever he wanted. He'd stashed enough money away over the years to live comfortably for the foreseeable future. While some people might have found those prospects inviting, Monarch felt as if he'd had too much freedom already. Twice before, extreme liberty had come to him like an earthquake cracking open the earth, leaving a fissure— sudden, fathomless, and dark. Each time he'd been cut off from his prior life, leaving him to figure out a way forward.

That's how Monarch felt at some level as he climbed through the old city, cut off from his friends and support, alien and adrift and, he assumed, pursued. The boys at Langley must have figured out he was not dead by now. Someone would come searching, wanting to talk. Monarch decided that when that happened, he'd be honest; he'd tell them that he had no intention of going back inside the fold. As far as he was concerned, when the earth cracked open like this, it left you on one side or the other.

Monarch's thoughts broke when he noticed a group of seven teenage males coming down the narrow street at him. He caught the hunger in their eyes and recognized its flavor. They were a pack. They were hunting.

The urchins swarmed around him, bumping him and turning him as they passed. Monarch spun with them, keeping his pockets just ahead of their fingers, his own hands plucking a wallet from one and a wad of cash from another. He held both up and glared at the boys.

"Rule #6: Know your target," he said to them in Arabic, and then tossed the wallet and the cash back at the stunned pickpockets.

Several of them began to laugh and clap. One of the older ones, a boy with a gold tooth, asked, "Where you from? Where'd you learn to do that?"

"Rule #13: Keep your secrets secret," Monarch replied, and then turned and strolled away from them, happy that his skills had not dulled.

In his office in Langley, Virginia, a cheap prepaid cell phone rang in Slattery's pocket. He got out the phone and answered.

"Yes," he said.

"We've located the cat you lost," a woman's voice said in a mild French accent. *"As you suspected, looks like he's heading to Rafiq's."*

Slattery nodded, pleased. "It's where he would go in Algiers."

"And so he has," the woman said. And the line went dead.

Slattery left his office and climbed down a metal staircase into the agency's operational command center, which featured three tiers of desks and a wall of video monitors. CIA Officer Agatha Hayes was sitting on the top tier, headset on.

"Agatha," he said, "give me Lynch's feed, split upper left."

Hayes typed on her keyboard and the upper left quadrant of the screen jumped to show the view out the window of a car travelling past the Grand Mosque of Algiers.

Slattery spoke into his headset, "Lynch."

"Right here," a hoarse male voice came back. *"We've checked the manifests on the docks, but—"*

Slattery cut him off. "I think I know where he might go. A fabric shop west of *Boulevard de la Victoire*, due south of you, up the hill, no more than four kilometers."

He gave them an address, then said, "Get there and sit on it."

"On our way, boss," Lynch said.

"No fireworks," Slattery said.

"We're just there to assist him home."

Slattery took off his headset, feeling pleased with himself. The choreography he'd just set in motion felt pitch perfect, all of it logical, acceptable, and defensible.

Agatha Hayes was watching Slattery. She asked, "What makes you think Monarch will be going to this fabric store?"

Slattery replied, "He entered Algiers under one of his known aliases, which means eventually he'll have to seek a new identity. That fabric store belongs to Sami Rafiq, of the Beirut Rafiqs. The family has fabric shops all over Africa and the Middle East. The Rafiqs are also the finest document forgers in the world, and Sami is one of their best. We've used him quite often in a pinch as a matter of fact."

"The agency?" Hayes asked, surprised.

"There's a push from above to outsource everything these days," Slattery said. "Keeps the overhead low."

Rafiq's Magazin de Tissu Extraordinaire bustled with clerks and customers, women mostly, some modernly dressed, others in traditional robes and veils, examining bolts of expensive cloth stacked on long, short-legged tables and in bays attached to the walls. Monarch paid it all little mind as he headed to the rear of the store to a door and a staircase that led up to an office that overlooked the sales floor.

He climbed the staircase, hearing a man barking at someone in French, "You call Sami thief? I gave you a fair price. I always give a fair price. Sami Rafiq is no thief! I am an honorable businessman!"

Monarch rounded a corner to look into the office, where a short, portly Lebanese man with glasses, a shirt opened too far down his hairy chest, and a rash of gold chains around his neck was listening to his cell phone. He shouted, "You slander me!"

He thumbed off his cell phone and slammed his fist off his desk.

"That temper of yours will get you, Sami," Monarch said in English.

The fabric merchant's head rose, and his face broke into a grin. He lurched to his feet, his arms open. "Robin Monarch!" he cried. "My dear, dear friend! How are you?"

Sami came around his desk, shaking Monarch's hand warmly before appraising him. "Who lets you wear these clothes? Come, we go to the floor and pick out a fine light linen and—"

"—I'm kind of in a hurry, my old friend," Monarch said.

"Of course!" Sami cried, before bustling around his desk. He retrieved a padded envelope, and handed it to Monarch. "Six, just as you ask in your e-mail."

Monarch opened the pouch and fingered through passports from Chile, Brazil, Canada, Morocco, India, and Australia, seeing his face over names he would soon learn to respond to flawlessly. He studied several of the other documents in the pouch, and then nodded, satisfied. "Beautiful work, Sami, as always."

The fabric merchant beamed a moment, then remembered to lean over to another drawer. He pulled out a bundle of blue cloth that smelled of oil. He tossed it to Monarch, saying, "Wasn't easy to find this particular make and model on such short notice."

Monarch caught the bundle and felt a familiar weight and shape.

"H&K .45 USP," Monarch said, putting a hand to his heart. "I'm touched that you remembered, Sami."

The Lebanese merchant smiled. "The Rafiqs take care of old and dear customers."

"Ammunition?" Monarch asked.

Sami slid two boxes of bullets and two clips across his desk.

Before picking them up, Monarch tugged out a cashier's check drawn on the Bank of Algeria. "Your fee as agreed."

Sami took the check with a bow and quickly slipped it into his pants pocket. "Always a pleasure doing business, Robin," he said. "Can I interest you in some coffee?"

"It's Ramadan," Monarch said.

"I'm Christian," Sami said. "You?"

"A lost soul," Monarch said, as he was loading the clips with the bullets.

"A lost soul who drinks coffee?"

Monarch shook his head. "As much as I'd like to, Sami, I'm pressed for time."

"Where are you going so fast?" Sami asked.

"Trying to figure that out."

"You still with the agency?"

"Nope."

"Working freelance?"

"That's a possibility," Monarch allowed, taking a shopping bag advertising Sami's store off the windowsill and dropping the passports and the extra bullets inside. The gun he stuck beneath his shirt in his waistband at the low of his back.

"I hear of any jobs, I'll let you know," Sami said.

"Appreciate that."

Sami bowed again. "Let me at least walk you to the door, my old friend."

Back at Langley, Slattery paced inside the CIA's operations center. Agatha Hayes typed on her keyboard and a satellite image of Algiers popped up on the central screen. She zoomed in on the Kasbah and now Slattery could see a red dot flashing on the *Boulevard de la Victoire*. Lynch's position.

"Can you give me a visual on the shop?" Slattery said into his microphone.

"Coming at you," Lynch said.

A moment later, the screen to the right of the satellite image filled with the street scene outside *Rafiq's Magazin de Tissu Extraordinaire*, looking at the business from a block away at a steep diagonal angle. Pedestrians crowded the sidewalks on the store's side of the street. On the closer side, two women in dark robes and veils were moving slowly toward Lynch's position. A boy on a bike pedaled down the middle of the narrow street, with a taxi coming up behind him.

Through the front windows of Rafiq's fabric shop, Monarch saw the boy on the bike pass at the same time he heard the Muezzin's cry begin to echo out over the city, calling the faithful to pray and an end to fasting. He stopped inside the transom. He turned, meaning to shake Sami's hand and bid him farewell. But as he did so, ingrained habits forced him to scan the shop around him, looking at the customers and clerks.

All seemed well until he caught a woman in dark veil and robes standing up against the plate-glass windows at the far end of the store next to the other exit. She was trying not to show it, but she was watching him.

Monarch stuck his hand out to Sami. The forger took it and pumped it, saying, "You sure you would not like to buy some fabric? I have a tailor who could be finished with some fine clothes for you by noon tomorrow."

"Not this trip, Sami," Monarch said, releasing his grip and turning once more, letting his attention drift past the veiled woman. She was no longer watching him. She was looking out the window and nodding.

Monarch's attention slipped to the crowded sidewalk just outside the store, to the taxi honking its horn, and to the other side of the street where two other women in dark robes and veils were talking. One of them faced roughly toward the storefront. Something about the situation felt wrong, but he said, "Until next time, my old friend."

Monarch decided that the sidewalk was crowded enough to let him slip in, move with the flow toward the nearest mosque, and catch anyone trying to follow him. But he'd no sooner stepped out onto the sidewalk than he realized he'd emerged into a gap in pedestrian traffic. The taxi had turned onto the *Boulevard de la Victoire*, and the veiled women on the other side of the narrow street were reaching inside their robes and crouching to face him.

Their silhouettes dropping into athletic postures were enough to throw Monarch into action. He ducked, spun, and dove back toward the entrance to the fabric shop and a startled and puzzled Sami Rafiq. Monarch tackled the forger and drove him to the wooden floor of his shop just as automatic gunfire broke out, shattering the plate glass all around the entrance.

Slattery watched the surreal scene unfolding on the big screen inside the CIA's operations center. Monarch had clearly stepped out onto the sidewalk from the store. And then he had twisted and dived back inside as the two robed and veiled women drew machine pistols and opened fire, blowing out the shop's windows. The feed went shaky.

Lynch shouted into the covert ops chief's ear, *"Who the hell are they?"*

"No goddamned idea," Slattery shot back, transfixed by the veiled women moving in combat crouches toward the store, letting go with controlled bursts of fire.

"What do you want us to do?" Lynch demanded.

Slattery said, "Nothing you can do. Hold your ground."

"But they're trying to kill Monarch!" Agatha Hayes protested.

"Or Rafiq," Slattery shot back. "In any case I'm not putting my men in harm's way. We'll let it play out."

Monarch scrambled forward off of Sami Rafiq, and threw himself behind one of the tables laden with fabric. He retrieved the pistol and clips while customers and clerks screamed and ran for cover. Another burst sounded from the street, splintering the wooden doorframe.

Monarch got to his knees, threw the .45 up and over the bolts of fabric, firing three quick shots at the door and another two out the front window. Out of the corner of his left eye, he spotted Sami dragging himself under another table.

A burst of gunfire came from Monarch's far right. He heard it thudding into the rolls of cloth over his head. He sprawled on his belly, peering beneath the low fabric tables, and seeing a pair of dark sneakers beneath the hem of a dark robe. Monarch aimed at the sneakers and fired.

He heard her scream, and jumped up, seeing her let go of her gun, twisting, trying to get to the ground. Monarch shot her in the chest, then swung the pistol hard and fired twice in the direction of the street. He kept swinging, using the momentum to hurl himself away from the front entrance. He landed, slid, and then pushed himself up, running low toward the rear of the store and the door at the bottom of the staircase, the pistol aimed behind him, shooting the last two rounds in his first clip.

He'd almost made it to the door when the two veiled women attacking from the street opened fire again. Their rounds pinged off the metal staircase and blew holes in the drywall, but none hit Monarch, who barreled through the rear door to the fabric shop and out into a whitewashed alley. He cut hard to his right. More shots ricocheted behind him.

He ran, dropping the first clip and shoving it in his pocket, coming up with the second clip, and slamming it into the magazine. He reached another alley.

This one was more like a tunnel, with a roof overhead, and ancient stone stairs that dropped downhill. He ducked around the corner into the alley and waited, panting and refusing to let his mind seize on the obvious questions: *Who are they? Why are they trying to kill me?*

Monarch heard people shouting, and then police sirens wailing in the distance. He thought about fleeing, but felt compelled to take a look around the corner, back toward the rear exit from Sami's store. Before he could, a chicken came squabbling up the alley behind him. He grabbed the chicken, which scolded and clawed at him. He underhand-tossed it into the air about head high out in the main alley.

The bullets came immediately, spraying the alley side to side. Monarch shifted the pistol to his left hand, aimed it blind around the corner, and fired. On the second shot he heard the unmistakable punch of a bullet striking flesh and a soft cry, before the corner he hid behind exploded under fire. Shattered plaster and brick stung his face and hands.

He ran down stone stairs past a line of brightly painted Moorish doors. He reached a T where the covered alley ended, glanced back up the long stone staircase, and saw the veiled woman appear, her weapon held hip-high as she readied to fire. Monarch jumped out of her line of sight, but his shoe caught on cobblestones. He stumbled and fell, the gun clattering from his hand.

He struggled forward on all fours, hearing the po-

lice cars wailing closer now, and knowing that the
veiled woman was coming. He reached for the pistol,
but a sandaled foot stepped on it.

Monarch looked up and saw one of the pickpockets,
the one with the gold tooth.

"Follow me," the boy said in Arabic, and kicked the
pistol at Monarch.

Monarch snagged the gun and jumped up, sprinting
after the pickpocket, who dodged hard left into another
descending alley, with three- and four-story buildings
pressing in from both sides. The boy skidded to a stop in
front of a low, green, Moorish door, twisted the knob,
and pushed.

He went in and Monarch followed hard at his heels,
ducking so as not to hit his head on the low arch. The boy
let him pass, then eased the door shut and slid the bolt.
Monarch looked around himself. He was in the court-
yard of an old villa badly in need of repair. The boy silently signaled to a staircase that climbed the interior of
the wall to a small landing, before shifting directions and
rising to a second-floor colonnade.

The pickpocket stopped on the landing in front of a
small piece of wood carved in the same shape as the
door and set into the plastered wall. He hooked his finger in the iron ring attached to the piece of wood and
gently tugged. It pulled out, revealing two iron bars
that crossed the opening horizontally. Through them,
and from above, Monarch could see people coming out
onto the alleyway. He could hear their frantic voices
wondering about the gunfire. Then he spotted the last

veiled woman descending into the alley, her shooting hand tucked beneath her robes alongside her hip.

The pickpocket touched Monarch's shoulder. He twisted his head to see the kid with the gold tooth smiling at him, and holding his fingers to suggest a gun.

Monarch eased closer to the hole, watching his assailant move beneath and past him, hurrying by the other people in the alley and then out of his sight. It was many moments until he was convinced that she'd gone. He slid the cover back into the hole.

Monarch turned and looked at the pickpocket, who was watching him the way some might a master magician. "What's your name?" Monarch asked in Arabic.

"Bassam," he replied.

"Why'd you help me, Bassam?"

The boy shrugged. "Why they want to kill you?"

Monarch hesitated, and then said, "I don't know."

"Why didn't you kill her?"

"Because then you'd have a dead body outside your door and questions to answer. And I don't think you or your neighbors would like that."

Bassam seemed to respect that. "Who are they?"

"I don't know."

"Who are you?"

"Just a guy."

"Where you from?"

"All over."

"You got super-secret enemies then," Bassam said.

Monarch thought about that, came up with a short

list of possibilities, and then decided he had to flush out whoever was behind the attack.

"You want to make some money?" he asked.

The pickpocket looked interested. "What do I got to do?"

"I need clothes, scissors, a razor, and a cell phone off a tourist."

Slattery said, "Lynch, go have a look before the police cordon off the place."

"Roger that," Lynch said.

On the big screen at the front of the operations center, Slattery watched Lynch's point of view as the operator left the car, and crossed the street toward the six or seven people brave enough to look into the shop so soon after the shooting stopped. He could hear the police sirens coming.

"Hurry up," Slattery said.

Lynch's camera went to the front door and scanned inside. Glass lay all over the floor. Several people were wounded and moaning. A veiled woman in black sprawled dead on her back, half on, half off one of the fabric tables, blood pooling beneath her. Sami Rafiq climbed out from under one of the tables, brushing glass off himself, and trying not to break down in tears. He turned and looked right at Lynch.

"Who are you?" Sami demanded.

Lynch pivoted without answer and left the shop, moving through and away from the crowd building outside.

"Did you see Monarch?" Slattery demanded.

Lynch crossed the street to the car, saying, *"That's a negative."*

Slattery snapped, "Circle the Kasbah. There are only so many roads where you can drive. He'll head for one eventually."

With that, the covert ops chief threw down his headset. He looked over at Agatha Hayes. "I want everything our other people in Algiers can find out about what happened inside that store. A.S.A.P."

Hayes was new to Slattery's team and shocked by the violence she'd seen explode on the streets of Algiers. She nodded dumbly, but then said, "Shouldn't we alert the Algerians to the threat?"

"What threat?"

"Monarch?"

Before Slattery could answer, the cheap prepaid cell phone buzzed in his pocket. Without speaking, he turned away from Hayes and stalked out of the room. He climbed the staircase to his office, digging for the phone. He flipped it open, entered his office, closed the door, and growled, "What happened?"

"He killed two of my best operators and escaped," said the woman with the French accent, sounding tense, exhausted, and angry.

Slattery felt like kicking something. Instead, he squeezed his free hand into a slow, deliberate fist. "I warned you he was good before you took the job."

"Not that good," the woman said coldly. *"It will take me at least six months to replace them. So I'm out. And I damn well expect final payment."*

Slattery said, "For a botched job? Not fucking likely."

He clicked off the phone, sat down hard on his leather couch, and stared at the ceiling. The game had changed. Monarch knew he was being hunted now.